AGAINST THESE POWERS

GROUP X CASES

BOOK 3

J. A. BOUMA

PROLOGUE

America! America!

Where have you been all my life?

With all of your vices and vainglory; your back-biting and back-handed, two-faced compliments; your mix of moxie and maleficence; your exaltation of every passion and proclivity, every impulse and injustice the Good Book itself decries—having your fill of unrighteousness, wickedness and greed; envy, murder, strife, deceit, and malice; gossip, slander; insolence, arrogance, and boasting; untrustworthiness, faithlessness, and mercilessness.

You even go so far as to invent evil, with all the myriad of pronouns and identities that make even my comrades' heads spin with confusion—and that's saying something, because we've been looking for ways to undermine the essence of human nature for millennia. But that's another story, for another of my comrades to share.

My kind of peeps, you are! My kind of peeps.

I mean, I've heard tale of you, of course. Who hasn't? Oh yes, your reputation precedes you! Our kind have been watching you for centuries, ever since those pious, plucky Pilgrims plopped their pontoons upon those New World shores, marveling at your progress—from upstart, backwoods rebels to the reigning superpower.

Wasn't that long ago you dazzled the known world with your missives upholding the fundamental rights of mankind, with a slavish, pious devotion to not only the laws of Nature, but also of Nature's God.

Now your military bombs the snot out of backwoods regimes first then asks questions later, certainly garnering a reputation for itself. Not to mention your popularity as the purveyor of all sorts of high-class culture, from *Keeping up with the Kardashians* to Dua Lipa and Mickey D's to Coca-Cola. Because if the Reaper drones don't kill your enemies and maintain your dominance, cultivated stupidity and obesity certainly will.

Despite your military and cultural prowess, however, that's not why I sing your praises. I've only just arrived on your storied shores and already your stench is sending chills racing up my spine and through every appendage. Which is saying something, because my kind can't smell worth a lick!

No no no! What I smell is different from a steaming cup of Seattle's Best earthy joe or a Philly cheesesteak sandwich piled high with sautéed onions. What I'm talking about is the smell of a little word that gives me that warm, fuzzy feeling deep in my bowels every time it wafts my way.

It goes by many names, many stripes, most of them too fancy-schmancy to be of any use to me.

Angst, anxiety, apprehension.

Despair, dismay, dread.

Horror, terror, worry.

What gets me going, what gets me tingling every time a whiff of it blows my way is a little thing I like to call *fear*.

So, here I stand, taking it all in—taking you all in America! Honest Abe at my back and the National Mall spread out before me under a clear, blue sky portending fantabulous things to come. With Georgie's Monument down below and the People's

House farther beyond—a world of possibilities stretches out before me.

Because boy, I tell ya, America: You are positively swimming in my heart's desire!

Not that I can blame you. After a few years of panic-porn fueled hysteria from all corners of the airwaves and internet, cajoling you into masking up and checking your privilege, who wouldn't piss themselves silly every time they stepped one toenail out their front door? Add to that a bear tearing through the stock market and the Bear, Mother Russia, rampaging through Eastern Europe, it's any wonder you haven't all just kicked back the Kool-Aid Jim Jones style!

Don't worry. I'm here to help. Because, see, fear is what I live and breathe. What flows through my veins, in fact. Have cut my teeth on it, yes I have.

Violence and war, cultural subversion and incitement, they aren't the ways I roll. But fear…now that's my jam, as all those American teenyboppers say.

Taking a breath and surveying the breadth of my new assignment, I'm giddy as a clam for what lay before my eyes.

Spacious skies. Amber waves of grain. Purple mountain majesties above the fruited plains. Gleaming alabaster cities undimmed by human tears!

I laugh at the thought, my breath exploding from me with a guffaw that would set Wormwood's teeth on edge! Hates laughter, he does, the Principal much too serious for my taste. Live a little, pal! After all we've been through, humor is all our kind has.

Now, where was I. Oh, yes. Those gleaming alabaster cities undimmed by human tears.

Just wait till I get through with ya!

Or rather, we. For this operation is a multi-layered one, with Semjaza himself, the cosmic Prince over this swath of geography that has become my new assignment, kicking it into high gear to shackle the land he's been commanding since the cosmos were birthed—once and for all.

One of the original sons of God whom the Shining One appointed himself as Chief Geographical Regent, the Watcher has been watching the borders change from tribal savages to European ones, then into the Fifty Nifty United States—fomenting rage and chaos and despair, especially through recent efforts from my comrades that haven't turned out so well.

I aim to do better. I *will* do better!

So, here I stand. Election winds at my back and a country spread before me to tear limb from limb.

More than that: a Church to put under the spell of my enchantments and turn against itself.

The world is my oyster! Or at least one slab of its geography. Semjaza has been its overseer, and he expects me to bring results. Same for Wormwood, who had quite the chat with me about those expectations before my arrival, given what Chaos and Despair wrought the past half a year—or didn't...

No matter. Those two have nothing on me. For I wield a weapon of war far more powerful than mere chaos and despair.

America! America!

Just wait and see what I've in store for thee.

For ruin your good and ravage your brotherhood, I will.

From sea to shining sea...

CHAPTER 1
WASHINGTON, DC.

Elijah Fox was not a happy camper. And that wasn't only because he hated camping.

The sun was not yet peeping through his curtains, it was his day off, he had the beginning of a head cold, and his blasted alarm was squawking to beat the band!

Hank, hank, hank it had sounded, like some impatient mama calling for her child Hank to catch the morning bus.

He'd rolled over and smacked it, thinking he'd shut the dang thing off.

Nope.

Nine minutes later, it was squawking back up again, sounding like that annoying parrot from his childhood orphanage that drove him crazy!

Was a pet to that nasty headmistress Ursula, her pride and joy. That's right, like the half-woman, half-octopus villainous sea witch she-witch from *The Little Mermaid*. With those overly mascaraed eyes beshadowed a sickly blue, and those lips painted whorehouse red, and that black dress spilling out into eight long tentacles—the woman strutting around like the love child between Marilyn Monroe and Marilyn Manson.

Except Ursula the Terrible from those years in Appalachia

Virginia was no blonde 1950s bombshell! Ursula from *The Little Mermaid*, she was—to a T. Same eyes, same lips, same gargantuan backside stuffed in black leggings that made her look like an octopus. Even had the laugh down, a husky chuckle that jiggled her jowls from smoking a carton of Camels a day.

Most single ladies her age whose daily attire consisted of either gray sweatpants or purple moo moos tend to be the cat kind, breeding them like rabbits and filling the house with the varmints.

Nope, not Ursula.

She was a parrot lady, letting that green and red and orange varmint have the run of the joint. Somehow, it always ended up perched outside Elijah's door.

Sounding like that dang alarm squawking like Polly the Parrot (originality wasn't Ursula's strong suit).

"Sweet mother of Melchizedek…"

Must have forgotten to turn it off. Elijah fumbled in the dark with the dang thing again, but only managed to half fall out of bed and knock his head onto his hardwood floor. Lucky for him, he had a nest of dark, curly hair to soften the blow.

Woke up his Jack Russell rescue, though, prompting him to lick his face something fierce!

"Dexter…" Elijah moaned hanging out of his bed upside-down while getting slobbered.

Tried swatting him away with one hand while balancing out of bed with the other. That only made the pooch go at it even more. Added a bark and a yip for good measure, thinking it was a game.

"It's too early for playtime, Dext! Let's go potty instead."

That seemed to work, his Jack Russell trotting out of the room and leaving behind a tinking trail of nails on hardwood down the stairs to the back door. Must really have to go.

Tumbling out of bed, Elijah stood and stretched, yawning and reaching for a Kleenex, then blowing.

That felt good. Except for the fact it wasn't even 8 o'clock!

Just wanted one lazy morning off from saving the day. Just one day, when the fate of the supernatural world wasn't hanging in the balance and threatening the Church.

Guess he'd have to take a rain check on that proposition.

Probably best, anyway. Never could sleep in. Probably that Protestant work ethic beat into him at the orphanage. Which was ironic, since he was ethnically Jewish but had embraced Jesus as his Messiah thanks to his Baptist pastor adoptive father married to his Catholic adoptive mother.

Only in America.

Suppose his only saving grace was the fact Group X headquarters hadn't been the one to drag him out of bed with some panicked case of demonic possession or a murdered pastor. His new gig as the director of the upstart investigative unit sure had given him a run for his cryptocurrency, that's for sure.

Not that he wasn't used to the supernatural crazy. He'd seen his fair share gumshoeing it as an agent for the FBI's special unit of unexplainable phenomenon. But the Feds had nothing on the Church's X-Files!

He'd stumbled into the upstart ecclesial investigative unit after being dragged into a special-ops case involving his hobbyhorse: alien abduction stories, unexplained aerial phenomenon, and their connection to the supernatural worldview of the Bible.

There he was, minding his own business teaching at a Midwest graduate school for pastors, when Silas Grey, Master of the Order of Thaddeus (or former Master, given he was currently MIA), came calling thanks to his former-turned-current partner Gina Anderson who'd made the connection. Before he knew it, a rogue government agency had blown up his place of employ, and he was dragged into helping the Church's special-ops arm, SEPIO, expose an alien government cover-up (long story; don't ask). The operation had revealed an obvious incursion from the Unseen Realm of Fallen Ones (more don't ask; read Genesis 6:1-4 for the 411 on *them*!) that had lit a fire under Silas's behind to launch an investigative unit to take on the supernatural crazy.

Group X was its name, taking on the Church's *inexplicitus* cases with a supernatural edge. And Elijah was its director, along with his former partner from his FBI days back in the day, Gina.

The pair had cut their teeth on solving similar inexplicable cases of the more paranormal variety that stumped Uncle Sam's men in black. Alien abductions, cultic ritual abuse, shape-shifting serial killers, mind-reading con men. You know, your run-of-the-mill criminal crazy with a supernatural edge.

And there he was: back in Washington, DC, and back in the saddle of an investigative arm solving cases of the more super-natural variety—only this time for Jude Thaddeus, or at least his long-lost religious order.

The Lord sure does work in mysterious, if ironic, ways.

Dexter was barking to beat the band downstairs, shaking him from his lazy out-of-bed getting.

"Yeah yeah yeah. Hold your horses!"

Elijah swiped his phone from his nightstand and sauntered out of his bedroom on the second floor of a half-million dollar fixer-upper in the Adams Morgan district along the 18th Street corridor in Northwest DC. Had landed his lovely abode after a bidding war that ended with one of those impassioned letters that actually worked.

Floors were nice and sturdy, throwing up not a creak or a complaint. Had spent the summer sanding them down and freshening them up. Still smelled of stain and varnish, along with the walls giving off fresh paint. Slate gray, in every room. A nice middle-ground to his black-and-white obsession. The world had enough high-definition color to overload the senses. Why invite the overwhelm into one's abode?

Elijah reached the back door where Dexter was doing a little jig on the tile floor, the all-white pooch with a light brown patch on his left eye almost ready to let his bladder rip.

Nope. Not on his day off!

He reached for the door to let him out, when his foot stepped in something wet.

He looked down, and muttered a curse.

"Sweet mother of Melchizedek…" Dexter had piddled on the floor.

Supposed he couldn't be too cheesed at the little fella. After all, he had warned him. But Dext was still carrying on—which meant round two was nigh!

Elijah promptly threw open the door, and Dext bounded across the flagstone patio, nearly careening into the red-clay chiminea at the end before sliding into the thick green grass and squatting.

While his pooch fertilized his lawn, he swiped the paper towel roll from the black granite countertop and cleaned up the mess.

Finishing, he fished out his phone and swiped it to life. Greeting him was a news item on the upcoming presidential election.

Elijah rolled his eyes but figured he should do his civic duty by reading the headline.

Hated politics. Had no time for it. Maybe because all it had ever gotten him was an orphan and adoption system so unchecked and dysfunctional that it nearly did him in. That was the personal side of it, but having spent half a decade working for Uncle Sam as an FBI agent, he saw firsthand the seedy underbelly of a bureaucracy bent more on institutional self-preservation than national service—a posture replicated across all three branches of government.

Yep. Color him cynical.

Bartlet for President, all the way! Was why he spent each election cycle binge-watching *The West Wing*, one of his favorite TV shows. Item numero uno for the day. Jed, the fictional president, reminded him when times were more honorable, as fictional as it was.

He smirked. Honor. In politics and government. Those were the days.

The news item featured a wide-shot photo of President

Robert Santos and his two other contenders: Debby Gallego and Lenny Levin. It was one of those non-newsy news stories touting the closeness of the race, with all three poling tightly together within the margin of error.

The current President was a Democrat Elijah actually liked. A strong practicing Catholic man who was America's first elected Latino. He'd had some missteps, like the scandal involving the alien conspiracy from a year ago. And he'd bungled the corona-crazy pandemic that set the country on fire—more economically and socially than epidemiologically—but Elijah thought he might cast a vote his way.

The others…not so much.

The Republican candidate was a Texan tech magnet who'd taken a Lone Star State-size branding iron to the wall separating Church and State. Aimed to "Take America Back Again," as her conservative splinter cell was called.

To what, Elijah wasn't sure. Figured back to the time autistic people like him were shut away in mental institutions because they didn't fit some definition of normal. Another way to read it, he supposed, was to reclaim America again from the clutches of imagined evildoers, something her campaign boldly announced in a favorite talking point: "Reclaim America for Christ Again."

The irony in that cheerful slogan was that it spelled *raca*, a biblical word meaning 'worthless' or 'empty.'

The other one running as an independent wasn't much better, a flaming socialist who made Che Guevara look like a Trappist monk. Promised free tuition, free health care, free housing—even free marijuana for the needy. Of course, after printing all that money to pay for it, America would be the next Venezuela. Details, details, details.

A yipping bark from Dexter nosing the door back inside yanked him from his phone. Dexter jumped up and down outside the glass door, tongue hanging out with joy, like he hadn't seen him in ages.

Reminded him of that too-on-the-nose proverb about the

difference between dogs and cats. Dogs think they're humans; cats think they're gods.

Reason 623 why he was a dog person.

He shoved his phone in his pocket and let Dexter inside. He scooped him up in his arms and fought back the pooch's kisses again while he walked to get him some breakfast.

Speaking of which…a late start to the morning always called for eggs and bacon. Or rather, begs and acon, as Dad had always called their Sunday morning breakfast.

Without fail, his adoptive father had cooked him and his mom cheesy scrambled eggs with thick-sliced bacon and raspberry-jellied toast. Said it gave him the fuel he needed for his sermonizing gig that stretched two services. Was a good preacher, too, doing the Lord's work unpacking the historical context of the Bible while applying it to his parishioners' lives. That is, until a crazed gunman off his meds stormed down the center aisle of their country church and shot him in the face.

The surfaced memory spiked a rise in Elijah's anxiety, sending him for his stimming tick.

Thumb to index finger, thumb to middle, thumb to ring finger, thumb to pinky—then rinse and repeat.

Had learned early in his life how to manage the overwhelming emotions and anxiety that threatened to lay him flat. Actually, he'd stuffed them so far down inside a black hole in his mind that it wasn't until a Group X case just a few months ago forced him to reconnect with his emotional self.

Go figure.

He'd been beaten and mocked, taunted and threatened so many times at that dang Virginia orphanage that he'd disassociated from his emotional self. When he did, the floodgates opened, and now he actually seemed to feel almost physical pain from emotion when it spiked.

Hadn't realized it until years later when he was adopted by a mother who moonlighted as a psych-ward specialist that he was neck deep into the autism spectrum. Those not in the know would call him a high-functioning person with autism.

Nope. He was just Elijah Fox, autistic person extraordinaire.

Over the years, he'd navigated well enough his...condition, as some people might be tempted to call it. Him, he came to understand he was fearfully and wonderfully made by the God of the universe who liked him just the way he was—imbuing him with a "superpower" as both Dad and Mom had framed it.

Thanks to his father pastor, who'd offered a biblical and theological faming of himself, and psychologist mother, who'd offered a medical and psychological explanation for his unique struggles, Elijah had actually come to accept himself.

Almost.

Because he hadn't always liked any of those framings—whether the biblical and theological one, that God had specially formed him in his Jewish birth mother's womb; or the psychological one, that he was merely a non-neurotypical person who experienced the world in ways that were different and unique, not bad or wrong; or the paternal one, that he had some sort of superpower that let him engage the world in ways he could uniquely help people.

Nope, never liked them one bit. Mostly because he'd never believed any of the bulldookie people shoveled his way to make him feel better about himself. He knew better, because he knew his brain better.

Instead, he'd cursed God for the inner life that never shut down—how his brain skipped from one piece of information into a spool of synaptic connections that sometimes made him want to throw up with whiplash; how he would obsess over some new insight or random factoid or squirrelly interest, plunging deep into a rabbit hole that spun out into a bazillion different rabbit trails (yeah, mixing metaphors there, but go with it); how his emotional connection to people had been shut down thanks to his childhood, only to open back up again into a pain that often clawed at his chest.

Eventually, he'd come to be at peace with himself. The Father, Son, and Holy Spirit had been good to his heart and mind.

Why his mind was suddenly consumed with his personal identity after his pooch laid a deuce was beyond him. There'd been a lot of that lately, actually. Ever since taking on his new gig standing against the darkness.

Wasn't one to find a devil behind every tree, but investigating the Church's cases that smacked of the cosmic powers of this present supernatural darkness had opened up something in him —or perhaps exposed himself to something that not even his days at the FBI tracking down cult leaders on the lam or possessed serial killers had exposed.

It was like those powers from the Unseen Realm were lobbing kryptonite at his brain, trying to distract and detract and discourage him.

Why couldn't he have gone into roofing instead? Now there's an honest day of work without getting in the way of the Devil's carefully laid plans to ravage the world.

Then again, he was afraid of heights. And nail guns. Throw buzzing bees and the stifling high-noon sun into the mix and his ecclesial private eye gig wasn't looking so bad. Would've gotten a wicked tan slinging shingles, though. Chicks dig that sort of thing.

Why he was contemplating his career choice was beyond him. Nothing a little begs and acon couldn't solve.

First things first, he tossed a heaping scoop of dog food into a shiny chrome bowl near the back door. Then he went to his medicine drawer at an island in the middle of his generous kitchen, searching for Zicam and Airborne tablets. His cold remedy of choice.

He filled a glass of water and popped in the Airborne tablet, drawing it to his nose and smiling.

Smelled like that one family road trip to Disney World through Tallahassee, Florida, orange capital of America. Was flat amazed at all the groves lining the state highway. Went on for miles! Convinced Dad to pull over on the side of one of those roads to take a tinkle. Really, he just wanted to run amok through the grove. Dad didn't like that too much, but it did smell of Tropicana, his favorite smell in all the world.

The tablet stopped fizzing, the bubbles no longer tickling his nose. He gulped down the orange liquid fortified with a week's worth of vitamin C and antioxidants, then promptly pressed the Zicam tablet on his tongue. It let off a similar fizz that sent a tingle down his tongue, along with the taste of orange sherbet.

More Tropicana heaven…

Which made his tummy rumble something fierce! For OJ, for breakfast.

Begs and acon.

While Dexter munched on his pooch chow, Elijah slung two HexClad non-stick pans up on his KitchenAid stove. None of that pedestrian Calphalon nonsense. Gordon Ramsey best for him. Because according to the master chef, not only are they beautiful pans, their hybrid technology cooks to absolute utter perfection.

And only utterly perfect begs and acon for Elijah Xavier Fox.

He retrieved a pack of applewood-smoked Wright bacon from his cousin KitchenAid refrigerator, appreciating the polished stainless steel and thinking he needed to leave a little extra cabbage for his house cleaner for the spic-and-span shine. Following up with a half-empty carton of brown eggs (none of that pedestrian white-egg nonsense), he schlepped the goods onto the island (a good Yiddish word for ya) and finished his retrieval effort with a quarter-drained half gallon of milk and stick of salted butter.

Because perfectly cooked scrambled eggs were all in the salted butter. None of that I Can't Believe It's Not Butter vegetable oil nonsense. Butter from a cow, not corn.

Lighting his gas stove (actual fire like cavemen you can control was where it was at; none of that hippie electric nonsense), he tossed three strips of slaughtered pork into the heating pan and got to work on the eggs. He cracked open three of the brown suckers into a bowl and added a dash of milk, then cranked a hand salt grinder times three, followed by double the crankage for the matching peppercorn grinder.

Satisfied, the kitchen filled with the scent of frying bacon now, he lit a second burner under another pan, let it heat up half a minute, then smeared a goodly dose of salted cow butter on the HexClad and poured in his concoction. Waiting for the eggs to do their thing, he popped down a slice of wheat bread in the toaster then an Ethiopian pod into his Nespresso Vertuo and set it to lungo size.

A few minutes later, the bacon was cooked to a perfect crisp, the eggs were fluffy and smothered in melted sharp cheddar, and his darkened bread (no, not burned; darkened) was smeared with raspberry preserves (no, not jelly; preserves). His coffee was hot and steaming and smelling oh-so caramelly and nutty.

He went for that first and took a sip.

Nearly choking on it at the startled sound of a shrilly *bring-bring-bring* from his pocket.

He yanked out his squawk box and startled.

Mama.

He frowned. Of course things get worse just as he's about to scarf down breakfast!

Back to Mama…

Calling this early? On a weekday? And smack dab at the start of her patient hours, which always ran from eight to four?

Did not compute.

Which could only mean one thing.

Something was afoot.

So much for a lazy morning off.

CHAPTER 2

Gina Anderson wanted to go back to bed. It was turning out to be a terrible, horrible, no good, very bad day.

She'd overslept her alarm, woke with a wicked, pulsing headache thanks to some gluteny pasta she had eaten the night before (and maybe thanks to a bottle of Bordeaux), and America was barreling toward an election that had the makings of Civil War II!

And actually, the pasta was brought on by the latter. She'd watched the final presidential debate with her cats and a bowl of that gluteny pasta smothered in vodka sauce, piled high with artichokes, Kalamata olives, and prosciutto—joined by a bottle of Bordeaux. All of it, too. The night called for it.

President Santos was running for his seat again, a Democrat Catholic who'd governed far more at the center than the left wing cared. He'd rocketed to the White House after a major scandal broke four years ago the last go around. Apparently, the Mormon Church had tried to install their choice presidential candidate with the help of some wackadoodle Evangelical powerbrokers. Said Mormon Church had filled said wackadoodle Evangelical powerbrokers' coffers with certain…shall we say, helpful donations in exchange for their support.

As they say, money talks and dollars sing, and all that jazz.

All of which was super ironic because there'd been a not-too-subtle anti-Catholic streak running through the last time those Protestants made a play for the White House. So the fact they were canoodling with a non-Christian, bastardization of historic Christianity was too weird for words.

But politics does weird things to people. She should know.

Gina's mama had always been a political junky growing up. Was never an ideologue. Much more into kitchen-table issues that had a direct bearing on their Toledo double-wide parked in the armpit of Ohio. The cost of milk and bread, the per-gallon price of gas, which candidate pledged to eliminate cigarette taxes and legalize marijuana.

Basically, whatever served her needs, she was on board. And on board she was. Had pounded the pavement for nearly every candidate since Gina was a child—sometimes the same ones from different parties during the same election!

Probably why Gina had been roped into the mosh pit of politics, catching the bug and not giving up. She followed all the major players just as her mama had, and her father had followed football—knowing who was who, what district they represented, how far down the line of succession they were in the Presidential Cabinet. Had even memorized the U.S. Constitution as a second-grader, much to the chagrin of her parish priest, who couldn't get her to spend as much mental energy on her catechism and Scripture.

She'd made up for it since, tucking both away in that noggin of hers. But the American government, and all its checks and balances, separation of powers, guaranteed rights fascinated her.

Understood someone needed to make sure the gravy train delivered to the right people the right goods at the right time for the right reason. Same for the crazy train, knowing there were human forces in this world who needed to be stopped and locked up. Was why she'd joined the FBI when they came a calling after some muckety-muck read her doctoral thesis on cultic ritual abuse.

Anyhoo, back to the cray-cray conspiracy to elect a Mormon President. Wouldn't've been so bad, and probably would've gotten away with it all, had they not assassinated the independent candidate. Something straight out of *All the President's Men* it was! Would've worked, too, had the Order of Thaddeus not intervened, sussing out the political conspiracy that rivaled a Robert Ludlum fever dream and bringing down the whole house of cards.

The same actors who just happened to be her new employer.

The employer she was running late to!

Whatevs. It was Elijah's day off, technically her boss, the director of Group X. So while the boss was away, Gina colada (her partner-in-crime's affectionate nickname, so bestowed after her fave Caribbean piña colada drink) would eat cake. Red velvet, to be exact, a tradition her grammy had started way back when, eating cake and coffee for breakfast. Though she preferred a strong cup of Red Rose black tea.

The special blend of black pekoe, with their malty and spicy, smoky and rich taste was a perfect match to the mild cocoa and vanilla flavor of the slice of red velvet—joined by that oh-so-good smooth, soft, tender and light creamy cream cheese icing!

Figured she deserved at least one late-morning start after all that had gone down the past few months anyhow. The Church's X-Files were far more cray-cray than the FBI's ever were. And that was saying something after she and Eli had gone up against a Vegas serial killer targeting prostitutes who was possessed by one of the Devil's minions.

So far with Group X, she and Eli had exposed a drug cartel that moonlighted as a devil-worshiping death cult and laid bare a plot to sow the seeds of despair in the hearts and minds of unsuspecting women through social media. All with the cosmic powers of the Unseen Realm as puppet masters.

Too weird for words.

So, take it easy she would, propping her feet up on her desk in the bowels of the Basilica of the National Shrine of the Immaculate Conception in Northeast Washington, DC—the former headquarters of the Order of Thaddeus back in the day and current HQ for Group X.

But first things first: cake!

She'd made it the night before after chowing down on that pasta she'd made (humongo mistake) just after halftime during the presidential debate. Had to. Couldn't keep her hands idle after the network broke for commercials after the foreign policy section. Would lead this country into World War III, those three would!

One candidate wanted to go all in on Eastern Europe, hoover up all the non-NATO nations and rally the old Western order together again after Comrade Crazy Pants with the ushanka tore it to shreds. The other wanted to pivot to Asia, batten down the hatches with our Asia Pacific allies and go all in on going toe to toe with the Red Dragon on Taiwan. Still another wanted to pull back entirely to take America back again by doing nothing at all.

Gina couldn't take the stress anymore, so she whipped up the red velvet cake that sat under the glass cake stand sitting on the granite island in her red-and-pink polka dot kitchen.

It was a perfect contrast to her partner's, which was the saddest kitchen she'd ever seen. Nothing but gray walls and stainless steel appliances. No way, Jose! Not for Gina colada.

Slipping into plush pink slippers that made her feet tingle with the happy-happy, she wrapped a matching silk robe around herself (her skin tingling with the same feeling) and made for her kitchen. Nearly tripped over Baxter—a Maine Coon cat that doubled as a tiger wannabe. The brown striped oaf complained, loudly.

"Yeah yeah yeah, right right right. I'm as famished as you are."

Gina scratched his head, the cat throwing up a famished meow and weaving between her legs—nearly sending her to an early grave again! She gave him a slipper to the backside and sauntered into her happy place.

The kitchen was the real selling point of the joint. It was big enough to do some serious culinary damage without taking up the first floor. A little nook sat at the back, with floor to ceiling windows peering out into a backyard garden edged by towering oaks and maples with a little pond of half a dozen koi surrounded by flowering bushes and flowering—well, flowers. Another selling point.

She'd managed to buy the joint after saving up her earnings over the years. No, not on Uncle Sam's dime. Lady Luck's. After that cray-cray Vegas case, she had unwound at a black jack table at Caesar's Palace. Dad had showed her a thing or two growing up when Mom wasn't looking, and she put those moves to good use.

Several times over.

Who knew her autistic brain would come in handy? She sure hadn't. Always counted it more a curse than a blessing, the way the synapses of her noggin fired off from one thing to the next like a squirrel on speed. Didn't help matters that same brain was also socially awkward, finding it difficult to connect with people —facial avoidance was definitely a thing; still was, but she'd learned to work around it thanks to Doublemint gum.

But where other autistic people would ride those synaptic waves down the rabbit hole into the nether of factoid upon factoid, she was more a wave rider, skimming along the surface from detail to detail, which happened to server her needs just fine both at the FBI and on the Vegas Strip.

No, she wasn't Rain Man autistic; no Ray Babbitt savant running through her veins. More a Roy G. Biv kinda gal, seeing the world in high-definition, seven-part rainbow colors where everyone else just saw red, green, and blue variations.

That knack for detail is what set her sailing at the Bureau, as well as the Vegas Strip. Details like eye movement and facial ticks, both in the interrogation room and at the card table. Details like when someone licked their lips just so, or reached for a drink of water when their mouth went dry.

Details like cards, and counting them.

Which the Vegas security type didn't much like the more she kept on winning. Nearly got run out of the Bellagio, too. But a quick wit and even quicker mouth, not to mention the flashing of her FBI badge, managed to let her squeak by without incident.

After that run-in, she'd put her card-sharp paws to pasture and quickly invested her earnings in real property.

Like the three-story fixer-upper on Embassy Row that had once belonged to some African banana republic that hadn't seen one of those yellow fruits since the Pangea was a thing.

A narrow pink refrigerator sat nestled in the kitchen corner between the sink and a purple stove. Yeah yeah yeah, both the dishwasher and the microwave were stainless steel, but the walls more than made up for those drab things.

And the granite island! A beautiful, colorful, swirly mélange of turquoise and canary and rust and burnt orange. Made her brain fire on all cylinders just glimpsing it from the hallway.

Along with the glass cake storing her red velvet cake.

Baxter was moaning something fierce now, so she slopped two cans of Friskies pate in a bowl for him and his cousins. Not sure where the others were, Angel and Patches and Cookie, but the sound of breakfast usually was the only dog whistle they needed to kick it into high gear. Or cat call, as was the case.

Uncovering the glass lid, Gina's senses were instantly flooded with strawberries and dark chocolate, joined a beat later by buttermilk and vanilla.

Heaven…

After filling her electric tea kettle with water, she prepared her mug with a single cube of sugar and tea bag. Could never get the ratio of sweetness to bitterness just right with the granulated variety, either mixing too much or too little sugar with her Red Rose. Would go through cups and cups of it in frustration, her brain and buds not letting go until it was perfect.

The cube was her saving grace, thank the Lord Almighty!

In a minute the water had boiled to perfection, and she poured herself her one and only cup. Then she promptly cut herself a piece of cake the size of her foot.

The day called for it.

She went to bite into the luscious piece of happy-happy when she gasped.

"Almost forgot!"

Her fork dropped to her plate with a clatter, and she bounded down the echoey hardwood hallway then out the front door to retrieve her *New York Times*.

A whipping fall wind bit at her ankles, and leaves were strewn about the postage stamp-size front yard. She shivered and waded into the yellows and reds and oranges, trying her darnedest to swish away the wet fallen leaves and avoid her neighbor's dog poo. Managed the latter but the leaves clung to her slippers for dear life.

"There you are, ol' Gray Lady..."

Gina snatched her paper and darted back inside, hunger rumbling through her tummy now for that cake and her frigid body hankering for that Red Rose.

Although the *Washington Post* was the city's go-to paper of record, she wasn't too keen on The Bezos having his fingers in the news-generation pie. So ol' Gray Lady was her go-to paper of record.

And the actual paper kind, too. Smelling of ink and pulp, the newsprint staining her lily-white fingertips black from use. Hadn't been averse to tech, and was more than fine with saving a few trees getting her news online. Until her last case, that is. Given what her phone had done to her—and nearly drew her into doing—let's just say she and iPhone had a DTR that redefined their relationship, and Mother Nature would have to cough up a few more saplings for her news.

Drawing back to the granite island, she unfurled the newspaper—and gasped.

"What the what?" she shouted.

There was a triptych shot of three photos, one from each of the three presidential candidates and dueling—or was it trieling, trueling?—rallies.

The first was President Santos, a healthy crowd chanting "Four more years!" with raised four-finger fists pumping with delight. Whites, blacks, Latinos, Asians—a real diverse crowd he had packed in some Hilton ballroom.

Then there was the Republican nominee, Debby Gallego.

Every rally parroted what she had expressed on the campaign trail: the second-classing of the American Dream to the globalist agenda, which had sacrificed our jobs; border security and national security; the destruction of traditional family values in the interest of the progressive social agenda; the transformation of Washington into a swamp of special interest elitists who had grown richer and more powerful, which she vowed to drain.

And America was eating it up.

Slowly but surely, the conservative base was opening up to the lady who was on her third marriage. Even Evangelicals had taken notice, having thrown their support behind her early in the primaries after it was clear the other Republicans were sure losers against the incumbent Democrat president. The mainstream media had taken notice, too, but in a different way. Polls had her neck-and-neck with the two other candidates, but they all poo-pooed the idea of another populist rising to power a second go around. Said that ship had sailed and America had learned its lesson.

The rallies said otherwise, especially what people said about her.

"She gets what's got us down," represented a common refrain. As did: "She understands me." Her successes in the business world had also ratcheted up her support: "She's the woman to get the job done. After all, look at her success with those tech start-ups! With that history of success, just think what she can do for America."

When asked about her nominal Christianity, especially all those divorces, most of those interviewed were incredulous. "We're not electing a Pastor-in-Chief," one supporter said. "If she takes America back again, I don't care who she's married to —or if she's married at all!"

There was another one of those rallies—and Gina could hardly believe what was staring back at her. Or rather, *who* was staring back at her.

Gwen Anderson.

AKA: Mama.

Decked out in a slinky U.S. flag...something! Looked hand-made, whatever it was. And whatever it was was showing way too much cleavage for a sixty-something woman.

At her left was some dude with a Don't Tread on Me patch on his jean jacket and handlebar mustache and a port-wine stain on the right cheek. On her right, some other dude, a black man with a clean-shaven face stood in pleated pants and a T-shirt with some triangle thingy. Behind them was a sea of Midwest faces— young and old, fresh and weather-worn, middle class and working class.

Mama's kind of people, it was, the whole crowd.

Probably blaring Springsteen's "Born in the U.S.A." along with Lee Greenwood's "God Bless the U.S.A." And there she was: smack dab in the middle of a mostly white crowd in a large circus tent flashing her smiling pearlies and a double OK ring sign, her thumbs and index fingers joined into a circle, wearing that silly dress and a TABA hat.

Take America Back Again.

"Oh, mama..." she groaned. "Just what I need. You on the front page of the *New York Times* to mess up my breakfast!"

A quiet day at the office was just what the doc ordered after that frightful sight. Nothing but paperwork and bonbons for this investigator.

Taking a sip of tea, she went to take a bite of cake when the doorbell rang.

"For the love…"

It rang again. Twice, then again.

"Coming!" she yelled, shuffling down the hardwood hallway again in her pink puffy slippers.

She could see the silhouette of a tall man through the frosted glass of her front door. Bet it was Elijah checking up on her, wondering why she was running late.

Always on time, that Eli was. And always late, she was! Razzed her for it, too. And pestered and picked on and finger-wagged. Was a constant theme of theirs when they were working at the Bureau together. Her always running late, him always complaining about it.

But…hold the cheese stick.

Today was his day off. A personal day to binge-watch straight through his *The West Wing* collection. Had a little thing for Jed Bartlet (no judgment there; who doesn't?) and every four years he binge-watched his favorite show.

So why was he on her front stoop?

Now a hard knock at the door sent Gina scurrying, and cussing, to twist her burnished bronze doorknob.

"Eli, one of these days I'm gonna—"

She opened the door. Her jaw literally dropped at who was standing on the other side.

"Oh my heck!" she exclaimed.

"Hey, Gina," the man in a black suit said, waving.

A familiar face was flashing her a nice set of pearly whites. Hadn't seen Calvin Dobson since college—her boyfriend for all four years! And now vice presidential candidate for President Santos.

But…

What on earth was he doing at her door?

CHAPTER 3

With one hand, Elijah started up his stimming tick again. With the other, he answered his mother's call.

Why was Mama calling? She knew it wasn't their normal time to call. He had things to do, people to see, cases to solve! Well, not that day but normally, both of them with things to do and people to see and cases to solve—him the supernatural crazy, her the actual crazy with her counseling practice back home in Kenturkey.

But she didn't know it was his day off!

Besides, this was breaking the rules. Totally deviated from their weekly rhythm set in stone for, what, a decade now? Which she definitely would have known, and should be sticking to.

They had a weekly check-in phone powwow every Thursday evening. Was the day after the weekly *Survivor* episode, and they would begin by catching up on all the reality show drama. The long-running castaway competition had been a family tradition, Dad and Mom and him watching it from the beginning when that snake Richard Hatch took those other fifteen chumps for a ride. Afterward, they'd chit-chat about work and life and when

Elijah was going to give her grandbabies and get married—except the reverse order. He'd pester her about retiring from her practice and moving to Sarasota, Florida, and remarrying some wrinkly shuffleboard champ—in that order.

So…why was she calling? What did she want? What did it mean?

His buzzing phone yanked him back to the moment. Only a few seconds until it would go to voicemail.

Suppose he should answer the blasted thing and find out.

Elijah brought the phone to life. "Mama, why are you calling this early?"

"Well, hello to you too, Eli," she said in that sweet-sounding Southern twang of hers. Got him every time.

"Joyce, why are you calling this early?" he repeated, using his mother's name.

Now she scoffed. "Elijah Xavier Fox. How many times have I told you it's not proper for a son to address his mama by her first name!"

"A bazillion. Why are you calling this early, and well outside our designated call-in day?"

"Why does there have to be a reason?"

"You're breaking the rules."

"Can't a mama call her boy for a simple chit-chat about their week?"

"Nope. There's always a reason for your calls at—" he cranked his arm for a look-see at his watch "—8:23 in the morning."

"My lanta, child. You've always had a one-track mind!" She sighed, clearing her throat. "But you are right. Something has come up."

He waited for her to explain.

Mama heaved a breath and sighed. "It's about your father's church."

Nearly dropped the phone at the mention of his hometown

Kentucky ecclesial haunt—or rather, Kenturkey, as Elijah affectionately referred to his adoptive state, on account of all the wild turkeys running around their family property out in the Paducah boondocks.

Before his murder in cold blood during the Sunday morning service, Dad had pastored Seventh Baptist Church of Paducah (yes, the town's seventh Baptist church; it's the South) for two decades. Had just celebrated his twenty-year anniversary, too, picking up his only church gig straight out of seminary. So the fact Mama was calling about it…

Not good.

He asked, "What happened? Did it burn down?"

"Heavens no!" Mom exclaimed. "Although it'd be best if someone were to torch the place."

She'd never spoken ill of Dad's church like that before. Something must be bigly up.

Swallowing hard, his stomach churning more from dread than hunger now, Elijah adjusted his grip and plunged into the deep end.

"Mama, please don't tell me you're confessing to a pre-crime of arson, are you?"

"Oh, fiddlesticks, I'm not either."

Mama wasn't one to beat around the cherry tree. A straight shooter, she was. Even on the Thursday calls, there was no meandering, no throat-clearing before getting to the call's punchline. So it wasn't like her to not get to it, on top of calling outside their Thursday arrangement.

So, again, why the early morning call?

His anxiety ratcheted up a bit, and so did his fingers. Thumb to index finger, thumb to middle, thumb to ring finger, thumb to pinkie—then back through it again.

"Alright, lay it on me. What's got you so hot and bothered?"

"It's…well, it's that cotton pickin' pastor, that's what!"

Cotton pickin'? Uh-oh. Breaking out the Southern cuss words now.

"Reverend William Baron?"

"Reverend William—" She scoffed. "It's Pastor Billy now. A man of the people. And for good reason."

"What reason?"

"The man has remade himself into some sort of populist guru fighting against the evil forces of this nation to take America back again."

Elijah smirked. "Where have I heard that slogan before?"

"Exactly! That cotton pickin' political slogan. And suddenly our country church has become the epicenter of the war between good and evil. With him and the conservative populist uprising on one side and the socialist elites on the other."

"Except our struggle isn't against flesh-and-blood actors, *'but against the rulers, against the authorities, against the cosmic powers of this present darkness, against the spiritual forces of evil in the heavenly places,'* as Saint Paul reminds—"

"In the Book of Ephesians, I know," his mother interrupted. "Tell that to Pastor Billy. Do you know, he interrupts the regular worship service each week to go off on whatever bee has buzzed up his knickers?"

Elijah rolled his eyes. "Nice visual there, Mama."

"Diatribes, he calls them. Headline news, where the man riffs off of some political issue."

"Like what?"

"Like everything from forced vaccinations on schoolchildren to the IRS proposing more oversight of personal bank accounts."

"Neither of which are the best propositions in the world."

His mother scoffed. "But ones that're totally irrelevant to Sunday morning worship!"

"Touché. What else?" Elijah asked.

"He goes on and on about how the left has done a power grab to systematically dismantle religion and banish God from the lips, minds, and hearts of believers."

"Not the worst insight in the world."

"And again, totally irrelevant to Sunday morning worship!"

"Touché. Again."

"Then there's his diatribes about stolen elections from the last go around. Last Sunday, he demanded a full audit of all 50 states to find out the level of cheating and the level of manipulation that actually took place, for Pete's sake! People around me were cheering, hootin' and hollerin'. Wanted to spit, it made me so hoppin' mad how Billy had co-opted the Lord's Day to air Uncle Sam's dirty drawers—or grind their axes against those George Soros and Bill Gates fellas."

"Mixing metaphors there a bit, Mama…" Elijah complained, running a hand through his bed-head hair.

This was getting off the rails. Had no interest in politics, and definitely had no interest in jawing about it with his mother that early in the morning.

"That's not even the worst of it!" Mama exclaimed.

"It isn't?"

"Now, I'm not supposed to say anything," she went on, voice growing low and quiet and conspiratorial. "So don't you go flappin' your gums about what I'm 'bouta tell ya."

"Lips are sealed. Now spill the tea, Mama."

She took a breath, then a beat, then: "Billy Baron is fixin' to join the Republican presidential campaign!"

"That's some major tea spillage."

"You're telling me!"

Elijah asked, "In what way?"

"Beats me. All I know is, Patty Lee—"

"The chief elder's wife? What's his name?"

"Right. The chairman of the elder board, Eddy Lee. Anyway, we had coffee the other afternoon, and she told me Pastor Billy informed the church board just two nights ago. Just up and leaving to join Debby Gallego!"

"In what capacity?"

"Rumor has it it's something big. Like campaign manager, or maybe even a cabinet member if she manages to get elected."

Now that took the cheesecake.

Debra Gallego was part of a resurgent movement called Take America Back Again. Part nostalgic throwback, part populist uprising, the movement wasn't a political party per se, but rather a feisty wing of the Republican Party that was in open rebellion against the elites. She also happened to be the daughter of a Texan reverend who made Jerry Falwell of the '80s Moral Majority era look like a cuddly teddy bear.

For the Democratic Party's part, they had their own merry band of rebels: the Push America Forward Now. PAFN didn't have as nice of a ring to it as TABA, but they got their point across. Unlike the nostalgic populists clinging to the past, these activists had one aim: smash that past to pieces and dismantle it limb from limb—literally, too, tearing down statues and murals they deemed regressive.

Their fearless leader, Lenny Levin, was a septuagenarian with wild silver owl hair and a Basset Hound frown still stuck in the '70s, dancing to Joni Mitchell with a peace pipe filled with ganja in one hand and his other raised into a Che Guevara fist. Only he was running as an independent against the establishment Democrat, Roberto Santos, the current president.

Should be an interesting election, that's for sure. And why not? After lab-leaked viruses and murder hornets, uprisings that brought Pacific Northwest cities to their knees, crazed cancer-ridden ex-KGB dictators dismantling the Western order and $5.27 a gallon gas prices—why not carry out an election that officially turned America into a WWE spectacular spectacle?

With his childhood church's pastor now in the mix.

Elijah said, "I'm sure it's nothing to worry about, Mama. Passions are fleeting. Things will cool down after November."

"I'm not so sure about that. Especially since the church board has been more than supportive of Pastor Billy. After all, the congregation has bloomed from a few hundred attendees to near a thousand!"

"Oh my cheeps. Where do you fit them all?"

"A tent erected out on the lawn. And that ain't even accounting for all the people who tune in online. Giving has increased six-fold, too. You can imagine it's made not a few old-time parishioners doing the happy dance."

Elijah sure did. Was having flashbacks to the handful of rowdy and insistent voices Dad had to deal with who didn't think he condemned "the gays" enough or organized protest marches against the lone abortion clinic in town across the river. Not that he didn't express God's creative intent for marriage or the Lord's love for all life, at all ages and stages. Just didn't come at it politically. His was a pastoral angle that cared for people's souls, not about political scores.

He said, "Well, I'm sure it'll be alright, Mama. Might even be a good thing, this Billy dude moving on. You know what Dad used to say. *'God doesn't bite his fingernails over any of this—'*"

"*'Neither should you,'*" his mother finished. "I know what your daddy used to say, but this is different. Something deep is going on, something unsettling."

Elijah's stomach threw up a grumbly complaint, his innards near well about to start eating themselves if he didn't get to his bacon and eggs.

He said, "What do you think I can do about it?"

"Aren't you the Church's policing agency or something?"

"Nope. We investigate the Church's inexplicable cases perpetrated by the cosmic powers of this present supernatural darkness."

"This darn well near seems like the workings of those cosmic powers of this present supernatural darkness you speak of! Especially the way Billy Baron goes on about the battle lines being drawn between good and evil, and we're standing on the brink of a coming war—a Great Awakening, he calls it. Where all will be exposed, the light will pierce the darkness."

Elijah went to retort, but held his tongue. Perhaps a first.

Instead, he went with: "Has a crime been committed?"

"Not that I'm aware of, but—"

"Anyone been murdered?"

"Of course not!"

"Any severed goat heads left on the church's doorstep or exsanguinated bovine carcases end up on the altar?"

"My lanta, heavens no!"

"Sorry. Can't help you."

"Fiddlesticks!"

Elijah went silent. No sense arguing with Mama when she's sunk her teeth into something.

"Eli…" she said, her voice low and demanding. Got that way when she was fixin' to make a move.

Could feel those eyes of hers burrowing into him from hundreds of miles across their 5G network connection—those penetrating blue orbs beneath a furrowed brow, one of those well-plucked eyebrows raised just so.

A shiver ratcheted up Elijah's spine. Had to get off the phone before her powers of mama persuasion overpowered him.

He said, "I suppose I could jump on the interwebs, see what's what."

"That's all I ask, dear," Mama replied, sounding like a victorious smile had spread across her face. "In fact, why don't you see for yourself? It's been ages since you've visited your mama."

Elijah chuckled. "I'm a little tied up here with…umm, things."

She huffed but didn't press it. "Just pray about it, would you, dear?"

He smiled to himself. Pray about it. The Southern way of asking someone to acquiesce to one's demands. After all, how can you say no to the Holy Spirit?

"Sure, Mama. I'll pray about it, and I'll get back to you."

He heard an audible sigh on the other end. Almost of relief, as if the idea he might step in and check things out back home set her mind at ease.

Ending the call, Elijah leaned against his sink, the soft crunch of dog food from his munching pooch the only soundtrack to his distracted mind.

Was unlike Mama to get so worked up about something like this. Loved their old congregation to pieces. How could she not after her husband had served it so faithfully and so long before his untimely death? Still carried a mother hen way about her with the church, but she was always so even keel about life. She trusted Yahweh Almighty to take care of things according to his plan, as Dad had always reminded.

And yet...

Some of what she'd shared did sound serious, the way his teenage church was being used as a campaign soundstage for the powerful ends of the State. Not inexplicable serious, just crazy serious.

Felt the urge to channel his inner Rudyard Kipling: Oh, State is State and Church is Church, and never the twain shall meet.

At least, that's how it should be. Although he liked the early Church father Tertullian's framing of it better: *'What indeed has Athens to do with Jerusalem? What concord is there between the Academy and the Church? What between heretics and Christians?'*

In this case: What does Washington have to do with Rome, the White House to do with Christianity?

DC to do with some Podunk, Paducah country church?

Didn't quite know.

Dad sure did, believing the machinations of this world were super tempting for the Church, using might and power to further its agenda—and getting caught up in its web of corruption.

And he preached against those powers. Refused to bow to them or get entangled in them. It's what Elijah liked about Dad, how he carried on with his simple ministry at his simple church, standing against the powers of this world.

Perhaps he should too.

Perhaps...

That could wait. Cheesy eggs smothered in shredded cheddar with three thick slices of bacon and a side of raspberry-jellied toast toasted extra dark were the first item of business.

Then he'd mossy into Group X HQ and see what he could find out about his hometown church.

CHAPTER 4

T ime stood still.

There Gina was, standing in her slippers in her nightgown in the middle of the threshold of her row house.

And Calvin freakin' Dobson standing on her front stoop!

With that light brown skin of his and those freckles that had stolen her breath back in the day, the characteristics of a mixed marriage between a black dad and Persian mother. And those gleaming white teeth blinding her behind a wide grin that had made her all hot and bothered from plenty of make-out sessions in the back of his Lexus. Not to mention that shiny bald head she loved racing her fingers across, and those wide shoulders and killer cannons that had landed the Wolverines a national championship title.

Not that he was at the University of Michigan on a football scholarship, mind you; she tired from over-wrought minority clichés like the rest of them, herself being written off as an unfeeling zombie and social nincompoop for being autistic. Nopety-nope! His way was paved with a full-ride in the University Honors Program. Football just happened to be one of the many talents that plused that cool brain of his.

And there he was…Calvin freakin' Dobson standing on her front stoop!

Took throat clearing and a gust of frigid fall air riding up her nightgown to snap Gina back to the moment. Nearly unfurled the thing before Cal's very eyes.

She blushed and tightened the hold on the tie keeping the only thing standing between the two in place. Her silk nightgown!

"Caldo the Magnificent?" she said on a disbelieving breath.

He chuckled. "The one and only!"

Gina literally double-blinked to make sure her eyes weren't deceiving her.

Nope. Caldo was still standing on her porch, the nickname she'd given the man their freshman year at Michigan (go Blue!). Reminded her of that Waldo character, on account Calvin always wore striped shirts of one variety or another. One of those Abercrombie & Fitch rugby things. Boy, did he sure look hot in them then.

And now, his black suit and white shirt fitting him perfectly, along with a regimented tie. Again, striped. Blue background with diagonal thick crimson and narrow yellow stripes.

Sun still sets, tides still come and go; some things never change.

Sounds like a country song.

"Calvin Dobson." Gina smirked, crossing her arms and leaning against the doorjamb. "Or I suppose I should say, Congressman Caldo. Maybe even Veep!"

"Hopefully," he said with a chuckle.

"But what on earth are you doing here? Haven't seen sight of you since college."

Now Gina noticed the man had company. Two men in black.

Strike that: Government-issued men in black. Very, very familiar with them type, given her decade with the FBI.

What were they doing perched outside her door? Mystery compounding mystery…

Calvin glanced behind, noticing her gaze. Then he gestured toward the door, face drawn and serious.

"Would you mind if I step inside?"

She crossed her arms. "What's shakin', Caldo?"

The two suits at the bottom of the stairs turned their backs on them and widened their stance—a classic protective posture. Like security guards.

Now Gina saw an earpiece winding down behind their necks, the clear wire disappearing into those black suits.

Yep. Definitely security. Except…

What was going on that Caldo needed such protection? Probably Secret Service, given he was a VP candidate and all. Which was a super-odd turn of things in and of itself, the former Veep being run out of the White House after it came to light he'd been the one responsible for a massive government conspiracy involving aliens and UFOs—or rather, UAPs as Eli would surely have corrected her, unidentified aerial phenomenon.

So, the Latino President had tapped the up-and-comer congressman representing Michigan's 9th congressional district. No, not Detroit's congressman. Bloomfield Hills's, the wealthiest enclave in the Mitten State, his hometown.

Now she saw a few black Chevrolet Suburbans anchored at the other end of the street, blocking traffic, joined by three other men in government-issued suits across the street.

Her college boyfriend leaned in now, brow furrowed.

"I need your help, Gina." He gestured inside. "Please, inside."

So much for paperwork and bonbons.

Gina drew in a measured breath and stepped aside.

"Sure thing, chicken wing. I've got cake."

Cal chuckled. "I'd forgotten that about you. Rhyming all the timing, you were. Loved that about you, too."

She giggled, completely forgetting about that frigid fall now, the temperature ratcheting into the stratosphere.

Shoving a stray lock of ginger hair behind an ear, she gestured inside.

"I'll need to change a minute. Make yourself at home."

"And unfortunately," Cal said, "my men will need a minute to sweep your house. Protocol and all."

"Sure thing—"

She stopped herself, blushing again at his recollection of her rhyming peculiarity.

"Whatev. Just mind my cats and let me change in peace."

They did while she slipped into a pair of dark jeans and a white blouse. Nothing fancy, but fancy enough for a congressman who could very well be America's next Vice President. Thought about adding a string of pearls and a dash of Chanel No. 5 behind the ears, but didn't want to overdo it.

The suits finished their thing just as Gina finished her thing. Bounding down the stairs, her cherry red patent leather pumps clattering away. Perhaps a little overkill, but he was the Democratic VP candidate, for Pete's sake!

One Secret Service agent stood at the door, another at the entrance to her living room. She nodded at the man; he remained impassioned, motionless.

Taking a breath, Gina bounded in to see Cal—and found him, fork in hand, mawing on a piece of cake. Her cake!

"Thith ith good," Cal said with a mouthful, the man shoving in another bite.

She smirked. "Make yourself at home, why don't you. Want a glass of milk to go along with your cake?"

"Yeth, pleath!"

She frowned, putting a hand on her hip.

He swallowed and grinned. "Never mind."

"Good man."

Wiping his mouth with a napkin, Cal set the cleared plate on her glass coffee table. Gina joined him on the leather couch, Baxter bounding onto her lap and sitting on it protectively and throwing Caldo a pair of skeptical cat eyes.

Good cat.

The pair adjusted their positions on either end of the couch, pivoting toward one another. That's when the morning light streaming through the bay window behind them caught Cal's hand just right. Something glittering, something glistering, the morning light glinting off a gold ring on his left hand, second digit in.

A wedding ring.

Gina was suddenly seized with a heart-rending sense of what could have been. The two of them, hands clasped and taking on the world—together. Her heart raced, her breath grew heavy, her head swam with regret.

Damn Mama…

"Thanks for seeing me," he said, shaking her back to the moment. "And so unannounced."

"Out of the blue, more like it! Last thing I ever heard from you was that sorry dear Jane letter breaking off our relationship."

He shifted, frowning. He said lowly, almost out of earshot of his protection, "Obviously you know why…"

Gina joined him in that frown.

Yes. Yes, she did.

Mama had hated she was dating a black man. Insisted it wasn't natural, that God himself had ordained the "coloreds," as she'd crassly put it, were meant to stick to their kind. Even quoted Scripture to defend her nonsense. Could still recall good ol' King Jimmy's translation: *'Be ye not unequally yoked together with unbelievers: for what fellowship hath righteousness with unrighteousness? And what communion hath light with darkness?'*

Her ears burned just thinking about how God's Word had been twisted toward racist ends—and by her mother, no less.

None of what Saint Paul wrote in his first letter to the Corinthians had anything to do with keeping God's creatures with varying shades of melanin from marrying one another! Was about the relationships between followers of Christ and those outside the Church. She'd certainly given Mama a piece of her Scripture-informed mind about the subject, but she was having nothing of it.

So, one day, Mama had gotten hold of Cal and given him a piece of her mind. Pieces Gina cared not to recall in that instance. Boy, was the temperature cranking to beat the band!

Between her and Caldo. Between her and Mama. They were never the same.

Gina adjusted Baxter on her lap and crossed a leg over another, pushing that stray lock of ginger hair back into place and wanting a taste of that frigid fall air again. It was sure getting hot in there!

"Yes, well, that was a long time ago. But you…look at you! VP candidate."

"If I don't get lynched first, maybe…" he muttered.

"For the love…" she complained.

"I'm serious!" Cal exclaimed now, eyes flashing wide along with his nostrils. Not in anger or irritation. But…was that fear she'd glimpsed?

He heaved a breath and raced a hand across his bald head. "Sorry. I didn't mean to offend you with my careless comment. And certainly apologize."

She waved a dismissive hand. "No, it's alright, Caldo. But… what's this about?"

Now she gestured toward the suit guarding the living room before waving it between them, Baxter yawning widely and throwing up a bored squeak.

Cal nodded, finally looking ready to talk.

"I need your help."

"You already said that, but all you've helped yourself to is my cake." She threw him a wry grin and a wink.

"Which was amazing, by the way."

That heat returned to her neck, and she worried it was blooming pink in her cheeks now.

"What sort of help?"

Cal leaned toward her. "The Bureau kind."

Gina startled. "The Bureau kind?"

"The Bureau kind."

"Is there an echo in here?" she said with a smirk.

"Specifically, your experience with cultic ritualistic killings, like your doctoral dissertation was on."

"How did you know about that?"

Cal shrugged. "I read it. Couldn't help keeping tabs on you after we…well, parted ways."

Now Gina really did blush, and grinned. Widely. Couldn't help it!

She shook her head, more to shake away the embarrassment but also to signal his mistake.

"Sorry, partner. I'm not at the FBI anymore."

His face fell, and he leaned back with a slump. "You're not? But I thought you were working down in the bowels of the Hoover Building. Something to do with cases about unexplainable phenomenon."

"You're a little late to that punchbowl, I'm afraid. It's been a few years since those days. I was down at Quantico helping out at the Academy when…"

Gina trailed off, not wanting to touch that crazy with a ten-foot pole. Getting chased by rogue government agents sent by the man who'd formerly filled his VP shoes wasn't high on her small-talk list!

"It doesn't matter," she went on. "I left the Bureau last year."

"I see…"

Disappointment draped his face, dejection even, like he'd been denied some saving grace.

What was going on?

Gina put a hand on his leg; he flinched, meeting her eyes.

Leaning forward, she asked lowly, "What does this have to do with my thesis, Cal? What's going on?"

He glanced at the Secret Service agent still standing outside the living room and leaned in himself. She could feel his breath brushing her face, warm and minty. Just like she recalled from nearly two decades ago.

"Something's happened. Something not even the press knows about."

"OK…"

"It's why I showed up at your house like this, unannounced. Sorry about that, by the way."

She smiled. "No prob, Bob."

He grinned back, that bazillion dollar smile sending her heart soaring—and pulse racing, joined by that dang heat again.

"Anyway…" Gina said, trying to move it along.

Cal cleared his throat. "I was needing a friend on the inside of the Bureau. Someone with your expertise who could handle a delicate turn of things with the campaign."

She frowned. "Sorry to disappoint, but I'm all ears if you'd like my…expertise, as you put it."

He scooted closer now, saying lowly, "You need to swear to secrecy, Gina."

"Uhh, alright…"

"If word got out, things could get…complicated. There are forces at work that would have a heyday with what I'm about to tell you."

Now she giggled. "Got a tin-foil hat hanging out in that suit of yours?"

He pulled back, his nostrils flaring again. "I mean it, Gina. This is serious!"

"Sorry. Yes, alright. Sworn to secrecy, I am. But now you're scaring me. What's got you so riled? What happened?"

Cal took a breath, then a beat. Could see the wheels turning in his head, behind his eyes—that noggin of his deciding whether to spill the tea to her.

Then those gears clicked into place; he'd made his choice.

He said, "A head showed up on my front lawn."

"Egads!" She jumped. "A head?"

"Well, a goat head. Impaled on a pole."

"For the love..." Gina moaned, a shiver ratcheting up her spine at the thought.

"That's not all."

"As if an impaled severed goat head wasn't enough?"

He shifted, explaining: "I discovered the...lawn ornament early in the night after spotting an orange glow outside before bed."

Gina leaned in, interest growing alongside dread.

"And?"

"And...there was a fire."

"On your lawn?"

"Nothing major, but someone had taken lighter fluid and drawn—here, let me..."

Cal withdrew his phone from his suit coat and swiped it to life, then brought up his photos and spun it around for Gina's viewing.

No severed goat noggin, but there was the faint impression of a burned, upside-down triangle. Grass was charred, blackened to a crisp in a messy pattern.

Sliding his phone back in his jacket, he continued, "Got to it with my lawn hose before it did any damage, or drew any attention from the neighbors."

"I didn't see the—" Gina swallowed "—goat head in the photo."

"Stuffed it in several garbage bags. It's with the FBI's hate crimes unit."

She nodded, leaning back against the couch, emotion suddenly seizing her throat and pricking at her eyes—that same sense of what could have been rising.

"I came to you because of your expertise in these sorts of things."

Gina snorted a laugh. "You mean a severed goat head impaled on a pole in a ring of fire?"

He laughed. "Something like that. Seriously, though, this smacks of the occult, don't it?"

Heaving a breath, she nodded. "Sure does."

"What can you tell me about it, the head, the fire?"

"Well, in a cultic sense, a goat head has been associated with Baphomet."

"Baphomet?"

"A supposed symbol of balance in various occult and mystical traditions, originating with the Gnostics and Templars."

"So it's definitely occult."

"Definitely occult. A recently unveiled statue at the Satanic Temple in your neck of the woods in Detroit, Michigan, depicted the satanic character with a goat head."

Cal slumped back with a sigh. "That's what I thought—what I feared."

"Are you sure this wasn't some sort of racial thing, an intimidation tactic by the Michigan Militia or something?"

"Not that the FBI can gather."

"But you said the head is with their hate crimes unit."

"And the Secret Service. Or at least they're trying to claim jurisdiction. A real pissing match between the two, it's been."

Gina smirked. "A men in black sword fight. Gotta love it."

"Except when my family's life is on the line! Thank God my two girls were sound asleep. But my wife…Vivian hasn't been able to get the sight out of her head."

"Suppose not…" Gina said softly, that sadness over what could have been renewed at the mention of his family.

"So far, from what I can gather, there are no known white supremacist groups that do that sort of thing." Cal snorted a laugh and shook his head. "They're much more liable to stick a cross on my front yard and light it on fire than an impaled goat head!"

Gina shivered at the thought of anyone using Christ's cross in such a hateful, wicked manner. Much less anyone, her Caldo the Magnificent, being intimidated and harassed like that.

"Suppose you're right about that," she said. "But I do wonder…"

"About what?"

"About how I can help."

Cal shrugged. "What can you do, you're out of the Bureau?"

"Not entirely…"

"I don't understand. You said you'd left the FBI."

"True, but not the profession. I've joined an investigative agency called Group X."

He laughed. "Group X? Sounds a little too on the nose, don't you think, Gina Anderson. I think Gillian Anderson wants her Dana Scully back."

Gina crossed her arms. "Ha-ha. Very funny, Cal. But we're a serious agency, my partner and me."

"What's this…agency of yours with? Never heard of it before."

"A subgroup with the Order of Thaddeus, a religious order, that takes on the Church's inexplicable cases."

Now he raised a brow. "What, with the Vatican? Like the Holy See's X-Files, or something?"

"We're an ecumenical group, but you could say that. We actually carry on a lot of the work we did at the Bureau, looking into just this sort of unexplainable phenomenon."

"Like severed goat heads smacking of the occult showing up on a sitting U.S. congressman's front lawn?"

She smiled proudly. "Exactly!"

Cal took a breath and rubbed a hand across his head. "I don't know. Sounds pretty hinky to me…"

Gina scoffed. "I'll have you know we solved the minister serial killer case from last year."

"The one with the priest and the AME minister and megachurch pastor?"

"Sounds like a bad bar joke, but yeah. That was us. Along with the suicide cluster in Mill Creek Junction from your home state."

Now he whistled. "Dang, girl. Sounds like you still got game."

"You know it!"

"And you can take on this case?"

She shrugged. "I'd have to talk it over with my partner, Elijah. But there's enough going on to look into it. Enough elements that smack of the spiritual—the cultic elements I know all too well—to warrant at least a peek, even though it's not the Church's business, per se."

Cal went quiet, staring off into the ceiling.

"This partner of yours," he finally said, "can he be trusted?"

"Implicitly."

"Can he keep this confidential?"

"Absotutely!"

Cal turned to her now, drawing close. "And you think you can make sense of this. That there may be some—what, some underlying spiritual power behind this?"

Gina shrugged. "In my line of work, Caldo, everything is spiritual."

His face tightened, jaw locking with a mixture of resolve and dread. Then he nodded and stood, opening up for an embrace.

She joined him, the pair sharing a quick, professional hug between two long-time friends.

Cal told Gina he would have his people coordinate with her and Eli, giving them access to the details of the investigation. She said she couldn't promise anything, but she'd sure try her darnedest. He seemed relieved to have a friendly face on what was understandably an unnerving and downright terrifying ordeal—and on the cusp of a presidential election that could very well tear the country apart.

Gina watched Calvin Dobson, VP candidate extraordinaire, pull away from the curb in his black Chevrolet Suburban. Thought she caught him throw her a wave, but she wasn't sure.

She smiled and waved back regardless, disbelieving the turn of things. That sense of what could have been now shifting into a resolve to lean into what was—to help her friend, to protect him even.

Here all she'd wanted was a day of paperwork and bonbons.
That could wait.
Because Caldo needed her help.
Needed her.
Which was a pretty cool way to start the day.
Just hoped Eli agreed.

CHAPTER 5

lijah spent the rest of his morning poking at his begs and acon, not making much progress. Couldn't get his mama's phone call out of his mind.

Everything Dad had built—a focus on the Kingdom of God rather than the City of Man, as Saint Augustine had framed it; a Sunday morning of God-centered worship and the proclamation of his Word and Good News; a kind and loving community that might have had differences, but would come together to put on the best potlucks this side of the Mississippi to raise funds to help their brothers and sisters in need.

All that seemed to be at risk. All in the interest of gaining and maintaining political power.

No amount of cheesy eggs and salted bacon cooked to an oh-so-good crisp was going to make him feel better.

And yet…

Elijah knew there had been cracks even back then in the facade. Glimmers of political lines drawn in blue and red that gave Dad not a few sleepless nights.

His adoptive father still had to put up with divisive nonsense pastoring a Southern church that proudly displayed Old Glory alongside the Christian flag at the front of the sanctuary. Was a firm believer in the separation of Church and State after seeing up close and personal how politics compromises the faith. Mixes about as well as OJ and jet fuel.

Yet there were always those handfuls of congregants who didn't feel like he was preaching against abortion or gay marriage enough. Or when he did wade into social issues, like exhorting his country church to take care of widows and orphans (you know, the kind of religion Saint James says *'is pure and undefiled before God the Father'* a la his book on the subject, chapter numero uno), he'd be fingered as a commie pinko.

You don't get fingered as a commie pinko and survive another day in the South. Especially survive another day as a pastor of a Baptist church in the South!

But somehow he did, being available and faithful to the good Lord's calling on his life to shepherd his flock through the social and political crazy, which didn't even touch on the everyday crazy—cancer diagnosis, job loss, marriage splits, gossip and slander.

What Mama described—well, that Pastor Billy fella seemed to be taking things to a whole new level of crazy than what those handfuls of congregants had stirred up when Dad was at the helm. Seemed like he'd cloned them all and gathered them under a big-top bonanza—Ringling Brothers and Barnum & Bailey style.

A crazy that was threatening Dad's memory, threatening the church he'd built for two decades and given his life to—given his life *for*.

And Elijah Xavier Fox didn't like it.

Not one bit.

But what could he do about it?

He frowned at the thought. What could he do about it? He was the freakin' director of an investigative agency within a religious order founded by one of Jesus' disciples! With half a decade of law enforcement experience investigating the government's crazy, joined with another half decade of academic experience sharpening his biblical and theological chops.

If there was anyone who could make sense of what was going down back home—and then put a stop to it—it was him.

But should he? Did the crazy brewing in Seventh Baptist of Paducah rise to the level of inexplicable crazy?

A sudden thought pinged Elijah. A verse, actually. The one that sat at the heart of Group X, the one he and Mama had quoted.

'For our struggle is not against blood and flesh but against the rulers, against the authorities, against the cosmic powers of this present darkness, against the spiritual forces of evil in the heavenly places.'

Is that what was going on, back home—in this election even? Should he stand against these powers—the supernatural ones of the Unseen Realm? Were there powers to even stand against?

Perhaps he should find out. Poke around a bit and see what was what.

Which meant climbing onto his motorcycle and cruising into the office.

On his day off.

Such is life, he supposed, when the fate of the Church rests in the palms of your hands.

Or at least the fate of one small-town Kenturkey country church.

Elijah downed his coffee and jumped in the shower to wash away the night before throwing on dark denim and a black turtleneck. If Timberlake brought sexy back, no reason Elijah Xavier Fox couldn't bring turtlenecks back. The day called for it.

Revving his BMW motorcycle, he peeled out of a narrow walkway that served as a driveway and cruised on toward destiny.

And boy, did he love revving and cruising! With all of the potential power in those handlebars, and the 91 horsepower at 4,750 revolutions per minute propelling him forward, giving him all the control he needed to go wherever and whenever—and as fast as ever—he wanted.

Power and control.

The two things in his life he'd never had. Not over his life, certainly not over where it went—being an orphan and thrown headlong into the foster care system. Not even his own body, his emotions and brain and body triggered by stimulus and circumstances outside of his control, and leading to less-than-ideal reactions he had little power over.

But behind those chrome handlebars of his BMW R 18 racing through Washington, the world was his oyster bar!

Not one of those hippy Harley hogs that smacked of biker cliché. Not a Honda, either, or other Japanese variety. No Yamaha or Kawasaki for him, either.

What Elijah rode was the only motorcycle worth its salt.

A beemer. With two Es and one M. Not a bimmer, with one I and two Ms, which is the American bastardization for cars of the original moniker for BMW motorbikes.

Beemer, that's what he rode. Specifically, the throwback hog sporting the dexterity and temerity of a modern cruiser combined with the nostalgic sense of classic beemer design.

Beemer, not bimmer.

It was nearing the middle of the morning, 9:30 a.m. Had always insisted the day was pretty well over by the time 10 a.m. rolled around, and if he wasn't productive by then, the day was shot. But it was his day off, so he cut himself some slack.

The whipping air slapped his face like an angry mama, even though Joyce had never laid a hand on him; he'd gotten enough beatings from Ursula the Terrible to last a lifetime. There was a bite to it, the fall air laced with the dueling scents of dead leaves and woodsmoke.

Best. Smells. Ever!

Along with hot apple cider and cinnamon and pipe tobacco and wool—the smells of fall.

His fave. Season. Ever!

The clear sky and bright sun tilted toward the horizon just so, inflaming a cluster of clouds red and casting angular shadows across the road.

Never believed in those ridiculous sailor superstitions about the weather. Red sky at night, sailor's delight; red sky in the morning, sailor's warning. Was a bunch of hooey. The day was what you made of it, and he planned to make it a great day.

Arriving at his destination, Elijah pulled into a looping driveway off Michigan Avenue and turned into a service entrance on the westside of the Basilica of the National Shrine of the Immaculate Conception. The access driveway ran behind a stone wall and a thick hedgerow, leading to a keycard entrance into Group X HQ.

He loved his new place of employ. Much snazzier than the functional block of glass and concrete he'd worked in at the FBI, and even at that Protestant seminary. Never understood the Protestant fascination with de-ostentatizing their sacred spaces, whether schools or churches.

Strip-mall churches were well and good, carrying the good news of God's crazy love in Jesus to people on the streets. But the big-box monstrosities anchored along highways and spread across suburbs like Kohl's department stores? Why trade the stone and stained glass of the cathedrals their Catholic and Orthodox brothers and sisters built for fog machines and fancy light shows? Ostentatious design and architecture all the way!

While functional '70s architecture had been most of his church experience, now smells and bells were his jam. Probably had something to do with his Jewish people's penchant for cultivating sacred spaces that reeked of burning spices and gums from thuribles—those metal censers suspended from chains in synagogues with burning incense. Mostly, it was thanks to his experience of Anglicanism while studying in England.

He pulled into an empty spot next to a silver Audi sedan. Abraham Patel's car, their fearless techie who'd more than earned his keep. But...no candy apple red Honda Odyssey. His partner's ride of choice. Didn't understand her affinity with the Japanese minivan. Something about the tinted windows and bangin' stereo.

Either way, it wasn't in the parking lot. Which meant Gina wasn't at HQ. Where was his partner?

Leaving his helmet on his hog, he went to a heavy steel door anchored at the side of the cathedral, an old outpost for SEPIO, the muscular arm of the Order of Thaddeus. A Latin acronym for *Sepio, Erudio, Pugno, Inviglio, Observo.*

Protect, instruct, fight for, watch over, heed. Based on Jude 3, Saint Jude Thaddeus' exhortation to *'contend for the once-for-all faith entrusted to God's holy people.'*

Near the start of the Church's existence, the good Apostle Jude Thaddeus had already seen forces inside and outside the faith working against it. So, he launched a religious order about five centuries before that was a Christian thing, historians pegging the first Christian order with Saint Benedict in the 6th century.

For centuries, the Order had worked tirelessly to instantiate Thaddeus's vision for faith-contending—all the while battling nemeses from the shadows of history. Especially one particular bad actor who happened to be headed up by the Order Master's little bro, Nous.

Although formerly a Roman Catholic outfit, the Order of Thaddeus itself was an ecumenical mission, with members from every Christian denomination. Protestant, Catholic, Orthodox, even some Southern Baptists on the force.

And now a Messianic Jew who formerly taught at an evangelical Protestant seminary, partnered with a charismatic Catholic.

Who wasn't around.

He slapped his hand on the entrance security biometric pad when the whirl of an engine caught his attention.

Spinning around, a candy apple red Honda Odyssey rolled

into view from around the hedgerow. Elijah's face widened into a grin.

"Gina colada…"

The Honda braked hard in an empty spot next to his beemer, a soprano belting some operatic number heard through the tinted windows.

He darted to his partner as she climbed out of her pimped-out ride, those wavy ginger locks of hers falling past her shoulders, though the two didn't embrace.

Instead, they both waved a hand, the motion synchronized and almost touching, but not quite. A greeting they had practiced and perfected working together at the Bureau. Touching wasn't their thing.

"What are you doing here?" Gina asked. "Thought it was your day off."

"It was. Something's come up. Why are you late?"

"Something big showed up at my house."

Elijah frowned. "How big?"

"Former boyfriend big."

Took him a beat to get her meaning. Then he did.

"Congressman Dobson? The Democratic Veep candidate?"

"That'd be the one."

"Oh my cheeps. What did he want?"

"I'll tell you inside."

Repeating the security rigamarole, Elijah pushed through the entrance, and the pair were met by a short, sterile-white hallway leading to an elevator. Punching the lowest floor, the pair traveled three stories beneath the Catholic church down to Group X HQ.

Another palm-reading keypad stood guard at double doors, waiting for Eli's hand. Security rigamarole times two.

When one door unlocked, he opened it and led them inside.

Dimmed recess lighting around the perimeter shone down upon narrow tables lining dark walls commanded by workstations. Only one man was working away at one of those stations, Abraham Patel. A massive screen hung dormant at one end. A raised platform with a few chairs stood at the center awaiting someone's control. His.

Elijah recalled the history of his employer in his briefing with Silas Grey, his new boss and Master of the Order of Thaddeus. Or was, until some operation went sour.

His wife, Celeste, who also happened to be filling in while the chief was AWOL, headlined the more kinetic wing of the Order. Something called SEPIO. Sort of a Navy SEALs for Jesus with a team of former military and intelligence officers that surrounded the memory of the faith with a hedge, as the Latin *sepio* means. SEPIO was the operational arm of the Order of Thaddeus to fight for the Church's memory.

Group X was different, more an investigative agency. X For *inexplicitus*, Latin for unexplainable—along with inexplicable, incomprehensible, inconceivable. Also had the advantage of mirroring the Greek letter *Chi*, which was the first letter for Christ, an X. They took on the Church's X-Files, so to speak.

He and Gina had worked their own set of *inexplicitus* cases for the FBI, the kind of the more paranormal variety, giving them a unique edge and perspective standing against the darkness. They had been handpicked by Silas to work the same magic for Group X after assisting with a SEPIO operation that unveiled an uprising from the Unseen Realm, the cosmic powers of this supernatural darkness pressing against the world in greater, deliberate measure.

"Good good good!" Abraham exclaimed, standing and offering a *clap-clap-clap*. "I have been wondering when you two would be showing up."

Elijah said, "Why? It's my day off."

"Oh, I am being sorry. Director Bourne—erm, Bourne-Grey. Or is it just Grey?" The thin man in brown slacks and a red argyle sweater threw up a scoff, then his hands, before adjusting his thick, black glasses. "Celeste has been looking for you. Expressed an urgency, she did."

Before Elijah could respond, there was a *brong-brong-brong* sounding through the room.

"Egads," Gina said, pressing her hands against her ears. "What is that ungodly sound?"

Abraham answered, "It is being the teleconference indicator. I have patched you through to the Order Master's study."

Celeste suddenly appeared on the large screen. Abraham wasn't kidding.

She was clacking away on a computer, face pinched in concentration and turned away slightly toward another monitor. Didn't appear to notice they'd teleconferenced into her Order HQ digs beneath the Washington National Cathedral.

The soft clattering of her keyboard continued filling the room, along with an awkwardness at their voyeuristic intrusion.

Elijah cleared his throat, and Celeste jumped. She glanced at them and nodded.

"Jolly good. You're there," she said in a perfectly posh British accent.

He said, "I take it Master Grey is still MIA if you're in his chair. The other Master Grey, I mean."

Celeste frowned, a slight crimson rising to her cheeks. She and Silas were now a mister-missus pair. She'd been given the reins to the Order on a provisional basis, and rumors were swirling that her hubby Silas was gone for good.

"Yes, well, that's neither here nor there. Where have you two been?"

"It's my day off," Elijah explained.

"And I was held up," Gina answered.

"By the VP, no less."

"The Vice President?" Celeste exclaimed.

Gina ribbed Elijah for letting the cat out of the bag; he yelped.

"Calvin Dobson," she explained. "The new VP candidate with President Santos. He was an old friend who came looking for a favor."

Elijah smirked. "Old *boy*friend, more like it."

Another jab to the ribs; another yelp.

Celeste said, "Regardless, I'm in need of your assistance on a matter that's—"

"Nope," Elijah said.

She frowned. "What do you mean, nope?"

"I mean nope."

"Nope what?"

"Nope nope."

"Stuff and nonsense…What are you going on about?"

"I think what he means is," Gina said, taking over, "we have a case."

He turned to her. "We do?"

She shrugged. "Maybe. It's what I was meaning to share."

Celeste leaned back in her chair, the dark wood walls and bookshelves of the Order Master's study visible now. "Go on."

Gina recounted what the congressman had shared, the whole bloody and fiery affair. Was something straight out of a Stephen King fever dream!

Which was just what the Group X doc ordered.

Except…

"That's odd," Elijah said, something about her story striking him.

"What's odd?" she asked.

"My mother called this morning talking about the same thing."

"What thing?"

"That thing. About the cosmic powers sticking their nose in our nation's political business. Same thing is going on back home."

"In Kenturkey?"

"What's this Kenturkey business?" asked Celeste.

"She means Kentucky," Elijah explained. "My hometown of Paducah."

"What about it?"

"My mother called and said something strange has been going on in my childhood church."

Gina asked, "The one your daddy had pastored before he passed?"

"Right. A strange mixture of biblicism and patriotism. Then there's the juicy tidbit the lead pastor is joining the Republican ticket as some high-ranking muckety-muck."

"What the what?"

"But I was sworn to secrecy. So don't say anything."

Celeste sighed. "We don't have time for personal side projects."

Elijah turned to her. "It's not a side project. There's a strange nationalism affecting the Church. Not to mention some cultic crazy infecting the election."

"I don't want you focused on that. I need you—"

"Silas never dictated to us the cases we took."

Celeste threw him a lock-jawed grin. "I'm not Silas, mate."

"I know. You've got better legs."

Gina groaned, putting her hand against her forehead and giving it a shake.

"What? She does. Not that I'm making a move or anything."

Celeste bit her lower lip, looking like she was either holding back an irritated retort or a laugh. Hoped it was the latter; definitely could be the former.

She finally said, "I'll give you one day. That is all."

"A day?" Elijah whined.

She stiffened now and leaned in toward the camera. "Shall that be sufficient, Agent Fox?"

"It shall," Gina said. "Right, Eli?"

She threw him eyes that told him neither the time nor the place to squabble; to say yes and move on. Sometimes she had to do that.

Elijah sighed but nodded, saying nothing more.

"Right. Keep me apprised," Celeste said, "of anything you find. We'll reconvene here tomorrow."

She signed off with nothing further.

"Stuff and nonsense is right," Elijah muttered under his breath. "Who does she think she is barging onto our screen and telling us what to investigate?"

"Uhh, our boss!" Gina replied.

"Provisional!"

"Cut her some slack, would you? She's up to her neck in crazy with the looming election on top of her new hubby's struggles. Not to mention the Order's with their leadership turned upside down."

"Suppose you're right. Maybe I should send her a gerbera daisy, maybe gummy bears. I hear ladies like that sort of thing."

She smiled. "That would be a nice gesture."

"Except…" Elijah cranked his wrist for a look-see. "We've got T-minus twenty-three hours and fifty-eight—no, wait, strike that. Twenty-three hours and fifty-*seven* minutes to see if there's anything *inexplicitus* to this made-for-streaming political conspiracy."

Gina turned to him with a grin. "You know what this calls for, don't you?"

"Nope. Already ate. Well, sort of."

She scoffed. "All I've had is a piece of red velvet cake."

"Suppose that's better than cheesecake."

"We all know how much you detest *that* dessert. Come on, we do our best work over eggs and bacon."

She was right on that one, but he'd lost his appetite mulling over what Mama had called about. Although…it was nearing the hour Elijah turned into a pumpkin if he didn't get a bagel and coffee. Supposed they should get to it.

"Fine," he said. "But you're driving."

She folded her arms and grinned. "Fine. Cracker Barrel it is."

CHAPTER 6

ina basked in the glory of Pavarotti as she drove the twenty minutes to Cracker Barrel a few miles outside the District. Sort of pedestrian, more preferring contemporary operatic heavyweights like Netrebko and Bartoli—some women with pipes, they were, who'd make her feminist mama proud. But sometimes the moment called for the simple, the mundane, the pedestrian. The Pavarotti.

Traffic was surprisingly light, so they arrived at the über-Americana joint in no time flat. Wasn't Gina's first choice for work powwows, the place giving her the heebie-jeebies. Didn't help the place reeked of cinnamon sticks and apples and lilies thanks to a wall of scented candles. Then there was the olden-day kitsch that was supposed to spark a nostalgic love for a simpler American life the century before last.

Never understood that sentiment in the slightest. Who'd want to go back to an age without refrigerators and microwaves, where the quickest transportation produced gas instead of guzzling it and you had to churn your own butter? Gina sure didn't, that's for darn tootin'! Mama sure did. Which was probably why she hated the joint so much.

Their Toledo double-wide was filled to the brim in the same

sorts of antiques that decorated Cracker Barrels strewn across America. Kerosene lamps and wagon wheels, washboards and crank radios, even horse bridles and saddles. Mama thought it made their mobile home look sophisticated. Gina thought it made it look like, well, a Cracker Barrel—cheap and trashy!

Had never told Elijah that until this past year. Knew the place meant the world to him since his adoptive parents had taken him to it first thing after their adoption papers were signed. Cracker Barrel was a thing for him and his folks, which became a thing for him and Gina as well, the restaurant becoming their go-to place to ponder the details of their FBI cases. They'd solved more than their fair share at those tables meeting over plates of pancakes and cheesy eggs, bacon and steak, fried apples and grits. Far more than any of their former Bureau colleagues packed into fluorescent-lit conference rooms with burnt Folgers and Krispy Kreme donuts.

At least they made a mean breakfast, which Gina was hankering for after being interrupted by Caldo the Magnificent and his severed goat head. Too weird for words, it was—all of it. Calvin Dobson showing up at her house like that seeking her help. The story about the freakin' severed goat head—impaled inside a burning triangle!

Again: too weird for words.

Thankfully, a proper breakfast was just around the corner.

Gina pulled her candy apple red Honda Odyssey into the Cracker Barrel parking lot, sandwiching it between a massive Ford pickup and an aging, sagging Chevy Bronco. In fact, hers was the only foreign car in the joint. Made sense for the CB clientele.

Climbing out, the scent of burning wood hung heavy, along with grilled meat and something sugary. Stomach rumbled something fierce now on their march across the parking lot, her head feeling faint with hunger.

Just her luck there was an hour wait. Elijah complained loudly about the decline in the American service industry. The hostess encouraged him to write his congressman, with a wink and a chuckle; he said he would, in all seriousness.

Across the street sat a small diner called Sunny Side Up. Looked more accommodating, so they made for that instead.

Suited Gina just fine because the memory from earlier in the year at that same Cracker Barrel was still fresh. Had come to pore over their first case only to have some demon-possessed psychopath shoot it up.

Had no interest in a replay of that crazy again!

They took a booth at the back along a bank of windows flanking the parking lot and within darting distance of an emergency exit. Because if there was anything they'd learned at the FBI it was to be within eyeshot of an exit. Never knew when the shiznit would hit the fan, and a quick escape would be needed.

Their waitress was a rail-thin co-ed in a pink shirt and matching skirt with a giant poodle on it. Clearly, the place took its own nostalgia for America's glory days a little too seriously. It was like American corporations were selling memories more than food.

The young woman named Taylor took their orders.

Tea with a plate of three buttermilk pancakes, scrambled eggs, and thick-sliced bacon for Gina. Coffee and a raisin bagel for Elijah, a mid-morning routine she'd learned not to mess with.

Their new powwow place bespoke a good-'ol-days vibe Gina knew never really existed. Oldies played softly in the background, powered by an old-school jukebox with hits stuck in the 1950s and '60s. Walls were white with baby blue and soft pink booths edged by chrome. A long countertop of beige Formica ran the length of the joint, with little round chrome-padded stools. A few people sat there reading iPads and munching on muffins and plates of eggs.

Gina rested her elbows on the table, fresh cleaner wetting her skin and tickling her nose. She frowned, but at least cleanliness was their policy.

Elijah glanced around with a sigh. "It ain't the Barrel, but I suppose it'll do."

"Selling the same nostalgic charm," she said.

"I prefer mine packaged in rustic pioneer, not this Golden Age nonsense."

She scoffed. "You sound like my mother."

"So," Elijah started, "back at it again."

"Suppose so. Though I'm not sure what *it* is."

Waitress Taylor brought them their tea and coffee and promised their food was on the way.

The Beatles started in with "Help!" and Gina settled back in her seat with her tea. Wasn't Pavarotti, or Bartoli, but the food joint could do worse than John Lennon. Except that horrid "Imagine" song. Hated that nonsense with a passion that burned bright and strong.

Elijah asked, "What do we got so far?"

"Let's see here," Gina began. "One severed goat head impaled in a flaming triangle on a sitting U.S. congressman's front lawn."

"A congressman who happens to be the VP candidate for the current setting President."

"That smacks of the occult."

"Sure smacks that way. Though I'm not sure I can recall satanists using triangles as their symbol of choice. Usually the pentagram type."

Gina frowned. Had to give him that.

"True, but the goat head is certainly a thing."

He nodded. "Baphomet."

"Which is definitely a satanist thing," Gina said. "In fact, the Bureau was all in a tizzy last year after several dead goats were found in El Paso. None of their eatable parts had been removed, and instead they'd been exsanguinated."

"Oh my cheeps," Eli said. "Drained of blood?"

"Righto. And fire rituals have also been part of cultic traditions."

"You said the Bureau ruled out racial intimidation?"

"That's what Cal said."

"But I'd be surprised if there wasn't at least some racist motivation. How could there not be? You've got a black VP with a severed head and burned triangle symbol on his lawn!"

"Except them type," Gina replied, "are more apt to burn crosses than lighter fuel-fueled triangles with severed goat heads impaled at the center."

"Touché," Eli said, folding his arms and leaning back with a sigh.

"How about on your end? You said something about your childhood church getting mixed up in the election."

He sat forward again, ready to engage.

"Yuppers. Mama said Daddy's church has been transformed into a Faithful Majority convention!"

"What the what?"

"The bozo who took over for Dad seems to fancy himself the next James Maxwell."

"The leader of the Faithful Majority."

"Bingo. It's like that political action committee has taken over my hometown church!"

"How?"

"Pastor Bozo doesn't seem content enough to let the Bible inform his sermons. Instead, his Sunday morning services are infused with politics, plunging the church into this good-versus-evil showdown. Makes me want to puke thinking about it."

She could tell, Eli's face falling and his shoulders slumping.

"That's not even touching on the fact the dude is slated to join the Republican presidential candidate as some muckety-muck."

"Yeah, what's that about?"

He shook his head in silence, his face brightening red with a rage she'd seen before.

Taylor arrived with their food, giving them a hard reset.

Gina attacked her pancakes first, spreading the butter around and smothering them in syrup. Both were the fake stuff; no real butter or Canada's best for this joint. She didn't mind. They were blueberry, her fave, and the tart fruit with the sweet-and-salty garnishes did her tastebuds good.

Eli sat in silence munching on his raisin bagel, the cream cheese thick, and taking slurping sips of his coffee smelling like a gym bag. *Blech!*

After a few beats of eating in silence, he said, "So let me see if I got this right. We've got a Veep candidate dogged by weirdness that smacks of the occult. Then we've got a small-town, small-time pastor joining a rival political party and using his stage as a political soapbox."

"Sounds about right," Gina said, shoving a forkful of eggs into her mouth—the cheddar sharp and eggs peppery.

Elijah gulped down a mouthful of brew. "What do you think is going on here, Gina colada?"

"I don't know. Hopefully not a conspiracy on the level of last election."

"Oh yeah. Remember that Drudge Report scoop?"

"Do I ever. The man had posted recordings of some cray-cray conversations between religious wackadoodles conspiring to bring down the Republic!"

"Don't forget those two attention-grabbing headlines above the fold: MORMON REPUBLICAN PRESIDENTIAL CANDIDATE PLEDGES U.S. DOWNFALL," Eli said, spreading his palms and waving them above his head like a marquee billboard. "And TREASON: YOUNG THEOCRATIC HOSTILE TAKEOVER."

"Joined by," Gina went on, "the site's trademark blue-and-red spinning police strobe light. Yeah, I remember those."

"Pretty much re-established Drudge's reputation as a first-to-press alternative to the mainstream media reminiscent of the Monica Lewinsky scandal that catapulted the site to notoriety back in the '90s."

"Like I said, hope this ain't a conspiracy on that level of cray-cray."

Eli leaned forward, elbows on the table. "So, where does that leave us?"

"Especially given Celeste's instructions to pop a squat or get off the pot."

He twisted up his face. "I think you're mixing metaphors there, Gina colada."

"Whatevs. My point is, how is any of this *inexplicitus*?"

"Well, that goat head seems pretty unexplainable!"

"Which is for the FBI and Secret Service to figure out. Doesn't affect the Church in the slightest."

"I'm not so sure about that. Daddy always said that behind every earthly power is a heavenly one."

"What did he mean by that? That God was sovereign, or what?"

"Definitely that. Because as Paul wrote in the Book of Romans, *'there is no authority except from God, and those authorities that exist have been instituted by God.'* He also meant the spiritual kind."

Gina nodded, understanding his meaning. "The principalities and powers of this present supernatural darkness."

"Bingo."

"But you can't go looking for the Devil behind every political candidate."

"What about every impaled severed goat head?"

Gina went to answer but snapped her mouth shut.

Elijah grinned and took a large, satisfied bite of bagel, snorting a laugh.

Chewing, he said, "Did I jutht render the venerable Gina colada speechleth?"

She threw her napkin at him; he yelped. "Oh, go choke on your bagel."

"Hey, not nithe!"

"Well then, Mister Smith Goes to Washington," Gina went on,

regaining her footing, "what about the Kentukey nonsense your mama phoned about? What's that got to do with those principalities and powers? Surely the good pastor is doing the Lord's work, whipping up believers to take their own stand against the secularizing dark powers—spiritual or not."

"Nope. Politics has no place in churches."

"None?"

"Nope. None."

"Hold the cheese stick just one second," Gina said, leaning forward now with interest.

The two had never had anything remotely smacking of a political convo, so this was new. And could get ugly.

"You're seriously suggesting Christians don't have a place in the public square, that the Bible doesn't have anything to say about the myriad of political issues that our country is wrestling through?"

Eli held up a finger. "I didn't say that Christians don't have a place in the public square, that the Bible doesn't have anything to say about the myriad of political issues that our country is wrestling through. I said politics has no place in *churches*."

"Why?"

"Because all it ever got my dad was a nastygram from some disgruntled parishioner whose pet issue wasn't addressed proper! Tore him up something fierce, too, the way people went at it every two or four years, as if America were on the verge of collapse every election cycle."

Gina understood more why Eli was so interested in poking around this case. It was personal. These things often were.

She heaved a breath to loosen her tensing muscles. No need to get her knickers in a twist over political differences. Especially on the cusp of a case that was bleeding red-white-and-blue!

"I sympathize with your daddy," she said, "but it seems to me the Church has been called to bring its prophetic voice to bear on whatever social issue is tearing us apart, political or not. After all, that's what it means to be prophetic in the first place.

To articulate moral truth. And if the Church ain't articulating, someone else is."

Elijah opened his mouth to answer, but shoved the last remaining piece of his bagel down the hatch instead. Good lad.

Gina smirked. "Looks like I'm not the only one who's speechless. Which brings me back to the beginning. What do we have that we can bring Celeste to justify taking this nonsense on as a Group X case?"

"In other wordth," he said chewing, "bupkith."

Gina took a sip of tea. "Looks like we've got diddly when it comes to Group X."

"Bo diddly…"

Elvis filled the silent void, going on about a weepy hound dog.

Until there was a commotion from behind. At the hostess desk near the door.

Raised voices, gasps, now a scream and a string of curses.

Something about a gun.

Gina turned around for a look-see, and added a gasp of her own into the mix.

"What the what?"

A tall man with broad shoulders and a generous gut was flapping his arms around, trying to make some point or press some case. His hair went with them, what little of it was left. A silvery-brown comb-over with a bad dye job skittered about the man's head. His eyes were wide and frantic. He was wearing a black suit and black trench coat, like he was either an insurance salesman or a crime syndicate kingpin, or maybe an insurance kingpin.

"Eddy Lee?" Elijah said on a disbelieving breath.

Her partner had slid out from the booth, mouth open as if in a question. Understood the feeling.

Gina pivoted toward her partner then back toward the newcomer.

"Wait, you know that fella?"

Elijah heaved a breath. "You could say that…"

"Where?"

"From back home."

"In Kentucky?"

"Kenturkey…" he corrected in a whisper before shaking his head and giving her wide, confused eyes. "Paducah, but yeah, from back home. The chairman of the elder board of my child-hood church."

"The one your daddy pastored before…"

Gina bit the bottom of her lip, cringing at bringing up the painful memory of his death that fateful Sunday morning.

He swallowed and nodded.

Eddy was getting more animated now, his meaty palms waving like he was telling a story about the big-ass sea bass he'd caught that one time. Was muttering to beat the band, too, caught a few words about President Santos and something about kids and leaked emails and bacon and eggs. Didn't make a lick of sense!

Gina said, "What's he doing a thousand miles from home?"

"Seven hundred and ninety-eight miles, actually. But…yeah. What indeed."

Either way…Gina instinctively reached for the Glock concealed at her waist.

With one thought running through her mind.

Sweet Jesus, please, please, please not again…

CHAPTER 7

Elijah hated to admit it, but Gina was right.

Well, hate might be the wrong word. Gina was often right about so many things. Had been responsible for uncovering the clutch clue to plenty of cases in their FBI days. And he never shied away from giving credit where credit was due.

No, what she'd been right about was the Church's role in articulating moral truth, as she'd framed it, in the public square. To offer a prophetic voice of defense for the equal treatment of men and women, for babies still inside the womb, for the stabilizing force of moms and dads in every household, for caretaking the rivers and oceans and trees and animals, for caretaking widows and orphans.

None of which were political; they were biblical.

Standing up for these things—these principles, these people—was moral because they were all close to the heart of God, close to his righteous heartbeat.

From Elijah's perch in the world, what had made all of those things political were the powerful forces who'd wielded them over the years to gain and maintain leverage over the Other. Democrats over Republicans, conservatives over liberals.

It was against these powers that Elijah Xavier Fox stood—whether the earthly ones using the Church and its moral mandate like a cheap whore or the heavenly powers behind the political ones looking to strengthen their hand.

He was about to say so, too. But then something curious happened.

There was a raised voice—a shouting male—followed by the shrilly shriek of some startled woman.

Before he could assess the situation, Gina had turned for a look-see then placed a firm hand at her hip.

At her Glock.

Which meant whatever she'd seen, whatever was going on behind her was firearm serious. He trusted her intuition enough to follow her lead.

Easing his arm back, he planted his hand firmly on the grip to his Gen 5 Glock 17 semi-automatic pistol. Not the same as the 17M model from his Bureau days, but close enough.

Straightening and craning over Gina, Elijah saw what his partner had seen.

There stood a tall man, suited up for a funeral or sales gig with Cutco Cutlery (hopefully the former wasn't because of the latter!). Shoulders broad, gut generous. Was gesturing wildly, arms flapping like a pelican in heat. And shouting red-faced points at some poor lass with big eyes rimmed by too much black eyeliner. Dude looked like a cross between Arnold Schwarzenegger and Sylvester Stallone. Big man, all neck, a silvery-brown comb-over with a bad dark-brown dye job.

And very, very familiar.

"Eddy Lee?" Elijah said on a disbelieving breath.

He slid out of the booth and stood, his backside throwing up a vinyl squeak that would normally have made him blush. Didn't pay the flatulent sound half a mind, because things were about to get real.

Had seen that red face before. Lots of times. But in a very different context.

Backyard barbecues and church basement potlucks. Teaching Sunday school and coaching Little League baseball. Up front praying and leading the evening hymn sing for Seventh Baptist of Paducah, then at his family home eating and laughing around the Fox family campfire pit. He'd treated Elijah well, too, showing interest in his hobbies and life, being patient with his autistic outbursts—even talked him through a meltdown during one Sunday morning service. He was the model family man, model citizen, model Christian. Eddy had been Elijah's hero.

So this...

This didn't make any sense. What was Eddy doing here—in some Northern Virginia no-name diner with passable food and throwback songs, carrying on like some schizoid off his meds, storming around like King Kong with a bad comb-over?

A *rat-a-tat-tat* suddenly erupted. Livid and terrifying.

The white walls splintered puffs of drywall from the assault, along with glass frames and ceramic dishes. Another firehose of bullets barged down the center aisle as people took cover, the strafing fire chipping until it landed smack-dab in the jukebox and killed the King of Rock and Roll, for a second time.

Thankfully, no one had been hit that he could tell.

Yet.

But it sure did activate Elijah. He whipped out his Glock and took aim.

"Eddy Lee! I order you, in the name of Virginia common law, to lay down your weapon and put your hands where I can see them!"

Yuppers. Was fixing to make a citizen's arrest, all on his own. With Gina colada as backup, of course. Risky legally, but he figured the law was on his side.

Not only because Old Dominion's Supreme Court held in *Hudson v. Commonwealth* that an average Joe Blow like Elijah who witnessed a suspect breaching the peace—like, say, opening up a can of AR-15 on a '50s throwback diner—gave citizens a legal right to make an arrest. But also because Eddy was committing a felony and lives were in danger, and he and Gina were the only sheriffs around to keep the peace. Didn't even care whether common law was on his side.

Because Eddy Lee had a revolver in a holster at his hip along with an AR-15 rifle slung around his shoulder that he was wielding like Rambo.

The man Elijah knew as a kindly church elder shuddered to a stop, the tinking of shell casings the only sound to be heard. His command seemed to have sunk in somewhere in Eddy's noggin.

But…

Dude looked Woodstock stoned. Eyes were wide and blood-shot, staring off all cross-eyed. That bad-dye comb-over was going all Bernie Sanders cattywampus, sticking up like he'd jammed his finger in a light socket.

Which gave Gina a window to leap from her booth and whip out her own piece, taking aim and repeating Elijah's call.

Eddy staggered forward, lowering his weapon and turning toward the two Group X agents.

Yuppers. Higher than Steve Miller Band's "Fly Like an Eagle"!

Or maybe…something more sinister. Something darker.

Something the two agents had encountered more times than Elijah would care to count—first with the FBI, then Group X.

Demonic possession had been something of his specialty while working at the Bureau, earning him the nickname Spooky Eli. He'd also undergone special exorcism training thanks to an ecumenical exchange program put on by the Vatican several years ago.

So Elijah knew demonic possession. Had studied it, had seen it up close, had cracked cases with such supernatural possession at the center.

But this…

The man looked possessed alright, but not by anything from the Unseen Realm. He was far too alert, far too on a mission, far too in-control to be wielded by demonic puppet masters.

What was Eddy's deal?

The sound of silence was punctuated by heavy breathing and soft whimpering.

Until: "Eli Fox?"

Eddy Lee was looking at Elijah as if he'd seen a ghost, some echo of a distant relation that had long passed. Looked as if someone had taken a frying pan to the man's face, too, jolting him awake from whatever had taken over his mind.

Now he laughed, slapping his leg and whistling with a wide grin.

"Then you know, too! I knew the good Lord would send me more patriot soldiers to suss out that Mexican varmint!"

Elijah twisted up his face in confusion. Know what? And patriot soldiers, Mexican varmint? What the blazes was he yappin' about?

Jostled from Eddie's recognition and his confusing nonsense, Elijah faltered his aim some but kept at it. No telling what came next, but the recognition was an encouraging sign.

"That's right, Mr. Lee. Elijah Fox here, and I don't want anyone to get hurt. So let's put down the weapon and have ourselves a chat about what's going on."

Eddy's face crinkled with confusion. "I'm not here to hurt anybody. I'm here to save them!"

Now that didn't compute.

"Save them?" Gina asked at his side.

Eddy shifted his gaze, eyes wide and frantic.

"Yes, that's right. *SAVE THEM!*" he yelled, voice high and heady and cracking like an adolescent boy.

The echo of the raging lunatic sent a shiver ratcheting up Elijah's spine. The visual and the audio rang such a discordant tone within, the present clashing with past memories of what and who he knew this man to be.

"Save who, Eddy?" Elijah asked calmly.

The man shifted, spinning around and craning his neck in

search, muttering under his breath and running a hand through that bad comb-over of his.

"Stay with me, Mr. Lee. Save who?"

He spun back toward Elijah. "It's a conspiracy, I tell you. That man Santos. It's all his doing!"

"President Santos?" Gina asked, throwing Elijah confused eyes.

Eddy nodded, his rifle rattling. "Right right right! Santos, I tell you, Santos! You know he's an illegal, don't you? Read it online, I did. Which means he's not even a legit president."

"What the what?" Gina exclaimed, startling the man.

"Harvesting adrenochrome from kiddies to whip up an elixir of eternal life, he is!"

Now that took the cheesecake.

Thought he was going to shoot up the joint again, with his partner in the crosshairs, but Eddy held firm. Only twisted up his face with surprise, as if he were Barney the Dinosaur.

Eddy stiffened and cleared his throat, staring off above Elijah's head. "*'No Person except a natural-born Citizen, or a Citizen of the United States, at the time of the Adoption of this Constitution, shall be eligible to the Office of President.'* Article 2, Section 1 of the You-nighted States Constitution, that's what that was! And Santos ain't natural born, I tell ya."

He heaved a breath, then screamed: *"NOT. NATURAL. BORN!"*

Elijah couldn't believe the racist nonsense this guy was spewing—what Eddy Lee was spewing! The guy who'd taught him about Jesus' love in youth group, who'd listened to him quote Bible memory verses, who'd had the Christian sex talk with him and some of his other friends, for Pete's sake!

Yet, here he was, positively cuckoo for Cocoa Puffs. Didn't have the slightest clue what to make of this—of Eddy! All he knew was that a few dozen people were in the crosshairs of this man's crazy. No way would he let that happen.

Weapon still fixed on Eddy, he shouted, "Alright, everybody out!"

Eddy didn't move, except to heave a breath and dart his eyes around. Hand gripped the trigger of that AR-15 again, but he didn't raise it, didn't put up a fuss or protest.

Elijah was fixing to keep it that way. Or else…

Parents and children and employees rushed past him outside, right past the man—screaming, crying, even still chewing. But he wasn't doing anything about it. Wasn't stopping them, wasn't targeting them in the slightest.

Instead, by the time the last few patrons darted outside, he got to work.

Started moving through the restaurant, muttering something under his breath and pacing back and forth. As if searching for something—maybe for someone.

A man on a mission he was. Gina commanded him to lay down his arms and put his hands up, to wait for the authorities to sort it all out. Didn't pay her any mind. Just went from booth to booth searching underneath, getting down on his hands and knees, with that assault rifle scrapping along the tiled floor.

Then he stood and repeated the process until every last one of the booths had been checked.

Elijah was too dumbstruck and confused to do anything about it.

By now, sirens were blaring in the distance and fast approaching. Didn't matter to old Eddy Lee in the slightest. He'd left the dining area and barged into the back, fixing to complete whatever it was he'd come to do.

The coppers and a full-on tactical unit—no, wait. Three full-on tactical units and nine county mounties were barreling into the Sunny Side Up parking lot, complete with a massive charcoal fire engine-size truck that read 'Mass Casualty Incident Unit' on the side.

Great. Just his luck to be caught up in a mass shooting event—on his day off!

With Eddy Lee, of all people, at the helm.

Men and women and some teenagers cleared the area while the authorities set up shop. And set up shop they did.

Rifles, shotguns, pistols were all aimed at the entrance. Now some muckety-muck got on the blow horn and started barking orders for them inside to come out with their hands up. It was then that Elijah realized they might be mistaken as co-conspirators, caught in the crossfire if the county mounties came barging in.

"What the what?" Gina blurted.

Elijah spun around to find his partner gawking from an open doorway into the back kitchen area.

He hustled to her side, joining her in her confusion.

"Oh my cheeps!"

Eddy was at a locked door next to a large walk-in refrigerator, butter knife in hand, trying to pry the dang thing open. Figured it was a closet of some sort, storing who knew what.

Money maybe? The office sat behind it though, a door closed and locked and a window with drawn shades.

Drugs? Maybe he'd gotten wrapped up with some Kenturkey narcos back home and was sent to retrieve a stash from a rival gang.

A sudden *pop-pop-pop* jolted him from spinning out even crazier scenarios.

Eddy had given up knifing his way inside and was firing several rounds from his revolver into the doorknob.

It clattered to the floor and soon the elder was inside.

Behind the door was a small storage closet. Filled with brooms, a dirty mop bucket, bleach and other cleaning supplies.

No money, no drugs.

"What in tarnation..." Eddy said before storming inside and waving his revolver around with a mumbly mutter.

Then out came the brooms, one by one. Followed by the containers of cleaning agents, the plastic bottles tossed haphazardly behind. Joined by the mop bucket, which sloshed about before tipping over and dumping the gray-green water all over the floor.

"Where is it?" he demanded.

Gina turned to Elijah. "What the bleep is that man going on about?"

Elijah shrugged. "Beats the crap out of me!"

"Where *IS IT?!*" Eddy screamed now, huffing and puffing like he was about to blow the joint down.

Then he dropped to his knees, scratching at the tiled floor before attacking the back wall. Like a rabid animal searching for prey, or some junkie whacked out of his mind possessed by some strong meth cocktail that would make Walter White envious.

Or possessed by something far, far worse…

That was it. Time to end this crazy.

Elijah stepped up to the plate by stepping inside the closet, weapon at the ready but not taking aim.

Yet.

"Where is what, Eddy Lee?" he asked.

"That Roberto Santos feller."

Took everything inside Elijah not to roll his eyes or go off on the man for his renewed racist birther nonsense.

Instead, he took a breath and asked, "What about him?"

"Running that child sex ring out of this here diner, he is!"

"What the what?" Gina said from behind. Then a whisper: "Did he just say what I think he said?"

President Santos. A child sex ring. Run out of some mom-and-pop diner?

Yes. Yes, he did.

The accusation was so preposterous and zany and ridiculous and cray-to-the-Z that Elijah forgot to breathe for several seconds as the synapses of his brain tried to compute what the what—as Gina colada had said—Eddy was going on about.

Then he did, heaving a breath before it escaped in a full-on mouthy belly laugh Elijah didn't see coming.

Was afraid Eddy would crack at being mocked like that. Just

sat there instead with his legs crossed in that rumpled suit of his soaked with sweat, head bowed and mumbling to himself.

"Sweet mother of Melchizedek! What the blazes are you talking about, Eddy?"

"It was all in the emails," Eddy replied. "The emails, I tell ya. Surely you know that."

"What emails?"

Eddy went to his knees, then stood. "WeLeak. The ones from that former White House chief of staff, the chair of Santos's presidential campaign. This restaurant is all over those messages. And some god-fearing people have put two and two together to prove ritualistic child abuse is going on down in the basement!"

"Here, in Sunny Side Up?" Elijah couldn't make heads or tails of this nonsense.

"That's what I've been trying to tell ya! Modern day patriots have sussed out that Santos feller was hiding these kiddos in the basement of Sunny Side Up."

"But there is no basement!"

"References in the emails," Eddy went on, ignoring him, "to 'eggs' and 'bacon' are code words, you see."

"Code words?" Gina asked.

"For 'girls' and 'little boys.' But you already know that since you're here!"

"For the love…" Gina leaned in and whispered: "this man is in deep doo-doo, my friend."

"Saw it with my own eyes, I did," Eddy went on. "The eye showed me! Separate the goats from the sheep, he will. Even their heads!"

Gina startled. "Did you say goats?"

"And heads?" Elijah asked, throwing wide eyes at Gina.

She swallowed, asking, "What's this eye you're talking about?"

"And where?" Elijah followed up.

"Revealed all on WeVid, he did," Eddy muttered. "Trust the

plan, he said. Arrests will come. You can bet they will after I'm through with this place!"

This was astounding. Eddy drove hundreds of miles to some rando mom-and-pop diner because of some conspiracy theory video he watched on WeVid?

About Santos, a child sex ring?

Sweet mother of Melchizedek. He should have stayed in bed. Slept in and let Dexter pee all over his kitchen floor. Did anyway, so why not add a deuce to the mix? Would have been far less stinky than the crap he was dealing with now.

"I just knew," Eddy went on, "I had to sacrifice the lives of a few for the lives of many. Had to fight this degenerate, corrupt system that kidnaps, tortures, and rapes babies and children in our own backyard! There's a cabal of powerful elites abusing children—and they're getting away with it!"

Elijah's head was spinning now, not talking, barely processing what this man was saying.

Gina did the talking for him: "What the what are you talking about?"

"Secretive and untouchable. *A CABAL!*" Eddy shouted.

"What cabal?"

"Lefty-lefties. Tied to Democrats. Joined at the hip to Santos. Who wasn't even born in this country. Did you know that? And he's part of a narco death cult, yes he is!"

Gina bit her lower lip and eyes went wide, watering even. As if doing everything in her power not to repeat Elijah's outburst.

"But we're in the know."

"Who is?" Elijah said now.

"We're small but swelling, a band of patriots fighting back! So is he."

"Who?"

"Eye."

"Eye?" None of this was computing. "What eye, Eddy? What—"

"The intel on this was a hundred percent," Eddy Lee exclaimed with wide, pleading eyes. "One hundred percent!"

Never got around to getting an answer to that question about the eye, or whatever. Because suddenly a switch flipped. Something snapped in Eddy's brain. It was like he came to from some nightmare, from some coma state.

He said, "Never was my intention to harm or frighten innocent lives, but I realize now just how foolish and reckless my decision was."

The light returned to his eyes, his breathing got regulated, he talked in hushed, gentle tones now. The Eddy Lee Elijah knew from childhood seemed to have returned. At least some spark of what was left.

"I also know what I need to do."

Eddy spun toward the door leading back out into the dining room.

Elijah followed him, Gina close behind and gripping her Glock for them both.

The man opened the door, the red-blue lights from a bazillion cop cars flashing across his sweaty face—along with the commanding calls of a bazillion cops for Eddy to lay down his weapons and surrender.

He obeyed, without incident.

Setting down his firearms, the clatter of the assault rifle and revolver echoey and menacing, he walked out the door and surrendered to the police festooned in black tactical gear who had by then secured the perimeter.

It was over, just like that.

Eddy was dragged away in handcuffs.

And Elijah was left with a bazillion unanswered questions.

CHAPTER 8

ina sat on a stiff padded bench nursing a Styrofoam cup of Lipton tea in a tactical command center that smelled fresher than she recalled from a decade of law enforcement service, like Clorox wipes and Pine-Sol. Tea wasn't the best in the world (after all: Lipton!), but she appreciated the hot drink on the cold October day after the cray-cray morning.

Elijah sat next to her, nursing a similar Styrofoam cup of coffee. He was quiet, contemplative. Barely said a word after the tactical team barged in after Eddy surrendered. And barge they did.

Angry shouts, rough hands, menacing M-4 assault rifles pointed at their faces.

Made sense, since they were the ones left inside while the rest of the joint cleared. Could have been working with crazy Eddy for all those burly SWAT teammates knew, especially since they were wielding Glocks in a state that had soured on their open carry laws. Still legal, but frowned upon, especially by men in black tactical gear trying to make sense of another potential mass shooting event that turned out not to be as catastrophic as the two-hundred some real ones that had roiled the nation that year.

Once it was clear who they were after waving their

Vatican diplomatic credentials around (creds that were coming in handy more than Gina thought they would), and once it was clear they were victims like the rest of the diner bunch, she and Elijah were brought to the tactical command center to await a debrief with the local FBI field office liaison.

Gina took another sip of tea, grimacing at the chalky, cardboard black-tea taste but grateful for the caffeine jolt to ease her buzzing brain. Still couldn't get over what she'd heard—what that man Eddy Lee had said. All that nonsense about President Santos not being American, then the even crazier nonsense about him leading some sort of child sex ring cult—in the basement of some '50s throwback diner?

Too weird for words.

How does something like that happen? This Eddy guy seemed to be so middle class, so Midwest normal. Yet he sincerely believed that children were being held hostage as sex slaves in a Northern Virginia diner!

Again: Too weird for words.

Elijah heaved a sigh and stretched out, gulping down a mouthful of his caffeinated beverage. Wondered how he was holding up, this blast from the past barging into his present with tales from the funny farm.

Wanted to wrap an arm around his shoulder and give it a squeeze. She didn't, both because it would've been a professional faux pas as well as a personal one, neither of them caring for personal touch. Instead, she settled for an ask.

"How are you holding up, Eli?"

He gulped down more coffee and shrugged. "About as good as you could expect after discovering your childhood hero is cuckoo for Cocoa Puffs."

"Sorry about that."

"I just can't get over how something like this happens. Makes me think Mama was on to something."

"Back home in Kentucky?"

He took another sip and nodded. "Nothing like that grows in a vacuum. Not that level of crazy, anyway."

"Suppose not."

"And I dismissed her as paranoid."

Throwing back the rest of his coffee, Elijah shook his head and tossed the empty cup in a wastebasket.

"I wouldn't be too hard on yourself," Gina said. "Not sure I would have done anything different. Plenty of patriotic churches and you don't see their parishioners barging into a diner looking for a pedophile ring run by the president."

"I suppose," Eli said glumly. "But she's my mama. I should've listened to her!"

"For what it's worth, I would've dismissed my own mama's ravings as paranoid as well."

He snorted a laugh. "Yeah, but that makes sense. She's a loon. My mama treats the loons."

Gina giggled. Oh, Eli. Blunt as always, to a fault. But he was right.

She sighed and took a sip of tea gone cold. *Blech!*

Setting it in the wastebasket, she asked, "So where does this leave our investigation?"

"Is it any question?" Elijah asked, straightening and turning toward her. "A church elder targets a sitting president during an election season with wild, conspiratorial accusations. Not to mention barging into a diner and discharging a firearm while threatening to mow down the joint. A committed crime sits at the heart of all bargain-bin mystery yarns, you know that. Pretty sure this case takes the cheesecake on that criminal front."

"But is it *inexplicitus*?"

"How do you explain it?"

Gina shrugged. "Beats me, but Celeste will want to know to justify our involvement."

"Celeste..." He sputtered his lips and slumped back. "Silas Grey hired us and gave us our charge—"

"Who is MIA and whose wife is our boss."

"Provisionally."

"Even so, we can't leave her in the dark on this."

"We won't," Elijah said. "She gave us a day, and a day we'll take."

Gina rubbed her temple, an ache beginning to needle.

"Suppose you're right about that, but that only leaves us—"

"Twenty-one hours and twenty-seven minutes."

"Precisely?"

Elijah nodded. "Precisely. Besides, you're leaving out the other *inexplicitus* elephant on the soccer field."

"What elephant?"

"Hello? The impaled severed head!"

"That was a goat, not an elephant."

Eli sputtered his lips again. "Same diff. But definitely *inexplicitus*."

"And not at all connected that we know of."

"Not connected? What about Eddy's nonsense about the eye separating goats from the sheep?"

"For all we know he was just making reference to Jesus' teachings on the final judgment in Matthew's Gospel."

"Maybe…" Eli slumped back and crossed his arms. "Too on the nose, though, don't you think? A goat head shows up as some lawn ornament at your friend's house, and then Eddy goes looking for child sex slaves in a diner he thinks is connected to the Santos campaign—the very campaign your friend is a VP candidate for?"

Gina had to admit it all did sound too coincidental—too connected.

There was an interruptive knock at the command center entrance.

She and Elijah both turned to see a familiar face climbing inside.

A woman in your standard government-issued black pants suit and white blouse with blond hair cut pixie short. Brittany

Armstrong, from their first Group X case earlier in the year. She was alone but bearing a smirky smirk.

"Well well well. If it isn't my two favorite Christian crusaders."

"Nope. Navy SEALs for Jesus," Elijah deadpanned.

Gina herself smirked, glad to see her partner back somewhat.

Brit laughed. "Sounds about right. But how is it you two got wrapped up in something like this?"

Eli shrugged. "Just out for a mid-morning jaunt to your friendly neighborhood diner when the crazy showed up."

She sat on a bench opposite the pair and turned to Elijah. "I was told you knew the suspect."

He glanced at Gina and frowned. "That's right. An elder from my childhood church who served with my dead dad."

"Dead dad?"

"Well, dead pastor dad. Long story."

"I see…"

"Eli's father," Gina explained, "was the minister of a church in Paducah, Kentucky, who was gunned down during one Sunday morning service."

"You have my sympathies," Brit said softly.

Eli offered a curt smile, saying nothing.

Gina continued, "Eddy Lee served on the church council as an elder."

"And drove all this way," Brit said, withdrawing a small notepad, "to commit an act of domestic terrorism."

"Apparently."

"So you knew him pretty well, then, Mr. Fox?"

Elijah nodded. "Well enough."

"Would you say something like this was out of character for the man?"

He laughed. "Out of character? Last I knew he was a dedicated father and devout Christian. A man who went out of his way to care for others, even training as a volunteer firefighter. Not a bit character from *One Flew Over the Cuckoos Nest!*"

Elijah paused to catch his breath, heaving a lungful of air and huffing it out in disbelief.

"I knew this man. At least I thought I did. Tried to date his daughter once, too. Maggy Lee. But she didn't take."

Brit paused her questions to take some notes.

"Was there any indication of this level of psychosis from back in the day?"

Eli shook his head. "Nope. None that I can recall."

"What was he like, that you can recall? What were his known associations?"

"He'd gone on a mission trip to Haiti, an earthquake-response team with our local Baptist Men's Association. He'd always exhibited the actions of a person striving to learn the Bible and apply that biblical truth to all of life. To his business, giving deep discounts to his auto repair shop to the needy. To his community, volunteering to coach Little League baseball. To his family and church."

Brit finished taking her notes and leaned back, gesturing outside the command center.

"Then what was all this about? I was briefed by the lead investigator who filled me in on your testimony. So why would someone as sane and normal and Midwest average—"

"Southern average," Eli corrected.

Gina suppressed a laugh. Always one to correct, he was.

Brit chuckled. "Sorry. Southern average then—why would this kind of person commit such a crime?"

He shrugged. "The eye told him, apparently."

"The eye?" she said with raised brow.

Gina explained, "That's what Eddy had said inspired him to barge into the diner. Said some eye character showed him what to do and where to go."

"Where?"

"WeVid."

She wrote that down but didn't make any remark.

Finishing, Brit asked, "Anything else you think I should know?"

"Not that I can think of."

"Suppose there's the congressman," Elijah said.

Gina sucked in a startled breath. Eli…

"What congressman?" Brit asked.

"Nothing," she said, jabbing her partner in the ribs; he yelped.

FBI Lady looked from her to him, frowning.

"What's going on, what else is there I should know about?"

"It's nothing," Gina said.

"I don't know if I'd call a severed goat head nothing," Eli muttered, easing his arm back to shield any further blows. Smart man.

Brit startled. "Severed goat head?"

Gina huffed a sigh and threw Eli a not-very-happy pair of eyes; sometimes she needed to do that. Supposed the cat was out of the bag now. Or goat head, as was the case.

"A friend of mine," she started, "Congressman Calvin Dobson—"

"Wait wait wait," Brit said, putting her notepad down. "*Thee* Calvin Dobson? As in, vice presidential candidate Calvin Dobson?"

"You know of another Calvin Dobson?" Eli asked.

She frowned but let it go. "What is this business about—" she swallowed, giving her head a shake "—a severed goat head?"

"Impaled severed goat head."

Gina could wring that boy's neck! But she didn't, instead explaining the sorry story Caldo had shared that morning.

"It's important," she said, "that this stays strictly confidential."

Brit nodded. "I understand."

"Because the congressman had asked for my help, outside the watching eyes of the media. You can understand how the press might have a field day with something that smacked of the occult—let alone white supremacy."

"Certainly, but I'm not sure how this is connected to this case."

Elijah explained, "Because Eddy Lee had mentioned something about separating the goats from the sheep. Even the goats' heads from their goats' bodies."

Brit stiffened at that. "Interesting…Do you think Eddy was responsible for the congressman's lawn ornament?"

"Who knows. The connection was too on the nose not to notice, though."

"Sounds relevant enough." She took some more notes, then looked to Gina. "I'm going to have to follow up on this with the congressman. Discreetly, of course."

Gina didn't like it one bit, betraying the confidence of her friend and all. But she nodded anyway.

Brit thanked them both and said they were free to leave, even though they were free to leave to begin with. FBI Lady led them back outside, where Eddy Lee was being prepped for transportation to lockup.

The police had him in handcuffs and were transferring him from a squad car into a large armored vehicle for prisoner transport. His rumpled suit coat was off, and he was wearing a T-shirt. Barely paid the man a passing glance.

Until he turned just right, and she caught sight of something.

"What the what?" she whispered, peeling away from the group and padding over for a closer look.

She bobbed and weaved around a few police officers and bent back and forth to get the right viewing.

"Where's the fire, Gina colada?" Eli asked from behind, following.

She ignored him, making a beeline for the transport truck.

Then saw it. And gasped.

"That's it!" she exclaimed, stopping dead in her tracks.

"What's it?" Eli asked, coming to her side.

"That symbol. I've seen that before."

He glanced from her to where she was pointing—to Eddy, who was sitting inside the transport vehicle now.

"On the T-shirt?"

"You saw it too?"

"What, the triangle doohickey with some line in the middle?"

"Right."

"Where else have you seen it?"

She turned to him. "On the front page of the *New York Times*. Next to my mama."

"Your mama?" Elijah asked.

"My mama."

"Is there an echo in here?"

"Eli…" Gina moaned, not in the mood.

"What are you going on about, Gina colada? What symbol is this?"

"I don't have a cotton pickin' clue! All I know is, she was plastered on the front page of ol' Gray Lady standing next to some dude at some political rally with the exact same T-shirt."

"What political rally?"

"For Gallego."

"The Republican presidential candidate?"

"Exactamundo!"

"And Eddy was wearing the same wackadoodle T-shirt with the same wackadoodle symbol—a man from my mama's church and another from your mama's political rally?"

The heavy doors to the armored prison transporter closed with a shuddering clang, and soon the beast grunted to life and pulled out of the parking lot, joined by the rest of the police cars.

Elijah sighed. "And our only lead is gone."

"A lead that connects both of our mamas…" Gina sighed, trying to make sense of the turn. "But how?"

"And why?"

Why…good question.

The pair watched the cavalcade of law enforcement vehicles

leave the parking lot. Along with their only lead to an *inexplicitus* case that seemed to entangle both their mamas. A political entanglement that smelled rotten.

Eli finally broke the silence: "You know what this calls for, don't you?"

She folded her arms, knowing completely.

"I see a road trip in our future."

He nodded. "Kenturkey or bust."

She nodded back. Time to get some answers.

CHAPTER 9
PADUCAH, KENTUCKY.

Elijah Xavier Fox hated driving.

Strike that.

Elijah Xavier Fox hated driving in cars. Especially the kind that reminded him of his days with the FBI. Those big-boned, government-issued bruisers from Detroit painted black that were the mainstay of every Bureau grunt.

Much more preferred the power and control of a motorcycle—the wind smacking him in his tinted face shield and skating across his leather jacket with a slipstream that threatened to carry him overboard; the wide-open possibilities of an open road stretching beneath his wheels and promising endless routes to who-knew-where; the feeling at his fingertips of an engine pumping out a robust ninety ponies of peak power at 4,750 revolutions per minute, the twin-cylinder motor grunting and growling through his head; the gravitational pull against his body banking into a sharp turn.

But he didn't have an extra helmet, and his beemer (not bimmer; two Es and one R) was neither big enough for two nor the kind of vehicle you wanted to drive in across the country in the fall.

Especially with an impending snowstorm that was no longer impending.

The first pair of snowflakes smacked into the windshield like a couple of horseflies bloated with his childhood blood buzzing around that orphanage back in the day.

Smack! Double-smack!

Then, soon enough, a blanket of the white stuff was whipping across the road and bringing visibility to nothing but nothing.

"Knew we should've gone south through Tennessee..." he muttered as he flipped the windshield wipers to life.

Perhaps it was providential they hadn't taken his hog. Didn't want to argue with Gina colada that early in the morning anyhow. A five o'clock wake-up had been rude enough, especially with the puddle of pooch urine that greeted him for the second time on his way to make a cup of joe. No need to spoil the morning with an argument about road-trip choices.

Gina had driven halfway and Elijah took over just on the other side of the West Virginia border. Didn't like it one bit, and she would've kept going, but she wasn't a fan of snowstorms, so he took over a few hours ago.

Was just happy their vehicle was European made. A Mercedes G Class SUV pimped out with supple leather that smelled like a baby lamb and a bangin' system that rivaled what he'd grown up with thanks to Dad's hi-fidelity tastes. Was a curious vehicle of choice. Heard something about one of the SEPIO jarheads, Matt Gapinski, being responsible for stocking the Order of Thaddeus's fleet.

Wasn't a motorcycle but at least it was smooth and comfy, and wasn't flying. Both he and Gina had a phobia about it, in fact. Mostly brought on by claustrophobia, the thought of zooming around through the heavens in a metal tube breathing other people's air on top of other people's germs (yeah, add germaphobia into the mix), combined with speeding hundreds of miles an hour thousands of miles above the ground—he was dumbfounded there weren't more people who were averse to flying!

So, drive he did, with another hour or so left before home, sweet home.

At least he had Dizzy Gillespie, Ray Brown, Milt Jackson, and Hank Jones to keep him company, along with a packet of sunflower seeds. Picked them up at a convenience store after a potty break outside of Lexington and used Alexa to bring up the Charlie Parker tribute concert from Montreal featuring those jazzmen. Supposed at least one good thing came from the Great White North.

He popped a handful of seeds into his mouth and hummed with pleasure. The mild, nutty flavor and firm but tender texture salted to perfection was the centering anchor he needed to drive the final leg. That and the singsongy notes from the vibraphone Milt Jackson could work like a Swedish masseuse works calve muscles.

As the master hammered away at the metal bars, it struck Elijah how nostalgic it was of him to choose that album, among others, for the final leg home. He'd bought that album for his dad one Father's Day. The first Father's Day, actually, after he'd been adopted.

Dad had introduced him to all the great jazz artists thanks to three mint-condition turntables and McIntosh hi-fidelity floor speakers that cost as much as a year of college tuition. Had played everything from New Orleans and Chicago-style Dixieland to swing and big band. Bop, cool, and hard bop. Then on into free jazz and avant garde of the 1960s through to fusion jazz of the 1970s and the eclecticism that rounded out last century.

Chief among his favorite artists was Charlie Parker, the American jazz saxophonist, band leader, and composer who'd been a highly influential soloist and leading figure in the development of bebop. The Bird's fast tempos, virtuosic technique, and advanced harmonies had been the mainstay of Dad's man cave, and when Elijah discovered the tribute album—one of the few Parker album's Dad didn't have in his massive thousand-record collection—he convinced Mom to get it as a gift.

Dad had been over the moon for the double-vinyl feature. Said he'd never heard of the album and couldn't believe he'd missed it. Immediately popped the blue translucent disk on his turntable and struck up the band, Dizzy's dizzying trumpet lead joined by Brown's humming bass and Jackson's singsongy vibes and Philly Jones's drums filling the house.

The next month, Dad returned the favor, gifting Elijah an all-in-one record player housed in a wood contraption with built-in speakers for his fourteenth birthday. Meant the world to him, Elijah hauling it to college, then his first job with the FBI, then across the ocean to England during graduate school, then back again to his graduate school office before landing as the center-piece of his living room. What a journey it had had.

What a journey he'd had! Good Lord…

And there he was. Slowing to a crawl behind a Toyota grocery getter that had no business being on the highway during a snowstorm, red flaring across his whitening windshield and face flashing hot with road irritation on his way back home to investigate the Bride of Christ groping for trout in a peculiar river—Uncle Sam's trousers! (Blame Shakespeare for that graphic metaphor.)

Elijah gripped the steering wheel and cranked his neck to the side, then the other, trying to relieve a mounting tension brought on not only by the worsening road conditions but also by the fast-approaching childhood hometown he hadn't visited in years. A town that had been Elijah's true birth, coming into the world anew by coming into a family—that family, the Fox family—that had loved him with a purity he'd never known existed. Loved by a father he hoped he'd made proud.

Because sometimes Elijah wondered whether he'd made the biggest mistake of his life climbing on the pony that had led him to that highway heading home. Wondered whether Group X was the right course for his life—and what Dad would think about his choice.

Dad had always supported him in whatever he did, without question. The one thing he did hammer home, though, was seeking the Lord's direction—then go after it with all availability and faithfulness. A nugget of wisdom from the Book of Proverbs had been Dad's North Star:

> *Trust in the Lord with all your heart,*
> *and do not rely on your own insight.*
> *In all your ways acknowledge him,*
> *and he will make straight your paths.*

Solomon's wisdom was true enough and fine enough. But Elijah had always found it so dang hard to figure out whether he was on the right path to begin with!

Grand Rivers Theological Seminary had offered him a solid restart after he was given the boot from the Bureau—one of the most painful seasons of his life after his pastor had suffered a similar fate as his father. Training up the next generation of pastors was a real honor, a way to honor Dad and his memory.

And yet, he'd also grown in his awareness of the Unseen Realm. His interest had been sparked by his work at the FBI and furthered during graduate work at Cambridge and his hobby-horse project following UFOs. Some people collect baseball cards as a hobby (puke); some people hunt to while away the hours (double puke). Elijah went to contactee conferences and made connections between alien abduction stories and the Bible.

So, when Silas Grey had come a calling, joined by an equally strong calling by the Holy Spirit, Elijah had known it was the next leg of his journey—both professional and personal. Helping lead an investigative arm that took seriously the Church's struggle against this present darkness felt right. Because if he wasn't waging war against the Fallen Ones still ravaging this world, investigating the supernatural struggle making itself known and surfacing in ways humanity hadn't seen before, who would stand against the darkness?

A bridge caught his attention, snow covered and stretching over a frozen river. Not *thee* river, mind you, the Ohio River that separated his hometown from the Land of Lincoln. Nope, the Tennessee River, a narrow, winding band of rushing blue that spilled down into Kentucky Lake—another memory marker reminding him of summertime fishing with Dad.

Elijah Xavier Fox was home.

A screechy yawn yanked him from his thoughts and sent him jumping in his seat.

"Sweet mother—you scared the bejeebers out of me!"

"Sorry." Gina brought her seat upright, rubbing her eyes and throwing up another yawn. "We there yet?"

"As a matter of fact, we are. Home to a former uranium enrichment plant thanks to the U.S. Atomic Energy Commission as well as the National Quilt Museum."

"Sounds homey."

"It's something alright…" Elijah said, butterflies starting to do the conga line in his stomach at the sight of his old stomping grounds emerging now through the snowy onslaught.

Brake lights flared up ahead just over the bridge, and he could see the faint outline of a train of dim orange headlights snaking through the slushy haze. Traffic slowed to a crawl, reason 623 why he hated driving.

Great. Just what he needed. A sea of incompetent drivers mistaking the gas pedal for the brake pedal, driving as if they'd never seen a lick of snow in their life!

Interstate 24 wound past a Cracker Barrel anchored just off the exit that tempted Elijah something fierce. Given all the traffic crazy, he sure could go for a Country Boy Breakfast right about now, but figured Mama would have something cooking. Besides, his brain was already buzzing with the memories of the place he hadn't seen in years. No reason to add another reason to meltdown after walking into his family haunt.

The snow turned into rain, those bloated horseflies slapping against the windshield nothing but Mother Nature's spit now. Highway was still crammed with traffic. Felt like the annual July Fourth Riverfront Festival. Now that was a traffic jam! And for good reason. Fireworks, carnival food, carnival games and rides.

Could do without the country music, but him and Dad had suffered on account of Mama. Billy Ray Cyrus and the Judds duo, Wynonna and Mama Naomi, had torn up the stage with their twangy tunes and gyrating hips one year that reinforced his distaste for the South's genre of choice. Nothing but songs about harvesting corn and getting drunk (often at the same time), joined by tales of lyin', cheatin' spouses who ran off with their dog, pickup truck, and American flag—often in the middle of harvesting season after draining a twenty-four pack of Bud. At least the songs had some religion to them. "The Night Jack Daniels Met John 3:16" was pretty interesting. Nothing like a Bible in one hand and a bone-dry bottle in the other to set the mood right.

"Watch it!" Gina shouted, bracing herself against her window.

Livid brake lights flared with warning, waking him from his memories.

Elijah slammed his foot on the brake pedal, the car skidding across the slick road. Nearly kissed the bumper of some Detroit-bred sedan, but Elijah managed to steer their oafy SUV off the shoulder.

"Egads, that was close…" she huffed.

Understood completely. "Sorry. Mind got caught up elsewhere."

"I guess so. Want me to drive?"

"Nope. I've got this. Just distracted is all."

"Care to share?"

"Not really, but I know you want me to."

"For the love…"

Elijah steered back onto the road, then said, "It's this road."

Gina shifted toward him in her seat. "I know you hate driving, but you're usually better at dealing with traffic than I am."

"True that. But it's not that. It's the bridge, too."

"The bridge?"

"And river, where Dad and me went fishing. Then the Harbor Plaza where I'd get a mean Blizzard at the DQ downtown."

"The DQ?"

"Dairy Queen. Vanilla with York Peppermint Pattie and Reese's Pieces."

"Mint and peanut butter?" she said with a shudder. "Eww!"

"Don't judge, Gina colada."

"Sorry. But I hear you. Whenever I get back to Toledo, I get all distracted as well."

"They say absence makes the heart grow fonder. More like absence makes the heart go yonder."

Gina gasped and spun toward him again. "Hey, I loved loved loved that game."

Now he gasped and spun toward her, catching his reference to the title of his favorite childhood computer game.

"You played *King's Quest V*?"

Gina scoffed. "Of course! I was a child of the '90s with nothing to do."

"Surprised you had a computer in that double-wide of yours."

"About the only thing we had. But, yeah, I hear you. You leave a place and you'd like to think you take a piece of that place with you. But then you come back and realize how much you've left behind. For good."

Elijah flipped on his turn signal and eased off the interstate onto an off ramp that would take him toward destiny: his Mama's home in a suburban community just outside of town. Those butterflies began striking up the conga line again in the pit of his stomach, joined by his palms beginning to slicken on the steering wheel and his chest constricting with a rising anxiety. Felt like sipping air through a stir stick, too.

It wasn't just coming back to a place he'd vowed he'd never return. It was also the fact Mama needed him, because his dad's church sounded like they needed him. Needed him to set them straight and figure out what manner of crazy had infiltrated it to bring Eddy Lee to the threshold of the *One Flew Over the Cuckoo's Nest* mental hospital.

Didn't know in the slightest what that might be, and whether he should even be there in the first place. Sure, he was an investigative agent with Christ's Church. But the *inexplicitus* cases that defied explanation, the kind that sprang from crimes and all manner of craziness flowing from the loins of the cosmic powers of this present supernatural darkness. Not the teachings of some loon pastor more beholden to political power than God's Word.

Rounding a bend in the country road taking them far outside the rest of civilization, a streetlight pierced through the rain and struck his windshield golden. Mama's light, flaring a few yards from her driveway.

Heaving a breath, Elijah swung a left and began trundling down the crunchy gravel drive. Had no memories to speak of in this place, Mama purchasing the home a few months after dad passed. All of his family memories had been made in the parish home that was part of their Baptist church. She couldn't stand to live in it another day without her husband, and the church needed it anyway for the next minister they called. She'd lived there alone ever since on an acre of land.

A pond sat off to the side of the drive, the beams of his headlights casting an orange glow across a sheet of thin ice. Towering oaks and maples still clinging to their colorful dignity surrounded the Tudor-style house at the end, a two story thing painted white with dark-stained wood trim and shutters. Frozen vegetable and flower gardens sat farther back at the edge of the property line. Mama always complained about the deer swiping her tomatoes and ruining her petunias.

Elijah parked in front of a generous attached garage and led them to the front door. Pressing the doorbell, he waited, but heard nothing from the other side. Must be out of order, something he'd have to fix before they left town. He knocked a few times, then a few more, growing impatient.

Gina said, "Maybe she stepped out for dinner or a book club?"

He yanked his sleeve back from his wrist and checked the time. "Too late in the evening for either."

A gust of frigid fall wind carrying spitting rain sent him fishing his key ring out from his pocket. He found the one he needed and jammed it into the lock. Opening the door, he gestured to Gina.

"After you."

She nodded and went inside.

Those butterflies resumed their choreography, snatching his breath and sending his fingers strumming up his stimming rhythm.

"Into the portal we go…"

CHAPTER 10

They say when life gives you lemons, go make lemonade.

Bah! Amateurs.

You know what I say? Suck 'em dry and plant the seeds! Might as well make the most of it by turning a profit on a grove full of them suckers. Sure, whip 'em up into lemonade, maybe even lemon meringue pie. Lemon bars, lemon cakes, lemon tortes—and my fave: lemon schnapps. Picked that recipe up during my last assignment in Deutschland fomenting nationalist sentiments to influence the makeup of the Bundestag.

But I digress…

Back to lemons.

Like the Good Book teaches: What the enemy meant for evil —I'll turn around and use for good.

My good! And the good of Semjaza, regional cosmic Prince, of course. Not to mention the grand schemes of the Shining One…

I'm fixing' to sow the seeds of an unfortunate turn of events into a ripe harvest for my ends thanks to two-thirds of the Three Amigos currently enroute. Held up by some such and such agent of the Nameless One, but no worries. Because boy, are those seeds sown. And in the most unexpected of ways.

You see, the one fella was just one seed. One easily malleable sheeple who gobbled up my seed—hook, line, and sinker!—before scurrying off to that diner to shoot up the joint in search of a pedophile ring.

Run by the President of the United States.

To harvest the adrenochrome from kiddies to whip up an elixir of eternal life.

I guffaw at that ridiculous notion. Guffaw, I tell you. Guffaw!

Who in their right mind would be dumb enough to fall for such a thing—fall for such a *seed*!

Sheeple, that's who. And the dumbest kind of sheeple on the universe's block: steeple sheeple.

All it takes is one little seed sown in just the right way to send followers of the Nameless One scurrying about. Scurrying to some dump in the Land of the Free in search of a president leading a child sex ring to harvest their blood!

Doesn't even take much. Just one of my seeds does the trick. And one choice seed above all. My specialty.

The seeds of *fear*…

Fear ain't what you think it is, you know. No, siree, it ain't!

See, when most people think of fear, they think of that cold dread that skates through your veins at the sound of creaking stairs in the dead of night. Or a masked hoodlum shuffling up to your car moored at Pump Three while pointing a Glock at your kisser and demanding your wallet. Or the semi barreling into the side of your minivan after running a red light while taking your snot-nosed ankle biters to soccer practice. Or wondering how you'll pay for your teenager's braces while also supporting your Caddy's monthly payments and McMansion mortgage after getting the ol' heave-ho from your corner office thanks to some soulless corporate overlord.

You know. Good ol' suburban fear.

Except…that ain't what it is. Never has been; never will be.

Fear is reverence. It's awe. In the parlance of the steeple

sheeple, you might even call it *worship*. It's whatever sets your heart on fire.

Reverence and awe come in all sorts of sizes, of course. Any shoulder you put the weight of your world upon becomes the object of fearful reverence.

Safety and security in the dead of night. Neighborhoods with families that look like your own and livelihoods that keep the gravy train running. Again: Good ol' suburban reverence and awe for the status quo. For not only your family, but also your community, your country.

Especially your country…

And when that's threatened, when the good ol' days that were never all that good are in short supply because security and success is threatened by uncertainty and decline—well, then my work is halfway through. All it takes is a little push from me, a little seed sown into the hearts of sheeple to get the ball rolling for utter destruction.

But first, fear must take root. Which for steeple sheeple is all too easy.

See, it's not just your run-of-the-mill sheeple I've got at my disposal to reap sweet success, not just your average Joe and Jane Liberty. My sights are set on those—permit me to take a breath and gather myself, spitting the word out like a soiled garment—those *Christians!*

I sputter my lips and spit, wiping my tongue on my paws to rid me of the taste of that accursed word.

There, that's better.

Yessiree, those steeple sheeple are the most fearful lot on the planet!

I've been around the block enough to know they place primo value on the life they've known. The *earthly* life they've known.

The *American* life they've known…

You know the kind. Where father knows best and leave it to June Cleaver to set the table for a four-course meal. Where their morality's the majority and their religion commands a seat at the political sausage-making table.

And I threaten that. I threaten what they value. What they revere, what they bow before with worshipful awe.

So every four years, those followers of the Name-Who-Shall-Remain-Nameless run around with their hair on fire, fearful of the one who can take away all they hold dear.

Which is the great irony of ironies. Because the Nameless One himself had something to say about that. I know the Good Book well enough to know what they quickly forget. Part of our training, it is. Principal Wormwood has always insisted us Fallen Ones memorize it, chapter and verse. What better way to yank steeple sheeple around than use their own sacred text against them? Always been that way, it has.

Anyhoo, where was I? Oh, yes: the Good Book on fear. *'Do not fear those who kill the body but cannot kill the soul; rather, fear the one who can destroy both soul and body in hell.'*

Now, I am the first to tell you that hell ain't so bad. Sure beats the alternative. One big party, it is! But to see those steeple sheeple wilting in the face of all they think they'll lose—all they think will be killed off, even, as they cling to the sodding notion of their soul being saved…And they want to take back America again?

Bah! I guffaw in the face of such irony. Guffaw, I tell you. Guffaw!

But, I suppose, one can understand their transgression. After all, the cultural climate is certainly getting chilly for steeple sheeple. The Great Recession and now sky-high inflation has squeezed blue-collar believers across the Home of the Brave. More than that, the anxiety is amorphous, cryptic—and entirely manufactured by agents all too willing to do my bidding.

However effective your average Joe Pastorman—or pastorwoman, I suppose, given the day and age—might be at soothing their congregants for 45 minutes on a Sunday morning, keeping them on the straight and narrow and focused on the Nameless One, they ain't got nothing on me!

I've got them under my pretty little finger for hours, every day. Through podcasts, the twenty-four-hour news cycle, every single night on those pedestrian talking-head cable shows, at the supermarket jawing it up with their friends in conspiratorial whispers down the frozen pizza aisle or spittin' fire over beer and peanuts at the local watering hole.

The irony is that the most cited command in the Good Book is "Fear not." The Nameless One was quick to remind his original steeple sheeple of that!

But he and his promises just don't break through like they used to. Never will again if I have anything to say about it!

Knowing the Good Book like the back of my wings, I'm reminded how it teaches that fear is primarily reverence and awe. The sheeple people say they revere the Nameless One, that they hold him in awe. *Bah!* Not as much as they reverence the earthly, American life they've known. And when that's threatened, the roots of my sown seeds spread like weeds. Consuming, defiling, *destroying*!

Except there's one added lemon I did not anticipate, an added variable I had not known about until I was told moments ago after the little diner fiasco.

The Order of Thaddeus.

Those dastardly, despicable, dimwitted agents of the Church!

There's a long memory within our ranks of those buffoons, the guardians and defenders of the faith serving the Nameless One with pitiful subservience. Which is so ridiculous! You know you've already lost the battle for hearts and minds when defense is the default posture.

But I digress…

Most pitiful of all is that Christianity's Special Forces have solicited the help of Caesar's investigators. Group X, they go by, a pair of former FBI retards turned private investigators for the Church—sticking their schnozes where they don't belong.

In the Shining One's business. Semjaza's—*mine*!

But that's not even the worst of it. The Order I can handle. Even that upstart investigative agency. What are a pair of retards in the grand scheme of things?

No matter. I'll just water the little seeds of fear I've planted in my other steeple sheeple. Send my little miscreants on a mission to nip the lemon in the bud before it blooms into a tree ripe with yellow fruit.

If it doesn't work, I'll suck those lemons dry and scatter their seeds in a new field for my pleasure and purpose.

I can be most resourceful.

CHAPTER 11

Elijah stepped inside his mother's house, cringing at his footfall throwing up a creak from the hardwood floor. He was instantly wrapped in the comforting blanket of Mama's home.

The inside warmth (set at 74 degrees, God love Mama!) transported him to a world he'd forgotten, a world he'd never been able to imagine. Not only in general, this world a possibility that had existed for so long in the wildest fantasies of his orphan imagination. But specific to him, images of such a world pulsing through him and making his heart beat for them, yet so mercilessly out of reach from a world he could hope to inhabit.

The world of home.

And yet, Yahweh Almighty had seen fit to gift him one—gift him a home with a mom and dad to call his own, a home filled with love and laughter, where gentle correction to steer his life right joined by an encouraging word to keep him going were never in short supply, and a hot meal and rousing game of Monopoly were close at hand.

This world, the home Mom and Dad had crafted with care, was the only one he'd really known—the true kind. Sure, he'd stayed in plenty of *houses*, played the part of temporary guest in eleven of them. And that was after playing the part of prisoner in that Virginia orphanage. Asylum, more like it!

But as a foster kid, he'd been shuttled and shuffled around between families like a used coat passed from Goodwill to customer, only to be schlepped off again (as an ethnic Jew, he had rights to that sort of Yiddish expression) to some poorer excuse for a secondhand store, discarded to the heap of used goods only to be taken up again by another set of playacting parents cashing in on Old Dominion's coffers.

None of them had been home. He'd always been an outsider. A snot-nosed beggar whose face was pressed against the cold, frosted glass looking into a world that would never be his, a world so foreign, so alien.

Until a Kenturkey couple who couldn't conceive children of their own invited him into their house, to be their family, to make a home. With them.

A passage from Scripture suddenly sprang to mind. From the first letter of the Apostle John, chapter 3: '*See what love the Father has given us, that we should be called children of God, and that is what we are. Beloved, we are God's children now; what we will be has not yet been revealed.*'

Emotion sprang to Elijah's eyes just as suddenly as that passage. For it was because of the love of his earthly father that he had any chance of discovering that heavenly love, much less understand it. It was that love that had helped him heal, helped him grow, helped him finally come to terms with who he was—and be OK with it.

Alan Fox had been the father Elijah had always wanted but had never imagined in his wildest dreams he'd find. And it led him into Yahweh's arms, finally becoming God's child by recognizing and then embracing Jesus as his Messiah, the one his Jewish people had been waiting for their whole lives.

Elijah understood more than most why so many people rejected organized religion, why they rejected God even. It wasn't merely, or even mostly, because of intellectual reasons.

Yes, there's some of that, but those intellectual walls were usually just smoke screens for the real reasons.

It was that they couldn't conceive of God being *that* way, the way the Apostle John spoke of—a Father of lavish love who adopts us as his own, inviting us to make a home with him. Whether because of their own crappy fathers or because the Church had never offered a vision of God as a good, good Father. They're the snot-nosed beggar whose face is pressed against the cold, frosted glass looking into an alien world that would never be theirs. Fatherless. Homeless.

Just as Elijah had been.

Had been…

What a pair of words those were!

That heat was a merciful reminder of that past perfect tense. Even though this house hadn't been his house, it was still his home, because it's where Mama lived. Family.

It was also a merciful relief from the frigid fall outside. A dry heat that instantly warmed his face and hands and began to dry his wet, shaggy hair. The house was dark, except for faint light coming from the kitchen through the narrow hallway that stretched past a set of wooden stairs rising to the second floor. A single banker's lamp was also lit at a rolltop desk just inside the threshold to a modest living room with a bay window obscured by plastered snow and lace curtains.

A traditional grandfather clock droned on from the other side of the room. *Tick-tock, tick-tock.* Right before it struck a set of chords he hadn't heard since he was a teenager. It ended its tune with an announcement of the hour: seven o'clock. The hickory timepiece, elaborately carved and detailed with the familiar bonnet crown, was joined by complementary antique furnishings. A red velvet rounded arm sofa with a matching Victorian parlor chair of the same fabric. A large crystal vase of white roses sat atop a mahogany tilt top tea table. A curio cabinet filled with Mama's tea cup collection.

The living room, replicated across the house—from the

dining room to the bedrooms, the bathrooms to the three-season porch—matched his parents' provincial, throw-back Cracker Barrel tastes for a time and place in America that was never coming back again.

Elijah breathed in deep, centering himself and taking it all in, then smiled.

Potpourri and Pine-Sol, joined by chocolate chip cookies and ginger and apple cinnamon. The smells of childhood. He reveled in them, the sensations already doing wonders on his nerves, settling them down and setting him at ease.

"Doesn't look like anyone's home," Gina said, interrupting his reveling.

"Looks that way…"

He led them down the hallway past a bank of framed family pictures.

She stopped to look, giggling and pointing. "Aww, little Eli Fox."

"Nope. Teenage Eli Fox."

"And an adorable teenybopper, you were. What were you here, fourteen?"

"Fifteen."

"Look at you with that shoulder-length hair and those wide-leg jeans."

"My grunge phase," he said before continuing into a modest kitchen of cottage-style cabinets and black quartz countertops.

Where an apple pie was sitting on the stove! Looked fresh, too, made just that day.

"Oh, apple pie!" Gina exclaimed. "And are these cookies?"

She eyed a plate covered in Saran wrap he hadn't seen.

"Help yourself," Elijah said.

Famished from the drive, he went searching for a fork but couldn't remember where Mama kept them. He went from drawer to drawer, pulling them and riffling through their contents. Found three potato mashers, two sets of spatulas of various sizes, more measuring cups and spoons than should be legal.

But no fork.

Munching on a cookie, Gina complained, "You're gonna wake the dead with all that racket. Besides, where's your mom?"

"Dunno. Need a fork."

Last drawer in the joint and he finally found one.

Grinning, he padded over to the stove and dove in, scooping a large bite from the middle and shoving it into his mouth.

Nirvana…

Tart and tangy baked apples softened from the oven danced across his tongue, joined by cinnamon and a dash of nutmeg and Mama's secret ingredient: ginger.

He went for another bite.

When a creak was thrown up. From behind.

Then the hallway light flipped on.

Showing Mama in a purple bathrobe with wet silver hair and large pink curlers holding a candlestick above her head that was ready to strike.

Elijah and Gina threw up a startled scream. Which sent Joyce doing the same.

"Elijah Xavier Fox?" she said, clutching her chest with more drama than he thought necessary.

"The one and only." Elijah pointed at the still-raised weapon. "What were you planning to do with that, stick us with hardened wax? Never worked in Clue. Lead pipe or wrench, maybe. Never the candlestick, and almost always the revolver or—"

"My lanta, child! Does your mouth never stop running?"

Gina said, "I've been asking that question for years."

Mama set the weapon down on the black quartz island and leaned against it.

"Nearly gave me a heart attack, you did!" she exclaimed, catching her breath with a hand on her forehead.

Elijah frowned and hung his head. "Sorry, Mama."

"Thought you were the Devil himself with all that bangin' and clangin' I heard from upstairs."

"I was looking for a fork."

She eyed the utensil and leaned around for a look over his shoulder. Then gasped. "You desecrated my pie!"

Elijah shrugged, licking the fork. "I was hungry."

"Oh, fiddlesticks. That was for a friend."

"Well, Gina stole a cookie."

Gina jammed an elbow in his ribs; he yelped.

"Thanks for covering for me, partner…"

"Hey, Gina," Mama waved with a smile before a scowl returned and she crossed her arms. "Thought you were a burglar come to ransack my house. What in tarnation are you doing here?"

"Helping," Elijah said.

She sputtered her lips. "Helping yourself to my pie, more like it."

"Well, what were you doing creeping around?"

"It's my house!"

"But where were you? I was looking all over for you."

"Taking a bath!"

Elijah shuddered. "I don't want to know."

"After what happened yesterday," Gina explained, "we left this morning to make it by evening to get the ball rolling on our case."

Joyce looked up. "After what happened yesterday? You alright, Eli?"

"Yuppers. Eddy Lee, though….not so much."

Now she stood straight, magically recuperating. "What about Eddy Lee?"

He turned to Gina, then gestured to a table in the nook beyond the kitchen. "You might want to sit down for this one."

All three did, Elijah taking point to retell the sordid tale of Eddy's cuckoo for Cocoa Puffs mission to suss out President Santos's underground pedophile ring.

For her part, Mama sat with her hand covering her open mouth, as if trying to speak a bazillion questions but unable to squeak a single one out. Understood the feeling.

"So, you see," Gina added when he was finished, "we figured we should make good on your request and make a trip."

Elijah nodded. "Figured if something was going on at Daddy's old church, I should check it out."

Mama smiled. "Appreciate that, son. But you could've called first."

"Wasn't time. Had to act."

She turned to Gina. "He was always this way, you know. Wasn't cocked and loaded until he made his mind up. And when he did, he went in with both guns blazing. Ready, fire, aim was his way."

"Still is," Gina said with a wry grin.

"Gee, thanks," Elijah replied. "Anyway, where should we start?"

Mama stood. "First things first." Sauntering into the kitchen, she added: "You've already gotten into my apple pie, but care for some soup?"

"Yes, please!" they both said together.

Throwing open a cupboard, she grabbed a saucepan—

When the doorbell thew up a *ding-dong.*

Mama bolted upright, wide-eyed and glancing toward the front of the house.

Elijah stood, as did Gina.

"You expecting company?" she asked.

He smirked. "She was bathing. What do you think?"

Mama batted the air his way. Her way of telling him to shush it. She went to the front, Elijah and Gina following along.

Whoever was there was now rapping a mean beat against the door and calling her name.

"My lanta, is that Patty Lee?" Mama said, reaching the door.

"Patty Lee?" Gina startled. "Eddy's wife?"

Before he could answer, Mama opened the door and in flew

Patty. A bat out of hell, she was, storming all of her five-foot-four, ninety-pounds-soaking-wet frame into the narrow hallway.

And right up to Elijah. Looked like she was about to clock him too, her narrow lips pursed tight and eyes matching in angry slits. The large leather Louis Vuitton handbag slung around her shoulder certainly could do the job!

"Uh, hello, Mrs. Lee," he stammered, backing into the living room.

She followed in close pursuit.

"How could you, Elijah!" Patty screamed. "How could you turn on Eddy like that, handing him to those fascist brownshirts? After all he did for you when your daddy died!"

"Patty Lee," Mama gasped. "My lanta, woman. How could you accuse Eli like that?"

"Because it's true!" the woman sobbed. "My Eddy is jailed after doing his patriotic duty to protect this country. *And he's to blame!"*

Elijah's head flooded with panic, his mind swirling with a spiking anxiety sailing into the stratosphere at being confronted like this. In this way, by this dear woman who had meant so much to him during his childhood.

Couldn't think, couldn't speak. The synapses connecting his brain to his mouth were gummed up something fierce at the social confrontation.

Was never any good at that sort of thing, avoiding social situations in general thanks to a wicked combo of the wiring of his brain that made social interaction difficult and binding chains of his crappy childhood. The social detachment had usually served him well, letting him imprison his emotions to drill down into a state of hyperfocus—on cases, on hobbies, on research.

Until it served him wrong.

Social confrontation, the likes of what he was facing now, was not his cup of tea.

The woman drove him all the way back to the parlor chair.

The back of his legs thudded into it, and it scraped across the hardwood floor until he sank into its comforting velvet.

Except, Bat From Hell Lady was fast approaching with that handbag!

Thankfully, Gina quickly intervened.

"Calm down, ma'am," she said, putting up a gentle hand to force Patty Lee to stay her steps. "How did you hear about this?"

Patty Lee was shaken at the question, and she turned to Gina. "Why, I read it on the internet!"

"The internet?"

"The internet!"

"Is there an echo in here?" Elijah complained.

"Right after Eddy called me—" Patty turned to him, face growing red and shaking from a clenched jaw, and screamed "—*from JAIL!* Rushed over as soon as I heard to give your mama a piece of my mind. Saw you instead standing in her hallway. Just my luck!"

Then she did something entirely unexpected for the ninety-pound-wet woman.

She slapped Elijah. Clear across the face.

Heard it before he really felt it. A sharp *smack* resounded throughout the living room before the right side of his face bloomed with pain.

His breath left him, and a coldness flooded his veins. More from horrifying disbelief than embarrassment.

Didn't react, didn't respond. He couldn't. Besides, what could he do? Had to have a hundred pounds on her and almost a foot. So he sat. Still, unmoving, unfeeling. Shoving his emotions back into that prison where they belonged.

"You've ruined him!" she screamed again before doing a second unexpected thing.

She reached into that side saddle of hers and pulled out a gun.

Not just any gun, either. A Smith & Wesson M&P 9mm.

Elijah was too stunned for words. Too stunned to do anything.

Gina wasn't. She instantly whipped out her own weapon, the same Glock she'd pulled on Eddy Lee.

Life was repeating itself.

Mama threw up a startled scream, adding a whimpering sob and muffled pleas. "Patty…put away the gun before you hurt someone. Before you hurt my baby!"

Patty was huffing—big, deep, heaving breaths. Her entire teeny, tiny frame shuddered with each pull. Worried she was about to kill him.

His bigger worry was that she would do something to Mama.

"Ma'am, put down the weapon," Gina commanded, stern and steady.

Patty paid her no mind.

"If Eddy had wanted to shoot up those people," she huffed and puffed, "he would've brought this. Not that Ruger *revolver*! That was all for *show*! To prove he meant business."

"Ma'am, just put down the gun," Gina repeated. Louder, more insistent, with her own weapon trained on the woman.

Didn't worry in the slightest she would misfire. Always calm, cool, and Gina colada collected, she was.

Now Patty…that was to be determined. And yet he knew his partner wouldn't let it come to that.

Patty lowered the weapon to her side now, and something came over her. She swallowed and heaved a breath. Then a calmness washed over her face and shoulders, both falling with either resolve or resignation.

"We're standing on the brink," she whispered, licking her lips and closing her eyes, "this country of ours. At the junction of good and evil we stand. A Great Awakening is coming where all will be exposed. Light in the dark, dark to light!"

Sweet mother of Melchizedek! What the hot Hades was she talking about?

Sure sounded like what Mama had explained over the phone

when this whole crazy *inexplicitus* case started, what Billy Baron was teaching his congregants—Daddy's congregants! So, another connection to whatever was going on at his childhood church. Still…

What the hot Hades was she talking about?

"Patriots, that's what we need. Courageous minute men who think for themselves, who have eyes to see."

She snapped her eyes open, a shuddering jolt of fear rippling through him.

"The eye. Knows and sees all, he does. The eye of God!"

Eye? That was the exact nonsense Eddy had muttered on about at that diner.

"Separate the goats, he will. Expose them, he will. And spare their lives he won't!"

Finally, in one, sudden, shuddering motion, Patty stuffed the handgun back inside her bag and turned to leave.

Striding three paces twice her size, she spun back around.

Thought she was about to whip out that piece again and finish what Elijah feared she'd intended.

Instead, she had one final, parting word: "Debby Gallego will take America back again. Just you wait and *see*!"

And with that, Patty left the way she came, the front door shutting with an echoey slam in her wake.

CHAPTER 12

*D*id that just happen?

Gina stood at the threshold to the front door, breathing hard but still—stunned and silent. With her hand firmly clenched around the butt of her Glock.

She'd followed Patty Lee to make sure the lady didn't pull any funny business on her way out, but she left without further incident.

Now she watched the woman clickety-clack down the sidewalk to her Lexus LS sedan—an odd choice that maybe explained a bit of her rant against all the change sweeping America; those with the most to lose are often the ones who fear the future, especially when the winds of change are a blowin'. The car roared to life, and a beat later gravel was thrown up and clattering beneath the Lexus's undercarriage as Patty Lee peeled backward and on toward destiny.

Didn't even want to think what that destiny might be, given both her and her husband's crazy.

Holstering her weapon, she promptly withdrew a packet of gum. Wrigley's Doublemint.

The fraught moment fraying her nerves called for it. And

here Gina thought her hometown was filled with a bunch of kooks!

She promptly withdrew two sticks wrapped in shimmering foil and unwrapped them to reveal the white sticks of heaven. Then she shoved them in her mouth. Both of them. One might be enough for your run-of-the-mill Jane, but two was what the moment required.

The gum helped center her. One of the ways she stimmed, or stimulated. The act of chewing two pieces of gum, with the work it took to grind them into a chewy pulp, the fresh spearmint dancing across her taste buds, the smell of minty heaven filling her nostrils—all of it helped focus her attention away from the moment and back toward a centering calm.

The curse of being an autistic person, just like Elijah. She'd managed well enough, her personal spectrum wheel not as complicated as some people she knew similarly challenged with neurodiversity.

But gum helped.

It also reminded her of those silly '90s commercials from childhood, the ones featuring twins and that "Double your pleasure, double your fun" slogan. She could still recall the slogan song, and she began humming it to herself. The one she and her twin sister Grace had sung together, dancing arm in arm and twirling in their double-wide mobile home in a Toledo trailer park.

Until her untimely death…

Elijah was the closest thing to family now, her and her mother not the best of friends and dad out of the picture after running out on the family.

Her head felt lighter now, her nerves less tingly, even as her jaw ached, but in a good way. She chomped on her gum faster, the ache at her masseter, temporalis, and medial pterygoid jaw muscles stabilizing her and the minty freshness of the salivary buildup a balm for the rising overwhelm from the confrontation that was dialing back to zero.

Swallowing, she went back inside. Where the rest of the trio stood as still, as stunned and silent. Joyce knew her son well enough not to have a hand on Elijah and give him space, but she was whispering comfort to her son anyhow while dabbing away the emotion in her eyes with a tissue.

"You alright, partner?" Gina said, coming up to Eli.

He looked at her and nodded, slumping down into the chair. Gina took up the piano bench while Joyce herself slumped down on the couch near her son.

"That was weird, right?" Elijah finally said. "What Patty said, what she did?"

Joyce whimpered into her tissue and shook her head. "The way she treated you, Eli, was ugly."

"Just feel bad about Eddy, what happened to him."

"Eddy Lee made his bed, not you, darlin'."

"Yeah he did," Gina added. "And then took a big, stinky doo-doo in it."

Elijah smirked. "Colorful, Gina colada. But that's not what I meant."

"Then what?"

"Feel bad about what drew him to commit such a crazy crime to begin with. Something deep happened to that man."

Gina nodded toward the front door. "And clearly his wife. Almost a mirror to Eddy's nonsense ravings. The country being on a precipice. The battle line drawn between good and evil. Goats being separated!"

"That's 'Merica for ya," Eli said with a snort, shaking his head.

"And you caught the eye reference, right?"

"Oh, yeah. The eye of God. Same cryptic mumbo-jumbo as her husband."

"Did she look possessed to you two?" Joyce asked. "Not that I'd know. You're the experts in that sort of thing, after all."

"Possessed by something, that's for sure."

"By fear..." Gina said, staring off into the ceiling.

Eli turned to her. "Insightful. And as we've been saying all along: What the blazes happened to her to gin her up with such crazy talk?"

"What the bleep happened, is right! How does someone get drunk on so much fear?"

"Fear makes people do strange things."

"Suppose so."

"Well, I for one," Joyce said, "think you should hop to it."

Elijah snapped his head to her. "Hop to what?"

She motioned toward the door. "Go see for yourself. After all, isn't that what you came for?"

He sucked in a startled breath. He flashed Gina Did she say what I think she said? eyes after growing large. An instant transformation joined by his fingers snapping into motion.

Thumb to index finger, thumb to middle, thumb to ring finger, thumb to pinky—then rinse and repeat.

Gina chewed faster just seeing her own partner's anxiety spreading through his body. For what reason…she'd have to drill down into that. Stat.

Swallowing, he asked, "See what for ourselves?"

"There's a rally tonight at the church," his mother explained. "You should go."

"Go?"

"Go."

"Go go?"

Gina smirked. "Like the '70s rock band?"

He threw her narrowed neither-the-time-nor-the-place eyes. Which was odd, because usually she was throwing him them sorts of eyes. Clearly startled by something, he was.

Elijah returned to his mother: "Go where?"

She rolled her eyes in a huff. "Like I've been saying, the church!"

Elijah's eyes darted about the ceiling, and he kept at his finger-stimming tick. Worried he'd start flapping his hands too. Didn't do that often, neither of them did. But when the anxiety ratcheted up into the stratosphere and his emotions got the best of him—well, there was no telling what came next.

Like now.

Gina cleared her throat, taking over: "What kind of rally?"

"The political kind," Joyce explained. "With Debby Gallego herself."

"Egads! The Republican presidential candidate?"

"That's right. And the rumor mill, being what it is, has been turning out a doozie for what will be unveiled."

"Billy Baron as Gallego's campaign manager, or something. Eli told me."

Mama threw Elijah irritated eyes, but she left it alone.

"At any rate," his mother went on, "they're pulling out all the stops, inviting a whole host of musical acts to rev up the audience. The media's supposed to broadcast the whole thing, though there's been some disagreement on whether to let them kind inside. Even having a bit of praise and worship, too."

Elijah smacked his forehead. "Sweet mother of Melchizedek! They're using Daddy's church building to host the whore of Babylon?"

"Watch your mouth, Eli. I'll have none of that talk in this house."

"Sorry, Mama…" he dipped his head, his fingers intensifying his stimming.

Thumb to index finger, thumb to middle, thumb to ring finger, thumb to pinky—then back to the start.

Joyce continued, "Besides, I'm not sure slandering Debby Gallego as a whore is all that Christian."

"Nope. Not what I meant," he answered, shaking his head. "The Whore of Babylon—"

"From the Book of Revelation," Gina said.

"Yuppers. The center of imperial power coming against the Church in the last days."

Joyce said, "Irregardless—"

"Nope. Not a word."

"Oh, fiddlesticks," she huffed. *"Regardless*, then, you should see what I'm talking about. Will open your eyes, it will."

Gina threw Eli a shrug. "Suppose it couldn't hurt none. And, after all, we did drive all this way to get the 411 on the source of Eddy Lee's psychotic break."

"Suppose it couldn't hurt none?" he said, eyes going wide again and jaw dropping.

Elijah snapped it shut, clenching his jaw and leaping to his feet.

"Fine. Let's go."

Then he left the way Patty had gone.

Out the front door in a huffing rush.

Leaving Gina confused. And concerned.

———

Gina thanked Joyce for the cookies and pie before running after her partner.

Who was seated in the passenger seat of their Order-issued SUV. Knew he hated driving anything with more than two wheels, so she let it go. For her part, she hated driving anything other than her Honda Odyssey, but she saddled up for the rodeo anyway.

Bringing the Mercedes to life, she turned the car around then asked, "Where are we heading?"

Eli pointed down the long gravel drive. "That way."

"Thanks Mr. Specificity Pants…" she muttered.

She lumbered down the drive and turned out onto the road. Where Eli promptly jutted a finger at the windshield and hooked it to the right.

Right it was.

Then, a block down the road at a stop sign, he repeated his directional gesturing: His left arm jutted out, with a finger hooking to the left.

Silent, stewing, still. Except for his finger-stimming tick with his other hand resting on his lap strumming a rhythmic beat: thumb to index finger, thumb to middle, thumb to ring finger, thumb to pinkie—then back at it again.

Gina followed his directions and went at her own stimming tick, grinding those two double-your-pleasure-double-your-fun sticks of spearmint gum. Worry rose at Eli's response to his mother's suggestion that they go and check out what was going down that evening at his childhood church. Wasn't that the whole reason for their trek across a quarter of the country? So why the stimming tick, brought on by overwhelm, right after a weird reticence at his mama's suggestion?

Didn't take a psychologist to see that something had gotten him riled, that's for sure.

Wait, that's right: She was a psychologist! Judging by his response, it stemmed from a case of avoidance brought on by the suggestion they visit his childhood church. No doubt connected to the severe trauma of having his only real father shot—in front of his very eyes. The kids she'd dealt with during grad school exhibited such responses to objects and places connected with psychological harm or physical trauma. But they were in the thick of a case, which didn't leave room for avoidance.

She would have to get to the bottom of this before things spun out of control. Before something else triggered Eli into a meltdown she knew his brain would need to sort through the neural mess, but one that could seriously derail their investigation.

After several more rounds of arm jutting and finger hooking, Elijah's directions silent and halting, Gina heaved a breath and went for it.

"Eli, you're brooding."

"No, I'm stewing," he replied, not missing a beat in his finger-stimming tick.

Thumb to index finger, thumb to middle, thumb to ring finger, thumb to pinkie—then rinse and repeat.

"Alright, stewing then. What gives?"

More silence, more stewing, more stimming.

Which she couldn't blame him for, not in the slightest. Stimming or stimulating for autistic people was like drinking water. Couldn't not do it when the thirst came. Some hand-flapped, waving their hands and arms around to work through the neural impulses triggered by overwhelm. Eli's was a lesser form of that, more controlled but still as vital. Others were more tactile, loving to finger silly putty or immerse their arms in macaroni—or in Gina's case, work those masseter, temporalis, and medial pterygoid jaw muscles with a wad of gum like it was nobody's business.

A long country road stretched before them, slick and wet. So they had miles before them until they reached Paducah proper.

Gina respected his need to work through his anxious overwhelm. But when it came to a case, and their personal baggage got in the way, autism or not, the skunk needed to be yanked from the bag.

She decided to go a different direction: "So, what was that back there?"

"What was what back where?" Eli said in a rush.

Gina sputtered her lips. "Back at your mama's house!"

He opened his mouth, his chest heaving a breath. Then it snapped shut, his chest falling and breath hissing through his nose. Could tell he was deciding whether to spill the tea or not, his fingers continuing their stimming rhythm while his eyes darted about.

Held his cards close to his chest, Eli did. Couldn't blame him, given all the trauma he'd experienced at that dang orphanage growing up, and being shuffled around from foster family to foster family. During her PhD program in psychology at the University of Michigan, she'd moonlighted at an adolescent mental health facility for her clinicals. And the stories those kids told her—dark stories that shattered their connection to humanity, let alone *their* humanity…

Gina shivered just thinking about those kids and what they'd been through. What Eli had been through, even.

Combine that trauma with the mental wiring in his brain that thwarted his ability to process and understand his emotions—made total sense he found it difficult to trust people, to open up to them.

But Eli did, explaining, "Couldn't believe Mama suggested such a thing. Go there."

He jutted his arm right, his pointer following his sudden directional gesture—down a road ten feet away!

Gina slammed on the brakes and jerked the steering wheel. "Maybe a little more lead time next time?"

Eli only shrugged as she completed the turn.

"What do you mean about your mama suggesting such a thing? What, that we go to the rally at your church—"

"It ain't my church!" he shouted, snapping his head to her with wide, wild eyes. He sucked in a startled breath and let those eyes fall, his face turning a shade of crimson before turning away.

Looking straight ahead, he held out his hand to her, palm up. "Here's your head back."

Gina giggled. "No prob, Bob. But give it to me straight, would ya? What gives?"

"Mama must be smoking some strong wacky tobacky to suggest I step back into the scene of Dad's death that sounds like it's been turned into a den of thieves!"

He pounded a clenched fist against his door. "Haven't set foot in Daddy's church since his face was blown to smithereens."

Fingers were really stimming now. The one hand was joined by the other pressed against his leg, moving up and down in a rhythmic stroke.

"Couldn't do it," he went on. "Still haven't in a *looooong* time. Thankfully, Mama had understood. I was bound for college the next year anyway, so it made it all the easier to excuse myself from Sunday morning service."

"But I'm sure this is gonna hurt something fierce anyhow," Gina said softly, a thumping bassy sound thudding their way from up ahead.

"Nope," he replied. Then Elijah turned to her. "This is gonna hurt bigly."

He turned back to regard the quickly emerging scene out on the road. The massive tent glowing a burnt orange anchored to the field butting up against a modest brick church with a sloping roof; the ocean of cars arranged all cattywampus around the gleaming tent; the loud music and cheers and revving Harley-Davidson motorcycles coming from the other direction and peeling into the parking lot—a whole mess of them that gave Gina the heebie-jeebies!

"In there," he simply said, stating the obvious without any accompanying jut this time.

Gina nodded and guided their own chariot toward destiny.

A smooth blacktop drive led to a large lot of the same. Bright yellow parking lines dutifully arrayed were filled with trucks and sedans and similar SUVs. A one level building of dark brown brick jutted off toward the left from a large hall with a sharply peaked roof and an annex extension growing from the right side. Looked like the sanctuary, a tall cross proudly anchored to the roof at the far end. Looked like a whale with a spout of holy water spraying from the top.

Next to the handicap parking spots that were all taken, she found a single visitor spot that was still empty. Figured they fit the bill, so she slid inside. Besides, they were on official ecclesial business sussing out a case that smacked of the *inexplicitus*.

Throwing the vehicle in *Park*, Gina turned off the car and turned to Elijah.

"You ready for this presidential-campaign circus?"

Eli took a breath and a beat, then another before his stimming suddenly stopped. Both hands, his strumming fingers and fidgety hand.

"Ready?" he said, snorting a laugh. He shook his head and turned to her, smiling. "No, not in the slightest. But I'll go."

"I understand," she said with a nod. "For the Church."

He shook his head. "For Daddy's church."

Her heart literally skipped a beat, and a cold, empathetic pain skated through her veins—blooming in her head and spreading through her body. Her hyper-empathic nature ached for her partner, her friend, whose own heart had left a piece of it behind in that church when his father passed. Still cared for that community of believers, was still fighting for them.

Boy, was she proud of Eli for facing his demons!

Gina put up a hand, palm facing Elijah. He immediately followed, the pair of hands facing one another but not touching. A gesture of solidarity that had served them well as autistic people averse to physical touch.

"Let's go, partner," she said.

He grinned. "Together."

She matched it.

Yes, together…

CHAPTER 13

Was Elijah Xavier Fox ready to go?

Ready to step onto the grounds of the church that had stolen the only father he'd ever had, shredding his heart and obliterating his forever family? Ready to face down whatever had stolen itself inside that sacred space, rewiring people in a way that sent them sailing headlong into the loony bin? Ready to possibly confront the man who had made it all happen, Billy Baron?

Nope. No bananas on all those fronts.

Everything within him was screaming to run away. Screaming to hitchhike if necessary back to the quiet comforts of his DC Adams Morgan row house. With Dexter sprawled on his lap while listening to Dexter Gordon honk away on that tenor sax of his, a mouthy Meritage generously poured in one of his wide bell-shaped Zalto Burgundy wineglasses imported from a small Austrian town near the border of the Czech Republic—its size and shape letting the deep, earthy, blackberry notes of his favorite red breathe and bloom in his nose and mouth, joined by a charcuterie board of Dubliner hard white cheese, prosciutto cut onion-skin thin, and Kalamata olives.

But he couldn't. Had a job to do.

For the Church, yes, as Gina colada had said. But more than that, for Daddy—for the church community he had cultivated like the shepherd he'd been. For the body of believers who had loved him so well when he arrived from Virginia. Even tolerated him so well, his autism rearing its ugly head in ways that would send most allistic, neuronormative people scurrying for the closest exit.

Nope. Not the small family of followers of Jesus Christ at Seventh Baptist Church of Paducah. They'd shown him what it meant to give and receive love, truly living out the Apostle John's exhortation about love in his first letter: *'We know love by this, that he laid down his life for us—and we ought to lay down our lives for the brothers and sisters.'*

They'd laid down their comfort, their neat-and-tidy Sunday morning world, their box they'd manufactured for what was neurally normal—all for a scared and scarred teenager who couldn't look people in the face when they talked to him, his eyes avoiding facial contact; who recoiled and yelped at the slightest touch, and had melted down a time or two because some rambunctious teenager just wanted to include him in his roughhousing; who couldn't give the same love back because he didn't know how.

Now something was off about the place, wrong about the churchy dynamics. Something had stolen itself inside this beloved community. A wolf in sheep's clothing, as Jesus had warned.

'Beware of false prophets,' Jesus taught in Matthew's Gospel, chapter 7, *'who come to you in sheep's clothing but inwardly are ravenous wolves. You will know them by their fruits.'* Only question was, what sort of fruit was Seventh Baptist now producing?

Elijah Xavier Fox aimed to find out.

"Eli..." Gina whispered, yanking him from his contemplation.

He snapped his head to her. "What?"

"You ready for this?"

Swallowing, he nodded. Then threw open the door and marched toward destiny. Which was nothing like he remembered as a child—starting with the church grounds. Quite the sight to behold, they were.

A tent, larger than any Elijah had ever seen in his life, was erected at the center of a massive plot of flat land. Looked like something a circus would use, though he wouldn't know. Never got to one as a child.

Perhaps the only saving grace to this trip down memory lane returning back to Dad's church was that Billy Baron's holy-roller politics party was in a Ringley Bros. and Barnum & Bailey big top sprawled across what used to be a soccer field back in the day. Didn't know what he would've done had the circus been set up inside the main sanctuary where Dad had been murdered.

Was real impressed by the parking lot, though. Nice, fresh blacktop that had always been cracked and breaking apart, like the rocky land of Mordor Dad had complained about growing up. Never had enough money to replace the thing; barely had enough money to repair the thing. In fact…

Elijah stopped short, Gina nearly plowing into him.

"Egads!" she complained. "Where's the four-alarm fire?"

"Five alarm," he corrected, spinning around to take in the church grounds.

"Huh?"

"You said four alarm, by which I assume you mean to indicate a raging fire of the highest order. Except five alarm is the highest alarm for a raging fire of the highest order."

"For the love…What I meant to indicate was—what's the matter?"

Elijah threw his hands on his head, emotion rising at what his peepers were now adjusting to.

"It's all not right!"

"What's not alright?" Gina asked, craning around the parking lot.

Elijah waved a hand around the parking lot, toward the church building, toward the tent and the other things he'd glimpsed that had sent his pulse soaring.

"It's all changed!" He spun around, disbelief and disgust mixing in a sickening stew.

"What's changed?"

"This!" He flung his arms wide and waved them around, Gina ducking out of the way.

"Well, what did you expect? It's been, what, eighteen years since you've been back?"

"Nineteen."

"There you go."

The church had a new roof and a large new wing jutting off from the sanctuary—Dad's sanctuary, where he'd preached and baptized, married and buried his people for two decades. Looked to be twice the size as before, which meant at least twice the size of the previous congregation.

Dad's congregation!

Then the fountain at the entrance he didn't pay much mind to until he also noticed a massive swimming pool in the back— probably for baptisms, which was just sacrilege to his kind. Every Southern Baptist knew a baptism wasn't legit if it wasn't performed in a sanctuary or at a private lake of one of the parishioners, complete with a potluck. Not in some—suburban *swimming pool* that probably cost as much as Daddy's year of salary! John the Baptist was rolling in his grave.

That wasn't even touching on the parking space that marked it as belonging to *'Pastor Reverend William Baron'* (Dad never got his own parking spot! And wasn't Pastor Reverend redundantly redundant?); the massive chrome cross anchored to the roof like a whale spout (barely could afford a wooden one, which Dad had cobbled together from some local hardware-store boards, sanded and stained himself); and the gargantuan tent glowing and humming like a U2 concert dwarfing the church—

Daddy's church!

"Eli!" a voice shouted.

Elijah snapped his attention toward it. Toward Gina, who was standing before him with her hand raised.

He did the same, putting it next to hers but not touching it. A singular act of solidarity that already was helping the overwhelm of emotion that actually felt painful. Like someone had taken an ice pick to the center of his head—a sharp, jabbing pain blooming between his eyes—then scrapped a barbecue grill brush across his skin, the stainless steel bristles jabbing and throwing up a needly pain.

A clamminess joined the pain, as did drops of perspiration pushing toward the surface. His head swam with livid confusion at Dad's memory and legacy being sent down the crapper, made all the worse by the thumping, thudding bass and cheering, singing crowds inside the big top.

But then a voice broke through.

Singular, stabilizing, strong.

Gina's, who was muttering a prayer. A psalm, actually. Psalm 121.

> *I lift up my eyes to the hills —*
> *from where will my help come?*
> *My help comes from the Lord,*
> *who made heaven and earth.*
> *He will not let your foot be moved;*
> *he who keeps you will not slumber.*
> *He who keeps Israel*
> *will neither slumber nor sleep.*
> *The Lord is your keeper;*
> *the Lord is your shade at your right hand.*
> *The sun shall not strike you by day*
> *nor the moon by night.*
> *The Lord will keep you from all evil;*
> *he will keep your life.*
> *The Lord will keep*

> *your going out and your coming in*
> *from this time on and forevermore.*

Her prayer sieved away the fraught, freighted moment to nothing, all of the emotions and neural triggers, the head pain and tightness in his chest and garbled, confused mind all floating away.

The prayer worked wonders. He was back, safe and sound. Thanks to Gina.

"Giddy up, partner," Elijah said, shoving through the rows of cars.

And quite the rows they were!

Cars of every kind, new and old, were arrayed around the tent.

A thumping bass and the whine of an electric guitar, followed by the *rat-a-tat-tat* of a rock star drummer, floated toward them as shouts and whistles and claps joined the chorus floating their way.

All of it looked and sounded unlike any political rally he'd ever seen. In fact, it felt more like a Christian revival meeting than a political one! That chorus flooding through the rows of cars sounded vaguely familiar. A tune he'd heard on the local Christian radio station while skimming through the stations on his way toward the local NPR one for the *Basically Big Bands* show. Didn't pay attention to it; didn't pay attention to any of the newfangled tunes that sounded more like Jesus was some boyfriend to fulfill all our heart's desires than the Son of God who was to be worshipped. But that was just the cranky old soul of his that much more preferred old hymns—definitely Dad's doing, and the Southern Baptist Convention.

Gina muttered, "Sounds like the last Bruce Springsteen concert I went to."

"Nope. No way do these peeps have anything on the Boss!"

The grass lot was emptying of the last of the strays, most of Debby Gallego's supporters having been holed up inside that tent hours ago for the revival meeting—or wherever it was. The few stragglers they'd followed into the fairgrounds were dashing toward the entrance, Elijah and Gina close behind.

"Hey, check this out!" she exclaimed, smirking and shaking her head as she pointed at a vanity plate slapped on the backside of a Chevy compact.

It read: TABA

"TABA?" Elijah asked, twisting his face in confusion.

"Take America Back Again. You know, Debby Gallego's mantra, her campaign slogan."

Elijah scoffed and shook his head. "Nostalgia is for the birds." He was getting impatient at the music ramping up now. "We should get to it. Don't want to miss all the fun."

Weaving through the cars, they made it to the opening, tent flaps suspended back and letting in a view of a large crowd singing and clapping away inside, lit by flashing multi-colored lights—along with letting out a clearer hearing of the chorus blaring from the song revving up the audience:

> *Breakthrough, breakthrough, breakthrough-oo-oo.*
> *Breakthrough, breakthrough, breakthrough-oo-oo.*
> *Breakthrough, breakthrough, breakthrough-oo-oo.*

"Catchy," Gina said, head bobbing back and forth.

"It's something alright..." Elijah grumbled, arms folded and frowning. "Let's try and get a closer look."

Pushing through the clumps of people standing at the back, they made it to an aisle stretching down the center. They elbowed their way to two empty seats several rows on the aisle near the middle, Elijah slipping in first next to a Latino woman. Just as the next verse started:

> *It's your breakthrough-day*
> *God's showing the way.*
> *Health and wealth by right they're yours.*

It's your breakthrough-day.

Gina gasped. "I know this song!"

"You do?" Elijah said.

"It's called 'Breakthrough.'"

He smirked. "How original…"

"We sang it at my charismatic Catholic church. Was real popular, too, coming from a pair of charismatic evangelicals who were eventually busted for peddling deadly hope."

"Sounds about right."

She turned to him. "Why is an Evangelical Christian song being sung at a political rally for a Republican presidential candidate?"

Good question.

Elijah took a deep breath as the chorus struck up again, the place smelling of dirt and straw and ripe bodies, surveying the place that was unlike anything he'd seen.

A stage anchored the front of the vast space, red and blue and white lights flashing on a band leading the audience in song. Then they panned around, flashing on the audience standing and swaying and waving their arms. Chairs stretched the length and width of the vast space, all filled with those standing…worshippers. Guessed that was the right way to frame them. The characterization sent a revolting jolt skittering up his spine.

What sacrilege, seeing all these Christians bowing down before the golden calf of political power. Singing and swaying in some sort of syncretic stew that melded the Church and State.

Speaking of which…

It was striking who was there: men and women, young and middle-aged and sun-setters, black people and white people, Latinos and Asians—a real diverse measure of the spectrum. While he couldn't tell the income or education status, based on the cars in the parking lot and the clothes on those bouncing up and down, it looked like the political rally wasn't catering to the barefoot bumpkins, but middle-classers and even those on the upper end.

So many people. So many believers! Looking for hope in all the wrong places.

Sounded like a country song. Which was about right, given where they were.

Reminded Elijah of a passage from the Holy Scriptures, when Jesus Christ had gone about traveling throughout all the cities and villages, teaching in their synagogues and proclaiming the good news of the Kingdom of God and curing every disease and every sickness. The real kicker was what he thought of the crowds, his attitude toward them, his impressions: *'When he saw the crowds, he had compassion for them because they were harassed and helpless, like sheep without a shepherd.'*

Compassion. His default view of the crowds—of *these* crowds, this group of people.

He liked that about Jesus, the way he thought about people, viewed them. Sure, sheep were the dumbest animals on God's green earth. But Jesus didn't treat people that way. Instead, he wanted to shepherd them. Care for them and guide them. Be for them what they've been waiting for their whole lives.

Except...

Welp, sheep are the dumbest animals on God's green earth! So are people, who are still wandering like sheep, still searching for the shepherd who will give them hope, give them life, save them—searching in all the wrong places.

And suffering for it.

A shift in the singing mood snapped Elijah back to the stage. A radical shift, too, the Christian pop song melding into an a cappella version of "God Bless America."

God Bless America? On Daddy's front lawn?

That emotional overwhelm spiked again, his fingers getting to work: Thumb to index finger, thumb to middle, thumb to ring finger, thumb to pinky—then rinse and repeat.

"Santos is not Lord, and neither is Debby Gallego!" he

muttered, keeping at his stimming tick to deal with the anxiety. "The Declaration of Independence is not an infallible guide to the Christian faith and godly practice. Neither is the Constitution nor the UN's Universal Declaration on Human Rights. National righteousness isn't guaranteed through some original intent constitutional magical thinking. Old Glory is not the Old Rugged Cross of Christ. The Pledge of Allegiance isn't the Nicene Creed. 'God Bless America' is not a doxological hymn of praise to Yahweh!"

"Obvs," Gina said, turning to him with a nod.

"Yeah, well, tell that to these people!"

He huffed a sigh, running a frustrated hand through his hair, eyes darting around at the growing overwhelm—the growing disgust.

Yahweh Almighty, throw us a bone here!

"Quite the turnout, eh?"

Elijah jumped at the new voice, from his right. The Latino woman he'd sidled up next to. A striking woman, actually, tall with wavy chestnut hair that fell past her shoulders, wearing a white T-shirt and jeans. His troubles washed away at what he saw written on her shirt.

Bartlet for America.

A kindred spirit.

"Nice shirt!" he shouted over the din of patriotic singing.

She looked down and smiled. "You a fan?"

He scoffed. "Am I a fan? Was fixin' to start my biannual binge-watching fest of *The West Wing* just yesterday morning until—"

He stopped short, irritation replacing his anxiety at missing out on his favorite television show. With the way their case was going, he might miss out on his bingefest entirely until next election go-around!

The mystery woman said, "So, what's your interest in all of this?"

His face fell, the question throwing up his spidey senses. An odd question for someone to ask at a political rally. What did she think his interest was in all of this? Playing a game of tiddlywinks?

"Who are you?" Elijah asked.

"Dana Diaz. And you are—"

"What are you?" he pressed, ignoring her question.

Her mouth flopped open before snapping shut. She swallowed, glancing off toward the stage before straightening and taking a breath.

"A reporter with the *Global Times Wire.*"

Elijah furrowed his brow. "*Global Times Wire*? Sounds like a comic book rag."

Color matching Dana's lips flashed across her face.

"We're real. We're a new media outlet specializing in intuitively shepherding audiences through politics and policy, business and culture—"

"New media outlet?" Elijah interrupted with a chuckle. "Isn't that code for internet startup? A blog, right—you're a blogger, aren't you."

Frowning, Dana's face blooming all shades of crimson now, she slapped a hand on her hips.

"No, *muchacho*. Neither a blog nor a blogger. But, *sí*, a new media internet venture."

"And everything you read on the internet is true." He turned away. "Pretty sure we learned that lesson the last election rodeo. Fake news and alternative facts and all that jazz."

"Hey!" she protested. "I'll have you know I worked for the *Columbus Dispatch* before the *Global Times Wire.*"

Now Gina leaned in. "Did you say the *Columbus Dispatch*? From Columbus, Ohio?"

Dana nodded. "*Sí*. I was their star political reporter before—well, before leaving."

"What happened?"

"I...well, we had a mutual parting of ways."

Elijah scoffed. "Apparently not star enough. That's usually code for you got sacked."

"It was a corporate buyout, alright? Some vulture capital firm swooped in and—"

"Sounds like a real *telenovela, muchacha,*" he said, waving a dismissive hand. "A real soap opera. But we don't talk to reporters."

"Why not?"

"Because."

"Because…"

He went to answer when a sudden warmth flushed his veins, cluing him into something from the spirit-realm.

Sometimes a chill ratcheted up and down his spine when that happened, often the case of something malevolent poking its head up from the Unseen Realm. Like what had hit him in Cracker Barrel when that psycho had been killed on their first Group X case.

This was different.

Had always been a spiritually sensitive kid. Perhaps his time at the orphanage had hammered and honed his spidey senses (after all, Spiderman was his favorite comic book hero). Through the years, those senses had served him well, helping him stay out of trouble and generally walking the straight and narrow. Could have been from his innate desire to please, but it was more than that. The Spirit of God himself seemed to be upon him in a special way, cluing him into another dimension with an awareness that was as mystical and creepy as it was real and helpful.

Sure had served him a time or twelve during his years with the Bureau as well, his sensitivity to the working of the Unseen Realm breaking into their mundane world through violent acts of wickedness and evil. But also when the Holy Spirit was cluing him into something—a clue, a warning, a revelation-insight.

Like now…

And it seemed to be grabbing him by the ears and telling him that bone he'd prayed for had been signed, sealed, and delivered.

Third Person of the Trinity style.

Swallowing, Elijah went for it: "We don't talk to reporters because we're investigators who have a long, sordid history with them type."

Dana startled. "Investigators? With what agency?"

Gina cleared her throat. Loudly. A non-physical tell that was like a hand on his shoulder—yanking him back from the edge of spilling the tea.

Except he knew that wasn't the right call.

"Group X," he answered.

Dana crossed her arms and raised an eyebrow. "Never heard of it. What's that, some FBI basement-dwelling X-Files copycat?"

"The Church, actually."

She let her arms drop with a start. "The Church? As in, what, the Vatican?"

Elijah explained, "We're an ecumenical agency investigating inexplicable and unexplainable events that smack of being perpetrated by agents of the Unseen Realm."

Now she regarded him with skeptical eyes. "Unseen Realm?"

"Not important. What is, is that we're here—"

A new song started up with interruption, the volume and mood revving up as the Rolling Stones started belting "You Can't Always Get What You Want." Seemed both appropriate and inappropriate at a political rally on the grounds of a Southern Baptist church.

Dana smirked, shaking her head. "That *muy loco* song is a hallmark of Gallego's rallies."

"Odd choice," Elijah noted.

"Well, it may be a sort of screw-you to conservatives, maybe just a song that Debby likes, or maybe just one she knows her fans like, since that's what her playlist is all about."

"Suppose she is a woman of the people."

"Something's happening…" Gina pointed at the stage just as

the lights started going wild, joined by a raucous chorus of cheers and clapping, jumping and hand-waving.

Something sure was happening.

Nope. Not something. *Someone.*

Debby Gallego was happening.

CHAPTER 14

ina folded her arms as Debby Gallego strutted across the stage, one end of her mouth curling upward at the sights and sounds—even the smells and feeling of the place that was lit up when the presidential contender entered the room.

There was an energy about the palace, and not only because of the bassy thump in her chest from the ginormous speakers blaring to beat the band from the stage. It was the excitement, the anticipation, the—what was the word for it that sent all the hairs on her arms rising at attention?

She had it: Hope. Which was certainly fueled by all the other senses raging throughout the big top bonanza!

The rock-concert lights were going wild—blues and reds and whites blinking in a rapid pattern joined by the American flag on a massive digital display at the back of the stage. The band that had been a worship band on their arrival was now rocking out to the Boss's "Born in the U.S.A" (try that amalgamation of Church and State on for size!), the crowd going wild alongside the twangy electric guitars and smashing cymbals and *ba-da-bum* tom rack. Deafening, it was, and Gina worried Elijah would become overwhelmed, too much sound not his thing like too much smells weren't hers.

Speaking of which: major olfactory overload! Between the hay and horse dookie (which she figured was a Kentucky thing) to the scent of burnt accelerants from the concert fire machines shooting white sparks high into the tent like it was July Fourth. Worst of all were all the perfumes and armpits swirling around her, but she tolerated it all because of the energy of what all those five senses added up to: the thrill of the political rally!

Her ninth, by her estimation, not missing a single presidential election season since she was born. Had Mama to thank for that. Started with 1988 (Mama was a Dukakis fan; the only Dukakis fan) and ran straight through Bush Senior's second losing campaign (thanks to that Texan business-magnate spoiler), on to Slick Willey's re-election campaign (Mama volunteered for both, with Gina her sidekick). Then Gore the Bore (as Mama had nicknamed him) who spoiled her love for the Democratic Party (she punched the ticket both times for Dubya) until hope was renewed with the senator from the Land of Lincoln.

Now there was a political rally if there ever was one! Obama's hope and change fueled Mama's return back to the Dems (Gina joined her the first time, not the second) until that New Yorker with bad hair yanked her back to the Party of Lincoln (she never joined her mama on that bandwagon)—which was the oddest thing, because Mama had been a raging bra-burner during the '90s and couldn't wait to cast her vote for the first woman presidential candidate. Except, that's not what went down.

Mama was as fair-weathered of a fair-weather political animal as you could get, swinging and swaying to the man and movement that would benefit her best. So when Candidate Orange Hair showed up on the scene, despite his sketch record with the sisters of the traveling pants coalition, she was smitten. What had won mama over was the populist energy—the excitement, the anticipation, the hope—that wanted to stick it to the Man.

Much like what Gina was witnessing now.

There she was, Debby Gallego. The woman, the myth, the legend herself was taking the stage, her curly blond hair cut short glimmering beneath the klieg lights like a Marilyn Monroe lookalike. Mama would be proud.

The presidential candidate strutted to the center of the stage in a bright red, tight-fitting dress that sloped down past one of her shoulders and highlighted her curves. A bit seductive for a political rally, but she supposed that was probably the point. Throw red meat to the fellas and offer up a dose of aspiration for the ladies in the crowd. The power color also served to signal strength and power, energy and life for the sixty-something exec. Along with those killer calves and hips.

None of which men had to worry about! Could be old and fat and hairy, but as long as they promised to open up the gravy train, come down on criminals and the wealthy alike, pledge to fight for world peace while also pulling our boys from misad-venture warmongering—well, then they were golden. Flash a smile made of synthetic teeth, not do anything stupid (like brag about grabbing women by their hoohoo), even just hide out in your basement and stream your missives from the cozy comforts of your New England abode—well, that's all it took for men to grab the reins of power in the highest office in the most powerful country in the world.

Took much more work for women, a delicate balance between appearing strong without appearing bossy; appearing nubile enough to not look like last night's fast-food bag but old enough not to look naive; in-control without being intimidating —both for men and women.

Gina laughed. Sounded like her mama! Ever the feminist, she was. Had been swept up in Third Wave Feminism during her childhood, when women were fighting for new rights to party. Not that Gina was poo-pooing the movement of her sisterhood of the traveling pants forebears or anything. She liked voting and working like any run-of-the-mill male variety of the *Homo sapiens* species. She had Mama, in part, to thank for that. And Gloria Steinem, along with Madonna, Queen Latifah, and Mary J. Blige.

Watching Debby Gallego, Gina no longer thought Marilyn Monroe was the right comparison. Jane Fonda was more like it. How that octogenarian looked so good was some major Hollywood voodoo magic she wanted no part of. Probably a cross between yoga and Botox.

"Never trust a woman with short hair..." Elijah muttered as Gallego did her hand-wavy thing.

Their new friend, Dana Diaz, scoffed. "That's not sexist at all."

"Just saying. In my experience, them type drive a hard bargain. Although...have to admit, she is a stunner."

"And neither is that! Won't hear no woman go on about a candidate's nose or backside or hair, or how tall they are."

"What about the size of their hands?"

Dana went to answer, her mouth opening and closing like a trout out of water and searching for breath. She snapped it shut and turned back to the stage.

Gina just shook her head and buried her forehead in her palm.

Oh, Eli. Always the blunt one of the pair. Without fail. Got him into trouble a time or twelve. Too much trouble. Loved him to pieces, in the sort of brother-sister way. But she might have to play interference, like last time.

Because there was something about this new friend of theirs that piqued her interest. Couldn't put a finger on it, but a journalist covering this rally—of her caliber, and from her home state...something about it prickled at the back of her brain. Not sure what, but maybe she and Eli could use her for their own investigation.

As sexist as Eli sounded, the crowd sure seemed to agree

with his assessment, the sea of hootin' and hollerin' Gallego supporters sounding more like fans at a Stones concert than a political rally at a church. Or maybe a group of drunk frat boys at Hooters.

Gallego reached a glass lectern at the center front and gripped its side. Strong, commanding, in-control. She had a wide smile and perfect teeth that shimmered in the lights. Way too white to be real, that's for darn' tootin! But that hair—every one of them were put in its place, and perfectly coifed. And that dress, the color complementing her skin tone—

"For the love…" Gina complained. Now look what she was doing. Next, she'd be wondering about the size of her hands!

"Howdie, friends!" Debby crooned. "Nice party you're throwin' here!"

The crowd went wild, throwing up a gleeful cheer, with sustained clapping and hoots and hollers.

"Been to fifty of these things," Dana said, "and I have yet to hear her open with anything but that line."

"Catchy," Gina said. "And effective."

Elijah scoffed. "Patronizing."

"Maybe, but isn't that what the masses want? A patron to take care of them, one that gives them a show?"

"Suppose you're right. After all, there are only two things the people anxiously desire: bread and circuses."

"Who said that? Regan, Thatcher?"

"Juvenal, a Roman poet."

"I don't know about you," Gallego crooned, "but I'm in the mood to shut up and shut down the globalist, progressivist, elitist varmints and take America back again!"

The tent erupted with obligatory cheers and hollers and hand-waving, with phones raised and snapping in the moment to post on WeShare. Because we all know that a moment never happened unless it was put up on social media.

"It's America's moment, y'all!" the Republican presidential

candidate continued. "It's your moment. I'm fixin' to put fly-over-country back on the map and give you what you're due!"

"Give 'em hell, Debby!" someone shouted from down in front, their voice carrying at just the right lull in the adulation.

Without missing a beat, she jabbed her acrylic floozy-red painted pointer in the air and promised, "You're darn tootin' I will!"

More cheers, more hollers and hand-waving, more raised phones snapping away, joined by whistling and laughter at the exchange.

"But before we get into all of that, and I get into my hell raisin'—" She flashed a wry grin, basking in more laughter and cheers "—I want to invite my good friend and host of this here party up to the stage. Give it up for Pastor Billy Baron!"

Eli instantly stiffened, her partner crossing his arms and scowling. Made sense, given the man had taken over from his daddy and turned the place into a circus. Or a den of thieves, as some might suggest.

Also made sense Gallego would invite Billy Baron to the stage, given how much of a celebrity the man had become in the past year bucking liberalism and taking on the crazier wing of the Democratic Party. And if Eli's source was right, about him joining her campaign as manager, then this could be the moment of unveiling.

Billy Baron was a sharp contrast to the polished tech tycoon. He wore a dad bod with pride along with a flashy Hawaiian shirt that looked out of place in the South. Supposed it added to his of-the-people charm, along with his barely haired head that glinted in the klieg lights and the single diamond stud gleaming in his right ear. Was single too, never married.

Dana Diaz leaned in and shared, "What do you suppose that's all about?"

"Can't tell you," Eli replied, face hard and arms still folded.

"Can't tell me what?"

"Nope. Mums the word. My lips are sealed."

Gina scoffed. "Well, mine aren't. A source says he's joining the team as Gallego's campaign manager."

Elijah threw her a frown and shook his head. She didn't care. Sensed they might need this Dana Diaz journalist, and Gina was of the same mind as Ella Fitzgerald: You've got to give a little to get a little love. And she was hoping that little nugget got them enough journo love to help them solve this case blooming into something she wasn't quite sure of.

"Mama said not to tell anyone," Eli complained.

"No, she said for you not to tell anyone," Gina corrected. "Besides, the dog's gonna get loose soon anyhow."

"Let's just hope they're not the dogs of war…"

The pair stood side by side, hands grasped and raised high, Baron and Gallego basking in their followers' praise. Looked a little too cozy for candidate and campaign manager…

Hands still raised, and audience still cheering them on, Gallego announced, "I'm thrilled to be here with my good friend, Billy Baron."

More obligatory clapping and cheering, though it seemed like it was heartfelt. Like the good pastor was some sort of celebrity among these folks. "It is an honor to be speaking to you today and sharing with you my vision for this great nation. A vision that isn't only my own."

She paused, still smiling, taking a breath before letting the dog loose: "I'm pleased to announce Billy Baron as my vice presidential running mate to take America back again!"

There was a sharp dead zone in the moment. All noise and commotion, all cheering and hollering winding down to zero. If it had been one of those cheesy '90s sitcoms, there would have been an interruptive record scratch indicating the unexpected.

Then the lid blew off the place!

The applause was thunderous, the reverberations from the hundreds of supporters clapping their support thumping in Gina's chest. As was the exuberance of their vocal support clanging in her ears. Confetti fell all around them now, the colors of American patriotism—red, white, blue—and those rock-concert fire machines exploded with white sparks, high and exalting, the burnt residue washing across the hot tent.

"What the what?" was about the only response Gina could muster.

"*Dios mío…*" Dana muttered, her thumbs working overtime on that phone of hers.

"Welp, that takes the cheesecake," Eli said.

Gina turned to him. "Did you see that coming?"

"Nope," he said with a scowl. "But I'll tell you one thing, the worm has turned. Bigly."

"Far biglier—or bigger, rather, than campaign manager!"

"Suppose the Kenturkey gossip train isn't what it used to be."

"Can't say I'm surprised," Dana said, pecking away some post to WeShare.

"Why not?" Gina asked.

"Hold the cheese stick," Eli said, pointing toward the stage.

It was filling with people now. Men and women in white robes—the choir kind, by the looks of it. Billy Baron and Debby Gallego had stepped to the side, giving the center of the stage the audience's full attention.

A soundtrack began, and the choir members—as Gina gathered—started swaying. Now Pastor Billy joined them, microphone in one hand and the other raised toward the ceiling with eyes closed.

Then he crooned:

> *Well I'm just an ignorant Kentuckian*
> *But I want to take America back again*
> *So forgive my twang and don't worry, I'll be brief*
> *Here're some suggestions to the next commander in*
>   *chief*

"Sweet mother of Melchizedek…" Eli moaned, slapping a hand against his forehead.

Gina cringed herself. "Have to agree with you on that one."

Now it was the choir's turn:

> *Let's take America back again*
> *By making abortion illegal again*
> *Let's make the family in fashion again*
> *Let's take America back again*

"*Dios mío,*" Dana said, shaking her head. "Of course the first suggestion is a pivot to abortion and marriage."

"What did you expect?" Eli said. "Them issues are catnip to conservatives. Not that I can complain. Adoption is why I'm still alive."

"Conservative issues." Dana snorted a laugh. "Conservative Christians, maybe. Not this crowd."

"What do you mean by that?"

Gina shushed him as Billy Baron struck up the next verse.

> *I've been blessed to fly the continent*
> *From the Left Coasts through the Midwest*
> *We need a good dose of Providence*
> *To right what's wrong with America again*

"Nope," Eli said, shaking his head. "Providence doesn't rhyme with continent!"

Gina replied, "Not the only thing that's wrong with the bleepin' song…"

The choir was back, arms raised and voices booming out across the cavernous tent, the audience swaying now with raised phones, lights shining like digital lighters at a Stones concert. They crooned:

> *Not by might, nor by power*

But by my spirit, says the Lord
Not by might, nor by power
But by my spirit, says the Lord

"Come on, y'all—sing it with me!" Billy Baron boomed, storming across the stage, the ringleader whipping his supporters into a frenzy.

And frenzy they were! The entire place erupted with the bridge:

Not by might, nor by power
But by my spirit, says the Lord
Not by might, nor by power
But by my spirit, says the Lord

Billy Baron cut in: "And Debby Gallego is the one who'll—"
Then continued on into the chorus, joined by the choir again and the entire Ringling Bros. and Barnum & Bailey circus:

Take America back again
By bringing prayer back in schools again
Let's reclaim America for Christ again
By taking America back again

Gina's stomach clenched with sickening dread as Pastor Billy continued on into the next verse:

Ellis Island is where we start
Everyone is welcomed at the port
To shelter in the city on the hill
But nobody comes in illegal

"*Dios mío*," Dana said again, shaking her head before launching into a mumbled string of Spanish Gina took as something less holy. Whatever it was was drowned out by the Baptist choir again:

> *Let's take America back again*
> *Take our sin and shame to the cross again*
> *Let's make the Bible central again*
> *Let's take America back again*

Debby Gallego returned to the stage, joining her new vice presidential candidate in the final stanza:

> *Let's evangelize our oldest friends*
> *And point it out when they're backslidin'*
> *Remind them of the gospel and then*
> *We'll take America back again*

The soundtrack kept at its thing, while the choir and Pastor Billy kept at the chorus, singing the praises of America and their battle to take it back again.

"I think I'm gonna be sick…" Elijah moaned.

Gina nodded a sigh. "Agree. But not like you, I imagine."

He said nothing, hanging his head.

Felt bad for him. Real bad. His father's legacy being trampled like that. Which wasn't even touching on the Church's legitimacy being trampled like that! With a full-court mingling of the sacred and secular—with a bleepin' hymn of praise to America, to Debby Gallego!

The choir left and Gallego was back at center stage, jewelry gleaming and one hand waving while she gripped the microphone. She flashed her bright wide-mouthed grin that had won over so many Americans, the one that was slowly winning over Christians, as well.

"I'll tell you one thing," she shouted. "Not only are we gonna take America back again. We're going to take Christianity back again—protect it and set it back at the center of our great country. I can say that. I don't have to be politically correct!"

The crowd clapped and cheered their approval.

"Thank you. God bless you and this fine church of yours. And God bless America."

She stepped away, waving as her family met her on stage. Red, white, and blue balloons fell across the tent while the band played "The Battle Hymn of the Republic," a perfect ending to the full-court mingling of Christianity and politics.

Billy Baron strode onto the stage again. He was beaming. He grasped Gallego's hand tightly and said something to her. They both laughed and turned to the crowd, hands still clasped and raised now in solidarity. Stood that way for several beats until the preacher walked to the podium, face wide with a toothy grin.

The tent continued to offer their approval of Gallego and her political platform. Pastor Billy allowed it, before asking them to quiet down.

"The battle lines have been drawn!" Baron boomed. "Every institution of American society has been carved up by the Devil himself. This great country, this City on a Hill, is threatening to split into two over a second civil war!"

"Sweet mother of Melchizedek!" Elijah cursed. "What would the Prince of Peace say about such talk?"

"America is under siege, the barbarians are at the gates," Baron went on. "But today I have hope, because I've brought along hope. That hope has a name. Her name is Debby Gallego!"

More cheering and hollering, more clapping and hand-waving. Crowd was really getting revved up now.

"She will take America back again. It's time to play for keeps! Which is why I am thrilled to join her ticket as vice president. To not only take America back again, but to reclaim America for Christ again!"

"There it is," Elijah said, shaking his head. "The whole Christian-political syncretist taco."

Their new friend Dana smirked. "I think you mean the whole enchilada, *muchacho*."

"Nope. Taco."

Billy Baron flashed a double OK sign, curling both thumbs toward his index fingers and extending them high into the air.

Which Gina found odd. And familiar, the image of her mama flashing into her mind from that morning. The one with her mug on the front page of the *New York Times*.

Eli shoved past her in a sudden rush, throwing up his meltdown words of warning: "I need air!"

Just the rumbling stage, Eli edging toward the point of no return. But she knew what came next.

Gina went to intervene when something else caught her attention, up the way. The fleeting glimpse of something familiar—a slinky Old Glory dress, of red and white and blue running down a slim body with white stars plastered on the side.

More than something familiar was *someone* familiar.

Was that—

"What the what?" she said, stepping into the aisle.

Then it was gone. The familiar shape and hair and dress.

There was a sudden, slicing cry rising from somewhere in the tent.

Then a loud, rushing shout from several people in all directions of the rally, joined by a drumbeat and the ear-splitting *honk* of an air horn.

From all directions across the tent.

Something was happening.

CHAPTER 15

lijah couldn't believe the spectacle. The *circus* spectacle that was happening on Dad's old church stomping grounds—the grounds that had been a soccer field he'd built as a way to bless and love the community. Not to serve as a whorehouse for the Bride of Christ to get it on with Uncle Sam!

All of it was discouraging, disturbing, disorienting.

The rock-concert light show and patriotic symbolism—the red-white-and-blue confetti and balloons, the waving American flag. Especially the waving American flag. Dad had an especially hard and fast rule about displaying Old Glory in the sanctuary of his church just outside the big-top bonanza. Had paid for it, too, his parishioners pitching a fit about his refusal to properly honor the nation and its Christian heritage. But he hadn't budged.

He'd worried what would happen to his people's hearts when the symbol of the State was given pride of place alongside the symbol of the Church: the cross of Christ.

Dad's entire orientation had been one of placing Jesus at the center of his life. Made Jesus and all he taught and did for the world the center of his ministry—his teachings on neighbor love, his care for the sick and marginalized, his sacrificial death on the cross to pay our price in our place, his resurrection from the dead to pave the way for our own everlasting life with him and the Father and Holy Spirit.

Dad had also worried because of the other thing that was blaring from the stage: that blasted hymn nearly worshiping America—setting up Debby Gallego as some sort of golden calf that would bring the Church its salvation! Just like the first golden calf Yahweh's people had set up for themselves in the wilderness after their God had just rescued them from slavery.

The passage from the Book of Exodus, chapter 32, raced through Elijah's mind as the spectacle continued up front: *'These are your gods, O Israel, who brought you up out of the land of Egypt!'* Not much different than what had been promised just moments ago: Debby Gallego is your savior, O Church, your hope—the one who'll take back America and reclaim it for Christ again!

All of it led by Billy Baron.

Elijah had had a hard time looking at the man while the spectacle had unfolded. Couldn't believe, for one, that he would sacrifice his calling as a shepherd of Christ's flock in Paducah, Kenturkey, for the role of lap dog to Debby Gallego—why get fat and drunk off the scraps from Uncle Sam's table when you were gifted the chance to feed the world bread and wine, to offer it Christ's Body and Blood?

Couldn't believe, for two, that he would let the State use it like this, let a candidate of the most powerful country in the world reduce Daddy's church to a prop in a political theater that meant to do one thing and one thing alone: gain and maintain power. The Church of Jesus Christ was one more interest group the State used to further its aims—which Dad's church had been reduced to.

Nope. Strike that: Which Billy Baron himself had reduced Daddy's church to.

The reverend had to be in his mid-50s. Seemed gregarious enough, with thick jowls and a thinning wave of hair clinging to his shiny head and dyed a horrendous shade of black that did nothing for his dignity. Especially that floral shirt of his that was untucked over dark-blue jeans.

Dad was polished and buttoned-down. This blowhard Baron was ostentatious and loud. Dad was a traditional Baptist-church pastor, where people wore sweaters and sang softly. Now it was a charismatic monstrosity, with people dressing for a barbecue and hootin' and hollerin'! Dad was a pastor's kid and lifelong conservative who never had a sip of alcohol. But according to Baron's bio, he was a so-called "radical liberal" who once got so high on smack that he jumped onstage and grabbed a guitar at a Tom Petty concert.

The emotions were welling within Elijah, like magma building under the surface of Earth's crust. Running hot and livid, the pressure building and threatening to explode into a fit of screams and shouts, hand-flapping and arm-waving—like what had happened on that country road in Mill Creek Junction during the last investigation, when the bottled-up emotion from Dad's death erupted.

Now he was dealing with the bottled-up emotions from Dad's legacy—a legacy that had been spit out and trampled upon. Emotions that were fast spinning out into something that nobody needed in the moment—not him, not Gina, not the Group X case from hot Hades.

Meltdown.

Not a tantrum, as allistic, neuronormative people are prone to finger-wag. Meltdowns were the last leg in a slow burn when the overwhelm bloomed into an explosive outlet. What humanity didn't understand was they were as necessary as air for his kind.

It was the kind of combustible, pressurized overwhelm he'd had more times than he'd care to recall growing up in the Virginia orphanage—until the impulse had been beaten down by broom handles and coat hangers and frying pans. The kind autistic people sometimes struggle to keep at bay, but had reared its ugly head in Elijah's adult life only twice before—ironically, both having to do with Dad's memory.

First had come during his days with the FBI. It was the inciting incident that led to his dismissal thanks to Agent Pendergast yanking that terrorism case away from him. The one where a psychopath had shot up his Messianic Jewish community one Shabbat service, an event that smacked of what had happened to his father.

Next one came during the last case after a hella crazy turn of events. It was the final spark that sent the fuse blazing in a full-on race toward a totalizing, explosive end that had nearly done him in. There he was, right in a field of collard greens, screaming and flapping and spitting until Gina helped pull him out from the depths of despair.

And now it was happening again.

Understood completely what was going on, an out-of-body experience within Elijah's head that stood outside and above the rest of his consciousness looking in on his inner emotions boiling into a fierce frenzy. A physical welling inside that needed to escape. Like a vomiting sensation that found relief when one expelled the contents of their stomach.

Chest started tightening like a mother, his lungs and throat and mouth lurching into hyperventilation that threatened to bloom into screams and desperate cries to Yahweh Almighty wondering why this was happening to Daddy's church—to Daddy's legacy! Might even join the screaming prayers with a few choice words that would make a sailor blush.

It was just like the series of tremors before Mount St. Helen blew her lid. Elijah started rumbling; that's what they call it. Arms wiggling, hands jiggling, head nodding back and forth then side to side. And like the ol' gastrointestinal heave-ho, he needed air before things got real.

So: "I need air!" he announced, his code word to Gina colada that he was on the brink.

He pushed past Gina, rather abruptly and rudely, too. Didn't mean to, and she threw up a startled, annoyed cry at his arm brushing her back into her seat. Couldn't help it. Needed air.

Launching into the aisle, Gallego fanboys and fangirls spilling out all around him now with an oppressive suffocation of pressing bodies and stinky odors—tart and tangy and unwashed—he paced in a circle as Billy Baron went into one of his diatribes about the state of America and it being overrun by libtards. Worked through his thumb-to-finger tick, raising his voice but more pleading his case that all of it was whacked out. No one heard him above the din of adulation.

But then it shifted—his voice and movements. Until he lost it. Red-faced, spittle flying, cussing like a sailor, he was.

Those out-of-body eyes of his that were paying attention to the other part of him slouching into a meltdown understood completely what was happening, the inner emotion of losing control over his father's legacy on top of not understanding what the hot Hades he was doing back at his childhood church and why the hot Hades he'd taken this case that had nothing *inexplicitus* about it—all of it was boiling into a fierce frenzy until he couldn't contain it any longer. A physical welling inside that needed to escape.

"What the what?" Gina said as he tried to get himself under control.

Thought she was readying to reach in to help, by offering a word or prayer to bring him back to Earth. Instead, with furrowed brow, she took cautious steps past him. As if she'd seen something—something familiar, something haunting.

The shift in his partner's own countenance was enough of a trigger to reset his own head—the neurological synapses of his brain doing a double-take of interest and intrigue, of concern even, to right the ship and yank him from his own mental misery.

A sudden, slicing cry rising from somewhere in the tent cut off any chance for him to ask what was what.

Then a loud, rushing shout from several people in all directions of the rally rose, joined by a drumbeat and the ear-splitting *honk* of an air horn.

From all directions across the tent.

Something was happening.

Elijah shrank back from the shrilly blast, bending low and throwing his hands over his ears from the clamorous commotion. Was already maxed out with aural stimulation from the rally. His brain went bonkers from the wrong kinds of sounds—sudden, blasty, shrilly—like Gina's went sour from the wrong kinds of smells. So while he could handle the steady hum of loud music and cheers, for a time, the sudden addition of aural energy did not do his body good.

"You alright?" Gina shouted near his ear, bending next to him.

Taking a breath, he withdrew his hands from the side of his head and gave it a shake, then righted himself and nodded—searching for the offending addition that had tipped his neural scales into the red.

At first, it sounded like a rowdy group of college kids, the TABA YAGAs. The Young Americans for Gallego Activation that had galvanized the normally disaffected youth vote pledging to bear the Take America Back Again torch with gusto. Not the catchiest of groupie names, but it sure had caught the mainstream press by surprise, the diverse coalition catapulting Debby Gallego to the top of not only the Republican ticket, but also within winning distance over President Santos.

But when he glanced around, gathering the 411 on the shift—

What he saw said otherwise!

First, it was the men in black government-issued suits, hulking and bulky and running with purpose, who rushed Debby Gallego and Billy Baron from the stage. Which threw up all sorts of gasps and finger-pointing gestures and an immediate mood change from those standing across the vast tent.

Then it was the rush of hoodlums barging into the tent,

carrying signs of some sort, beating those drums and honking those air horns that had sent him recoiling.

Which set off a whole other rush. Not at first, the crowd too stunned for words to react, not knowing what they were reacting to. But then they did—men and women and their children, old and young scrambling to flee what they probably feared was about to become a mass casualty event that had become all too common in 'Merica the past several years.

Not Elijah, or Gina, who both stood still—discerning, intuiting, plotting their next moves.

Gina colada had always said there were three kinds of people in life when the shiznit hits the fan.

Freezers, callers, and runner-inners.

Three personalities baked into the lizard brain after generations of ancestors had been forced to stare down saber-toothed tigers and mastodons and half-naked men in loincloths bearing sharpened sticks. Not to mention car accidents and capsized fishing dinghies and psychopaths unleashing an AR-15 assault rifle on a country church.

Freezers freeze. Could be a third kind of F word to the famed fight-or-flight response baked into our bodies—our neurons working in conjunction with our adrenal glands to put up or shut up. But really they're fleers, their brain flat fleeing when disaster strikes. They do diddly when the shiznit hits the fan and are worth diddly. No judgment there. Just the facts, ma'am.

Callers grab the squawk box and, well, squawk! Whether for help from the police or fire and rescue, or plain ol' pops when a pipe bursts in the living room ceiling from a plugged second-floor toilet. Much more available than freezers, because at least they jump into the fight.

But runner-inners are the ones running into danger to pull grandma from the overturned Ford Fiesta or save the family cat from the burning bungalow. They're the heroes—often ordinary ones thrown into extraordinary circumstances—who rise to the occasion and save the day.

So, freezers, callers, and runner-inners. Three peeps who show up when the shiznit hits the fan.

Like a bunch of crazed loons trying to disrupt a political rally at his daddy's childhood church!

Long ago, Elijah determined who he was. Or more precisely: the Holy Spirit determined who he was, wiring him in a way that activated his feet and hands and brain to take the plunge into fate's furnace. A real irony, too, since the rest of the world figured his type wasn't the sort to save the day. The impulse had laid buried inside, and was triggered that fateful Sunday morning, Elijah the one who had sent a well-placed right hook dead-center kisser into the perp who'd taken out his father.

The same impulse that was ready to make dang sure Daddy's legacy wasn't tarnished by some two-bit carnival barker!

But instead of running toward the stage to stop the crazy that was taking over, he was determined to stop the crazy man that had taken over his daddy's church and an entire wing of the Church.

Pastor Billy Baron.

Clenching his jaw with resolve, and his fists to deliver his sentiments on the matter, he went to take off when something stopped him cold.

A man had mounted the stage. Looked real odd, too. Clad in furs, face paint, and wearing some animal head—was that a goat's? Too dark and far away to get a better read on his features —height, weight, race. A group of people joined the dude, all wearing white T-shirts with the most curious of thing displayed for all to see.

A capital I.

Looked like it had been written using duct tape (no, not *duck* tape; duct tape!), the wide strips of plastic adhesive shimmering silver in the klieg lights, the strokes of the ninth letter all crooked and kindergarten-like.

Was the oddest thing, the man jumping up and down on stage, with some big wooden stick like some sort of shaman. His followers doing the same and shouting phrases he could barely catch—except for one snippet.

"The Great Awakening is nigh!" they shouted.

None of it made a lick of sense—

Until it did.

The letter I!

"The letter I..." Elijah muttered aloud now. Then, turning to Gina: "I. I. I!"

"What the what, partner?" she said, the man carrying on now being cheered on by several in the crowd.

He swung an arm toward the stage, jamming his finger several times to put an exclamation point on the point that was lost on Gina.

"I—Don't you see?"

"See what?" Dana asked, poking her head in their business.

Elijah ignored her, pressing on: "Remember what Eddy Lee said, back at the diner?"

Gina squinted with a pinched face, following Elijah's still-extended arm and giving her head a shake. Clearly was processing the crazy he was spouting.

Until the gears clicked into place, and her face slackened and eyes went large.

"I..." Gina said with recognition. "Not eye!"

"What eye?" asked Dana again, her persistence becoming pesky.

Elijah turned to her. "Not eye—" He pointed two fingers at both ocular organs "—I!" He drew two parallel lines in the air with his finger then one straight down the center.

She scoffed and folded her arms. "This sounds like a bad Seinfeld bit."

"Nope. Abbott and Costello. But I get your meaning."

The jokers were going on about "a coming storm" and "a Great Awakening" that would reveal all—"the lines of good and evil drawn" and "patriots rising to fight the common cause of the people."

Dana yanked out her phone again and pecked away, muttering *"Dios mío…"* with recognition.

A lot of it seemed your standard Debby Gallego fare, but neither the Jane Fonda lookalike nor her new running mate, Pastor Billy Baron, were in sight.

What Elijah wanted to know was where they'd scampered off to. Specifically Baron, his dad's replacement, the one responsible for all this nonsense.

So he could confront the bozo.

Knowing the grounds like he did, Elijah had an idea where.

So he went with it.

Time to get answers.

CHAPTER 16

How could Gina have missed it?

It wasn't *eye*, as in her two peepers disbelieving all she was seeing go down inside that political rally that was more like the charismatic revival services her mama had dragged her to as a child.

I. I. *I*! As in the ninth letter of the alphabet and personal pronoun, just as Elijah had indicated.

The I showed me, Eddy Lee had said.

Now, what *I* was, or who *I* was—she didn't have a cotton pickin' clue!

Gina shook her head, cursing herself softly for missing it the first time. Not that she understood what it meant anyway, but she could have tried coaxing something from Eddy Lee. A name or book or website or WeVid video or organization—something, anything that could steer them in the right direction to help them make sense of the crazy train.

There was something familiar about it all that simmered in the back of her noggin. Something she'd heard or seen that connected with the spectacle on stage. Something professionally, from her FBI days—something personally, from her past.

The man dressed like a shaman wearing some taxidermist's

sombrero. The T-shirt with the crooked duct-tape I. The slogans promising a battle between good and evil, a Great Awakening ushering in the end times.

Freakin' Reverend Billy Baron signing up to Debby Gallego's crazy train!

But what it all connected to, what it all meant…she was trying to think but got nothing.

That wasn't even touching on what she had seen before Eli nearly melted down in the aisle. Had heard his watch phrase signaling his neuro-overwhelm. *I need air.* After he shoved past, she'd gone to make sure he kept his head on straight and talk him through the rumble stage before it erupted into a full-on purging event from what she figured was the aural and emotional overwhelm from the event.

Wanted to help and went to do so—

Until she'd glimpsed something that she'd definitely seen before, just the day before. Plastered on the front of the *New York Times*, wearing Old Glory with hands raised in the middle of a crowd flashing the same gesture Baron had.

Mama…

No doubt about it. In that slinky dress and long white hair, with that frame and gate of hers.

Then she was gone. Disappeared all Harry Potter style in the sea of bodies.

But not running away from the on-stage spectacle for cover, for safety—which was the smart thing to do given how disruptive politics had been; never knew when someone with an AR-15 was going to open up on a crowd. No, this woman—her mama, Gina swore—ran toward the on-stage spectacle.

Faces and bodies, arms and hands, legs and feet came at her in a tidal wave of panic, obscuring her view and jostling her from making purchase forward.

Went to shove through the crowd but was yanked back to the moment by her muttering partner in crime.

"Not on your life, pal..." Eli growled lowly, spinning around toward stage right.

Gina pulled back and gave him her attention. "Eli, what are you—"

"Come on!" he shouted, gesturing through the crowd to the other side of the tent.

"Wait, what are you—"

"No time, Gina colada. They're getting away!"

"Eli, no!"

It was too late.

Eli dashed between a mother and her teenage son, the crowd enveloping him in an instant, his mop of shaggy hair disappearing and leaving her alone.

"*Dios mío*," Dana Diaz moaned, pecking away at her phone. "This has turned into a *todo otro loco*!"

Gina turned to their new friend, wondering what other crazy thing this had turned into besides the crazy bananas. But she didn't ask. Wanted to, but she had bigger fish to reel back into the tank.

Like Eli!

"Nice meeting you, Dana, but I've got to go."

"Go where, *muchacha?*"

Gina didn't wait to explain. She needed to find out what the what was going on with her partner.

So she took off after him, Dana Diaz throwing up another questioning cry before it faded into the sea of shouts and screams of confusion.

She understood completely, the spectacle continuing up on stage. The crazy man with the furs and painted face, holding that stick and wearing some sort of head dressing that had an animal skull on it.

Darting down an aisle, she caught sight of Elijah—

Tussling with someone in a white T-shirt lying on the grassy ground.

"Eli!" Gina shouted, racing after him.

"Who are you—what are you doing here?" he shouted.

She found Eli on top of some tall, skinny white dude with scraggly facial hair. And a big, fat letter I on the face of his shirt —set inside a triangle!

An I. Or did it signal an *eye*? The eye of God, as Eddy Lee had said. And what about the triangle?

Either way, it looked like something significant. And with a possible connection to Caldo's own cray-cray.

"Get off me, punk!" the man shouted, teeth stained brown, two missing from the top right.

A hand reached past Gina and grabbed Elijah's shoulder, dragging him from the man.

He recoiled from the touch, skittering back and searching for the offender.

It was Dana Diaz, reaching out a hand to help him stand and gesturing with the other toward the exit.

"*Vamos, muchacho!*" she shouted. "Leave the man alone. We've got to get out of here!"

Letter-I T-Shirt Dude was now skittering away himself, scrambling up from the grassy ground.

"Not on your life, pal!" Elijah shouted.

He grabbed the dude's foot and yanked him back down, tugging him back for further interrogation.

Until the dude horse-kicked her partner—landing a solid, 12-size boot squarely in his jaw.

Heard his teeth clatter something fierce, and he fell backward, the perp scrambling with success now as Elijah recovered.

"Let him go!" Gina said, stepping in his line of sight.

Which she sensed ticked him right off.

Narrowing his eyes and clenching his jaw, he sprang to his feet and turned to Dana Diaz. "What'd you do that for? I had a lead."

"I know, and so do I."

"What lead?"

"I'll explain. Let's just go. *Vamos, vamos!*"

Elijah didn't move. Instead, he brushed past Gina, picking up his pace.

She didn't dare grab his shoulder as Dana had. Yeah, because of his aversion to physical touch, but also because it wasn't her place.

Instead, she shouted: "Where are you going?"

He shouted back, "T-Shirt Dude wasn't the man I was after."

"Then who?"

He took off again, bobbing and weaving through a gauntlet of onlookers to the second spectacle of the night on stage. The shaman, or whatever he was, was addressing the room. Recycling many of the same talking points as Billy Baron, actually, and Debby Gallego.

Which didn't make sense. They'd disrupted her event.

Gina raced after her partner, eyes on Eli but ears on the stage. Again, more nonsense about some Great Awakening and a coming storm, about battle lines drawn between good and evil and patriots rising to meet the challenge of the New World Order.

Lost Eli in the crazy, but when she finally glimpsed him, he was reaching the canvas wall.

"Eli!" she shouted, but he didn't pay her any mind. Instead, he raced along it and disappeared through an opening into the night.

"For the love…"

She raced after him down the side aisle toward stage right, catching a better glimpse of the shaman figure jumping up and down with the I on his T-shirt.

And something else.

On his head. That animal skull. Which wasn't just any animal skull.

It was a goat head.

She gasped.

Like the severed one that had landed on Calvin Dobson's front lawn in a ring of fire!

"Egads!" She halted her pursuit at the edge of a set of stairs leading up to the target.

The I-man, wearing a goat head.

Clues from both sides of the *inexplicitus* case had come together in this one figure.

A frigid breeze gusted through a flap in the tent wall, the opening snapping in protest like the riggings of a sailboat drawing her outside.

And glimpsing Eli racing across the grass toward some destiny that worried Gina more than the clue that was prancing around like some pagan shaman.

She let it go, spinning outside and racing after Eli. Dana called after her to hold on, but she didn't pay her any mind. All that mattered was her partner.

Who was drawing near a line of cars idling on a service road behind a massive addition to the rear of the modest building that had been Elijah's childhood church, and his dad's.

Five of them, actually. All black, all Chevrolet Suburbans.

All looking like government-issued vehicles that would transport government personnel. Like presidential candidates and their security detail and staff.

Which meant one thing.

Eli was going after Billy Baron!

"For the love…"

Panic swept through Gina as she glimpsed several people running far down the lawn, the apparent escape route for security breaches like the one that had cut short the Gallego-Baron for President powwow. Could literally feel the frigid fright of adrenaline skating through her veins, blooming from the two glands chilling atop her kidneys and spreading cold throughout her body.

He was liable to get himself arrested for pulling such a stunt.

Or worse…

Forgot her partner had run cross-country during college, Eli and those long, lanky legs of his carrying him far ahead. Was the perfect sort of sport for autistic people who would rather participate in recreational sports without social interactions that might cause stress. Same for skiing, hiking, golf, cycling, and track— her own specialty during high school and college.

So she kicked it into high gear and raced after Eli.

Who was beelining it for the middle SUV, where the middle doors were open and a pair of suits were ushering a large man with a Hawaiian shirt inside.

That frigid fright returned, an anxious dread flooding her veins at what came next—jumpstarting her ticker to an even faster gallop and activating her legs to do the same.

Had to stop Eli before he messed everything up. Before he messed himself up.

Reaching back into all those years on the track team, she hiked up her legs and pumped her arms, tearing after her partner.

"Billy Baron!" Eli shouted up ahead.

There was a moment when the sound waves clearly met the main target, along with his handlers.

Everything stopped. No movement. No shuffling the veep candidate inside, no protecting Gallego from would-be assailants, no shuttling the protectees off to their next gig.

Until it all started back up again, on a dime.

The reverend tried turning back to see who was calling his name, but a large meathead handler shoved Billy Baron in the back with insistence to get him inside the Suburban.

While three massive gorillas in matching black suits and white shirts and black ties—all neck and shoulders, no nonsense and no fun—spun around and positioned themselves like linebackers ready for a fight. Or maybe the offensive line gearing up to make sure the quarterback completed his pass. Either way, Eli was in for a world of hurt.

Gina reached him just before he arrived at the line, his legs and brain not at all interested in rationality as he barreled toward his target.

She saw it before it happened, her already shallow breath from the sprint catching in her chest with horrifying anticipation.

"No, wait—"

The middle of the three, a real big-boned bruiser Secret Service agent, stepped forward and stiff-armed Eli from getting closer as one of his partners followed through on the protective play to get Billy Baron inside the SUV.

Elijah didn't get the message, or maybe he didn't care.

His chest slammed into the massive, meaty palm, all the while screaming after the reverend.

"What the hot Hades have you done to Daddy's church!"

The agent drove him back, Eli's arms grabbing fistfuls of air for any sort of purchase forward to continue his pursuit but getting nowhere.

"Pastor Baron!" Eli shouted. Then again: "William Donald!"

At that, the reverend spun around away from the Secret Service agent handler and craned for a look.

"Elijah Fox?" Billy Baron said with disbelief.

"Let me go, you lily-liver, chicken-hearted lickspittle!"

Elijah backed away in a huff, throwing his hands on his head and spinning in a circle—gulping down heavy, heaving, frustrated breaths. Face was crimson and beads of sweat edged his brow.

Was really rumbling now. Was really afraid he would burst.

The one agent stepped back and stiffened, throwing his massive arms out onto his side. A cross between a gorilla and an NFL linebacker, he was. Which also gave an opportunity for two other Secret Service agents to get into formation.

"Sir, back away!" they shouted in unison, weapons extended.

Billy stepped forward, placing a hand on one of the agent's shoulder. "I know him, it's alright."

"Mr. Baron, we've got to—"

"No, it's alright!"

Elijah spun back to his target and went to lunge forward.

When Gina placed two hands on his shoulders and held him fast.

His whole body tensed at the touch, trying to recoil but making no headway with Gina's firm hold. Didn't do it often, and only a few times before, but the situation called for it.

"Good to see you, Eli!" Pastor Billy said, smiling. "Didn't know you were in town. Glad to have you back at your old stomping—"

"Judas, that's what you are! Betraying my father's legacy like this—with your carnival, the golden calf to Beelzebub, the pride of political power. Or maybe it's Jezebel, the fork-tongued, honey-coated temptress!"

That smile quickly faded, crimson showing in the light of the SUV's headlamps.

Billy Baron said lowly, "I'm sorry you feel that way, son. I knew your father well."

Elijah stiffened. "You did?"

"That's right. You might not recall, but I pastored a small country church down the road from your daddy's."

"Don't call him that!" Eli snapped.

Billy just shrugged. "Wanted to keep the peace and preach the gospel, he did. Never dirtying his hands with politics or social concerns. But look at this place!"

The reverend spread his arms across the grounds, swiveling his hips and heaving his body toward the massive new addition to the old church and back to the tent.

"We've got a chance to make a real difference in this country! To take America back again—for Christ! Your daddy just didn't have the vision. Was never all that bold or courageous."

Elijah's entire body tensed under Gina's grip at that slight. Every muscle hardened into a ready position, and his shoulders heaved up and down as his lungs fueled them with oxygen for what came next.

Which was entirely unexpected.

That same jutting arm Gina had come to know that evening

from their drive over suddenly took a swipe at Billy Baron. A slapping *smack* sliced through the tenuous church grounds, followed by a very disbelieving reverend and an even more distraught Secret Service detail.

It was over, just like that.

Gina was thrown back, caught from stumbling to the ground by Dana Diaz.

Elijah was flat on his back before being rolled to his stomach, two Secret Service agents pinning him down and wrenching his arms behind his back while he screamed and kicked and pitched a foul-mouthed fit.

She knew it was more than just the turn of events, the fear of arrest or freighted neurological weight of being constrained and suffocated by two government-issued goons.

It was the frustration of losing his target, of his confrontation being cut short with the man who had trashed his dad's legacy, who tore it to shreds, and then tapped-danced on its remains—and who was now secure inside the government-issued vehicular vault and readying to speed away.

But not before Gina had caught a glimpse of the oddest sight. Eli's fingernails had dug just right into the man's face. Rather than scraping at his skin, he'd managed to smear a layer of pancake foundation clear off his upper cheek—revealing the traces of a birthmark that smacked of the familiar.

With the sudden revving of engines and the whirling of the reds-and-blues and honking of crabby sirens, Billy Baron and his political mistress sped off.

Leaving Elijah in their dust, and Gina in the dark.

The worm had turned, with Eli riding its back.

"You can't do this!" Elijah pleaded. "We've got diplomatic immunity!"

Didn't matter worth a lick, the agents slipping heavy-duty plastic zip ties around his hands and feet with restraint. He bucked something fierce, but it was no use.

Gina took over pleading his case: "He's right, we've got diplomatic immunity."

Not a card she ever thought she'd have to play, that's for sure.

"And former FBI!" Elijah added.

One of the agents, a real Hulk Hogan—with a mane of golden locks and massive wide shoulders stuffed in that government-issued black suit of his—approached her, breath surprisingly minty for a Fed.

"Who are you?" he growled.

"Gina Anderson." She nodded toward her hog-tied partner. "He's my partner, Elijah Fox. We're investigators with Group X."

"Never heard of it."

"We're an agency with the Order of Thaddeus—"

"Never heard of that, either."

The agent turned and spoke into his wrist, walking away.

Peeved Gina right off, him brushing her off like that. So she channeled her feminist Mama, hiked up her big-girl pants, and plunged back into the deep end going toe-to-toe with the meathead.

Whipping out her Vatican credentials, she stepped in front of the agent. Nearly plowed into her, he did, but he jolted to a halt. She flashed those creds in his face with one hand, along with a satisfied smirk, while the other was firmly planted on her hip.

His face hardened with narrowed eyes, but he took in the credentials. Grunted and muttered, then shook his head and sighed before crossing his arms with stiffened restraint.

"Fine. Talk," he barked.

Taking a breath, she nodded, then dove into an even deeper end to rescue her partner, her friend.

Took some mighty fancy tongue work to get Eli out of his sticky federal wicket. Helped they'd both been former agents with the FBI, and Gina was able to call in a favor from their former special agent in charge, Agent Pendergast, to explain a few things that filled in the blanks, including his autism that fueled his reaction. Hated leaning on his neurological makeup like that, as if it were wicked fairy dust that exempted him from social mores and the rule of law.

But, hey, Eli was in a sticky federal wicket, and she'd use anything to save his backside.

She also explained the situation with his father, which seemed to have a stronger effect. Surprisingly, as Gina told the story, the hardened agent's face softened. As his narrowed eyes darted between her and Elijah, they eased open with compassion. He heaved a heavy breath, as if the weight of the revelation had taken it away. In the end, the agent understood and let him go, but would leave it up to Billy Baron whether or not to prosecute the assault.

Gina thanked the man, but she wasn't worried. Diplomatic immunity granted them a surprisingly wide berth of protection from all sorts of crimes, a principle of international law by which foreign government officials are exempt from the jurisdiction of local courts and other authorities for both their official and personal activities. Including smacking a veep candidate, as was the case.

Released from his restraints, Elijah scrambled to his feet and shuffled away from the agents, shaken and shaking from the encounter. They backed off and sauntered off.

"Now what?" he said, massaging his wrists.

Gina sighed, shaking her head. "Beats the bleep out of me."

"*Como dije,*" Dana Diaz replied, gesturing toward the parking lot, "I have answers, just like I was telling you before. At least, I think I do."

"What answers?" Gina asked, skeptical to trust anyone after what had just gone down.

"About the Eye of God."

"Eye of God?"

"Don't you mean *I*?" Eli said.

"*Sí.* Both." She took a step, then another, motioning them to follow. "*Vamos!* We may not have much time."

Didn't know what that meant, not in the slightest. Just thankful the good Lord above had put this woman in their path—literally, plopping them right next to her in the row of that bleepin' church tent.

Because it was as clear as Mama's crystal Precious Moments figurine collection that they were going to need whatever help she could offer.

CHAPTER 17

Elijah sat quietly in the passenger's seat while Gina drove. Still and silent. Numb, really, from what had gone down at Daddy's old church.

The political rally on church property he never would've let happen as long as the sun burned hot and bright. Probably doing somersaults in his grave at the blasphemous syncretism of the Church and State! But that wasn't all.

What pastor becomes the right-hand human to a presidential candidate? One so drunk on power that he'd rather shill for the Empire than shepherd Christ's sheep, that's who. And everything Elijah had read and heard about Billy Baron—well, that pretty much fit the bill.

Made him dread the season that much more, seeing how it had taken over his childhood church—Daddy's church!

Flat dreaded election season. A season filled with battle lines being drawn and awkward Facebook memes that vilified the Other. With neighbors giving passing glances and muttering to themselves at lawn signs and friendships severing over differences of opinions—and candidates. With the Church of Jesus Christ anointing their Chosen One, and the secular press christening their own, while the Bride of Christ turned tricks at Uncle Sam's beck and call.

Soon it would all be over. For another two years.

That is, if they survived the *inexplicitus* crazy!

All agreed alcohol and a midnight snack was in order after what they'd been through.

Nothing but your run of the mill capitalist conglomerate kitchen joints as far as you could throw a goat in those parts. Logan's Roadhouse, Applebee's, Buffalo Wild Wings. Was never a fan of those sterile staples of suburbia.

Navigating the streets while Elijah sat slumped in the passenger's seat, Gina managed to find something way better: My Old Kentucky BBQ Home. Apparently, it was a regional chain dishing Southern-style barbecue and sides in a cowboy-themed space. BBQ and cowboys seemed just what the doc ordered after a night from the loony bin.

Elijah trudged to the door while Gina met Dana Diaz at her arriving Honda hatchback, and he realized how hungry he was. Didn't expect much from the joint anchored across from the Kentucky Oaks Mall, but the noise and light and smells reaching him a good thirty paces away said it should be an interesting watering hole. It also reminded him how hungry he was, so he quickened his pace.

Opening the door, a horde of sensory forces smacked his face.

First thing he noticed was how packed it was—and loud, a jumble of conversations fighting for a hearing above the din of some country group crooning and twanging from a stage. Every table was filled and then some, with men and women packed in the aisles, milling about and roaming from table to table, conversations fevered and drowning but seemingly respectful—so far. No way was the place minding fire-code regulations!

Second thing was the smell. The air was thick with the staples of American cuisine: fried potatoes and grilled meat; lots of fries and hamburgers, some fish thrown in for good measure; the tang of garlic and onion and cabbage. Riding alongside it all was a hefty dose of barley and hops and wheat. Which meant lots of booze was flowing that night. Figured. People were gearing up to either drown their sorrows or celebrate in the coming weeks.

Third thing was the decor. Definitely cowboy themed, with saddles and stetsons hanging from the walls. Along with red and blue poster boards tacked up, yucky off-white paint showing from behind. Dragged out their July Fourth garland from the back storage, too, clumps of red and white and blue hanging from the ceiling. "Born in the U.S.A." was starting up from the band now, completing the Americana vibe.

A college-age kid with a blond mullet greeted them. Elijah almost asked if he'd brought his pet ferret to work with him, but thought against making a crack at his hairdo that went the way of Atari. Didn't want his mouth to catch a venereal disease from Mullet Man's payback in the rack of ribs he was hankering for.

Their hostess with the mullet-mostest left menus and left to fetch their drink order—a round of H2O for the table, along with a Pepsi for Dana and Dr. Pepper for Gina. Pabst Blue Ribbon was on the docket for Elijah, the only beer worth anything in those parts of Kenturkey, unfortunately.

Before Elijah could steer the convo, Dana leaned in: "*Primeramente*, I do have to ask you—" She turned to Elijah "—what was all that about?"

He raised an eyebrow. "What was all what about?"

"Back at the church rally. The…well, I'm not sure how to say this but—"

He interrupted, "The hand-flapping and walking in circles, the muttering and screaming?"

She laughed nervously, running a hand through her hair. "*Exactamente.*"

Elijah smiled, betraying a rising annoyance at not only having to explain himself—that part of himself. But also at that part of himself *being* part of himself.

He sighed and explained, "I'm autistic."

He could tell the word landed hard. Dana tensed, her back stiffening and eyes flashing wide, her brow furrowing and mouth narrowing into a contemplative, confused thin line.

Hated those looks. The uncertain ones that quickly morphed into pity before painting him as broken, disabled, disordered.

Less than.

"Meltdowns," Gina explained, clearing her throat, "are a way for autistic people—" she turned to him, one end of her mouth edging upward, adding "for people like the two of us to cope with overwhelming conditions that can be difficult to express in other ways."

Dana leaned back, bringing a hand to her chin and nodding, one end of her mouth curling upward. Didn't seem like pity now, which Elijah appreciated. More like curiosity, appreciation even, at meeting a different kind of species from the human spectrum. As if she was saying, Nice to meet you; you're alright.

Gina went on, "It happens when someone becomes completely overwhelmed by some situation and temporarily loses control of their behavior, expressing this overwhelm verbally or physically—"

"Or both, as you heard," Elijah explained.

Gina nodded. "I understand it may look like a temper tantrum, something bad and naughty."

"Nutty, even," he added again, discomfort growing with the silence and being put on display like some frog to dissect. "And, for the record, that wasn't a meltdown. Well, at least a full-on neurological disintegration. More an advanced rumbling than anything, perhaps with an added measure of pissed-offness."

Gina giggled. "Suppose you did have the right to be—*ticked*, as I would frame it, Mr. Potty Mouth."

Mullet Man returned with their drinks. Elijah promptly reached for his PBR bottle, apparently with German roots. Go figure. He took a swig of the wheat beer and grimaced. Tasted like soggy bread. Pissweizen, is what it was. But it would have to do.

"Perdóneme," Dana asked, putting up a hand and taking a sip of Pepsi, brow scrunching in on itself again, "but…rumbling?"

"Part of the meltdown cycle," she explained. "Behavioral changes that indicate discomfort and overwhelm. Tensing muscles, bouncing—"

"Hand-flapping and walking in circles," Elijah added. "Muttering and screaming. Though, again, the latter was that added measure of pissed-offness I referenced."

"So, what," Dana said, "you've got Asperger's or something?"

Elijah shook his head. "Nope. That's not what it's called. Not anymore. At least, not after revelations about a certain German, Herr Asperger, launched a number of experiments on children for the Nazi Great Cause. Society switched things up real quick after that little nugget of revelation, making a switcheroo to the Autism Spectrum Disorder lingo."

"I see…"

He gulped down more PBR, discomfort growing at being probed like a pig.

Earlier in his life, he had simply been called a retard. And a difficult, out-of-control retard at that. The kind who drove his birth parents to the brink, and then made the guardians at the Commonwealth of Virginia's orphanage and his eleven foster parents want to pull their hair out.

And beat him with the backs of their hands, and their belts, even copper pipes and coat hangers when they were within arm's reach.

"So, you're a person with autism—"

"Autistic person," Elijah corrected.

"Isn't that what I said?"

"Nope."

"Umm, alright…"

Rolling his eyes with a sigh (because he was in no mood to explain his diverse neurological condition and developmental disorder that affects how he interacts with others, communicates, learns, and behaves—but knew setting her mind at ease was important to the case at hand), Elijah explained, "If I was carrying a baby in one of those Norwegian papoose thingies—"

"Bjorn," Gina corrected. "Papoose is Native American."

"It's Indian. Indians prefer Indian, or their tribal name. Native American was a linguistic invention of Ivy League educated East Coast white people with a colonialism complex."

"For the love…"

"So, what are you," asked Dana, "some sort of savant or something?"

"Nope. That's a common misconception. Only point five percent of autistic people are savant. I'm not one of them. I suck at math. And solving Rubik's Cubes."

Gina chuckled. "Modest that one is. Eli does have an eidetic memory, so he might as well be a savant. But how about we close up get-to-know-the-autistic-person hour, alright? You good with us?"

Dana took a sip of her Pepsi before nodding. "*Sí. Bien.* Just wanted to understand who my new partners were in this *caso muy loco.*"

"Crazy case is right," Elijah said. "But I think this crazy train is just getting started. And I, for one, am glad to have a journalist on board."

"Cheers to that!" Gina added, raising her glass. The trio clinked their drinks together and Elijah promptly drained his PBR.

Mullet Man returned with their food and another bottle of beer for Elijah. Surprisingly attentive for a regional Southern BBQ joint.

It was burgers for the ladies, piled high with all the fixin's, though Elijah thought it a bit boring given they were patronizing My Old Kentucky BBQ Home. It was a full rack of ribs for him, with thick baked beans and coleslaw dripping with a special mayonnaise dressing. The brick of cornbread was a nice touch, too. He went for that first, smothering it in butter (the real kind, the good kind, the kind only worthy of cornbread; from a cow, not corn) before squeezing a pile of honey on top.

Chewing, his mouth full and thick from bread and honey, he asked Dana, "Tho how did you get into thith gig of yourth?" Swallowing hard, chased by a swig of PBR, he clarified, "Chasing down the crazy at political rallies?"

Gina added, "And a religious-political rally at that?"

Dana swallowed her burger and slurped some Pepsi. Shifting, she explained, "I have *mi papa* to blame."

Elijah nodded. "Ahh, the sins of your father haunted you into journalism. Say no more."

"Word," Gina agreed, swiping another bite of her burger. "Do tell."

"*Mi papa* was a card-carrying member of the Faithful Majority, you see—literally, with a laminated card and all signifying his membership in the group."

"Whoa! Now there's a throwback to an era I didn't think I'd hear again."

Elijah tore into his ribs and snorted a laugh. "Yeah, I think the '90s are calling for their religious right political activism back."

He regarded the bone picked clean, his taste buds dancing with the tart and tangy, yet smoky, BBQ sauce. And then he stiffened, recognizing that name Diaz now.

"Diago Diaz…*He's* your father?"

Now Gina regarded her. "Egads! Paul Maxwell's right-hand man?"

Dana's cheeks flushed pink and she pushed a stray lock of hair behind an ear, clearly embarrassed at the recognition.

"*Sí.* Papa did indeed help Paul Maxwell and others found and build the group."

"Build the group." Elijah snorted a laugh again before shoving a bite of baked beans into his mouth. He hummed with pleasure. Smokey! "You make it sound like they were just a bunch of pals chumming it at some weekend game of poker. This was the premiere organization that gave Christians a seat at the political table!"

"Melding the Republican party," Gina added, "to the interests of the Church. At least the Evangelical, conservative variety."

Dana took a slurping sip of her Pepsi, then explained, "Yes, well, back when papa believed there was an honorable alliance between Republicans and the conservative Christian movement. He believed their values would ultimately prevail, come what may on this Earth, whether we win or lose some election."

She paused, looking outside through a large bay of windows, as if searching for a memory—whether sweet or sour, it wasn't clear. She shook her head and returned to her burger before adding, "But over time, there was a shift. Losing was no longer an option. It became all about winning. Good people were taken in by this stuff. They really believed they were doing the Lord's work, saving the country and ushering in Christ's kingdom."

Elijah said, "I sense a *but* coming…"

Gina nodded. "Like you're not so sure about that legacy."

One end of Dana's mouth curled upward, and she shifted in her seat. "But…well, let's just say I saw a different side of the beast than papa."

Elijah leaned in, eager to hear more. "Do tell…"

She explained, "Not only had I applied myself to government studies at the premier Christian university for such things, Freedom University—"

"Hold the cheese stick," Elijah interrupted. "You're talking about Jimmy Maxwell's college, right?"

"*Sí*. Papa had also been one of the key vice presidents of the university, giving me free college tuition."

"Must be nice."

"After graduating with my nice, shiny undergrad degree in political science—"

Elijah smacked his hand on the table. "Knew we were

kindred spirits! I studied philosophy with an emphasis in political ideology. Sorry, go on."

"Well, after graduating, I moved to Washington on nothing but a buck and a prayer with the aim of making my Jesus-stamped mark on Capitol Hill."

"Jesus-shaped mark on our nation's capital?" Gina said with a raised brow.

Dana laughed. "I know how that sounds."

"Like the Taliban?" Elijah said.

She furrowed her brow. "Now that you mention it, sort of!"

They all laughed.

"But I didn't mean it like that."

"Phew!" Elijah said, adding a dramatic hand against his forehead. "Good to know Dana Diaz wasn't about to inaugurate a theocratic takeover of the American government."

"You'll have to excuse Elijah," Gina said. "He's a bit skittish when it comes to the whole separation of Church and State thingy."

"Me too!" Dana said.

"Like I said. Kindred spirit. Carry on," Elijah said, waving a hand for her to continue.

"Given papa's political connections with the Speaker of the House's office, I was able to get a prominent legislative job."

Gina turned to Elijah. "Don't we know someone who worked there a decade ago or so?"

He nodded. "That guy from Mill Creek Junction. Peter Young."

Dana's face brightened. "You know Peter Daniel Young?"

Gina replied, "You know Peter Daniel Young?"

"Is there an echo in here?" Elijah said, taking a swig of PBR. "So we established our world is small. What happened on Capitol Hill?"

Dana said, "I started getting glimpses of the seedy underbelly of the political beast, that's what."

He shivered. "Two things you never want to see being made.

Sausage and—"

"Legislation," she finished with a chuckle. "Yeah, and my experience pretty well lines up with that maxim. The memories sitting in on meetings and being part of conversations and witnessing backroom deals still makes my stomach turn. By the grace of God, I'd gotten out of that gig, the whole experience leaving a *muy mal* taste in my mouth. Had zero interest in anything political anymore. At least from the inside."

"What changed?" asked Gina.

Dana shifted, explaining, "After the midterm elections one year, this trade magazine for politicos asked Members of Congress, *'If you could ignore one special interest group without having to worry about the political repercussions, whom would you ignore?'* For Democrats, it was the environmentalists, unionists, and abortionists—in that order. For Republicans, it was the National Rifle Association, National Right to Life, and Religious Right—in that order."

"See, that's what's wrong with politics these days!" Elijah complained, easing back on his stool and crossing his arms. "Just a bunch of interest groups clawing for power and a handout."

"Pretty much," Dana said in agreement. "And after I read that poll and experienced too many closed-door, off-the-record meetings, I'd had it. I was through trying to tear down the wall separating Church and State—I was ready to reinforce it at all costs."

Elijah pulled another bone from his mouth, having polished off its pork. Mouth full, he said, "Knew you were a kindred spirit the minute I met you. But you didn't explain how you got into this journalism gig of yours."

"After I left the Hill, I returned home to Columbus and got the job with the *Dispatch*—and was sent packing back to the District."

"To cover politics?" Gina asked.

"*Sí.* It wasn't at all my plan to return to that world. But as they say, man plans but God laughs."

Elijah shook his head. "Nope. That's not Scripture."

"*Yo sé eso.* It's Yiddish."

"It is? I always thought it sounded Scottish."

"Anyhoo…" Gina said. "So, back to Capitol Hill."

Dana nodded. "Back to Capitol Hill. I saw it as a way to keep everyone accountable. Including backroom-dealing Christians. What I've found in my reporting research since—especially this election cycle…well, let's just say it explains a lot."

Elijah wanted to know more about that, but Gina interrupted with a question of her own.

"Whatever happened to your father? I recall something about him having some sort of falling out with the group."

Taking a deep breath, Dana nodded. "*Sí.* Papa began to have misgivings about the manner in which Maxwell and the Faithful Majority were going about their work."

"Such as?"

"By then, he'd begun pastoring a church. It was then he became convinced that it wasn't Christianity's job to make our pet social policy illegal. Rather, seeking first the Kingdom of God and his righteousness, that's where our heart should be."

Elijah snorted a laugh. "A laudable goal, but there ain't much power or prestige in that sort of gig."

"No. His vision was much more about a heart-level change in people than ramming laws through Congress or in getting the right number of justices on the Supreme Court. But even as papa became more vocal, he was being drowned out by other voices."

"Let me guess. The Billy Barons of the world."

"*Exactamente.* It was more than that, though."

"What more?" asked Gina.

She went to answer when a cheering whoop was thrown up from the stage. All three turned toward the sound, an image on the large screen behind the country crooners drawing from them a collective groan.

Billy Baron was back.

And bigly time.

CHAPTER 18

Behold, America, I stand at your door and knock. He (or she, as the case may be) who hears my voice and opens the door—I will be more than thrilled to let you suckle from my teats. After all, you've been suckling since your founding and you didn't even know it!

First, there were those intrepid religious zealots who shoved from shore over four centuries now, fearful their religious right to party would be snatched from their mousy little Christian hands. Have to give it to 'em, though, braving the oceans blue in all its cold fury and battling the natives in all their naked glory.

Then there was that incident in the harbor, the one that sent all that tea overboard. Feared you'd lose your political right to party on your own terms, so you created a party all your own. Which lit the fuse that started the whole American adventure in the first place. Props to you for having balls of steel to go toe-to-toe with King George!

Of course, it didn't end there. No no no! Because my nectar drove you to pit brother against brother in a pitched battle for a way of life you feared losing for good—not to mention the gears to an economic agricultural engine that would cast the South in a sorry state compared to their industrialized Northern brethren.

I could go on—especially with the Devil deals your steeple sheeple have made. Oh, yes. Them deals have been brokered off a 100-proof purity from the milk of my loins, the Church drunk on not only the potential power of having a seat at the table, but also of preserving its way of life.

No no no! Not in the veins of that silly handmaid's tale nonsense spun from that Canadian's feminist fever dream. Although, that may be my next act of generosity should my plans succeed this go around. I'm talking about basic survival. Worrying about losing your job for wrongthink or whether your kiddos will be asked their pronouns. Worrying about steeple sheeple steeples closing down or burning down for running askance the ruling authorities—political, cultural, corporate, you name it.

Suppose you did claw back a minor win from the cold, dead fingers of a dying breed of bra burners thanks to six Black Robes. So, props to the steeple sheeple for going toe-to-toe with the Venus Industrial Complex! Even then, it's no sure thing your hold on culture will last. Especially when I'm through with you, and my sown seeds begin to blossom into a ripened harvest in the hearts of so-called birthing persons (can't take credit for *that* turn of phrase, but boy, oh boy, is it a right hook into the Nameless One's kisser sullying his designs for sheeple!). When Americans fully realize all they've lost—their power, their freedom, their autonomy—who do you think they'll blame?

And who do you think they'll come after?

Oh, yes! Your entire land is ready for the biggest, boldest, ballsiest experience of my kind from the Unseen Realm—all led by *moi*! And a few of my compadres.

Fear, it's what's for dinner in these parts, during these days.

And I'm just getting started.

I'm also here for good, having been commissioned by Semjaza himself, America's cosmic geographical prince. Apparently, his orders to bind these lands to the fruit of my loins comes straight from the tippity top.

Oh, yes. *That* top. From the Shining One himself.

I shiver with a giddy glee just thinking about the privilege!

Speaking of the Shining One, that reminds me of a story. One of those yarns passed around through the millennia around campfires of yore extolling the stupidity of the Nameless One.

You see, once upon a time, us kind were part of Elohim the Most High's ruling counsel. Yessiree, we were. *Bene Elohim*, we were called. Sons of God. Chief amongst that divine council was the Shining One, sitting near the right hand of Yahweh—not at the right hand, mind you, but close enough to catch a whiff of the 100-proof good stuff, the stuff of raw power.

Anyhoo, after a rather comical episode of a breach of heavenly decorum—some of our kind leaving the cozy confines of the Unseen Realm for the earthly one, deciding to take matters into their own hands by raising up a race of supermen upon Earth by copulating with their women; don't ask—combined with an equally amusing one where earthlings sought to rend a tear into the Unseen Realm, building a tower to reach the heavens, our kind were given dominion over the nations, the ones scattered about by Elohim the Most High himself.

So, you see, our kind—the Principals, at least, the Fallen Ones —hold the keys to the kingdoms. Literally, presiding over the nations in glory and dominion, power and authority. We are the principalities and powers of this age. And we've been biding our time, America!

Until now…

The past year has been Year Zero for the Unseen Realm, our kind launching an assault against the steeple sheeple that has gone unmatched from ages past.

With me and a little help from my friends at the center of all the action.

Thankfully, my newest report indicates those retarded Fed rejects are none the wiser to my schemes. A real testament to their pathetic sleuthing skills! For my helpers haven't been as careful as they should have been, leaving too much exposed for those with eyes to see and ears to hear.

Especially one in particular, with that unfortunate connection.

Anyhoo, I won't worry my pretty pair of wings about that now. Because it's go time. The moment has ripened to pull the pin and toss the next salvo into the cesspool that is America. Aimed right, it will stop those Group X agents in their tracks.

I've rustled up a few of my compadres for a demonstration. Chaos and Despair. The Three Amigos, we are, sowing the seeds that will bind America to the collective will of our brethren and sow discord within the Church. Maybe even bring it to its knees. The Shining One knows it's already got one foot in the grave as it is.

Wormwood wasn't too keen on my plan, given their—*ehem*, mistakes from the past year. Semjaza overruled him. After all, it is his territory, and he thought the three of us should be let loose.

And let loose we will be. America won't know what hit her.

From sea to shining sea.

CHAPTER 19

Elijah's belly churned something fierce, and it wasn't because of those Southern ribs and coleslaw and baked beans. Not even because of the PBR, though he was beginning to seriously regret that decision.

Good ol' Benny Franklin might be right that beer is proof that God loves us and wants us to be happy, but Pabst is a reminder that mankind has enough free will to mess up even those generous gifts from above.

Same was true for those who led us—whether in government or in the Church.

There he was. Billy Baron. Still festooned in that ugly Hawaiian shirt of his that made him look like George Costanza at a luau.

Joined by his new running mate, Debby Gallego, still looking her dashing self in that Vegas Strip dress of hers. Now that he thought of it, she reminded him of a case from back in his FBI days. A string of victims who were unlucky enough to meet a demon-possessed drifter targeting ladies of the night.

Hoped she didn't meet the same fate.

Back to the TV, where the pair were waiting for something to begin.

The shot was perfectly framed, wherever they were. Nothing but a phalanx of American flags forming a backdrop to the couple who would be the county's king and queen.

Except...

Now the picture panned out, and Elijah gasped. He shot straight to his feet, kicking his chair back with a scuffing screech before it tipped backward with a falling thud.

"Oh my cheeps!"

Air was sure hard to come by, and his head began spinning with the implications of what his peepers were peeping.

No...It couldn't be!

But he knew it could, because he knew that room like the back of his hand. And there it was, festooned with rows and rows of Old Glory.

"Where's the fire, Jerry Maguire?" Gina asked in her typical rhyming-all-the-timing.

Jutted out a finger without a word, pointing at the screen now zooming out to a wide shot of a room that was all too familiar—a red-brick wall showing from behind the row of American flags, along with the black Steinway Mama had played to accompany Dad's hymn sings and an electric organ, the wood backs of benches coming into focus too as the shot went wide.

"Is that a church auditorium?" Dana asked.

"Nope. Sanctuary," Elijah corrected on a disbelieving breath. "Daddy's sanctuary."

"*Dios mío*...What sacrilege."

He had another word for it. Bulldookie.

Surprised Baron's security detail allowed him to return back to the scene of chaos. But what was he doing there? Elijah didn't know if he wanted to know.

The picture suddenly shrank and pivoted to the right as the cable news network swung in for a hard look-see at its prized news anchor, Kai Renolds. It was a wide shot of a brightly lit news studio studded with America's colors and massive LCD panels. The main camera swooped in for a close-up of a dutiful-looking Kai, the mainstay of The Most Trusted Name in News. Though Elijah thought the motto's claim was as laughable as Fair and Balanced, but whatever.

"If you're just joining us," the well-makuped anchor began, dark brown hair slicked back and glistening under too many klieg lights to count, face stoic with a set jaw and earnest eyes, "this is a CNN breaking news report with Mara Mitchell standing by at a church in western Kentucky."

"Egads!" Gina exclaimed. "Why is CNN showing up at Billy Baron's church?"

Heat raced up the back of Elijah's neck and it took everything not to snap at Gina for the slight. It wasn't Billy Baron's church. It was Daddy's church. Always would be.

Instead, he swallowed, strumming up his stimming tick to quell the rising anxiety at the point of her observation.

What was so newsworthy that the news network had shown up?

Dana answered, "Looks like we're about to find out."

Elijah folded his arms and widened his stance, furrowing his brow with confusion, and concern. That Kai dude looked intense, his eyes narrowed and forehead creased and jaw locked, even with all that pancake plastered to his face and those lights and CGI tech making him a decade younger.

"Isn't that right, Mara?" Kai said, shaking him back to the moment.

An equally well-makuped woman, hair blond and blown, lips glistening cherry, appeared on an 80-inch screen mounted next to the CNN anchor. On the other side of the screen sat an image of Baron and Gallego, the pair waiting for….whatever it was they were waiting for.

Except now it looked like something bigly was going down. In the moment between Kai's question and Mara's response, Elijah glimpsed an array of tripod studio lights flooding the stage with white light where Daddy had preached, and cameras were jutting their noses out toward the pair, along with a very dutiful Mara Mitchell clutching a microphone and nodding somberly.

Elijah understood what was happening now. That stage—the one where Daddy had preached the Word of God for years, where he had baptized and married and buried his parishioners, where he'd even played Joseph to Mama's Mary one Christmas pageant—it was now a soundstage for Billy Baron's introduction to the world as a politician and comeback from the interruption.

"That's right, Kai," Mara said, her hooker-red lips glistening under the klieg lights matching a silk dress in a similar shade of red, brow furrowed and pinched with the seriousness of plastic. "A dramatic scene at the site of a Debby Gallego rally hosted at the church of Billy Baron, one of her staunchest supporters whipping up support from the religious right. In fact, the minister had just been introduced as her running mate when all hell broke loose."

"Not what you'd expect at a church, that's for sure," Kai said with a chuckle and a wink. Elijah rolled his eyes at the pitiful attempt at humor.

"Nor a political rally, which appears to have been overtaken by overzealous fans of the pastor-turned vice presidential candidate."

Kai leaned towards the massive display holding Very Serious Mara with his own very serious stare—as if the fate of the Republic rested on their two shoulders.

"What's the latest, Mara?"

"As you can see—" the woman gestured behind her as Gallego and Baron stepped forward to a wooden pulpit "—the Republican presidential candidate and her new running mate arranged a hastily arranged press conference to…well, I think we're about to find out."

"Arranged a hastily arranged press conference—" Elijah snorted a laugh. "Nice reporting, Mara."

Gina shushed him and pointed at the large screen at the far

end of the festive dining room rapt at attention—where Debby Gallego herself eyed the patrons through the CNN broadcast that had now firmly given her its full attention.

"My fellow citizens of America," the woman began, "we are now joined in a great national effort to rebuild our country and restore its promise for all of our people. Together we will determine the course of America, and the world, for many, many years to come. We will face challenges. We will confront hardships, but we will get the job done."

She turned to her new running mate, Billy Baron nodding and grinning like a moron. He took over, centering his gaze straight ahead at CNN's camera. Almost as if he knew exactly where to look, exactly who his audience was.

"Every four years," he began, "we gather to vote to either maintain a white-knuckle hold on power or to transfer power from one failed administration to another, or from one party to another. Well, we have something else in mind, don't we, Debby?"

"Sure do," she said, nodding and grinning at America with those tech-money teeth. "To transfer power back to you, the people."

"That's right!" Billy added, pounding the podium. "The clouds of wickedness have been gathering over Washington for some time. The storm is upon us!"

There was a rowdy disturbance at the entrance, several people entering into the already packed joint. Loud, ornery, looking for trouble.

Elijah spun toward them, sucking in a disbelieving breath while his ticker sank to the sticky tiles beneath.

"Sweet mother of Melchizedek…"

"What—" Gina herself twirled toward the newcomers, throwing up a gasp of her own. "Goat Man!"

"*Que es?*" Now Dana joined the fun, a round-three gasp adding to the mix of dumbfounded disbelief. "The *idiotas muy locos* who stormed the rally!"

"What the what?"

Elijah whispered, "More like what the hot Hades are they doing here?"

"The battle lines have been drawn!" Baron boomed, yanking all three back to the stage with the broadcast. "If you're not taking a side, you're on the wrong side. Jesus said, '*Everyone who belongs to the truth listens to my voice*'."

"Oh my cheeps," Elijah startled. "He's quoting Scripture!"

"From John's Gospel," Gina clarified, "in an exchange between Jesus and Pontius Pilate before his crucifixion."

Nodding, he threw her a frown. Didn't like that one bit.

The newcomers had barged far into the dining hall now. Goat Man in the lead, his headdress gone but still adorned by those furs and that red-white-and-blue face paint obscuring his skin tone. The others joining the shaman were dressed in the familiar white T-shirts emblazoned with those odd I letters.

Dana leaned in close, pointing with a whisper, "That's what I wanted to share. I've got a lead on something big with the Gallego campaign. And they're part of it!"

"Goat Man?" Elijah asked.

"I?" Gina added.

"*Sí...*" was all Dana said.

Elijah's fingers started back at his release valve. Thumb to index finger, thumb to middle, thumb to ring finger, thumb to pinky—then back to the start again in the face of Billy Baron using Scripture for his own ends.

His political ends.

"Listen to her truth," Baron returned. "Listen to her voice. And join us in this war for the soul of this nation! Because as God's Word reminds us, '*If my people who are called by my name humble themselves, pray, seek my face, and turn from their wicked ways, then I will hear from heaven and will forgive their sin and heal their land*.'"

"For the love..." Gina complained. "Whenever I hear Christians quoting the Book of Zechariah, I want to take an ice pick to my ears!"

Had to agree with her on that one. The most out-of-context Scripture quotation, that was.

Billy Baron went on, "The Lord God Almighty is ready to heal this land, America! He's ready to take America back again, and he's raising up a leader to do it. Like ancient Israel's Deborah before her, who showed all the men up when there were none to be found but a bunch of spineless, godless twerps —Debby Gallego is ready, willing, and able to take America back again! America's moment is now, and she will take us there."

The place erupted in hoots and hollers at that line, the crowd clearly taken by Baron and his sycophancy—those who'd been jawing it up upon arrival along with the newcomers, who looked pretty cozy with the crowd.

"Just like the prophetess of ancient Israel," Baron continued, "who had been raised up as a judge after the Israelites again did what was evil in the sight of the Lord and he sold them into the hand of their enemies—we have our own leader during these dark days, someone to right the ship and set us straight when all others have fled. Someone who will surely reap the same glory the Lord gave to Deborah for her courage, for her steadfastness, for her righteousness in not only taking America back again, but in making America great again!"

"All I have to say is," Dana started, "I want whatever that man is smoking."

"You and me both..." Elijah muttered, eyes fixed on Billy Baron who was handing it back to Debby Gallego.

"You're too kind, Billy! I'm proud to have you as my running mate. Together we pledge to all Americans that you will never be ignored again. Your voice, your hopes, and your dreams will define our American destiny. And your courage and goodness and love, will forever guide us along the way. Thank you. God bless each and every one of you, dear people. Especially all of my beautiful supporters who have been so supportive in supporting me."

Folding his arms, he smirked. "Eloquent."

"Good night, y'all. You will hear from us again soon. God bless America!"

With that, the picture faded to the familiar faces of cable news. Had no interest in their yammering about the implications of the event at Daddy's church and their response.

All Elijah could do was pick up his chair, slump back down, throw back a swig of PBR, and stew. Stew at struggling to make sense of what had happened to the place that had shaped him so. The place his father had poured his life into that had shaped so many. It was shocking to listen to this man—on Dad's turf!

He wanted to throw something. A punch, his empty PBR beer bottle.

Almost did until another raucous was thrown up from the entrance.

Elijah spun toward the disturbance to find another group had entered. Clothes were dark, with torn knees and patches at the elbows and wielding—

His eyes bugged out, and his breath caught in his chest.

This was no small group. A dozen or more men, some women. All wearing black—skinny jeans, face masks, hoodies, military boots. And were they carrying bats, spiked clubs?

"There they are!" one of the newcomers shouted, waving a bat around with accusation and looking for a fight—clearly not on the same political page as the I-Letter crowd.

The voice carried above the din, causing a sort of record-scratch moment with the crowd of oldcomers—the ones in the white T-shirts with the duct tape letter I emblazoned across the front inside a triangle; the shaman figure ensconced in fur, face painted the colors of Old Glory; the ones who'd been taken by Baron's message.

Kai and Mara continued yammering on the screen, none the wiser at the turn of things at the Paducah BBQ joint. Nobody but no one was paying them any mind. All heads had turned to the moment—time spinning down to zero as it dawned on everyone what was what. And who was who.

The mood darkened, the space suddenly cooled and constricted.

Then it turned. On a dime.

Each party surged forward. Was like that '90s *Gettysburg* movie, when good ol' Jed Bartlet was moonlighting as General Robert E. Lee and leading the frontline of his confederate troops to take on the Union troops hunkered down (no, not bunkered down; unless you're a golf ball that had the unfortunate luck of being hit into a sand trap) in that Pennsylvanian town. Except where bayonets had been fixed and readied to skewer some Yanks and Rebels, these local yokels were brandishing fisticuffs and those bats!

"What the what?" Gina said.

"*Dios mío!*" Dana cried.

Had to agree with the ladies. This could get ugly.

A crash from behind, followed by shattering glass, sent Elijah's hands to his ears.

Someone had thrown a chair into one of the windows, the glass splintering and skating across the floor like ice chips. Then food started flying and bottles were launched.

"Eli! Look ou—"

His head exploded with starlight before he saw it coming, one of those glass bottles launched from yonder tumbling to the floor with a clatter the only indication what had struck him.

Then down he went, the world spinning in a maelstrom of starlight before going all topsy-turvy and fading to black.

CHAPTER 20

And then it wasn't, the dining room fading back to high-definition color—except looking far different from when I went down for the count.

And smelling far different from when I went down for the count. Pee-yew!

Sulfur and smoke fill my nostrils even as my peepers still adjust to my surroundings. Joining it is the pungent smell of moss and rot, of wet newspaper and Dexter after coming in from the rain. More like a basement, actually. The basement from my earliest memories back at the orphanage. A hellhole, that place was. Smelling of the depths of Hades itself.

But what am I doing back?

The thought shakes me loose as I take in my surroundings. Which right now amounts to a cold tile floor. My head is lolled sideways, and my right cheek is pressed against its frigid hardness. From that angle, I can see all manner of grit and grime from years of neglect. Almost as if every chink and crack in the tiles and creepy, crawly dust mites and dropped crumbs and spilled sauces are popping out at me. Such clarity, such definition. Yet it looks all wrong.

Just moments ago, the floor was a horrid brown the color of Dexter's dog poo after a bad case of the runs. This floor is more like oatmeal that's been left out for too long, collecting a sheet of grayish green spores. Or maybe more like a block of white cheddar gone bad, square and white and covered with a grayish green patina of mold. Can't make sense of the scene change. Almost like making the reverse jump poor Dorothy and her little doggy Toto made: From high-definition Oz back to black-and-white Kansas.

But that isn't even the most interesting thing about what is going on.

My eyes adjust past the putrid floor and sharpen their focus to the rest of the world spread before my eyes. The black steel legs of tables and chairs. Gina and Dana's pant cuffs and girly shoes, looking more like smushed strawberries than the bright patent red from just before I cashed out.

Now movement. Feet looking like they're doing the Tennessee shuffle. A massive man falling to the floor in slo-mo—the last bit of hair in a wicked comb-over allowing him to cling to some semblance of dignity flapping high like a mohawk; his arms rising above his head, as if he were doing the wave; his belly jiggling something fierce, all the folds rising and falling; his head whacking against the end of a table with a muffled thud until he crumples to join me in my own sorry story.

Breaking bottles join him, as do tumbling chairs and toppling tables, along with soft drinks and burgers. All around me the rager is— well, raging! Again, in more slo-mo. The movements fluid and heavy and clumsy. The bodies and bottles and burgers, the flying fists and flying food.

Without any Dolby surround sound to it. Zip, zero, zilch. Just a straight-up aural void punctuated by a low-grade hum. As if the volume had been turned down to nothing but nothing. Or the sound had been sucked straight out of the atmosphere. Like a black hole, only the BBQ joint dining room letting everything out but sound waves.

But it is more than that. More than the sounds, more than the smells. It isn't even what I'm seeing unfold before my peepers that sends a chill flooding my veins. It's the feeling of it all. A frigidity, a weightiness, a—

Fear...

Suddenly, every hair across my skin stands at attention, a sheet of goose flesh skating in sync. The sensation sends me pushing off the floor in a sudden rush—but my body doesn't follow the urgency. Just sort of floats from the floor until I ease upright, the scene around me continuing in its chaos.

What the hot Hades is going on?

Where the hot Hades am I?

Clearly, I'm still in the Kenturkey BBQ joint. My freakin' unfinished ribs are still chilling on the table, along with my unfinished PBR! Maybe that's what happened. I had too much to drink. Passed out and hit my head, sending me into flights of fantastic supernatural fancy.

And yet...

All of this feels way more real than some drunken stupor. Because there are Gina and Dana, paying not a lick of attention to me but just as horrified at all the crazy swirling around us. Or maybe I slipped into some alternative dimension of the multiverse—somewhere inside the Unseen Realm, even...

Now there's a thought!

Pain suddenly lances through the middle of my head. A searing slice before spreading in a blooming movement that fills my head—now not in pain but in...voices. Like a tuning fork ting clarifying into a singular note. Except this is a cacophony! A stew of voices—shouts and screams, whimpers and cries—ricocheting inside the cauldron that is my head. All coming from around me, the people raging inside the Kenturkey BBQ joint.

'If we lose this election, women's reproductive health care will be set back a generation!'

'We have to hold the Senate, we just have to! Otherwise those woke, comie pinkos will make sure every damn one of us plaster our pronouns to our foreheads!'

'Without the Supreme Court firmly in our grasp, who knows what will happen to our rights!'

'Just like what happened in Canada when the State decided churches weren't essential services—they done shut 'em down! No telling what will happen to our churches if Santos remains in office.'

'Pedos—the whole lot of 'em are Satan-worshiping pedos!'

My body convulses from all the bad juju vibes and desperate voices hitting my consciousness—like poisoned darts, one right after another in a sickening rapid fire.

So much despair, so much chaos—so much fear! All of it coming in rapid bits.

'...globalists took my job and left me...now they're after my kids! Over my dead body...'

'How is it...daughter has less rights than I did back...? What the—'

'Already outlawed child-murder, but if we don't take back Congress for Christ, no telling what they'll allow those pedos to do to 'em!'

'Climate change...extreme weather...overpopulation...EPA!'

I can't take it anymore! I slam my hands against my head, my arms like leaden weights of jello on their way to my ears. Doesn't work worth a lick. The voices keep streaming through my consciousness—the complaints and concerns, the desperation for survival and panic for rights.

I start up my stimming tick to deal with the aural overwhelm, compounded by the emotion of their fearful pleas.

Thumb to index finger, thumb to middle, thumb to ring finger, thumb to pinkie—then back through the wringer. Can barely feel the touch of my tips, and the movement is as slow as the man with the bowl full of belly jelly slumping to the floor. But it's all I got in this world.

Something catches my eye—outside, through the bay of windows overlooking the highway that runs straight through my hometown.

I manage to shove off from the floor and stand, the sensation like walking on the moon—slow, plodding, exaggerated, weightless.

And my breath seizes in my chest. More like escapes my lungs altogether, with no purchase for more.

My brain can't conceive of what I am witnessing, can't process the...Beings that are hovering in wait out in the parking lot, in eager expectation for what is unfolding inside.

I blink. Then again. Now I crane my head forward and peel my eyes open to make sure what I'm glimpsing isn't just a bit of dust floating in *my aqueous humour, some apparition flaring from light hitting the watery fluid in my eye just right and causing the unbelievable sight.*

Nope. No bananas on that front. It's real as rain and wrong as rain.

There they are. The three of them.

Tall—maybe eight or nine feet. Skin leathery—snake-like, reptilian. Heads bulbous—like party balloons chilling on their shoulders.

I know these Beings.

Watcher-spirits…the disembodied souls of dead Nephilim. The bastard-born offspring of the sons of God and female humans.

Except…

What are they doing here? In my world, at this moment in time?

Do they see me? Can they sense my presence?

Doesn't seem like it. Because their attention is focused on everyone else. Their gaze turned, along with their bodies, to the newcomers and oldcomers who are brawling like modern Montagues and Capulets. Faces set with interest, mouths—or rather, the holes at the base of their faces, because it isn't certain they're mouths at all; perhaps breathing holes. Whatever they are, they're turned upward with satisfaction. With glee. With lustful delight at the ravaging fear and the unfolding chaos, at the songs of despair still ringing in my noggin like a dang klaxon alarm!

Except…

Wait a hot New York minute. What's that outside?

More apropos: Who is that outside?

Because there is someone else.

Something else…

I can see—him, it?—through the window at the far end whistling Dixi thanks to that chair that had crashed through earlier. The Being is set starkly against the sky glimmering red, glowing hot, glistening with a fiery, otherworldly undulation.

He is massive, and he is hovering, his face shrouded in the shadows, large appendages waving like sails from behind.

Instructing, commanding, directing what is taking place inside the BBQ joint. I see his—its?—arms raised and waving, as if a conductor setting the course for the events unfolding within.

And I am pretty sure I know who he is.
Then…then…

————

Then all faded to a mawing blankness even darker than the darkness Elijah had just witnessed.

Didn't know how long he was out until he felt his head being jostled. Then his name floating to the surface, faint and far-off, but there.

Eli…

Then again: *"Eli…"*

Now clearer: "Eli! Dear Lord Almighty, please let him be alright…"

It was Gina, and she was cradling his head in her lap, smacking his cheeks while rocking back and forth and muttering the Hail Mary to herself.

Elijah heaved a breath and held it, closing his eyes and throwing up his own prayer.

He was alive. He was safe. He was back home.

But—

What the hot Hades was that?

Didn't have time to noodle on the crazy because of a sharp smack to his face.

"Ouch. That hurt!" he exclaimed, wincing.

Gina gasped, yanking her hand away. "Sorry!"

Elijah groaned, rubbing his temple and heaving a breath. Did that just happen? The–The–Whatever the hot Hades that was?

"Qué paso, muchacho?" Dana said, the shouts and shuffling growing with intensity.

Gina gasped. "Eli, you're back! Are you alright?"

Was he? Didn't have a cotton pickin' clue. Especially after what had just gone down. What he had just experienced—witnessed, this ecstatic vision or revelation of the Unseen Realm.

Was it a hallucination? Did someone slip some shrooms in his coleslaw? Had the bang to his head jostled the synapses of his brain, sending it down into Crazyville?

He moaned, both from the pain blooming at his noggin but also at the confusion surrounding the rapid-fire questions.

Gina helped him sit. "Eli, talk to me, partner. What was that about?"

Swallowing, he heaved a breath, giving his head a shake. What was it about?

"I–I–I'm not sure…"

"That bottle must have hit your head pretty hard, the way you went down like that."

"How long was I out?"

"Just a few seconds."

That was stunning! He glanced at her, eyes wide. "A few seconds?"

"We raced to you as soon as you fell, then brought you back to the land of the living."

Boy, did that not compute. Not in the slightest! With everything he'd seen, everything he'd felt…all of the emotions of the room—the fears and despair—the chaos erupting all around compounded by the sensations. All of it felt far longer than a few seconds!

"*Vamos, amigos,*" Dana said. "This is getting ugly."

Someone was thrown across the room and landed on a table, the thing breaking and crashing to the floor. Screams and shrieks and shouts of injury and anger and menace joined more of the same crashing and clashing—it was absolute bedlam!

Helping Elijah stand, Gina answered, "No disagreement from me."

"No way, Jose," Elijah replied, widening his stance and readying for a fight.

"Now who's rhyming all the timing," she muttered before giving her head a shake. "Dana's right. We need to get out. Now!"

"Don't you see? This is the whole taco, right here!"

"Enchilada, *muchacho*," Dana corrected again.

"Nope. Taco. The veil was pulled back. I saw what this is about."

"But this isn't our fight, Eli!" Gina insisted.

"It's my fight."

"Why?"

"Because it's my town! And that bozo is the reason for what's going down."

The violence was through the roof now—literally, the ceiling at one end having collapsed from someone being thrown against the cheap tiles.

Elijah couldn't get that image out of his mind. Those...*Beings*! Arms high and tentacle-like fingers wiggling around. Then the other larger one standing on the sidelines, arms waving around like a conductor. Looking on with approval, with command.

As much as he wanted to stop the mayhem, Gina colada was right. This wasn't their fight—the flesh-and-blood part of it. The other part...the principalities and cosmic powers of this present supernatural darkness? The Watcher-spirits who were wreaking havoc in his town—now that was a different ball of ugly.

"Fine," he said with resignation. "But I don't have to like it."

The chaos was all around now, and the entrance was taken over by the band of hoodlums who'd come in at the end. Which meant only one recourse.

"Stand back," he said, heaving his heavy metal chair above his head.

"Eli..." Gina said. "What are you—"

He sent the chair sailing into the window behind their table before she could finish her objection.

It punched through with ease, shattering the glass before clattering outside on the cracked blacktop.

Cool air, laced by woodsmoke sparked the memory of his frightful experience. He shook it off and climbed into the void, slipping his hands inside his sleeves and rubbing his jacketed arm across the rim to clear the glass. Satisfied all was safe, he helped Gina and Dana through outside, then pushed through himself.

The trio ran to their cars and watched as the restaurant devoured itself.

Elijah shook his head, emotion edging to the corners of his eyes before spilling down his cheeks, his mind reeling with disbelief.

"What is happening to our country?" Gina said on a breathless whisper.

He glanced her way, the same emotion wetting her own cheeks. He nodded and swallowed, a far more potent, more personal question rising to the surface.

What is happening to my town?

The trio watched from the outside as the inside tore itself apart. The perfect fishbowl showcasing the perfect metaphor for the state of 'Merica.

Chaos, compounded by despair, fueled by fear.

CHAPTER 21

Gina followed Eli back up the front porch to his awaiting mother's home, the trio having returned to regroup after the cray-cray night.

Between Billy Baron's rhetoric joining Christ's Bride to the hip of Lady Liberty and the first rushing mob, compounded by the mayhem unleashed inside the restaurant when those bozos showed up along with the second rushing mob—all she wanted was to crawl under her cozy covers with a package of Toll House cookie dough and a glass of Moscato wine, maybe watch a few episodes of *Bridgerton* or *Dancing with the Stars* and call it a night.

Not gonna happen, not with their Group X case straight from an Aaron Sorkin fever dream. Didn't share Eli's love for his West Wing television flick, but she'd watched enough to know the starry-eyed, Clintonian depiction of optimistic politics was something from an era long dead. So perhaps their Group X case was much less *The West Wing* and way more *House of Cards*.

With Kevin Spacey's Francis Underwood pulling the strings!

Add a dose of Stephen King's *It* and you pretty much had the supernatural political stew that had been barfed up in My Old Kentucky BBQ Home. If King and Sorkin and Spacey had a baby, that's what their case was.

Sounded about right. Because what Gina felt in that dining room…the subzero chill, the vibrations of something unholy, the feeling of a wicked presence—even *presences*. Egads was there something mighty off about it all. What exactly, apart from the Christian-political syncretism rhetoric and the marauding brawlers, she wasn't sure. Especially wasn't sure about the Group X angle. Sensed there was one; knew it in her heart. But with the election fast approaching, time was running out and they had bupkis.

And bupkis could send America to the loony bin.

A cranky creak from the floorboards announced their arrival. A soft orange glow from inside beyond the screen door, along with a whiff of fresh-baked chocolate chip cookies, told Gina that Elijah's mother had waited up for them. Probably worried sick, given the news about Gallego's rally.

Joyce called out Eli's name and emerged from the shadows in a rush to greet them, throwing open the door before throwing her arms around his neck, pulling him close as only a mother could.

"Thank heavens you're alright," she whimpered, Eli stiff and straight under her grip. Knew a tingly anxiety from the touch was mounting but he let his mother have her way. "I was worried sick!"

"I'm fine, Mama," he said. "At least I was until you squeezed the breath from me."

She let go and wiped her eyes, then gestured inside. "In you go. Fresh cookies are waiting."

"And cream soda?" Eli asked with a boyish grin.

"Oh course! Always have your favorite on tap."

"Cream soda?" Dana muttered. "Who eats cookies and cream soda?"

Gina smiled and shook her head. That was Eli for you.

He and Joyce led the way, Dana behind, when her phone buzzed in her pocket. She yanked it out, face falling.

Calvin Dobson.

Hadn't chatted since the other day when he stopped by, and it was dang late to be calling. She wasn't sure she wanted to know why.

On the fourth buzz, she swiped her phone to life.

"A little late, congressman," Gina answered. "Does your wife know—"

"Thank goodness you answered!" he said in a whisper. There was a tremor to his voice, then a catch in this throat before a sigh. Not like Caldo at all.

"What's shakin'—"

"Bacon," he replied with a chuckle.

She smiled. "You remembered."

"How could I not. Always rhyming, you were."

"Still am."

"That's my Gina…"

He trailed off to silence, the void filled with soft classical music in the background that reminded her of this Italian joint they'd frequent in Ann Arbor during college. Cottage Inn Pizza, it was called, serving mostly gourmet pizzas but also calzones and this to-die-for lasagna. Played classical music, too, the violins and oboes and flutes and even opera an odd juxtaposition with the plain college-town decor. Bonded over their love of Roma tomato and artichoke pizza and Pavarotti. Was how Gina got into opera in the first place.

She shook away the memory and got to it.

"Where are you, Cal? What's going on?"

A beat, then a breath, then: "My office on the Hill. There's been another…incident."

The image of that severed goat head impaled on the pole at the center of a fiery triangle flashed through her mind.

She swallowed. "What incident?"

Back to the whisper: "A slaughtered goat lying in the middle of my personal office!"

"For the love…"

"And get this. The dang thing is missing its—" He choked

back a retching reply, heaving a breath. In between the setup and the reveal, Gina pretty much guessed the ellipses to his speech omission.

"Head," she said, finishing what he couldn't voice.

He grunted a "Yeah" and fell silent.

"You think it's the same one, the match to your early morning lawn ornament?"

Calvin said, "I don't know. Don't even want to think about it."

"Given what you've already dealt with," Gina said, "Can't imagine this is some sick joke."

"Can't imagine."

"Who had access to your office?"

"Just my staff. And maintenance, part of the Architect of the Capitol."

"Anyone else?"

"No one. Not even Vivian."

"How many is that, then, your staff?"

"No way it was one of them! They're loyal, to a fault."

"Just how many?"

He huffed a sigh. "Twelve here on the Hill, then another six back home in the district."

"Egads! You've got eighteen people working for you, Caldo? I got into the wrong line of work…"

"The only way I manage things. It's how we all work. Staffers are the lifeblood up here. Something like 28,000 of them running the show. A bunch of post-college kids."

Gina smirked. "Suppose that explains the sorry state of things. But if you're saying only they had access, apart from any housekeeping, you're sure it isn't one of your staff?"

"Nu-uh. No way."

"Some disgruntled assistant or jilted page?"

"Intern. Pages are high school students, which we don't employ."

"Shows how much I know…" Gina muttered. "Well, what

did the police say?"

Another beat, another breath, then back to the whisper: "I haven't brought them into it yet."

"What? Caldo—"

"I know, I know! Lay off, would you."

"Didn't know I was laying on…" Gina muttered.

He sighed again. "Sorry. You didn't need that. I came to you for help, so I should expect whatever word you dish—and be grateful for it."

Was always quick to confess when he was wrong. She'd liked that most about him.

"As you can imagine, this has been incredibly stressful on top of the campaign."

"Suppose not every day a severed goat head shows up impaled on a stake in your front yard—and then its other half in your office."

He laughed. "Suppose not. And I know I should be worried about my safety, but this can't get out."

"You're not the only one who should be worried."

He gasped. "You don't think Vivian and the kids are in danger, do you?"

"Not sure. I was thinking more along the lines of your future boss—or potential future boss, should you pull off the big W."

Caldo groaned and muttered a curse. "I didn't even think about President Santos."

"Gina colada?" Elijah yelled from inside the house.

Gina sighed, covering the phone and yelling back she'd be a minute.

"I've got to go, but if you have anything you could send along—pictures of the crime scene and any names that come to mind—that'd be great."

"I'll do that right now," Cal replied. "Any word from your end yet?"

"In process. I'm worried there may be a connection with the Gallego campaign."

"Debby Gallego?" Calvin exclaimed. A *bring-bring* from her phone interrupted any reply. A set of images he'd messaged her that took the cheesecake, as Eli would say.

There was a goat alright, splayed out on a navy rug, blood soaking and staining the seal of the House of Representatives anchored at the center. And branded on its white hiney was something that sent Gina's pulse soaring and adrenaline pinging her gut with dread.

The 9th letter of the alphabet.

Big and bold, searing and red.

The memory of Goat Man shaman and his merry band of Eyes or Is, or whatever they were, suddenly became super significant. If this didn't scream a direct Gallego connection, she didn't know what did given what had gone down at their rally!

Another insistent and persistent call from Eli sent her back to Calvin.

"Let me look into it. Can I reach you at this number?"

"Yeah. But hurry. I'm afraid we don't got much time left."

She said she would and insisted with Eli's same persistence to take care of himself and let at least the Secret Service in on the development. He said he'd think about it and the two hung up.

The inside was much warmer than the outside frigid fall, and warmer than she remembered from just the previous evening. Which she realized was almost half a day now, the midnight hour zipping into the early morning hours of the next day. She suddenly felt very sleepy, her arms and legs all wobbly and heavy with fatigue.

She was getting too old for this.

Joyce met her in the short, narrow hallway leading past the stairwell and gauntlet of family pictures on the way to the kitchen. She handed her a plate with two large cookies, the chocolate chips still glistening with gooey warmth and smelling of heaven.

She suddenly felt way less sleepy! Cookies were just what the doc ordered. Elijah was a lucky man to have a mama like Joyce.

Not only did she keep chocolate chip cookies in stock, she made them herself.

Her mama had certainly not been the cookie-baking type of mother. Always kept a package of Oreos lying around. Usually well past their use-by date, something she'd gotten from the local Catholic parish food pantry on her weekly trips keeping her and her sister Grace fed after Daddy had left. Always felt bad about it, too, knowing where the rest of their family's money went, supporting her mama's drugging and boozing habits. Why should they get Oreos for free when they could easily have been bought and paid by Jim Beam's and Bob Marley's specials?

"Want milk with those, dear?" Joyce asked.

Gina smiled. "Yes, please." Then followed her into the kitchen and took her place on a stool at the center of the granite island. "And thanks for the snack."

Dana and Elijah were already one cookie down. He asked, "What's shakin'—"

"Bacon," Gina finished with a giggle. Couldn't resist.

He shook his head with a chuckle. Glad he appreciated her quirks.

"Seriously, where were you?"

Before answering, she stuffed half a cookie in her mouth, the dough warm and soft and melting on her tongue, the moist, fudge-like center settling her nerves after the cray-cray phone call. She closed her eyes and allowed herself a moment to breathe, to savor.

"Helloooo," Elijah said. "Earth to Gina…"

Swallowing, she gulped down her creamy milk and wiped her mouth with a paper napkin. Apparently, she didn't have a moment.

"Congressman Dobson," Gina answered. "He rang."

Dana startled. "As in vice presidential candidate Congressman Dobson?"

"That'd be the one."

"What'd he want?" Eli asked.

"There's been a…development." She broke another piece off from the other half of her cookie and popped it into her mouth.

Swallowing her bite, she let the cat out of the bag—or the severed goat carcass—pulling her phone out and passing it around the island.

"*Dios mío…*" Dana said before shaking her head. "It's worse than I thought."

Gina wanted to ask her what she meant by that, but Eli interrupted.

"*Oof,*" Eli said with a grimace. "Takes the cheesecake, that does."

"That's what I thought."

"Welp, nothing we can do about that now. What do you make of what went down tonight?"

Gina put her phone away. "Cray-cray to the cray-cray, is what!"

"I don't know," Dana said with a shrug. "It wasn't so shocking. Having grown up around *mi papa,* I spent my life watching conservative Christianity change. Morph, really, from a theological and spiritual posture into a political identity that trumped both the Bible and the Creeds."

Elijah nodded. "Suppose you're right about that. It had been heartbreaking for Daddy pastoring a church in the South, the years leading up to his death after 9/11, and the radicalism that had overcome his small Kentucky church."

She turned to him. "How so?"

"Well, for one, good and godly people wanted to bomb the snot out of every last one of those overseas Islamic cities back to the Stone Age. Knew some elders who even gave full-throated endorsement to Dubya's use of waterboarding and other torturous nonsense—Eddy Lee, in fact."

"The *hombre loco* who almost shot up the diner in Virginia?"

"Yuppers. Never mind the fact those men in Guantanamo— whether they were actual terrorists or not, or merely fingered as potential ones from faulty intelligence—were made in the image of God, bore his likeness and were loved by a Savior who died for them. Nope. Didn't matter. All that did was defending 'Merica, exacting a pound of flesh with a two-ton bunker buster, and making dang sure nothing ever threatened their way of life again."

"Funny how that works," Gina said. "The teachings of Jesus and the principles of Christianity are tossed when it's inconvenient to the national narrative."

"God bless the U.S.A."

"It's what I was getting at," Dana said, "before we were interrupted by the *hombre loco* and his sidekick."

He turned to her. "Getting at what?"

"About fear taking root inside the church. What I saw around my own papa. Some of it made sense. Culture has turned on conservative Christians. The Great Recession was making it mighty hard for papa's blue-collar congregation, who were mostly migrant workers. But a lot of the anxiety felt far more manufactured. Papa kept reminding his congregation that the Bible's most cited command is 'Fear not.' It didn't matter. He could never break through the competing voices."

"Sort of makes sense, doesn't it?" Elijah answered. "Biblically, fear is primarily reverence and awe. We revere God, we stand in awe of him and his works. Or we're supposed to, rather, offering that reverence and awe to nothing and no one else."

Gina offered, "Got Israel into plenty of hot messes for messing that one up."

"Not only Israel, the Church as well. Just look at what went on inside that tent."

She considered this, thinking back to the evening's festivities. Then she had it.

"Reverence and awe."

He nodded. "And fear."

"That was *mi papa's* point," Dana added. "You can give your reverence and awe over to other things—anything you value, esteem. Among conservative Christians, there's a whole lot of value and awe being placed on the earthly life we've known."

"The *American* life, you mean," Elijah corrected.

"*Exactamente*. And anything that threatens what we value, what we give our awe and reverence—"

"What we fear," he said, finishing her thought, "then that's the whole soccer match."

"I think you mean ball game."

"Nope. Soccer match. Much less American."

"Point is, when something we hold in inappropriate awe is threatened, then we go *muy loco*. And there's lots being taken away, that's for sure. So what you see is panic inside the Church, inside churches, not to mention across the rest of the country."

"I like the way King Jimmy put it," Gina said.

Elijah replied, "You mean his Bible? Which wasn't translated by King James but—"

"I know, I know," she said, waving her hands. "But, yeah. Bingo. Paul's second letter to Timothy, chapter 2: *'For God hath not given us the spirit of fear; but of power, and of love, and of a sound mind.'*"

"Nope. Original isn't *phobos* but *deilia*. *Cowardice* or *timidity* is what the original Greek had in mind for *fear*, but I'm with you."

"Whatev. Whether fear or cowardice, the principle is the same. People who are filled with the very Spirit of Christ should not live life gripped by fear, or cowardice or timidity. Especially every two years, as if some election by some candidate in tube socks or pantyhose matters to God's providential plan."

"Word."

"Perhaps this is America's moment," Dana said, polishing off her final cookie. "Perhaps a twice-divorced billionaire tech magnet really will take the country back again. Will reclaim America *para Jesucristo*, just like Billy Baron promises."

Elijah snorted a laugh. "When hell freezes over. Besides, where she'll take it is still an open question."

"I'm not so sure about that, *muchacho*."

"What do you mean by that?" Gina asked.

Dana took in a contemplative breath, regarding her, then Elijah. Then she stood and started pacing.

"Let me explain what I've been finding out about Gallego's supporters." She stopped, looking dead at Elijah. "As well as where Billy Baron has been taking your church."

Then she snapped her head to Gina. "And what it all means for Congressman Calvin Dobson."

She didn't like the sound of that.

CHAPTER 22

Elijah definitely liked the sound of that!

Finally, answers.

He leaned against the granite island and popped the last bite of cookie into his mouth. "Hit me with it."

Dana nodded then did, getting down to brass tacks.

"I've been working on a story for this election season." She chuckled, tossing her hair back and gazing into the ceiling with a knowing grin. "Pretty certain it was more therapy than anything. An attempt to exorcize my demons from—"

"Dear ol' dad?" Gina said.

"*Tu viejo?*" Elijah added.

Dana blushed, pushing a stray lock of hair behind her ear. "Suppose they are my old man's, as you said. That obvious, huh?"

"I think we've all been there. Not because of Alan or Joyce," he quickly added, eyes going wide and glancing for his mother, who had left the trio to themselves. He explained, "I'm adopted. And have a string of foster family demons I'm still exorcizing. All thanks to two bio-parents who couldn't handle their neurodiverse child. So, yeah. Still exorcizing."

"Hear, hear," Gina added in solidarity, raising her glass of milk with a wink.

"*Entiendo*," Dana said with a nod before shaking her head. "Anyway, I've been documenting a new kind of conservatism."

Interesting. Elijah asked, "What kind of conservatism?"

"Represented by the elites that populate cable TV and Spotify and raising up an entirely different demographic than you may think. It is making itself known in ways we're just beginning to see. It is also distinctly different from the culture wars of the late 20th century. The ones *mi papa* waged from his place in the Faithful Majority. It reflects a broad shift in conservatism's priorities and worldview."

Elijah stood and went for the plate of still-warm cookies his mother had baked. Loved that about her. Pretty much every day coming home from school, the first thing he'd do when he opened the front door would take in a big lungful of air through his nostrils, sucking in a whiff of some treat she had baked. Usually she'd had a plate of her famous chocolate chip cookie recipe waiting for him (the secret was in the ginger and tablespoon of vanilla). His favorite, though, were the no-bake cookies she made. Honkin' mounds of pure cocoa powder and marshmallow and oatmeal and butter (cow, not corn).

He swiped one and took a bite, carrying the plate with him. Dana and Gina dove in for their own third helping.

Swallowing, he took another bite. "You were saying something about a shift in the new conservative movement?"

Dana swallowed her own bite, then downed a slurp of milk. "*Sí.* The conservative political project as we know it is no longer specifically Christian. The political issues are far different than the ones the Faithful Majority fought for." She smiled, taking another bite, then another swig of milk before adding softly, "*Por lo que luchó mi papá.*"

"And what did your dad fight for?"

"Oh, your run-of-the-mill conservative Christian issues.

School Bible reading and prayer, then against no-fault divorce and porn industry."

"All worthy battles," Gina said. "Christians have just as much right to a voice in the public square as anybody else. And if we don't stand up for justice, for righteousness, for the way God meant for things to be—well, then who will?"

"*Así es*," Dana acknowledged. "That is quite true. However, that's not the case for the new coalition. Their focus is on questions of national identity, social integrity, and political alienation. *Sí*, most conservative Republican Christians who have traditionally formed the electoral backbone of the Faithful Majority from the '90s support the cause. However, this new conservative movement is *social* conservatism rather than a religious one. Race relations, identity politics, immigration, and the teaching of American history are what's important."

Now that was an interesting insight. Elijah wanted to hear more about that.

He said, "You said before, back at the political rally, that the issues in that cray-cray song were speaking to conservative Christians but not necessarily to the conservative crowd."

"*Sí*, that's right."

"Care to explain?"

"What I have found, as I've studied the electorate this season, is that the culture wars of this era isn't between the religious and secular. Instead, it's an unlikely alliance between diverse religious folks, Middle American small-business owners, and skeptical liberal atheists who are all pushing back against the social agenda offered by progressives from the past few years. Instead of appealing to Scripture, now the appeal is to defending the American way of life that's threatened by all these outside forces."

Elijah nodded. "I've noticed that in the language used about education. Which isn't religious in the slightest but about American families wanting a voice into what goes on in the classroom."

"Exatamente," Dana agreed.

"But isn't all this good for American conservatism?" Gina asked. "For American Christians, even, to have this broad-tent alliance?"

"Doesn't matter. It's convenient. After Boomers have spent the past few decades suffering a long string of losses in the culture war, the potential for a new majority is nothing to sniff at. Some have misgivings. Evangelicals especially don't want their political priorities to be co-opted by functional pagans simply because they share a limited set of political objectives."

"So they're bound together in an uneasy partnership to fight the cultural left."

"Sí. However, they're going to butt heads at some point about the country's future. Mostly because of one glaring problem."

"What's that?" Gina asked.

"American church attendance has been declining, plummeting twelve points in a decade to 63 percent while the share of people who have no religious affiliation jumped ten points to 29 percent. Same has held true of the Republican Party, where those belonging to a church dropped ten points to 65 percent in 2020."

"Which means," Elijah said, "the influence of religiously minded folks in the conservative movement, the Faithful Majority kind, has shrunk."

"Sí. Recent nominees have ranged from flip-flopping on women's issues to not even being Christian to being a sexual libertine. Hardly surprising, then, that the Faithful Majority is no longer a relevant force in U.S. politics. Christians are mostly ignored."

"What's that done to the conservative cause?"

"It's changing their worldview," Dana explained, "where most culture warriors are now what one sociologist calls 'Middle American radicals.' Men and women who do not share the same religious moral commitments as their devoutly Christian counterparts—both politically and morally."

She polished off her cookie and gulped down her milk. Then got back to it.

"These voters are less likely to be married and more likely to be divorced. They're also more nation-focused and less interested in multiculturalism than their religious peers, not at all on board with free trade and open immigration."

"And you're saying," Gina said, "this fierceness of today's culture wars is actually tied to the decline in organized religion?"

Dana nodded. "Rightly or wrongly, political Christianity at least kept that war in check, moderating it with Christian virtues like humility and honesty and compassion. There was a humanizing Christian ethic that has been replaced by brute power protecting the middle and working class."

It was starting to make sense now. Elijah added, "In other words, to take America back again."

"*Exactamente.* These new conservative culture warriors rarely discuss matters of faith. Because this struggle isn't about faith. Yes, it's cloaked in good-versus-evil language, but the struggle is really about the powerful elites treading on the little man."

"A class struggle."

"And no clearer do we see this than in the Debby Gallego campaign. Which I started following even before she signed Billy Baron up at the last minute to be her running mate. And I have a suspicion why."

Elijah threw Gina a grin. Here came the goods.

He leaned toward Dana. "Do tell."

She leaned back, sucking in a contemplative breath. "How familiar are you with Gallego?"

He shrugged. "Just what the media has said."

"Did you know she was a major VC funder for WeNet platforms?"

"What the what?" Gina said.

"She means venture capital funding," he explained.

She frowned. "Duh! I knew she was a tech titan, but I had no idea her money was wrapped up in that social media nonsense."

"*Así es,*" Dana continued, "She is. Both. Not only did she pony up the pesos, but one of the underlying technologies to a sector of WeShare was developed by her technology firm, Etherium."

"Which sector?"

"WeChan."

Elijah squinted, not recognizing that part of WeNet.

"Never heard of it," he said, giving his head a shake.

"Not many have. It's part of the Dark Web, hosting anonymous communication channels, chatrooms and message boards, and even darker *disparates.*"

"What kind of darker nonsense?"

She visibly shivered. "You don't want to know. What you do is what I found lurking on WeChan following a lead for a different angle of the story. A cultish conspiracy movement called I-Og."

Now Elijah visibly startled. He threw Gina knowing eyes; she nodded.

Together they voiced the goat in the room: *"The 9th letter."*

"*Exactamente.*"

"What does it mean?" Gina asked.

"It's an anonymous handle derived from a mysterious figure who calls himself Eye of God posting on WeChan."

"The anonymous communication channel on the WeNet platform."

"*Sí.*"

"I think the '90s are calling for their internet tech back." Elijah snorted a laugh. "Back in my day, we just called those forums."

Gina added, "And had to dial into them with our landline modem."

"Oh, yeah! Did you have an AOL account?"

"*Psht.* CompuServe. We were too poor for that suburban nonsense."

Dana cleared her throat. Elijah and Gina turned their heads.

"Can we keep at it?"

Elijah bowed his head. "Go forth and elucidate."

"As I was saying, I've also seen it simply referred to as I."

"The letter."

"*Sí.*"

Gina asked, "And what is *it*, exactly? Where is it?"

"Near as I can tell, I-Og is a loose association of like-minded people. It has no physical location, but it does have infrastructure, literature, a growing body of followers, even merchandising."

Elijah said, "So I can drink from my I-Og coffee mug, wearing my I-Og knitted wool cap, while surfing WeChan on my I-Og mousepad?"

"Something like that."

"What is it they're pushing? What's the ideological glue."

"Simple," she said with a shrug. "They are convinced the last election was rigged, that the voting booths had been hacked. That Amos Young really had won the election against Santos, but a mix of China and the Deep State stopped it from happening. Claimed their person would be installed for life now, that liberals and traitors would be hanged and freedom will reign. Followers of I-Og believe they've been given the secret that will make America great again."

Gina said, "All of this is part of the—what, cult, populist movement?"

"Puzzle or community, a way to fight back against evil—whatever you want to call it. A wedge slicing countless relationships in half, domestic terrorist group, an everything conspiracy theory. But, *sí*, that's right."

"How many people are involved in this crazy?"

"Hard to say, but likely hundreds of thousands are buying into some parts, if not most of the complex I-Og mythology."

Odd word choice. Elijah asked, "Mythology?"

"The conspiracy movement revolves around an anonymous group of military intelligence insiders who refer to themselves as

I-Og. Patriots who are supposedly under orders from some Deep State counterintelligence agent to leak clues and breadcrumbs, as they're called, to reveal secret knowledge of a world-changing event called the Great Awakening. Anyone can read the breadcrumbs, but it's only the special and most fervent believers in I-Og that can discern their meaning."

He smirked, shaking his head. "Gnostic nonsense. This business of secret knowledge and cabals of power and a black-and-white war between good and evil. Head-shakingly bozo."

"That may be, but these hardcore believers insist they're at the center of a secret war between good and evil—where in the end freedom will prevail, America will be taken back from internal enemies, and those enemies will be slaughtered for their high crimes and misdemeanors. And it's growing in popularity every day, from every corner of the internet, mostly in secret back alleyways on WeNet."

Elijah scoffed. "Who takes this stuff seriously?"

Gina said, "Clearly, people in your childhood church…"

He frowned, shaking his head. Had him there.

"Ironically, it's baby boomers," Dana explained. "The over-50 crowd are most likely to share I-Og posts and stories. They're also the same cohort who are being milked for all they're worth by I-Og celebrities—including Billy Baron."

Gina laughed. "Sounds like my mother's perfect demographic. You know, I saw her plastered on the front of the *New York Times* the other morning?"

"Really?" Elijah said.

"Oh, yeah. At a Gallego rally. Even thought I caught her at Billy's—erm, your daddy's church."

Elijah smiled, appreciating her correction. But then something hit him, something confusing.

"If you're right, about a connection between this I-Og outfit and the now Gallego-Baron campaign—well, why did they storm the stage, disrupt the event?"

Gina shrugged. "Maybe overzealous fans?"

Dana added, "That, and maybe those fans were looking to leverage the new-found platform to broadcast their message."

"Or deny it," Elijah said. "Now that Baron has hit it big, Debby Gallego might want him to tone down the crazy. Or at least appear like he's distanced himself."

"Plausible deniability, that's what you're saying," Gina said.

"Yuppers."

Dana said, "Suppose that could be part of it."

"Or all of the above," Elijah said.

The women nodded, going quiet but for their munching.

"Troubling thing is," Dana went on, "most adherents look like any other American. They're mothers and college frat boys. Accountants, ophthalmologists, grandmothers. Evangelicals and Catholics."

"Christians?" Elijah was dumbfounded. "Why do people believe this nonsense?"

"This is the tricky part of my reporting." She took in another long, contemplative breath. "Are Eye of God followers true believers who really think they have been given secrets to the inner workings of the U.S. government by military intelligence figures about a secret war between good and evil? Have they been duped by Russian or Chinese intelligence operatives?"

"Perhaps trolls getting their jollies on riling people and stringing them along in some sick game? Or grifters milking people's fears and draining them of their savings to make a buck?"

"*Quizás*. Perhaps a mixture of everything."

"What about the deeper questions?" Gina asked. "What is it about I-Og that attracts such people? What's the void that it's filling, you know? No way it isn't filling a void that something else isn't filling—whether family, work, or friends."

"Or church," Elijah added. He appreciated her angle, which he would've expected from Gina, given her psychology background.

"*Exactamente!*" Dana answered. "Because nearly three in ten conservative Christians have bought into the *muy loco* movement."

"Oh my cheeps!"

"Think about why, though. I-Og leverages the concepts of spiritual warfare. Donning the armor of God is a standard line."

"Which has nothing to do with battling flesh-and-blood actors." He quoted:

> *Finally, be strong in the Lord and in the strength of his power; put on the whole armor of God, so that you may be able to stand against the wiles of the devil, for our struggle is not against blood and flesh but against the rulers, against the authorities, against the cosmic powers of this present darkness, against the spiritual forces of evil in the heavenly places. Therefore—*

"'*—take up the whole armor of God,*'" Dana continued, picking up the quotation from the Book of Ephesians, "'*so that you may be able to withstand on the evil day and, having prevailed against everything, to stand firm.' Sí,* I know. I memorized that passage from Saint Paul as a little girl. But it's been leveraged to activate I-Og followers."

"Twisted, more like it."

"Sounds like now," Gina added, "WeShare or WeChan or whatever is being used to shatter shared reality. To undermine civil society—to the point of whipping someone into storming a diner in search of children being held as slaves."

"Not at all surprising," Dana said dismissively.

"Why not?" Elijah asked.

"Because I-Og reflects modern America's susceptibility to conspiracy theories. Even its enthusiasm for them. From the Kennedy assassination to Elvis's death to Roswell—"

"Nope," Elijah interrupted. "Not a conspiracy."

She squinted at him as if he were mad. Gina knew better, but didn't correct her.

Shaking her head, Dana went on, "Anyway, I-Og has already morphed into something well beyond a loose collection of conspiracy-minded chat rooms on WeNet. It's a movement now on a mass scale. They harnessed the paranoia and fears of the American public and stoked them into embracing hope for salvation and warring against a common enemy. It's also apocalyptic, breathing life into preoccupation with the end of the world as we know it."

"But hey, at least they feel fine about it."

"This isn't a laughing matter! When you look into what is happening with I-Og, this isn't just a conspiracy theory about the Deep State and a cabal of puppet masters. This is the birth of a new religion."

That took Elijah back. Interesting way to frame it, as a new religion.

Dana sighed, crossing her arms. Looked like she'd been carrying the crazy for a while. And had not a lick of a clue what to do with it. Understood the feeling.

She said, almost in a whisper, "Ultimately, I-Og and the entire movement tells a story—one its followers want to believe, one they want to hear. It's a story that gives them hope, yes, but it's more than that."

"What's that?" Gina asked.

"What do all conspiracy theories offer?"

"Aside from hope?"

"*Sí.*"

Took Elijah a beat, but then he had it. "Control."

"*Exactamente.* A way to explain events that are out of our control. Which then, in turn, brings such things within our grasp, within our control."

"It puts order to chaos."

"A good way of framing it. Of course, none of this is original. It's no different than the New World Order fears of the 1990s, which was a new-fangled way of channeling fears about the

Catholic Church and Freemasons from the 18th and 19th centuries."

Gina added, "And now rejigged for the 21st century."

"Only thing is," Elijah said, "what do we do about it? Because clearly the crazy has come home to roost."

"Literally. In your hometown."

He didn't respond to that. Didn't want to. The truth of it stung too bad, too deep.

Gina said, "We've got to keep following the trail."

Dana nodded. "Which means following the Gallego-Baron campaign."

"You think?"

"*Oh, sí.* I am convinced they're at the heart of it. Though I'm not sure who is really fueling it, what it is exactly, other than winning the presidential election."

Elijah asked Gina, "Let me see your phone a sec."

She took it out of her pocket and handed it off. He jumped on their campaign website, searching for the next stop.

"Says here they've got another big throwdown at—" He gasped, shooting Dana disbelieving eyes.

She furrowed her brow. "*Qué es?*"

"It's..." He swallowed and whetted his lips, returning to his phone.

"For the love, Eli..." Gina complained. "What's the dealio?"

"It's at Freedom University."

"*Por supuesto!*" Now Dana laughed. "Of course it is! It all comes full circle. The Faithful Majority in bed with the Devil."

"The Devil who wears Prada..."

Gina said, "You know what this means, don't you?"

He glanced up from the phone, nodding but also smiling. Because he knew exactly what it meant.

"Road trip."

She stood, carrying her plate to the sink.

"Pennsylvania or bust, baby!"

"As long as you're driving."

CHAPTER 23
YORK, PENNSYLVANIA.

Elijah wanted to puke.

Saint Augustine had famously contrasted the earthly City of Man with the eternal City of God in his similarly titled book. The second-century early church thinker Tertullian had asked, "What has Athens to do with Jerusalem?"

According to James Maxwell, president of Freedom University, everything! At the premiere Christian institution of higher learning, the cities of Man and God were united in a sickening arranged marriage. And, by the looks of it, Maxwell was throwing the bachelor party.

After a few hours of fitful sleep, he and Gina and their new journalist pal were up early for another trip back to the East Coast—this time flying the friendly skies in a Gulfstream jet courtesy of the mother ship, the Order of Thaddeus. Picked them up just after sunrise from the small regional airport just west of town, the sky inflamed by the rising sun. Just hoped the old sailor maxim wasn't true: red sky in the morning, sailor's warning.

Didn't like it one bit. Not only the portent of bigly crazy to come—which was sort of a given, given where they were heading. But also because Elijah didn't like flying one bit. Neither did

Gina, the pair of them having issues with being catapulted through the stratosphere at ungodly speeds. The only saving grace was the luxe accommodations without any grimy passengers and wailing babies.

But they'd managed. Didn't really have a choice. The Gallego-Baron rally was mid-morning, so they had to hike it to make sure they got inside.

York, Pennsylvania, home to Freedom University, was similar to Washington during the fall. The temperatures dropped into the mid-50s. The leaves turned a palette of muddy browns and sunburst reds and burnt oranges and brilliant yellows, dappled by the autumn sun or drenched by autumn rains. Chimneys sprang to life with crackling fires beneath their hearths. Cable knit sweaters were brought out, as well as the mulling spices and sacks along with cheap bottles of red wine for his favorite fall evening treat.

So Elijah felt right at home as they drove through the historic town of 59,000 people.

Founded in 1741, Yorktown served as the temporary capital of the Continental Congress during the Revolutionary War and crafting site for the Articles of Confederation—making it the perfect spot for Freedom University to take root. From the arts to business to government, graduates were commissioned to "impact this world for God, bearing the torch of Christ's freedom in the legacy of our Founding Fathers." Taking over the family business, James Maxwell had grown it to be the largest private university in the nation—and boy, did it show!

Large poplars and maples blazing the colors of fall lined the road leading into the heart of campus. A large white dome peaked above the buildings that dominated the campus, forged in a Colonial Revival architecture that bespoke the founder's intent to serve as a beacon of hope for the country's Christian Golden Era.

Gina parked their car in a visitor's parking spot on the other side of campus. A group of students walked past laughing, and

Elijah almost missed his old life at Grand River Theological Seminary. But no time for reminiscing. They had to get to it.

By the time they arrived at the open-air Freedom Stadium, the sleepy college campus had been transformed into a carnival of political chaos.

Campaign volunteers were passing out "Gallego for President" and "Vote to Take America Back Again" posters. Women in colonial-era costumes were waving American flags. There were even men on stilts dressed as Uncle Sam passing out campaign buttons with Debby Gallego's face joined by Billy Baron's smiling mug.

Then there were the obligatory "God Bless America" bumper stickers, as if God had forgotten about 99% of the world. There were crosses draped with American flags where Jesus bled out, as if his blood ran red, white, and blue. Someone walked past in a green camo T-shirt with the words "God, Guns, and Guts. Made in America."

Elijah wanted to puke.

He hustled through a metal detector while Dana and Gina got frisked by a couple of female Secret Service agents.

While waiting, an ache grew in the pit of his stomach standing in the brothel of Christian-political syncretism, the "Battle Hymn of the Republic" now providing the soundtrack to the frenzy.

Had no qualms with the Church being actively involved in the public square. Christians should vote and make the best arguments for what was best for the nation, even lobby for policies that align with God's intent for human flourishing. Had no problem with believers working in government for the sake of the common good either.

But this political spectacle conjoined to obvious Christianity?

Elijah wanted to puke.

His phone intercepted any actual puking—but it also sent his stomach doing the Tennessee shuffle.

It was Celeste Bourne-Grey, their boss—well, *provisionally*. At least until Silas Grey got back from his walkabout. Probably wanted a status update. Which would have to wait.

"Who's that?" Gina asked.

He smirked, shoving his phone into his pocket. "Who do you think?"

"The boss?"

"*Provisional* boss."

"Eli, drop the tude about her checking in. She's just doing her job."

He looked away, noticing a squirrel-looking cloud floating overhead. Or was it a cat?

"Was she OK with our side trip to York?"

He shrugged. "Don't know. Didn't answer."

"For the love…If we get sacked, I'm blaming you."

"Agreed. Now, let's get the show on the rollercoaster going."

The trio pushed their way through the crowd making for the 50-yard line. At one end stretched a massive stage festooned with American flags. Below was a twenty-foot security buffer guarded by Secret Service agents. The field itself was packed with a standing-room-only crowd. On either side, the bleachers were similarly filled with committed Christians eager to hear their candidate—the twice-divorced tech magnate and her pastor veep partner. Had a lot of convincing to do, given the election was right around the corner.

The mood suddenly shifted when a new song started up from the stage. Not the piped Muzak from some soundboard off-stage. No, this was a full-on rock band—

And they were gearing up to serve up that dreadful song that had set Elijah's teeth on edge, starting with the chorus:

> *Let's take America back again*
> *By making abortion illegal again*
> *Let's make the family in fashion again*
> *Let's take America back again*

Someone who sounded like Charlie Daniels was the crooner this go around. Much more preferred "The Devil Went Down to Georgia" than this abomination.

> *I've been blessed fly the continent*
> *From the Left Coasts through the Midwest*
> *We need a good dose of Providence*
> *To right what's wrong with America again*

Then the chorus before transitioning to the blasphemous appropriation of the Book of Zechariah:

> *Not by might, nor by power*
> *But by my spirit, says the Lord*
> *Not by might, nor by power*
> *But by my spirit, says the Lord*

Like Billy Baron, the Charlie Daniels Wannabe shouted, "And Debby Gallego is the one who'll—"

> *Take America back again*
> *By bringing prayer back in schools again*
> *Let's reclaim America for Christ again*
> *By taking America back again*

"I think I'm going to be sick…" Gina moaned, drowned out by the cheers and hoots and hollers of the singing crowd.

"Word," was all Elijah could manage, someone catching his eye walking toward center stage.

"And all God's people said…" offered the arriving man.

The audience dutifully replied in unison: *"Amen!"*

"Amen, amen, amen!"

"That's James Maxwell," Dana pointed out.

Couldn't get a good look at the guy, which Elijah didn't like.

Because that meant they couldn't get a good look at the other guy, the one they'd come to see and hear firsthand.

So he pushed through a pair of co-eds toward the end zone.

Gina protested, "Eli, where are you—"

"Closer!" he shouted back.

"For the love…" she complained, but they followed.

"University family," Maxwell continued as they pushed farther down the field, "this morning I have for you a real treat. As has been the tradition of this school since my daddy founded it, we wanted to showcase the only candidate who can reclaim America for Christ again—along with your very own graduate!"

"I didn't know Baron was an alumnus of Freedom." Elijah stopped and turned to Dana. "Did you?"

She shook her head. *"No lo sabía…"*

Interesting…

He took off again as murmurs of anticipation rumbled through the audience.

Maxwell boomed, "Decades ago, when my father established this university in his church's basement in one of America's most important historic cities, he was guided by one verse from God's Holy Word. Galatians 5:1, which you all should know by heart since it's plastered all over campus, so let's say it together."

"It is for freedom that Christ has set us free!" the crowd roared in unison.

"Yes. This verse was the driving motto of all that my father did. Not only with establishing this university to raise up young men and young women to proclaim the freedom that comes when one has been brought into a right relationship with God through Jesus Christ's life, death, and resurrection. But also his work to secure the freedoms of this country by helping elect God-fearing, God-honoring men and women who uphold the values of God's Word and principles of our Founding Fathers."

Several students cheered, others clapped. The stocky man gripped the wide wooden podium like it was a Baptist pulpit. He continued his remarks like a Baptist preacher.

"That legacy is under assault in increasing measure from the left-wing, progressive policies of this administration. Santos was elected on the promise of hope and change. Hopeless change is what we got." Then his voice rose higher into a fevered pitch: "No, *godless* change is what we got!"

The crowd loved that line, and everyone else on the other side of the camera newsfeed would, too.

"Gay marriage has been the law of the land. Abortionists have been unmasked under this administration as trading in baby parts for profit. The communists are winning across Europe and knocking on our own door. The globalists want open borders that traffic in ideas totally foreign and subversive to our Christian way of life. We need to take America back again and stop the godlessness!"

He paused again. Like any preacher worth his salt, he knew when to ebb and flow the rhetoric to bring the audience to the edge of the homiletical climax. He was there, and so was his audience.

"And I know just the gal to do it."

The crowd went wild (overly cliché, perhaps, but it was true; hands waved, mouths barked the Texan vixen's name, feet danced), clearly all-in on Debby Gallego.

He leaned into the microphone now. "Today, I am giving my unequivocal, full-throated endorsement of Debby Gallego for President of the United States of America. And I trust you will join me in seeing that she is elected."

Elijah skidded to a halt, Gina throwing up a 'For the love…' and narrowly missing plowing into his backside. "That takes the cheesecake."

"*Dios mío…*" Dana cursed before actually cussing in Spanish.

He turned to her. "Did you know about this?"

"*No sabía nada!*"

"How could you not know anything? You're the daughter of one of the chief architects of the Faithful Majority."

She put a hand on her hip and narrowed her eyes. "*Was* one

of the chief architects of the Faithful Majority. He left. *Recuerdas?*"

"Hey, we're on the same side here," Gina said with intervention. "Clearly, this maneuver took everyone else by surprise." She waved a hand at the surrounding crowd, their glee-filled faces betraying a surprise.

Elijah said, "Guessing bringing Billy Baron to the ticket helped seal the deal."

"*Estás bien,*" Dana agreed. "Her poll numbers were in the red until she replaced her old veep running mate. I have it on good authority that his little 'health scare'—" she added air quotes before revealing "—was a total lie to kick his old behind to the curb and clinch the Christian vote bloc."

Gina added, "Still one of the largest there is in America."

"And William D. Baron was the hook that reeled that big fish into the fold."

"So it was all political, him joining the ticket?"

Elijah snorted a laugh. "What isn't these days?"

The stocky man smiled broadly and extended his hands outward, pushing them down to signal silence.

"Now, I know some of you may have misgivings about our guest. But we have much more in common than many might think when it comes to restoring America to its founding principles in the Christian faith, when it comes to ensuring freedom for all."

Elijah shook his head, that tingly tang of rising bile at the back of his throat threatening to jettison the hatch. They needed to get closer.

He went to take back off when a gasp was thrown up from stage right.

From Gina.

"What the what?" she cried out—

Before darting through the crowd.

What the what was right!

"Gina!" he called after her, seeing her ginger locks disappear between Larry Bird and Joe Dumars wannabes.

But their '90s basketball-legend height didn't dissuade him from pushing past them, the pair of jocks throwing up a complaint. His maneuver succeeded in catching a glimpse of Gina tearing off toward the front. Dana gave a similar cry, but he didn't care.

"It is my honor," Maxwell went on as he and Gina and Dana pushed and shoved farther on, "to introduce to you the next President of the United States of America. Debby Gallego!"

The Republican presidential candidate walked out onto the platform, the cheering crowd as intoxicating as ever. She stood stiff and straight in a dress of glittering, glistering gold, waving and receiving their admiration and praise, returning their offerings with her trademark wide, white smile and both fists raised high into the air.

Gallego stood to the right of the podium where the stocky man was still standing, taking in the cheering crowd and giving the cameras some good B-roll. Then she turned toward the man and took his extended hand. He grasped her shoulder, dwarfing the Texan, then whispered something that was probably insignificant into her ear, still displaying that bright grin.

Then she took over the lectern, and said, "Thank you, Dr. James Maxwell, for the invitation. And thank you, Freedom University, for your warm welcome!"

Gina reached the front first, followed quickly by Elijah with Dana close behind. They managed to push through just as Gallego began her speech. A barrier offered a motte of distance between the audience and the stage, Secret Service agents patrolling the grass.

And giving stern, suspecting looks to the petite lady in black pumps and a black leather jacket.

Elijah heaved a breath to catch his breath, then sighed. "Gina colada, where's the fire—"

"Jerry Maguire," she said, hands on her head and scanning

the crowd. She spun in a circle, face drawn with peepers wide and mouth gaping as if in a question.

And white. Her mug was completely drained of color. Not a good look for Gina, because it wasn't a good thing for their case!

"There!" she exclaimed.

"What there?"

"There there!"

He followed her pointer, a finger of chipped mulberry paint but nicely trimmed nails. But only saw the government-issued suits and a gaggle of press snapping pictures and giving very serious reporting while Debby still waved and winked at her adoring crowd.

"Oh, nuts! I lost her," Gina cursed, throwing her hands on her head again, looking this way and that again.

Elijah swallowed back annoyance again. "I don't get it. What were you chasing after, Gina?"

She swallowed and stared at him dead in his peepers with frantic, frazzled—even frightened peepers of her own.

He didn't like that look. Not often he saw it. Only time he recalled that face was when a crazed lunatic possessed by the cosmic powers of this present supernatural darkness stormed into a Cracker Barrel on their first Group X case—looking for them!

Hoped to Yahweh Almighty this wasn't that…

"Gina…I don't—"

"Not what," Gina said with interruption. "*Who.*"

"Who?" Dana asked.

She nodded, those frantic, frazzled, frightened eyes returning to the stage.

Elijah tried not to get annoyed, but they didn't have time for this.

"Gina!" he shouted.

"What?" she shouted back, snapping her head at him.

"Who?"

She took a beat, then a breath. "My mother, that's who!"

"Your mother?"

"Tu madre?" Dana added to the inquiry for good measure.

He sighed. "Echo, echo, echo…"

"Yes, my mother!" Gina said, scanning the crowd.

Dana huffed a sigh. "So, what? Didn't you say she was one of those types who clings to politicians like Mic Jagger fangirls?"

"Yeah, but—"

"Butts are for horses, I seem to recall," Elijah said with a grin.

She snapped her head at him with a confused scowl, held it for a beat before it faded and she busted a laugh through her clenched lips.

"Hey, that's my line!" Gina giggled.

"And a good one."

Eased the tension some, but she wasn't making a lick of sense.

"Slow down and spell it out, Gina," Elijah asked. "What's going on?"

Gina took in a measured breath before popping two sticks of Doublemint gum into her hatch. Her stimming tick.

Which meant nothing good.

Chewing her chaw a few beats, she explained, "You don't understand. Like I mentioned earlier, she was on the cover the *New York Times* at a Gallego rally, then I saw her again at your church. Now here? Does not compute!"

"So, she's a fangirl," Dana said, "what's the big deal?"

Gina didn't pay her any mind. Jaw was really going at it while her peepers darted about, clearly her anxiety and over-whelm through the roof. Knew things with her mom were bad, so he could understand why catching glimpses of her in situa-tions connected to their case would be distressing. But this—

"There!" She cussed and threw out that chipped pointer again past his chest.

Elijah followed it. Past the government-issued suits still roaming the grass like hungry bovine. Up on stage and past

Gallego, who was still basking in the adulation of her would-be subjects. Then clear into the off-stage nether where—

He did a double-take. That didn't make sense.

Because gallivanting with a very jovial Billy Baron was a woman who looked like a pruned version of Gina Anderson. A petite, svelte, ginger wearing a magical Old Glory dress that would put Katy Perry to shame. They were sharing a laugh, from the belly, with heads thrown back and nostrils flared.

Very chummy, they were. And clearly familiar with one another. As if friends of some sort, as if compadres, as if partners—

In crime…

A frigid fright skated through his veins, the kind that he'd felt a time or twelve on cases of a supernatural nature at the FBI and then the past year with Group X. Now, what it all meant—

Didn't flat know. Not in the slightest.

What he did know was that Gina colada was right. What the what…

The worm had turned.

All personal like.

Again.

CHAPTER 24

Gina stood still. Not a movement, not a motion. Not a blink, not even a breath.

This was not happening.

Mama and Billy Baron. Billy Baron and Mama. Laughing it up like a pair of high schoolers canoodling in the Natural History section of the library.

Gina gasped, clutching her chest. Were Billy Baron and Mama canoodling in the Natural History section of the library?

Now she clenched her eyes closed, banishing the thought. For all she knew, Mama was a fangirl who'd sneaked behind the security line to pal around with her latest political fixation. Or maybe Billy Baron had picked her out of the crowd back at Eli's childhood church and invited her to join him in the green room like some coked-out rock star assembling his posse of admirers.

Except she was the only one canoodling with Billy Baron. No other fangirls were around!

"What is your mama doing with Billy Baron?"

It was Elijah, leaning in close with a whisper, that coriander scent of his grounding her in reality. This reality. The one where Eli and Group X and this blasted case from the pit of all that was unholy was her reality.

The one she was commissioned to solve.

The one she was *committed* to solve.

Even if Mama was somehow involved…

Gina chewed her two sticks of Doublemint faster, her masseter, temporalis, and medial pterygoid jaw muscles really going at it even as the minty freshness of the salivary buildup served up a balm for the rising overwhelm at seeing her mama on stage with the Republican vice presidential candidate. She swallowed hard, the fresh spearmint dancing across her taste buds, the smell of minty heaven filling her nostrils.

"Good question…" was all she could manage under the circumstances.

Dana turned to her. "Wait, you didn't know *su madre* and the Republican vice presidential candidate were in cahoots?"

"No, no I didn't."

Elijah asked, "What's she doing with that clown?"

"I don't know."

She huffed a sigh, chewing faster to quell the overwhelm.

It was true. She flat didn't have a cotton pickin' clue about any of it. But it wasn't surprising, given Mama's fascination with all things political. Of course she found her way into Billy Baron's world! Maybe into more of Billy Baron's world than she cared to know about. Hadn't talked with her in quite some time. Months. Years? Forgot. She figured Mama had too. Forgotten about her. Forgotten about reality, given her penchant for the white pills that had numbed it all away.

And yet…

The woman in that slinky dress jawing it up and hamming it up with potentially the 50th Vice President of the United States of America looked nothing like the woman she'd last seen.

Actually, not true. She looked exactly like the woman she'd last seen. A few Christmases ago, in fact. Her height, her build, her freakin' hair color that she'd passed along to Gina through that genetic pool of hers. Could even hear her cackling laugh that reminded her of Fran Dresher's nanny from the same-named '90s sitcom—all high and heady and nasally and oh-so-nails-on-chalkboard grating. Laughing it up with Gallego's veep candidate!

But how did she get so clean? Last she left mama, she was half drunk and half broke. Had nothing to her name but a double-wide in Toledo and a flower bed—literally her old childhood twin headboard and baseboard stuck in the postage-stamp size lot like tombstones with a mishmash of cheapo garden aisle petunias and marigolds sandwiched in between (Mama had thought it was clever; Gina thought it was kitschy). So to see her there, backstage at a political rally for the next President of the United States of America—

Mama and Billy Baron, Billy Baron and Mama.

What the what?

Did not compute!

And Gina flat didn't have a clue. But she was sure going to find out.

She shoved her sleeves past her elbows and looked up and down the motte of astroturf that stood between her and Mama. She went to jump over the security barrier into no-man's-land when Debby Gallego started up her speech.

"Almost three hundred years ago," the woman began, "this city was founded as Yorktown. It went on to play a pivotal role in the life of this country, serving as the temporary capital of the Continental Congress."

Her booming voice reset Gina's head, lifting her out of the swirl of questions and confusion and planting her back on reality's firm ground.

What was she thinking fixing to jump through the security barrier like that? No way would those government-issued gorillas let her get more than five feet before tackling her to the ground. Definitely didn't need a repeat of what had gone down with Eli back at his childhood church.

"This city also witnessed a holy sight," Gallego went on, "the drafting of the Articles of Confederation and their adoption, which was the first legal document to refer to the colonies as the United States of America. This sacred document was a precursor to the American Constitution."

"Oh my cheeps…" Elijah said.

"What is it?" Gina asked, snapping her head at her partner. Forgot for a second she wasn't alone.

"I'm pretty sure this is the same speech that joker Amos Young gave four years ago."

Dana asked, "The Mormon candidate who went down in conspiratorial flames?"

"Yuppers."

"How do you know that?"

He tapped his noggin with his index finger.

"Right," Dana said. "Eidetic memory."

"So, what," Gina said, "the chick is plagiarizing his campaign speech?"

Elijah shrugged. "Suppose if it almost worked once, why reinvent the wheel?"

Gallego paused, scanning the front of the crowd, as if searching for something. Then she stopped and smiled, fixing some distant point with the gaze of her silver eyes.

Gina glanced behind to see the red light of stardom indicating the position of a camera feed broadcasting her message to the masses. She smirked. What a showboat.

Had to admit it, though: the woman sure knew how to play the game. Now the other woman, her mama, what on earth was her role in it?

Debby Gallego looked directly into the camera and continued, "The citizens of America are now on the cusp of a great national effort to rebuild our country and to restore its promises. We will get the job done!"

She leaned in closer to the microphone. "We will take America back again!"

The field erupted in applause and shouts of agreement, the adulation lasting for minutes. Sure did know her audience, knew the kind of red meat to toss her ravenous fans.

Gallego gripped the lectern again. "Together we will determine the course of America, and the world, for many, many years to come. We will face challenges. We will confront hardships, but we will—"

She paused, pointing out into the audience.

Which erupted on cue, as one: *"Take America back again!"*

"We're about to engage in one of our nation's most hallowed rituals. The election of the President of the United States of America. Every four years, we go through this rigmarole of electing a new president, and what has it gotten us?"

"Nothing!" someone shouted from behind.

"You're darn tootin'!" Laughter fluttered across the field, but Gallego kept going. "I aim to shoot higher than merely a transference of power from one administration to another, or from one party to another. No siree, Bob! I *will* transfer power—from Washington to Kentucky, from the two left coasts to the heartland. I'm not just taking America back again, I'm taking *power* back again—and giving it back to you, the people! Recall what two Corinthians says in 3:17, that's the whole ballgame, right there."

"Oh my cheeps," Elijah startled. "Did she just say *two* Corinthians?"

"For the love…" Gina moaned.

"Is that the one you like?" Gallego asked. "Two Corinthians, that's it. *'Now the Lord is the Spirit, and where the Spirit of the Lord is, there is freedom.'"*

"It's *Second* Corinthians, you moron!" Elijah shouted.

Even if she did hear him, she didn't pay him any mind. "Without freedom, what's left? Billy Baron and I will give you back your freedom by taking America back again from the special interests and globalists who are ruining this great country. But we can't do it without you. Folks, our Constitution is hanging on a thread. But there's hope. All because of four simple, but beautiful words—"

Before Gallego could voice them, the crowd finished her sentence. They shouted, *"Take America back again!"*

"You're darn tootin'! I want to invite my good friend and running mate to share more about what we have planned."

Elijah snorted a laugh. "This should be good."

Baron strode to the center of the stage. Gina didn't pay him any mind. Only thing her attention was fixed on was her mother, who was now chatting it up with two others. Both looked vaguely familiar but were hidden in the shadows.

"Thank you, Debby," Billy Baron said in his Southern twang, all chummy and familiar and of-the-people. "Right honor to be here, and a right honor to join our very own Deborah in fighting the forces of darkness for God's people!"

Gina huffed a sigh, shielding her eyes from the high-noon sun and squinting for a better look. Bupkis. So, she whipped out her phone and pinch-zoomed for a better peep at who her mama was jawing it up with.

More bupkis.

"The storm is coming, America!" Baron boomed. "Nothing can stop what is coming."

"Dios mío…" Dana cursed.

"What is it?" Elijah asked.

"Trust the plan," Billy Baron continued. "We are winning and we are on the cusp of the Great Awakening!"

Dana explained, "Those are the lines!"

Gina focused on the images she'd captured instead of Dana, one of them looking super familiar now. A black man she'd seen somewhere before, but she couldn't place it.

"What lines?" Elijah asked. "What are you—"

Dana answered, "I-Og!"

Gina looked up now. "I-Og?"

"I-Og!"

"Is there an echo in here?" Eli complained.

"All of them," Dana explained, "were offered from the WeChan site, in the breadcrumbs from the Eye of God to his followers."

"Together," Baron boomed louder, leaning into the microphone and raising a fist in the air, "we will take America's strength back again. We will take America's wealth back again. We will take America's pride back again. We will take America's safety back again. And yes, together, we will take America back again. It all begins tomorrow. Join us for our freedom march as we take on Washington, taking our grievances straight to the source—the U.S. Capitol Building!"

"The Capitol Building?" Gina said.

Elijah smirked. "Hype up a bunch of fearful, disaffected voters and unleash them on Capitol Hill. That's not a recipe for disaster at all…"

"God bless you," Billy Baron said. "And God bless America. Thank you. Now let's fight like hell to take America back again —because hell sure is fighting us!"

That was a new line. Catchy and effective. Crowd sure liked it, an ear-splitting cry rising from behind and all around. The voices of the people like incense before their Chosen One. Or Chosen Ones, rather, the pair serving as the conduit for the crowd's hopes and dreams.

Maxwell strode onto the stage again as the crowd cheered and crooned over their starlet. Baron was beaming. The university president grasped his hand tightly and said something to him. They both laughed as Gallego met them, placing a hand on each of their shoulders, grinning and joining in the laugh.

The crowd cheered on the Gallego-Baron ticket and political platform, offering a very familiar chant.

Take America back again! Take America back again! Take America back again!

Maxwell allowed it for several minutes, before raising his hands to quiet the crowd down.

"Wow, I must say, Debby," the man said, "there's a bit of a

Southern Baptist preacher tucked away in those Presbyterian bones of yours!"

The field erupted in agreeing laughter. Gallego threw her head back and joined the joke.

"Thank you for those inspiring words. We must take America back again, reclaim America for Christ again. Which is why I and the rest of the Faithful Majority would be proud to call you Madam President."

He turned to the audience now. "So go vote. Vote to take America back again!"

Another rowdy cry of approval from the crowd as the main attraction moved off stage, back toward where Billy Baron had been canoodling with Mama.

Except—

"For the love…"

Elijah turned to her. "What's up—"

"Chicken what?" Gina replied without missing a beat, her mind on auto-reply as her eyes launched a frantic search for what was missing.

Her mother!

She'd disappeared from her perch off-stage, the petite ginger who'd surprisingly carried her age well (them Anderson gals were said to carry the gene) no longer jawing it up or grinning or standing or doing anything from the sidelines of the political rally too weird for words.

Which was cray-cray to the cray-cray in and of itself! Gwen Anderson, Gallego-Baron fangirl invited to pal around with the Republican candidates.

A thought suddenly walloped Gina across the back of the head. One even weirder than the political rally itself.

Was Mama some sort of consultant or staffer for the campaign?

The thought consumed her as Billy Baron himself disappeared into the backstage void—and sent her off along the security barrier, Eli's questioning voice registering, but not enough to yank her back from the edge.

She needed to find Mama. Because she needed answers.

The screams and shouts of adulation made her wince, as did the bodies pressing toward the security barrier. But she pushed on, shoving past the supporters and squeezing along the barrier, those government-issued suits grazing like goats in the grassy no-man's-land that stood between her and those answers.

Finally managed to edge along the end zone just as Baron and Gallego disappeared into the mawing off-stage void—confirming what she'd thought she'd seen.

No mama.

Not good.

Which demanded a split-second decision she hoped she didn't regret.

Only way to get to the bottom of Mama's mystery was to hear it from the heifer's mouth. Or was it horse's? Either way, she needed to get to Mama. Which meant she needed to get backstage.

And there was one path toward that Mordor.

Curling her fingers around the cold black metal barrier sent a frigid jolt through her hands and up her forearms, enough of a second-guess impulse to check her wacky idea—and her commitment.

The crowd cheered and clapped on, with her name shouted above the din a few paces away.

Go time was now time.

She glanced left, then right to confirm a clear path through the government-issued suits.

Both sides had their backs turned to her—all of them, in fact, paying her neither heed nor mind.

Like the parting of the Red Sea, it was!

Which felt like a sign.

She took it, pushing off the barrier and hiking a leg overboard.

When she was yanked back by the collar.

"I don't think so, Gina colada!"

Ankle caught on the barrier, and she took a tumble backward, plowing into a tall, solid body before two hands hooked under her arms and set her on her feet.

"Sorry about that," Elijah said, cheeks flushed and a hand weaving through his hair. "Didn't want you to do anything foolish."

Heat raced up her neck in anger, a quick glance confirming the candidates and their handlers were nowhere to be found.

"I wasn't being foolish!"

"Yeah, right!" He snorted a laugh, which irritated the snot out of her. "Don't forget what happened to me last time."

Dana was at his side, crossing her arms and face etched with no small amount of irritation. "He does have a point, *muchacha*."

Gina huffed a sigh. Had a point. But so did she. The case ran through Mama, she just knew it!

Then she had it. Something, and somewhere, she should have done and gone instead of messing with the strategy that nearly put Eli in the clink. At the far end, she saw a large opening through the stands leading out into the parking lot haloed by the high-noon sun. An exit, leading to the getaway line.

Gina went for it. "Come on!"

Eli threw up his predictable complaint, joined by Dana.

Paid them no mind. Not with Mama on the lam and a Group X case from Dante's Inferno that had taken a wicked personal turn.

Shoving past a septuagenarian couple decked out in Revolutionary War attire, she scooted along the barricade with a keen eye for a quick exit out of the stadium. Hands pushing, arms gesturing wildly, legs carrying her forward on uncertain feet that didn't know whether they wanted to know what lay at the end of the road.

Took some doing, but she managed to pop out of the crowd

at a set of stairs leading up to the main entrance—a channel of mawing darkness tunneling under the stadium seating out to the parking lot that held the promise of answers.

Or the kiss of death, a right swift kick into the back of a government-issued Chevy Suburban as a person of interest with designs for domestic terrorism.

Irregardless—or regardless (never could get that one right)—Gina kept going, kept running, kept searching for her mama.

Through the tunnel, her feet slapping the cement with a wicked echo. Outside into a fast filling parking lot. Then tearing across the sidewalk edging the massive stadium on toward a fence at the far end where she figured the goods were getting away.

Black chain-linked, nine-feet tall, and hastily erected. The government-issued kind the Feds put up at high-profile events.

She beelined it now, throwing off her black pumps and putting those track-honed legs and arms into action and feeling not an ounce of embarrassment for running barefoot in the dead of fall. Had to dodge grannies and co-eds alike, along with middle-aged men in Dockers and Polos and frat boys giving her sideways glances.

But she made it, flinging herself against the fence just in time to glimpse a familiar train of government-issued vehicles. Looked this way and that for a way in, but it ran quite a ways down. Gave it a shake and stepped back to assess its climb-worthiness, but it was a solid, sturdy barrier. It also wasn't worth the risk ending up in the Secret Service clink. Besides, she caught a glimpse of all she needed anyway.

From the barrier was a sight she never, no, never, in all her years, expected.

Old Glory getting into the back of a black Chevy Suburban, the silver-lined ginger locks of a petite woman blowing in the wind before disappearing inside the mawing darkness, the hair and the dress.

And her mama.
What was going on?
Gina flat didn't have a clue.
And she flat didn't want to.

CHAPTER 25

I n Elijah Xavier Fox's thirty-something trips around the sun, and in his just-shy-of-a-decade experience investigating the crazy and fighting for justice, one of the surest bets was that each case smelled, tasted, and felt like an onion straight from hot Hades.

Without fail, layer after layer—or rather, scale after scale, the membranous outer ones giving way to the fleshy inner ones and down toward the center—would reveal more *inexplicitus* crazy than you'd find in a bargain-bin Kindle yarn.

Start with layer one: a childhood hero from his childhood church had nearly shot up a Northern Virginia diner in search of a secret pedophile ring headlined by the sitting President of the United States.

Add to that the fact that the pastor of his childhood church had not only fomented some sort of schizoid episode in Eddy Lee and who knew how many others—the bozo was fingered for the veep running mate slot for the Republican presidential candidate.

Layer two.

Then, come to find out (layer three alert), there was a connection between Billy Baron and Gina's Mama, who was not only a rally fangirl but looked to be some sort of sidekick—and, well, he was ready to call it a day.

Was more than ready to throw in the towel (for an extra measure of cliché), rent a car to get out of Dodge (or York, Pee-Ay, as was the case), cuddle up with Dexter (on the couch) and Jed Bartlet (on the idiot box) and a nice mouthy Meritage wine (the bottle, not a glass; the case called for such drastic measures).

But they had a job to do. He had a job to do.

Not only for 'Merica but for Mama—for her church, his childhood church.

For Daddy and his legacy.

Only thing was—

What they'd find next, when they pealed back another scaly layer, burrowing further down into the flesh of this case from hot Hades…Elijah wasn't sure he wanted to find out.

But he had a hunch.

And it was time to let the goat out of the box before this *inexplicitus* case got any crazier.

Probably the only glimmer of grace was the Cracker Barrel a mile away. Almost didn't jump at the chance for their Country Boy Breakfast, given the crazy that went down their last go around at the joint, but he did.

Which was where they were now, stuffed in a corner during a very busy lunch hour.

Noise was almost too much to bear after the stadium crowds, Elijah's neurological wiring nearly fritzing out from the aural overwhelm. But the meal in front of him helped: a plate filled with scrambled eggs smothered in sharp cheddar cheese; tart, cinnamony fried apples; a slab of sweet-n-smokey sugar cured ham; and a chunk of hash brown casserole drowning in ketchup.

Just what the doc ordered.

Gina predictably got a cheeseburger, and Dana surprised him by ordering up for herself the same breakfast platter. Like he knew from the start: a kindred spirit, she was.

After shoving a forkful of casserole into her mouth, Dana

pointed her fork at Gina. "So, about your mother."

"Whata 'bout 'er?" Gina answered, mid-chew.

"I take it you didn't have a clue about her association with Billy Baron."

She swallowed and slurped from her Coke. "Not a clue."

"What's going on here, then? The rally and the rhetoric, *su madre* and *muchacho muy loco*?"

"I might know something about that," Elijah said.

Gina turned to him, taking another swipe of her burger. "Really?"

He downed some brew, smacking his lips at the smooth, nutty taste and nodded.

"Well, not your mom per se, but the bigger picture."

"What bigger picture?" Dana asked.

Taking a breath, Elijah shifted, getting ready to unload.

"Do you remember when I went down for the count, back in that Kenturkey BBQ joint?"

"How could I not!" Gina said. "Scared me stiff."

Swallowing and heaving another breath, he answered, "Well, I think it was a vision."

"A vision?" Dana said. "What, like a trance or something?"

"Or something…" Elijah closed his eyes and shook his head, still disbelieving all he saw.

"What sort of vision?" Gina asked, brow furrowed with concern.

Taking a breath, he recounted what he had seen inside the BBQ joint—what he had smelled and felt, the Beings he had seen almost conducting the chaotic scene.

When he was through, the women leaned back in their seats and went silent.

"I don't know what to say…" Dana said.

"Ditto," Gina added. "What do you make of this—well, vision, as you framed it?"

Elijah answered, "I think it was a glimpse into not only the Unseen Realm, but the reality of America's cosmic geography."

Dana twisted up her face in confusion. "Cosmic geography?"

"Let me—" Elijah closed his eyes and took a breath, quoting from memory: "*'When the Most High apportioned the nations, when he divided humankind, he fixed the boundaries of the peoples according to the number of the gods; the Lord's own portion was his people, Jacob his allotted share.'*"

"What the what?" Gina said. "That sounds like the nations were given over to certain gods."

Elijah nodded. "That's because that's what happened."

"Where is that from?" Dana asked.

"The Book of Deuteronomy, chapter 32, where Yahweh, the Most High God, disinherits the nations. He gave them over to be ruled by the sons of God. Israel understood their entire national identity through this lens. Yahweh claimed them as his portion, while the other nations were assigned to other gods."

"*Disparates!*"

"Nope. Not nonsense. Think about the Book of Daniel, chapter 10."

"Huh?"

"Here's what one of Yahweh's messengers said to Daniel."

Elijah closed his eyes again and tipped back his head, taking a deep breath before quoting:

> *"Do not fear, Daniel, for from the first day that you set*
> *your mind to gain understanding and to humble*
> *yourself before your God, your words have been*
> *heard, and I have come because of your words. But*
> *the prince of the kingdom of Persia opposed me*
> *twenty-one days. So Michael, one of the chief*
> *princes, came to help me, and I left him there with*
> *the prince of the kingdom of Persia and have come to*
> *help you understand what is to happen to your*
> *people at the end of days."*

He explained, "This angel, sent with a message for Daniel,

was stopped by a cosmic power, a divine being that held sway—held *rule*, over the geographical boundaries of Persia."

"What are you saying, *muchacho*?" Dana asked. "What's the Old Testament getting at?"

"What we're both saying is that the Hebrew Scriptures describe a world where cosmic-geographical lines have been drawn."

"Cosmic geography," Dana said. "Like you just said."

"Yuppers. Israel, the nation and their land, was holy ground because Yahweh had claimed it for himself. It was his portion, as Deuteronomy says."

"Which would mean the territory, the land belonging to other nations—well, then it would belong to other gods."

"Including America," Gina whispered, bringing a hand to her mouth.

He nodded. "Bingo."

"Mind blown…" Dana marveled.

Elijah explained, "there is an Unseen Realm with Yahweh the Most High ruling over a divine counsel. Problem is, we aren't trained to view this Unseen Realm. Yahweh ruled with *beney elohim*, divine beings called 'sons of god' on his council until the corrupt *elohim* were punished, as Psalm 82 teaches. The end reveals these chastised gods were given a degree of dominion over the nations of the earth, a ruling task at which they failed miserably."

Closing his eyes, he quoted part of Psalm 82:

> *I say, "You are gods,*
> *children of the Most High, all of you;*
> *nevertheless, you shall die like mortals*
> *and fall like any prince."*
> *Rise up, O God, judge the earth,*
> *for all the nations belong to you!*

Taking a breath, he snapped open his eyes and continued,

"Here's the deal: Yahweh is among the *elohim*, sitting at the head of his divine, heavenly assembly, but he is superior to all other gods. He created them. He is their sovereign king. Likewise, since Jesus is Yahweh incarnate, he too stands apart with superiority from the other gods. He is the divine sovereign over all the *beney elohim*."

"This sounds *muy loco* to me," Dana muttered. "Yahweh and other lesser gods?"

"I hear you, sister!" Gina said. "Was for me too the first time I heard about it."

"Even if this was the case, what does any of this have to do with our investigation?"

Elijah chided himself silently. "Forgive my theological travelog. That was set up for the Watcher-spirits, the Nephilim offspring which I believe are the very Beings who have haunted the world from ages past."

She just stared blankly at him. He was disappointed in her lack of recognition.

"Nephilim. Those Beings birthed from the sexual union between the sons of God and human women. In Genesis 6."

Still nothing.

Elijah stifled a sigh before reaching back again into his eidetic memory. He quoted Genesis 6: "*'When people began to multiply on the face of the ground, and daughters were born to them, the sons of God saw that they were fair; and they took wives for themselves of all that they chose…'*"

"Is that from the Bible?" Dana asked.

Gina answered, "From the verses leading to the story about Noah's ark."

"I don't recall hearing nothing about that!"

"Most Christians don't," Elijah explained. "Sermons about Beings coming down from Heaven to mate with women, eventually birthing divine-human hybrids, the Nephilim, with the intention to rule over humanity with divine right—let's just say that don't preach too well."

Dana turned to Gina. *"Que dijo el?"*

"You heard me right," he said with a chuckle. "The sons of God mated with human women, breaching the established boundaries and falling from their heavenly positions. Other Jewish literature refers to them as Watchers. And now, the sons of God, or their offspring rather—they can appear in the flesh, manifesting themselves on Earth, and the Bible makes reference to some of these occasions."

"And these…divine-human hybrids," Dana said before offering a chuckle. "I can't believe I'm saying this, but you think they're responsible for all of this election nonsense?"

"Wouldn't put it past them in the slightest! Again, Jewish literature teaches that demons are actually the disembodied souls of dead Nephilim. Watcher-spirits that continue to plague and terrorize humanity, as ancient Jewish texts explain."

Dana threw Gina skeptical eyes; she just shrugged.

Throwing back a swig of brew, Elijah continued, "Psalm 82 says these lesser gods became corrupted and were not to be worshiped by Israel. The Hebrew Scriptures don't explain how they were corrupted, and why the other nations served these other gods instead of Yahweh, the Most High God."

Gina said, "I'd always thought that was odd, that other nations served other idols—"

"Nope. Not idols," he interrupted. "Gods. Real, genuine, spiritual beings from the Unseen Realm."

"Fine. Got it. Still weird."

"Sure thing—"

"Chicken wing," Gina finished with a wink.

He laughed. "Always rhyming all the timing, you are. Anyway, cosmic geography explains this. A prime example is when David is driven from Israel's territory by King Saul, lamenting his pursuers *'have driven me out today from my share in the heritage of the Lord, saying, 'Go, serve other gods.'"*

"Heritage?" Dana said.

"In David's mind, being driven from the land meant being

driven from the place where Yahweh could be worshiped. He wasn't driven from the Ark of the Covenant or from the Tabernacle. Nope. From Yahweh's *inheritance*, from the holy land of his God."

"So, what," Gina said, "you're saying David couldn't worship like he would want, or even should, if he wasn't in the land of Israel."

"Bingo. The other gods owned that other land outside of Israel. All of which was driven home by the military hero Naaman. After the prophet Elijah healed him, the man recognized Israel's God and asked for two mule loads of earth to take with him back to his country."

Took Gina a beat, but then she got it. "He wanted part of the land so he could properly worship the God of the land—of Israel, Yahweh!"

"Bingo, Gina colada. Naaman carted back as much holy ground as his mules could take back to Syria so he could still offer sacrifices to Yahweh on his land, in his territory, even though the god Rimmon was the territorial god of that land. All of which reflects what happened at Babel, and reinforced in the Deuteronomy 32 worldview."

"I'm still not clear on this worldview. And how does it relate to Babel?"

"Deuteronomy 32," Elijah explained, "teaches that God disinherited the nations as his people and inherited Israel, making for himself a new people. We see this immediately after the judgment at Babel in the Book of Genesis, chapter 11. This sordid tale —which is about much more than a building project and language confusion—is actually core to the Old Testament worldview."

"*Realmente?* I thought Exodus was central—with the parting of the Red Sea and Ten Commandments and all that."

"Umm, in a word: nope."

"Fine, *sabelotodo*. Explain."

"I'm no know-it-all, but I'll try to explain." He drained his coffee and dove in. "See, it was at Babylon where people sought to make a name for themselves by building the infamous Tower stretching to reach the realm of the gods. It's basically the height of human rebellion, and Yahweh finally had it. He's like, Fine, you want those other gods? You can have them! Then decreed he's not going to have a relationship with the nations. He would start over with a new nation, one that would be his."

"Israel," Dana answered.

Gina added, "Beginning with Abraham's calling."

Elijah nodded. "Bingo. Now, most English Bibles get this wrong here in Deuteronomy 32:8. They don't translate it right."

"How so?"

"'*According to the number of the sons of God*' is mistranslated as '*according to the number of the sons of Israel*' thanks to disagreements between Hebrew manuscripts. But we know from the Dead Sea Scrolls that '*sons of God*' is correct. Besides, it wouldn't make sense in the slightest for God to divide up the nations of the earth '*according to the number of the sons of Israel*' when Israel hadn't been formed yet!"

"Makes sense," Dana said. "But what happened to the other nations?"

Gina nodded. "And what does it mean they were assigned to the sons of God?"

Elijah shifted forward, leaning his elbows on the table and propping his fingers in a tent.

"This is where we bring home the bacon and cook it. And where we connect it to what I mentioned earlier about the sons of God. Because as remarkable as it may sound, these other nations were placed under the authority of members of Yahweh's divine council."

"The lesser gods?" Dana asked.

"Yuppers. And all the other nations apart from Israel were assigned to these lesser *elohim* as a judgment from the Most High God, Yahweh. Deuteronomy 4:19–20 makes this clear."

He took a breath and closed his eyes, quoting:

> *And when you look up to the heavens and see the sun,
> the moon, and the stars, all the host of heaven, do not
> be led astray and bow down to them and serve them,
> things that the Lord your God has allotted to all the
> peoples everywhere under heaven. But the Lord has
> taken you and brought you out of the iron smelter,
> out of Egypt, to become a people of his very own
> possession, as you are now.*

He explained, "The celestial bodies, the host of heaven, are common language for other gods. And here we're told God has 'allotted' them to the nations under heaven. He handed them over to the sons of God."

Gina said, "All because of Babel?"

"All because of Babel, God decreed that the other nations would worship other gods. Don't want me, don't want to worship me? Yahweh says. Fine! I'll play matchmaker and hook you up with your very own cosmic being, one tailor-made for your geography. He says, Adios, muchachos! then claims his own nation, making a covenant with Abram. Think about what Saint Paul said."

"*Qué es eso?*" Dana asked.

"The powers of this present supernatural darkness."

Gina added, "From the Book of Ephesians."

He nodded. "Same cosmic geography worldview. Principalities, powers, authorities, dominions. The ruler of the authority of the air. All of it is used in Greek literature for geographical rulership. Which mirrors the divine dominion concept of Deuteronomy 32—which Paul then leverages to pit Christ and his sons against the corrupt *elohim*, the sons of God."

Gina said, "The battle lines are drawn for a cosmic turf war."

"Yuppers. And this cosmic conflict is on full display in the New Testament. Everywhere Jesus goes, everything he says and does when he reaches these points of geography are framed within the context of the dark cosmic powers of the Unseen

Realm. A conflict we, the Church, carry forward as members of Christ's Kingdom."

"Standing against the darkness," Gina said with a smile.

Elijah returned the smile. That's what the two of them had been doing together for half a decade—first at the FBI and then coming back together at Group X.

He nodded. "Standing against the darkness. And in our case, 'Merica's darkness. Which is stoked by a principality and power. Just like all the other nations, 'Merica's territory and land was given over to the corrupt *elohim* sons of god."

"You think so?" Dana asked.

"Why not? If all the nations have been apportioned to the Watchers, why would America be exempt? You heard it yourself from the Book of Daniel. A Prince of Persia. A powerful divine being ruling over that nation. Why not the same for America— the most powerful nation in the world? Just like there is with China and Russia and Germany."

Gina added, "Only question is, which one?"

Elijah shook his head. "All I have to say is, must be a powerful one. On par with the Prince of Persia."

Dana said, "The kind that takes the same kind of heavenly power to ward off?"

He nodded, saying nothing more.

"What does this mean for our case then?" Gina asked.

"For one, it means this case of ours is right up our *inexplicitus* alley. That it matters to the Church, as much as to our own country. It also means—"

Elijah stopped short, not wanting to voice what he'd begun to feel the deeper they dove down through the scaly layers of their Group X case.

"It means..." Gina said, brow raised and wrinkled with inquiry.

Clearing his throat, he answered, "It means there's a spiritual thread weaving through both halves of this case."

She sat back, crossing her arms. "By spiritual, you mean *demonic*."

"*Diablos?*" Dana startled.

"And which halves are you talking about? You're being a bit coy for Eli Fox."

He shifted again, getting to it. "Mine and yours. Our halves. My childhood church and—well, your mother."

Gina's face fell, and her shoulders slumped. Her face registered more confirmation than revelation, as if she'd been feeling the same thing. That her mother was wrapped up in the Unseen Realm as much as his childhood church had gotten.

"What you're saying, then," she said, "is Toledo or bust."

Elijah nodded. "The Glass City does seem to be our destiny."

"*Espera un segundo,*" Dana said, holding up a hand. "Why Toledo?"

Gina answered, "It's my hometown."

The reporter muttered something to herself in Spanish, furrowing her brow and bringing a hand to her chin. She went quiet, contemplative.

Elijah asked, "Does Toledo mean anything to you?"

She looked up and nodded. "A source for my investigation lives there."

"A source…what, into this I-Og business?"

"*Sí.* Someone on the inside who had gotten out."

"Do you think he'd talk with us?"

Dana shrugged. "*No sé.* Worth a shot since it seems the road leads through Toledo."

Elijah looked to Gina. "You ready to go home, to face whatever demons await?"

Gina took a breath, then a beat, then nodded. Didn't say anything more; didn't need to.

What he did know was exactly what he himself had felt from the start.

As try as you might to escape the past, it always bites you in the backside.

CHAPTER 26
TOLEDO, OHIO.

h, Toledo, how I've missed you…

Not!

A coldness swept through Gina as she pulled the Mercedes G Class SUV off Interstate 75 onto State Route 24, the main drag that held the sorry excuse for a Midwest town together—barely. More like baling wire and duct tape (not duck tape, as Eli was quick to point out), along with tears and the tattered strips of broken promises stretching back through the collapse of the manufacturing industry.

Knew she shouldn't be too hard on the place—her place, the one that had shaped her. For good and for ill. Also knew her snootiness toward the city was more about her personal pain than anything else. Father left town the fall she started junior high. Twin sister died a few years after that from suicide. Mama had filled in the years in between and all around with enough baggage to give a shrink a lifetime of work. That wasn't even touching on how out-of-place she'd felt as a girl navigating life while both feet were firmly planted on the autism spectrum. Her only chance at freedom from it all had come from an unlikely source. Well, two.

The University of Michigan and Calvin Dobson.

As a born-and-bread Buckeye fan, the fact she went to Michigan was enough to get disowned. Was probably a subconscious desire influencing her to venture into the Wolverine State, a ploy to force Mama's hand to leave her be. Regardless, it was the singular move that had given Gina her wings and sent her soaring. The full-ride scholarship was truly a gift from the Holy Spirit himself, the providential workings of the Lord Almighty moving in her story. Almost like Joseph, that cistern strategically placed in the desert when he went to find his brothers—only to find himself tossed down inside and sold into slavery, catapulting him into another stratosphere of his personal reality.

Her story pivot wasn't as dramatic, and was far more sweet than sour, but was just as impactful. Especially when the Third Person of the Trinity brought along a certain black boy from a wealthy suburb of Detroit. Calvin Dobson. Caldo the Magnificent. Another pivot point in her journey that was probably another subconscious way out of her trailer-trash life, but was far more than that. It was love.

Now he was threatened, seemingly by her mother no less—someone else she loved but whose relationship was complicated by the past.

And there Gina was, caught between the two.

The *burp-burp-burp* of a semi's honker from behind jostled Gina from her contemplation.

"For the love…"

She stepped on it, jerking the SUV back down the cracked-pavement road lined with squat, derelict houses straight from *The Walking Dead*. Broken windows, moss-covered roofs, overgrown yards with rusted swing sets and faded Little Tikes cars, the red little plastic coupes with yellow roofs signaling sad childhoods. In other words, home.

GPS eventually took her to their destination, a bar in the heart of the zombie apocalypse—named, of all things, The Seedy Bar.

Now there was some good Midwest originality for you. Was on the nose though, the brown brick bar stuffed between a pawn shop and Goodwill that made Gina glad it was still daylight.

Parking, she and her two companions got out and shoved through a heavy, barred wood door.

"*Oof,*" Elijah complained. "Seedy bar is right…"

Gina understood completely.

It was dinner time, but it might as well have been midnight it was so dark inside. Didn't help matters the walls were painted a hideous shade of purple, with heavy black curtains shading two picture windows flanking the street outside. Decades of cigarette smoke still smoldered in the walls and maroon vinyl booths long after indoor smoking was banned from the Buckeye State. The stale, burnt tobacco stench was joined by an overwhelming scent of frying—well, everything! Beef, potatoes, onions, cabbage, you name it.

Place was packed though, so clearly the locals didn't mind the Hitchcockian landscape.

Dana dialed her contact, the soft ring and soft glow of someone's phone thrown up from the back corner. She announced their arrival, and a young man with long blond hair slid out from a circle booth and waved them over.

Their new reporter friend exchanged a greeting with her contact and introduced him simply as Chester. Name sure fit, the twentysomething with oversized blue eyes and a broad, lush-lipped mouth framed by Basset Hound hair looking like a jovial fella who moonlighted as a guitar player in an indie rock band. Probably on the very stage that sat behind them.

The pair slid into the booth, with Eli sitting next to Chester and Gina next to Dana. She introduced her new Group X friends, leaving their identity simply as investigators without going into more detail about the *inexplicitus,* supernatural angle to her and Eli's investigations. Appreciated Dana's discretion. The young man seemed fine enough with the intro but threw them both narrowed, shifting eyes.

An older woman with bright pink lips who looked like she was a Prohibition holdover sauntered over from the shadows, interrupting them for their drink order. A round of Bud Lights for them all and the woman slipped back into the seedy bar.

"As I mentioned on our flight over," Dana began, "I met Chester on the I-Og WeChan forum, where I stumbled across Eye of God and his followers. For the longest time I simply lurked, taking in the crazy talk and conspiracy theories without engaging."

She looked over at Chester, one end of her mouth curling upward.

"That is, until a certain channel member started hitting on me."

The young man's pal cheeks brightened pink, and those large eyes cast down at the wood table.

"I have a thing for *The Legend of Zelda*." Chester said.

Gina turned to Dana. "What's that supposed to mean?"

"She laughed, explaining, "Midna the Marvelous was my handle. And Cheshire ninety-nine, here, certainly made his move."

"Guessing that was your handle?" Eli asked.

"That's right," Chester said, cheeks bright red now.

Their server returned with a tray of beers, and everyone paused for a drink.

"Long story short," Dana continued, "I eventually learned that Chester had left the I-Og movement and was trying to pull others out of the burning building."

Chester added, "Was trying to offer some help, some logic to keep others from descending into madness."

Gina asked, "How did you get into it to begin with?"

Downing a swig of brew, the young man answered, "I got into it for the hope. I wanted to believe that the good guys were fighting the good fight. I wanted to believe in a better future—one I could bring in, one I could control. One that took us back to the way things were before—"

"Liberals messed things up?" Eli interrupted.

"Pretty much."

"What did it do for you?" Gina asked, intrigued by the mindset of someone who got wrapped up in the group. "Why were you attracted to the Eye of God—the man behind the handle, the movement?"

"What it did for me was brought me a sense of joy and control. You see, I graduated a few years back now from OSU—"

"A Buckeye, ehh? The Ohio State University."

Nodding, he continued: "Made me feel like I wasn't like everyone else. That I was a warrior, not a failure. I-Og makes you feel important, it gives you meaning and self-esteem. You're saving the world when you're an Eye."

"That's what followers are called," Dana explained. "Eyes. What higher way can you view yourself than that of a savior, someone who's helping slay the dragons? But there is a darker side, isn't there, Chester?"

The young man's face fell, and a jittery tremble took over his hand holding his beer. He took a swig, the glass rattling some against his teeth before he set it down and withdrew his hands beneath the table.

"I-Og cuts you off from society," he explained. "It uses that isolation to draw you in and keep you with like-minded people. You can't leave. There's no incentive to admit when things don't turn out as predicted. People in your life drift on. Relationships are damaged forever. Leads to addiction, too—in the bread-crumbs, the chit-chat online, the special feeling you're in the know, the hope in something better."

"What I don't understand is," Elijah asked, "why is it so compelling?"

Dana took over now: "I-Og believers see themselves as victims in the march of society that has re-written everything they've known. Especially for Christians, who have viewed America as a Christian nation. All the rules about marriage and decency and gender have gone up in smoke. And here comes

Debby Gallego, this sort of messianic figure touched by God to stop the march of this alienating and alien progress. They believe they're doing God's work—that Gallego is his Chosen One to take America back again. Only problem is, this sense of meaning and purpose cuts a fine line through the next stage of things."

"What's that?" Gina asked.

"Anarchy and violence. What happens when it all becomes less of a journey and adventure sussing out clues and bread-crumbs and more of a crusade?"

Elijah replied, "Suppose jihad is what happens. Like what we saw at the BBQ joint back in Paducah."

"*Exactamente*. Foot soldiers and Eye of God himself vow this global cabal will be eliminated—which waffles between an imminent demise and a far-off prospect that can only be accomplished by patriots, or Eyes, who search for meaning in I-Og's clues. To be an I-Og follower means you've rejected everything that's part of the mainstream, all of the major American institutions. Everything from the media and press to the expert class and, of course, government. Battling apostates is the number one cause. The apocalypse is imminent, where the world as we know it comes to an end and followers are invited to usher in the Great Awakening."

It was becoming clearer. And something about all of this struck Gina as familiar.

Mama familiar.

A chill swept through her at the thought. She brought her arms around herself and began to rub her shoulders.

Chester leaned toward Dana, whispering something in her ear she couldn't hear.

Eli leaned against the table, mouthing: *You OK?*

His sensing her discomfort brought her more warmth than her hands.

She nodded, then got to her thought: "You're saying these foot soldiers, the Eyes—they believe they're on the side of right-eousness, that their cause is good."

Dana nodded. "Not only good, but *just*. The storm is coming, as they say, where dark forces are rising on the horizon to throw the country into chaos. All set into motion by a small group of manipulators, operating in the shadows, pulling the strings of world events. Of course, the mainstream media are the enablers of the puppet masters. Along with Santos and the Deep State. On the one hand, Debby Gallego stands between salvation and oblivion. On the other hand, a clash between good and evil can't be avoided, a Great Awakening is coming."

She paused, leaning toward Chester and whispering something in his ear now.

Lots of secrets going on. Which Gina didn't like.

"Are you sure?" Chester said lowly. "Can they be trusted?"

"*Por supuesto.* Tell them."

Gina flashed Elijah skeptical yet hopeful eyes. "Tell us what?"

The young man took a breath, then a beat, then spilled the tea.

"One of the reasons I got wrapped up in I-Og was because my chosen profession moved overseas. Thanks to my nice, shiny undergrad degree in computer science, I was able to secure a cush IT job with a major accounting firm in Columbus, along with a mountain of debt."

"The 'Merican dream," Eli said.

Chester snorted a sneering laugh. "Yeah, until it was shipped to Pakistan."

"The globalist dream," Gina added.

"Which is what led me into the Eye of God conspiracy. Anyway—" Chester waved his hands before polishing off his beer, then: "—when I unhooked from the Matrix, or maybe when I hooked back into the Matrix. Whatever. Doesn't matter."

"You're stalling," she said.

He glanced at Dana, who gave a quick nod. Then he continued, "One of my burning questions when I left I-Og was who was the man behind the curtain."

Elijah said, "The Wizard of Oz."

"That's right. The Eye of God, who was dropping all these breadcrumbs of so-called military intelligence that would blow the lid on the Davos crowd and World Economic Forum and President Santos's kiddie sex ring. So I put that unused college education to work and hacked into the WeChan forum, launching a backtracking algorithm that brought me to the doorstep of the Eye himself."

"Oh my cheeps…"

"Never thought I'd say this," Gina said, "but go Buckeyes! Where's the doorstep?"

Another quick glance at Dana to confirm before: "Right here, in Toledo."

"What the what? Are you for real?"

"As real as rain."

Eli huffed a sigh. "It's as right as—"

Gina cut him off with a raised neither-the-time-nor-the-place hand; sometimes she had to do that.

Head swirled with the possibilities that her hometown was caught up in all the conspiratorial nonsense. Flat didn't make sense. Sure, Ohio was a bellwether for much of the mainstream electorate, the perfect cross-section of racial, religious, and professional demographics. It also was a crucial swing state. So much so that no Republican presidential candidate has won the presidency without it. Even Democrats have only claimed the White House five times without winning Ohio.

But Toledo, of all places? Again, what the what?

Dana said, "He's prepared to take us there if—"

She stood, now cutting off their new reporter friend. "I'll drive."

"Now?"

"Hippity, hoppity. Let's go!"

Dana laughed, opening her purse and throwing down a couple of twenties to pay for their drinks. "I like your style, *muchacha.*"

Gina hustled toward the front exit.

Time to get some answers.

With her at the wheel.

CHAPTER 27

"Take this left," Chester said, a ripple of thunder rumbling overhead.

Gina took the left, trying not to be too cheesed that their new partner in *inexplicitus* cray-cray fighting was calling all the shots. In her town!

Suppose it was *their* town, but still. Was totally over the cloak-and-dagger nonsense, but he insisted on riding shotgun and spelling out the directions verbally. Didn't want anything written down so that none of it came back on him. Got that, but it still cheesed the snot out of Gina.

The sky moaned again something fierce, which tweaked the back of her lizard brain something fierce. Elijah poo-pooed putting any such stock in the portents of weather patterns. Not Gina. Didn't believe some mythical Mother Nature bestowed her providential workings through the universe or anything—none of that woo-woo pagan crap for her. Yet, in her experience, there still was something to be said about the rhythm of the day setting the course for how an investigation would turn out.

The sailors' warning about red skies in the morning and all that jazz weren't for nothing!

"There's something about all this," Elijah said from the back, her partner tolerating the car ride surprisingly well, "that I still don't get."

"What's that, *muchacho*?" Dana said next to him.

Chester threw out another left hook indicating another left turn. What was it with men and their jutting arms?

"I don't get how it all started?" Eli continued. "Like, I get there's this belief in this secretive and untouchable cabal with wicked intentions, usually tied to left-wing politicians like Santos and specifically to Democrats. According to the wack-adoodles, at least. But one day some random dude—"

"Or dudette," Gina said from the front, channeling Mama's feminist leanings.

He snorted a laugh. "I'm all for equal opportunity ne'er-do-wells—we certainly nabbed our fair share of those with the Bureau."

"But…?"

"But this has all the markings of a dude."

Dana scoffed. "That's not sexist at all."

"What, you want this conspiratorial perp to be a member of the sisterhood of the traveling pants? Anyway, my point was how we go from someone throwing up a conspiracy to a mass of followers."

She answered, "It all started with an anonymous post on a WeShare forum by someone calling himself the Eye of God."

Gina said, "And that's where the whole movement got its name."

Dana said, "*Sí*. Followers, the Eyes, have eyes to see—"

"And ears to hear, like Jesus talked about."

"Eye of God styled himself, or herself—no one is certain of the gender of this original poster. Regardless, they wanted people to think they were someone with a level of access to classified information within the U.S. government that gave them insight into highly sensitive material. Gave an air of credibility and Deep State machinations to the whole thing. When you look though I-Og's posts, the tone is clearly conspiratorial and quite ridiculous. *'I've said too much,'* he says, and *'Follow the money.'* Then: *'Some things must remain classified to the very end.'*"

"Take this right!" Chester exclaimed before jutting out another arm.

"For the love…" Gina slammed on the brakes and yanked the steering wheel toward destiny. "A little more warning next time!"

Taking the turn, she floored it in frustration, the rain rapping a mean beat now. She didn't care. Just flipped the wipers to full throttle and echoed their motion with the roar of their Mercedes M282 1.3 liter inline-four 16-valve turbocharged engine (had her daddy to thank for being a car girl).

"What's clear to me," Eli said, snapping Gina back to the moment, "is that these people are under the influence of some bad juju."

"What, like *marihuana y cocaína*?" Dana asked.

He shook his head. "Not wacky tobacky or nose candy. I'm talking about the rulers, the authorities, the cosmic powers of this present supernatural darkness."

Gina nodded. "Spiritual forces of the Unseen Realm."

"*El diablo?*" Dana said, voice betraying skepticism along with a raised eyebrow. Now she smirked and rolled her eyes.

Yup. Skeptical.

Not that she blamed her. Most Christians had never considered the influence the cosmic powers of this present supernatural darkness have over this world—especially the principalities and powers ruling over their specific nation.

Elijah answered, "Not the Devil, not Satan. I'm talking about Watcher-spirits."

Dana folded her arms and furrowed her brow. "*Dime más.* What's this Watcher-spirit business? You spoke of them earlier, but they did not make sense."

Gina had certainly heard plenty of Eli's theories of these Beings, about the Unseen Realm and its continued influence. Had seen plenty of that influence, too, to make her a believer.

"They are the offspring of the sons of God. It's what I was trying to get at when we covered this ground before. Other Jewish literature from the Second Temple period call them Watchers."

Elijah closed his eyes and tipped back his head, ready to unload what he'd stuffed away inside his noggin. He quoted:

> *Evil spirits have gone forth from their bodies, because*
> *they are born from men, and from the holy Watchers*
> *is their original creation. They shall be evil spirits on*
> *Earth, and evil spirits they shall be called. And the*
> *spirits of the giants afflict, oppress, destroy, attack,*
> *do battle, and work destruction upon Earth, causing*
> *chaos. These spirits shall rise up against the children*
> *of men and against their women, for they have come*
> *from them.*

"*Qué es?*" Dana asked.

"This was from an ancient Jewish text about Genesis 6," he explained. "Though not of this world, the Watcher-spirits have been wreaking havoc on Earth since the dawn of time. Afflicting, destroying, attacking humanity. Chaos is their aim. Same for sowing despair and fear into the hearts of humanity. It is against these powers that the Church battles."

"What does that mean?" Dana asked.

Gina answered. "Spiritual warfare."

Elijah nodded. "Bingo. Which isn't about commanding demons to submit or performing abracadabra magic tricks to put them in their place. Fundamentally, it is about conflict."

"What sort of conflict?" Dana asked.

"The kind that pits the Kingdom of God against the City of Man, as Saint Augustine wrote about."

"And the kind," Gina added, "that's reared its ugly mug this election cycle."

"Word."

"Let's say you're right," Dana said. "Demons are real, that these—principalities and powers Paul speaks of are wreaking chaos on our world. What does this have anything to do with this case?"

"What every Group X case has been about," Elijah answered. "The Gospel of John, chapter 10."

"*Qué es?*"

"*'The thief,'*" Gina quoted, "*'comes only to steal and kill and destroy. I came that they may have life, and have it abundantly.'*"

"And don't forget," Elijah added, "Peter's second letter, chapter 5: *'Like a roaring lion your adversary the devil prowls around, looking for someone to devour.'*"

Dana nodded, recognition dawning on her face. "The Devil and his minions."

"Rising up to destroy what is most precious to Yahweh, the very beings who bear his Image."

"*Hombres y mujeres.*"

"Bingo. You and me and all humanity."

"Growing up in the Church," she added, "I've never heard anything about Watcher-spirits and their influence on our world—on us."

Gina smirked. "You and me both, sister."

She went to offer a follow-up point when something caught her eye.

A dirty white building with a faded red roof. Boarded and shuddered, the four-car parking lot cracked and sprouting waist-high weeds. Looked like a sad loaf of white bread—or maybe more like a dinner roll.

Except...

She slowed, glancing around the neglected stretch of road—with overgrown sycamores towering overhead; Craftsman houses of various colors that were all the rage in these parts at the turn of the century, their porches slumping with rot and roofs covered in moss; a brown-bricked Lutheran church that looked shuttered; leaning telephone poles with strings of saggy black wire going this way and that.

Gina knew that building, a building from childhood. All of them were, but this one carried a special place in her heart.

The DQ.

Her neighborhood Dairy Queen.

Lots of memories at that place. Mostly of her and Grace peddling their Huffys the few blocks up the way from their trailer park for soft serve cones (vanilla-chocolate swirl for them both) and the swings on the playground at that corner Lutheran church next door.

But what was it doing here, on this road racing through her *inexplicitus* case?

Crucially: What were *they* doing here, on this road racing toward destiny?

"Alright, slow down," Chester announced. "We're here."

He gestured toward the left again, a sign coming into view behind a grouping of well-manicured evergreen shrubs.

Presidential Estates.

Her breath seized in her chest; that word—*here!*—jolted her to a stop.

A brake-slamming stop.

"What the what?" she shouted as the car skidded across the wet pavement, Eli and Dana and Chester throwing up shouts of protest. Good thing they were buckled up nice and tight.

"Where's the fire, Gina colada?" Eli asked.

Gina turned to Chester. "D-D-Did you say—"

She lost her breath, the words tripping dumbly over her tongue without any oomph to voice her question.

And the horror behind it.

She swallowed and slowed to a stop. Then she got to it: "Did you say we're here?"

Chester licked his lips and glanced back at Dana before pressing his back against his door and giving his head a nod.

"Egads, man! You didn't tell me we were going *here*."

Elijah leaned forward. "Gina, where's here?"

She threw him panicked eyes. Eyes that met his own—those wide, chocolate orbs yanking her back down to Earth and settling her heart some.

Swallowing again, she could only whisper: "Here is home."

Took a beat, then it registered.

"Oh my cheeps!"

No one moved; no one said a word. The only soundtrack for their rodeo was the continued *rappity-rap-rap-rap* of the rain on the SUV roof and Gina's heavy breathing.

Until the *honkity-honk-honk-honk* of some impatient nincompoop was thrown up from behind. Gina had half a mind to throw them the middle-finger salute but gripped the steering wheel tighter and confessed her unkind heart instead.

Then eased up on the brakes and motored toward destiny.

"Suppose now we know how your mama got involved," Elijah said. "Some crazy person with a DSL connection must have befriended her, sucked her into the vortex of his conspiracies."

"Yeah..." was all Gina could muster. Because she flat wasn't sure about that.

Regret welled within at the years that had passed since she'd last been in touch with Mama. Sadness roiled and boiled at the thought of all she could have done to keep her mother from the clutches of the Eye of God—keep her from red-pilling and tumbling down into the rabbit hole and any other well-worn cliché that sent her spinning into Crazyville.

Or the other thing she feared...

Chester gestured down Presidential Lane, a sad stretch of cracked pavement flanked by even sadder memories. Trees were taller than she recalled, the passage of time evident in the maples and oaks, along with the disrepair of the mobile homes lined along the road.

Not a one of them looked any different from last she recalled, memories peddling past them seared into her brain. From the siding colors to the flower boxes lining the weathered porches, the rusted basketball hoops to the tiny, weather-worn sheds. The still life of a former life that meant nothing good.

"Gina…" Eli whispered, shaking her loose.

"I'm going." She followed Chester's direction down the gullet into Presidential Estates. Right past Johnson and Taft avenues. Thought he was going to send her down Theodore Avenue for a second, but he was only going for an itch on his nose. At Nixon Drive, he sent her left.

Which sent her heart galloping into her throat and pounding in her head.

Went straight down the road clear to Eisenhower Drive, where Chester pointed dead ahead to a familiar double-wide and a flower bed.

Her bed.

And her childhood home.

It was nothing like she remembered it.

Looked brand new, with a fresh roof and bright blue siding. Some major cabbage did that, money Mama didn't have. A large satellite dish was anchored to the roof, too, sending and receiving who knew what kinds of transmissions.

Or breadcrumbs, as was the case with the Eye of God.

"See, that was their mistake," Chester said, pointing to the dish. "One of the most unsecured lines of communication, those things are. A little computer science know-how and several pizzas and cases of beer later and I traced the original breadcrumb to this here spot, where the Eye of God resides."

"B-B-B-But—"

There was that stuttering again, something that hadn't plagued her since childhood. Since finding her sister swinging from one of the rafters in that house!

"But *they* is my mother!"

"Your mother?" Chester asked.

"My mother!"

Eli snorted a laugh. "Is there an ech—"

Gina's hand flew an inch from his face, cutting him off at the pass. "Neither the time nor the place, Eli."

"Sorry..." He raked a hand through his hair and rubbed the back of his neck. "But if you're right...if Chester is, and this is your mama's house—then wouldn't that make her the Eye of God?"

Gina's head bloomed with the implications of the question. And the revelation. All of it.

The front-page photo. Seeing a fleeting glimpse of her at Eli's childhood church. The clear sighting of Mama canoodling with Billy Baron at the Gallego rally at Freedom University—right before she drove off in a bleepin' government-issued Suburban!

"Now what?" Dana said, snapping her back to the moment.

Gina knew exactly what.

"Now we get answers."

Easing the Mercedes forward, she crunched across the gravel driveway and threw the SUV into *Park*. Then shoved out into the rain toward Mama's house.

She took a faltering step, then another, reaching the stairs—the only thing left untouched from childhood. Gina grasped the rough, rickety two-by-four wood railing that led to the front door, took a breath, then a beat, then ascended.

Stairs threw up a familiar complaint beneath her adult feet, the same one that chimed under her childhood grayed over from weathered neglect. A pair of letters caught her eye, still etched into the corner of the top stair.

G + G.

Gina plus Grace.

Sisters forever bound by their twin identities, by their mutual love.

Her breath seized in her chest, her belly tightened with the sour memories and horrifying present reality.

She was not ready for this.

But she withdrew her keys anyway, grasping a faded metal house key and shoving it into the knob—hoping it still worked for the good of the case, but praying it didn't for the good of her soul.

The key turned easily, the knob along with it.

Taking a breath, she shoved inside, the air hot and humid, clawing and cloying with those scented candles Mama loved. Cinnamon mixing with rose petals mixing with grass.

And glue.

Lots and lots of glue.

A tremble seized Gina's body. Started in her head and neck and ricocheted down her spine and out her limbs into her hands —hot and heavy and heaving. Tried clenching them shut and making her legs go rigid, but it was no use. The synapses in her brain were firing on all cylinders and needed to release the neuro overwhelm at what her peepers were peeping.

She wanted to vomit. Could feel the bile rising at the back of her throat—sour and salty—even as her mouth salivated something fierce preparing the hatch for a major evacuation.

But it was more than that.

It wasn't so much a stomach reaction as it was a neural one, her body needing to expel the confusion and pain and fear and overpowering emotions welling within.

A meltdown was coming.

CHAPTER 28

Elijah wasn't prepared for what he stepped into. Not in the slightest.

Gina stepped through the portal first, followed by him, with Dana and Chester making up the caboose.

"Mama?" Gina called out without a reply. She hooked a left, shuffling into a large room before stopping cold.

He kept right, scoping out the other half, a far from impressive sight.

A kitchen with newish stainless steel appliances sat to the right—and a grimy mess of stacked dirty dishes in the sink, all caked with leftover macaroni and cheese; countertops covered in newspapers, articles clipped and pictures snipped; a nasty smell of onion and cabbage and spoiled beef wafting high on a hot, humid breath from the stove; bloated flies buzzing around carrying all manner of nasty.

Across the way was a tiny bathroom—which Elijah didn't even want to think about what was waiting for them, given the state of the kitchen. Down a narrow hallway was a closed door, which he assumed led to a bedroom. Again, didn't want to think about the state of affairs in that joint—unmade bed with covers strewn about, piles of unwashed clothes, soiled undergarments.

He shivered at the thought.

Not sure where the idea this abode was a double-wide trailer came from. Was flat false advertising as far as he was concerned! Far narrower and cramped than his DC row house, that's for sure—which was saying something, because his pet teenage goldfish (affectionately named Goldie) had more swimming room than they had right now.

Goldie also had more to look at. The whole place was dark and unlit. Didn't help matters that it was covered in cheapo faux wood paneling, making Ron Burgundy's bachelor pad look like a SoHo condo. Totally threw off the feng shui of a—

A squeaking startle followed by a mournful moan was thrown up.

Sounded like Gina.

He spun around. She stood at the threshold of what looked like the living room, more of that wood paneling plastered over the walls—but also plastered over by wall art. Couldn't tell what, because Gina was in the way.

And trembling.

Her petite frame looked like she was manning (womanning?) a jackhammer, her shoulders were jiggling so much. Same for her arms, which were elevated at her side but trembling. Same for her hands, which started flapping.

Uh-oh…

Elijah gasped. Knew exactly what that meant.

Rumbling. The precursor to a meltdown. Had never seen her slip into one while working together. Usually managed to keep her distracted and diverted during the pre-rumbling phase, calming Gina with fidgeting or music and guiding her from triggering neural overwhelm. But this didn't look good. Way further along than he'd seen her before.

But why? What had she seen, what overpowering emotional trigger had sent her reeling?

"What's with her?" Chester asked, those bug eyes of his shifting from him to Dana then back again.

Dana backed up against the countertop. "Elijah…what's gotten into—"

He threw up a not-now hand and shuffled after his partner.

Seeing what had set her off.

"Sweet mother of Melchizedek…"

It was the living room alright, filled with upscale furniture that looked out of place—a glass-and-chrome coffee table and end tables of the same; a long English tan leather couch with matching overstuffed chair. And covered in that putrid wood paneling, windows sealed with thick black plastic. Modest and cramped with that upscale furniture and piles of books, along with two large metal desks mounted by three computers shedding the only light they had on the situation from three large displays. Looked like they packed enough CPU horsepower to launch a tactical nuke.

Or a roving mob hellbent on taking America back again.

But that wasn't all. Not in the slightest.

The walls were scrawled across in big, bold letters—some red, some black, all definitely the hand of a woman. Not a sexist observation in the slightest. Just a flat fact, the letters delicate and cursive and precise.

And all super familiar.

> *Trust the plan.*
> *We are winning.*
> *Arrests will come.*
> *The storm is coming.*
> *The Great Awakening is nigh.*
> *Nothing can stop what is coming.*

All of the wackadoodle nonsense that had been spouted by Billy Baron.

But what were they doing in Gina's mama's house?

Joining those phrases were pictures—black-and-white print-outs on copy paper. Main Street storefronts, American landmarks, even some houses. Yarn was strung all over the place, from tiny pushpins in each of the pictures stringing out to more printouts—long text in tiny type, some to those wackadoodle phrases Baron quoted. A definite *A Beautiful Mind* vibe to the joint, something straight out of *One Flew Over the Cuckoo's Nest*!

"I-I-I..." she stuttered on a disbelieving breath, trailing off before heaving a lungful of air and trying again.

Nothing came. Mouth just flopped open like Goldie, a guppy searching for air to give voice to her questions.

Right before she threw her hands on her head with a *smack*. Fingers gripped her hair something fierce, those ginger locks of hers squeezing through her clenched fingers like Play-Doh and straining against her head.

Then she screamed. Bloody murder. A high and heady hysterical cry of dereliction, as if she had abandoned herself, losing her mind in the face of the overwhelming sensory overload staring her in the kisser.

Or perhaps it was the other way around.

She had been abandoned by the person behind the wackadoodle wall, her mama having taken leave of her brain and leaving Gina to pick up all the pieces. Because if Chester was right, Gwen Anderson was the Eye of God—and this was her lair.

Before he knew it, she was lunging into the room—leapfrogging over a pile of books and onto the glass coffee table before catapulting toward one of the walls.

And reaching for the ceiling with both hands before swiping them across the pastiche of wackadoodle printouts—

Ripping them from the wall with wicked slices through the paper.

Then again and again, grabbing for the pages in clumps and tearing them to shreds.

The evidence that would blow wide open their Group X case from hot Hades!

"What the—" Chester cried out before being interrupted by

Dana.

"No!" she screamed from behind. *"Basta, basta!"*

She shoved past Elijah and ran to Gina. "Enough, *muchacha!"* Then laid both hands on her shoulders.

Which was the wrong move, on so many levels.

Before either she or Elijah knew what was what, Gina spun around and threw a punch—the back of her hand swiping across the reporter's face in a hideous *smack!*

The sound was livid and wicked. It also looked like it gave Gina a momentary pause in her meltdown.

Which Elijah used to reset her neurons.

Stepping between her and Dana, he put up his hands. Both, not just the one they usually used to stabilize one another when things got saucy.

Took her a beat, but after half a decade of them both perfecting the neuro reset technique, her brain snapped into gear and mirrored his pose.

Elijah threw up a prayer of thanksgiving to Yahweh Almighty, grateful for his success.

So far.

He swallowed and heaved a breath. "It's me, Gina colada."

Wide, frantic eyes met his. Saucers of fear and confusion compounded by a mountain of sour memories. They were matched by flaring nostrils and an open mouth huffing and puffing desperate, stabilizing breaths, her chest heaving and hoing something fierce. The visual of his partner, his friend, in her trauma was made all the worse by her jittering body, her shoulders and arms, hands and fingers, legs and knees and feet all jumping and jiving to beat the band. A live wire, she was, crackling and sparking with a bazillion unaccounted feelings and emotions inundating her to the point of short-circuiting.

Could only imagine what was zipping along those neurotransmitters of hers and racing through her noggin. It was bad enough seeing Eddy Lee's reaction to the fear-induced hysteria, let alone his entire former childhood church caught up in the political madness. But to see her own mama at the center of it all —who was adding up to be the wackadoodle Eye of God figure who'd stoked a blazing scythe of fear across the country…

Was flat horrified and appalled at the atrocious turn of things in Gina's family tale.

Lord Jesus Christ, Son of God, may your peace that surpasses all understanding guard Gina colada's heart and mind!

No sooner than he had finished his prayer did Gina blink. Then again. As if waking from a dream, then landing smack dab into a nightmare. Now she swallowed and heaved a breath, easing it out of her nose before taking another easier one. You couldn't pray away autism, but Elijah had sure asked his Savior more times than he could remember to offer a helping hand through the overwhelm.

"I'm sorry," Gina said, looking Dana in the eyes, tears filling them before spilling down her cheek. "For assaulting you. For…" She trailed off, gesturing toward the wall she had torn apart.

The reporter nodded, a weak smile playing across her face. *"No hay problema, amiga.* No worries. I'd say I understand, but I don't. But…well, I understand."

Chester was standing in the entrance to the living room now, a deer in headlights. He said nothing, taking a halting step inside, as if to assess whether it was safe to enter, before making for the computers and clickety-clacking on a keyboard.

Elijah sighed, relieved the meltdown had passed. He threw up another prayer for good measure, taken from his people's prayers, Psalm 46: *Yahweh Almighty, you are our refuge and strength, a very present help in trouble. Help Gina not fear, though the earth should change, though the mountains shake in the heart of the sea, though its waters roar and foam, though the mountains tremble with its tumult…*

Tumult was right! Gina's entire world had just been shaken, turned all topsy-turvy.

Because things had just gotten real.

Bigly real because they were bigly personal.

He asked, "What is all this? What does it mean?"

Dana stepped over to the wall that Gina had worked a number on, kneeling and picking up a crumpled-up piece of paper.

And gasped.

"This is it…" she said with marvel, smoothing out the page before caressing it. "Ground zero." She turned to them, pointing at the printout. "It all began with a single post. This one!"

Elijah took it, a sheet of delicately scrawled letters, the kind a woman would make (again, not sexist; just the facts, ma'am), and twisted up his face in confusion at what he read:

RS extradition already in motion effective yesterday with several countries in case of cross border run. Passport approved to be flagged effective 10/30 @ 12:01am. Expect massive riots organized in defiance and others fleeing the US to occur. US M's will conduct the operation while NG activated. Proof check: Locate a NG member and ask if activated for duty 10/30 across most major cities.

"RS?" he asked, glancing at Dana.

"Robert Santos," she answered. "M means military. Since then, there have been thousands—literally thousands of breadcrumbs like these. Silly, conspiratorial bits of secret insight into what's supposedly coming to save the Republic. There's a date, too. They're all dated, all the breadcrumbs from the Eye of God written on single pieces of paper."

"Perhaps—" Gina's throat stumbled over itself. She apologized and swallowed. "Perhaps she copied them by hand from the interwebs, from the WeChan forum."

"Not likely," Chester said from the computer. His clickety-clacking had stopped, and he was pointing to the screen. "The originals are all right here, the whole mess of them strung out on a digital clothesline like dirty laundry in her personal WeChan account."

"Her personal WeChan…"

She huffed a sigh, bringing a trembling hand to her head. Then she slumped down on the couch, crunching into papers strewn across the cushions and leaning back to stare at the ceiling.

"Suppose this makes sense, though."

Elijah went to her, kneeling. "What does?"

"Mama had always been a fair-weather supporter, waffling across the political aisle when it suited her, following which way the winds were blowing."

"Clearly blew her off a cliff…"

She said nothing to that one.

"But this was all so manufactured," Dana said. "All of it, from these servers to the satellite dish, then clear through to the ravings and breadcrumbs."

She went to Gina now, still seated, still still. "Does this—any of it—make sense? Could your mama have pulled something like this off?"

Gina just shook her head and shrugged, too dazed and confused to process the personal turn of things.

Elijah didn't know what to make of it all, not in the slightest.

Lord Jesus Christ, Son of God, make haste to help us make sense of this…

"Now what?" Gina asked.

Good question.

The trio glanced about while their fourth wheel kept clattering at the keyboard.

"What the what…" Gina said.

She raced to a wall and snatched a picture. Wait, two.

Elijah joined her, scratching his chin. "What gives, Gina colada?"

She stood still, eyeing what she'd retrieved.

One was the front page of the *New York Times*, with a few politicos looking like they'd thrown back a few too many. An older white woman wearing an American flag dress sandwiched between a black middle-class desk jockey and a Colonel Sanders wannabe from Woodstock with a wicked birthmark staining the right side of his face. The second was a shot of the older woman and black man, both dressed to the nines.

"Who are they?" he asked.

"The woman, in the flag dress in the newspaper photo, then the fancy one in the other, is—well, it's Mama."

"Really? Quite the looker."

She threw an elbow into his ribcage; he yelped.

"If you're into that sort of cougar thing," Elijah said with a cough.

"*Tu madre,*" Dana said, "looks like she's at a political rally."

Gina nodded. "Cheering for Gallego. That's what the article caption says. Read it when this whole *inexplicitus* case started."

"And she's with that same black man," Dana went on, pointing at the second photo, "she's standing next to at the rally."

Gina nodded, saying nothing more.

"Who's the *hombre*?"

She shook her head. "Not a clue."

"Dude looks like he's getting fresh with Mama," Elijah said. "And at some fancy-shmancy dinner. Maybe a fundraiser, for Debby Gallego?

"*Psht!*" Gina scoffed. "With what money?"

"The plot thickens," Dana said.

Elijah nodded. "A riddle, wrapped in a mystery, inside an enigma."

"I might know," Chester said from the other end of the room.

Dana turned to him. "Know what?"

"About the money."

He was hunched over the monitors and motioning them to gather.

They did, sidling up beside the man pointing at the monitor.

Elijah asked, "What are we looking at?"

"Wire transfers," Chester answered. "Lots of them. In large sums of money."

Gina leaned over for a look-see. "To who?"

"To whom…" Elijah corrected, instantly regretting it. Sometimes he really hated his mouth and his brain for the particulars.

She didn't respond, but Chester did. It was a whopper.

"Your mother."

"For reals?" Gina exclaimed.

"For reals."

"But there's like hundreds of thousands of dollars in these transactions!"

Elijah said, "Suppose that explains the fancy furniture."

"And the new roof and paint job," Gina acknowledged.

"Along with the satellite dish," Dana said.

Chester added, "I traced them to an off-shore account."

"How?" Gina asked.

"Don't ask. I also traced that account to a super PAC—"

"Whose?"

"Not sure whose, but it's called America First USA."

Elijah scoffed. "That's not redundantly redundant at all…"

Gina grunted a smirk of her own. "If that's not clear who that cash cow belongs to…"

They all said as one: *"Gallego."*

"Probably."

"And it looks like," Dana said, "they've been paying your mother a bunch of pesos, too."

"The Eye of God, you mean," Elijah said.

Gina frowned, but nodded. "Now what?"

Elijah knew the first order of business. He snatched the

photos from Gina and whipped out his phone. A Jitterbug dumbphone he'd switched to after disavowing smartphones a few months ago. Still had a camera, so it was a win-win.

"Hey, those are mine!" she complained.

"They're Group X's," he replied as he snapped some pictures. "And we need help with them."

"What sort of help?" Dana asked.

"Our guy, Abraham Patel, is a genius with this sort of thing." He pecked out a message instructing him to figure out who that dude was. "If there's anyone who can locate and name our *mal hombre*, it's Abe."

"Good idea," Gina said, brightening some. "Still leaves next steps for us."

Elijah eyed the room. "Suppose we could sift through all this crazy."

"We don't have time, with the election looming and America a powder keg ready to blow."

"And Watcher-spirits ready with a Bic to set it ablaze."

"And that," Gina sighed, crossing her arms and tossing her gaze around the room again.

Until her peepers landed on something behind Elijah.

"What the wa—"

Then beelined it to the wall of crazy, snatching another picture. One of those old-school Polaroid photos of three people, arms slung around one another and looking plastered.

A young black man. A white frat boy with a port-wine stain.

And a Gina colada lookalike.

"Oh me cheeps! Is that our Three Musketeers?"

Gina said nothing, hand trembling at the reveal.

"Sure looks that way," Dana said. "Which means they knew one another, from a long time ago."

"How?" Gina wondered in a whisper.

He eased the photo from her hand. Taking out his phone, he snapped another picture and sent it to Abraham to check into their connections.

"Uh…guys?"

It was Chester, staring into a darkened closet behind those nuke-capable computers that looked like a hoarder's fever dream.

Dana went to him, peering into the void.

And threw up a startled string of Spanish.

Elijah and Gina turned to one another before darting to investigate.

They were not prepared for what they found.

Hoarder's fever dream was right! But the politico kind, with every manner of campaign poster and button and tchotchke for major candidates stretching back decades!

That wasn't all.

"Are those voodoo dolls?" Dana asked.

Elijah added, "For every. Single. Presidential. Candidate?"

Gina reached for one, a little cloth doll wearing a black skirt with short blond hair. "No, not every one. Just the ones who lost the past few decades."

"Sweet mother…" He trailed off. She was right. "It all makes sense!"

"What does?" Dana asked.

"I read about something like this during President Orange Hair's reign on the interwebs—"

"*Un momento!*" Dana complained. "I thought you scoffed about reading things online."

He smiled. "I'm a bundle of contradictions. Anyhoo, it was this exposé on witches drumming up spells to cast against the president. Even linked to this wackadoodle website to buy your very own presidential voodoo dolls. Clearly, Mama bought into the voodoo magic. They've even got needles shoved into their brains!"

The reporter turned to Gina. "Did you know about this?"

She swallowed, shaking her head. "Growing up, we were told to keep away from the closet on pain of death. Grace and I thought it stored her Precious Moments collection and Christmas decorations."

"There was a collection alright."

Gina set the doll back inside the closet, swatting at her eyes. "How does this happen…"

Elijah felt real bad, his partner discovering this secret about her mother, her legacy. Suppose it's true that kids don't know their parents like they think they do.

"I'll tell you how," he answered. "Clearly, your mama opened herself up to the cosmic powers of the Unseen Realm with this voodoo dabbling. But it was more than just mainlining the occult into her soul. The other drug did the rest, which she then peddled to the masses."

"*Qué droga?*" wondered Dana.

He shrugged. "What else but fear? I mean, look at this closet. She marinated in it. The political campaigns, the newspaper articles strewn about the joint. Giving her reverence and awe to Uncle Sam in this way, the perfect candidate winning, the right party owning Congress and the Supreme Court."

Gina crossed her arms, tipping her head in consideration. "Suppose she did talk about nothing else growing up."

"There's a reason the Book of Proverbs says to guard your heart, '*for from it flow the springs of life.*'"

"You are what you think."

"Bingo."

She turned to the closet, shaking her head. "Mama sure did stuff her heart full of this stuff. Stuff it full of fear."

"Only question is," Dana said. "*Ahora que?*"

Elijah nodded. "Now what is right…"

Gina answered, "Didn't Billy Baron say something about storming the Capitol Building?"

"That's right, some Gallego rally. One final college try before it's election D-Day."

Dana asked, "You suppose *tu madre* will be there?"

Gina laughed. "Is there any doubt?"

Elijah turned to her. "You know what that means?"

She nodded. "DC's the next stop on the crazy train."

"No, the *final* stop if I have anything to say about it."

Because something told Elijah the Capitol was the terminus.

The end point.

One way or another.

CHAPTER 29
WASHINGTON, DC.

The sky was spittin' angry that morning, sending down the kind of slapping rain that hurts your face and your feelings.

And Gina didn't like it. Not one bit.

She and Elijah and Dana had just gotten off the Federal Center Metro Station—which was quite the ordeal getting Eli to ride the dang thing! If she thought coaxing him to ride cross-country in the passenger's seat of an SUV was bad enough, cajoling him to get into a steel tube filled with who-knew-who who had been who-knew-where was the furthest thing from a tumbler of gin. Had to promise him she'd sit through his binge-watching marathon of *The West Wing* to get him to hop to it. That did the trick.

Good thing, too, because it was the only way into where they were heading: the National Mall, for Billy Baron's promised rodeo. Not only taking America back again, but storming the gates of hell to reclaim America for Christ again.

Greeting them was the storm from Dante's Inferno, the rain as cold as his 9th circle of hell. Chilled her right to the bone, but that wasn't even the reason for the frigid surface. Though the face-slapping rain was a pain in the backside hustling under an umbrella that had seen the sad side of the bottom of her closet, Mother Nature's rainy backhand wasn't the real bummer.

It was the vibe crackling through the air smelling more than the staticky electricity of the fall-time storm, joined by the scent of woodsmoke and dead leaves gusting in on a wicked breeze—a smell more than fall and more like…more like.

Gina had it!

Like grandma's sweaty armpits joined by that Pall Mall cigarette smoke that had burrowed its way into every nook and cranny of her own double-wide, with an added goodly dose of boiled cabbage and hamburger simmering in the high-noon sun.

It was the smell of rot, of desperation.

Of fear…

Didn't know where it was coming from, not in the slightest. But the sensation, along with the not-right feeling, had instantly assaulted her when they surfaced on 3rd Street. There'd been times throughout her life when she'd sensed things—like she was sensing now. Dialing into a mood, a *zeitgeist* (thanks high school German for the translation), a spirit of the age (and thanks Philosophy 101 for the deeper translation)—really a spiritual undercurrent permeating a space, even as large as the National Mall.

Maybe there was something to those sailors and their red-sky warnings of impending doom. Because when she was awakened by her mewing Maine Coon at the butt-crack-of-dawn, the horizon was on fire with a five-alarm red that spelled no uncertain doom before those gray, engorged storm clouds raced across the region.

Now she wished she hadn't skimped on a cheapo Walgreens umbrella and instead had sprung for a Burberry golf-style kind. Along with taking her Bible, a Rosary, and her Glock.

Because something told her she'd need all three in spades for the cray-cray that was waiting for them up ahead.

"You know, it's funny," Dana said as they reached the D Street crosswalk.

"What's funny?" Elijah asked.

"Back when I still worked in DC," she started, "Up ahead at the Capitol Building, I had what you could say was a vision."

"A vision?" Gina said, brow furrowed and growing impatient at the orange hand telling them to wait.

"About this place burning to the ground."

"Sounds like a shroom-style vision," Elijah scoffed. "That's not funny, that's creepy."

Gina smacked his shoulder; he yelped. She had to do that sometime.

"No less creepy, *muchacho*," Dana replied, "than your own vision of—what was it? The Unseen Realm and three demons—"

"Three Watcher-spirits," Eli corrected, "and a cosmic Prince directing their demonic traffic."

She smirked. "Whatever they were, you saw them after biting the dust and I didn't finger you for a kook."

"Touché," Eli said as the angry hand turned to a permissive white walker.

They crossed the road, a real crowd joining them.

"So, this vision of yours..." Gina said.

"*Bien*. It was springtime," Dana explained, "and the cherry blossoms had just fully peaked. The Capitol grounds were blooming with soft pink flowers and the air was tinged with a sweet scent. I remember walking out of the building one evening to a set of benches lining one of the walkways toward Constitution Avenue. I had just come out of a weekly meeting with a number of representatives from the Religious Right, and this time they were clamoring for my boss to do something about overseas religious persecution."

Eli shivered, saying nothing but saying all he needed to say.

"It wasn't like I didn't agree," she went on, "but it was the way they went about it that was exhausting and infuriating. So I took a stroll and had what I can only describe as an apocalyptic vision. Right there on a bench outside the Capitol Building."

"Sounds like shrooms to me," he mumbled again.

"Eli…" Gina said, throwing him a look as they reached another orange hand at C Street.

Dana continued, "I remember taking off my coat and stretching my legs out on the stone path, and I was staring at the Capitol Building when it hit me: *Dana, one day this is all going to burn.*"

"It's all gonna burn?" Gina asked, not understanding.

"What do you mean by that?" Eli echoed.

Dana chuckled. "I understand how crazy it sounds, especially after 9/11 and all the terrorism we've seen around the world. But I had this apocalyptic image of the Capitol Building crumbling to the ground and flames shooting from the Rotunda high into the sky. Again, totally crazy, but the bigger thing about it was that I realized all the glitz and glamor, the prestige and posturing didn't add up to a hill of beans. None of it mattered. It was all worthless."

"Word," Eli said.

Gina added, "Suppose that does put things into perspective. In the end Christ will be king, all other emperors be damned —literally."

"Couldn't have said it better myself," Dana said.

"What's that sound?" Eli asked, the white walking man giving them the green light to cross again.

Hustling across the street, Gina cocked her head. "Sounds like singing. A choir and some crooner bellowing."

"Yuppers. Def singing. Not just a choir, but a whole sanctuary full of people belting to beat the band."

The towering government buildings of functional, concrete eyesores from the mid-last century obscured the lyrics and blocked any visual of what lay ahead.

At least the rain died down, so Gina could put away her janky umbrella that was doing no good anyhow.

"Whatever it is, *amigos*," Dana said, "looks like we're about to find out."

Going with the flow of bodies cresting toward the National

Mall, a real swell of folks rallying for Debby Gallego and Billy Baron, they soon reached Independence, then Maryland avenues —the dome of the Capitol Building on the right, looking a pale reflection of its normal gleaming glory under the storm clouds; a stage coming into view dead ahead.

Along with those lyrics coming into a clearer hearing.

Eli groaned as they approached. "You may have wanted your vision to come true sooner than later, Dana Diaz."

"That *hombre loco*," Dana said, "singing that *muy loco* song of his."

Beginning with that crazy chorus that set Gina's teeth on edge. The one that echoed Gallego's campaign slogan: *Let's take America back again…*

A real crowd had gathered in front of a massive stage set up in front of the reflecting pool, the Capitol Building an apropos backdrop. Gallego-Baron fans galore packed the front and clear across 3rd Street and down the Mall toward the Washington Monument, with massive LCD screens as big as houses positioned along both sides for fans to see the action.

Billy Baron was back at it, clearing the second verse and belting the bridge now that was as blasphemous as his fake hair:

> *Not by might, nor by power*
> *But by my spirit, says the Lord*
> *Not by might, nor by power*
> *But by my spirit, says the Lord*

Then again, the crowd joining him in his fervor:

> *Not by might, nor by power*
> *But by my spirit, says the Lord*
> *Not by might, nor by power*
> *But by my spirit, says the Lord*

Holding the mic out to the audience, he joined them in

yelling *"And Debby Gallego is the one who'll—"* before jumping back into the chorus.

> *Take America back again*
> *By bringing prayer back in schools again*
> *Let's reclaim America for Christ again*
> *By taking America back again*

Gina led the charge pushing their way to the front of the pack at the stage. Got lots of sneers and dirty looks, even a few f-bombs, but they managed to reach close enough to see Billy Baron's spittle flying—just as he led his flock in the final stanza:

> *Let's evangelize our oldest friends*
> *And point it out when they're backslidin'*
> *Remind them of the gospel and then*
> *We'll take America back again*

The band did their twang guitar and *dum-ditty-dum* drum thing to wind down the song.

"Amen, amen, amen, tribe! Before I turn to the Word," Billy Baron announced, "I'm gonna do a little thing I like to call a diatribe."

"Go on!" one man yelled down the row. "Amen!" shouted a woman from behind.

And on he went—talking nothing about the forgiveness of sins, the resurrection of the body, or the life everlasting. Instead, it was politics all the way down. Perhaps not surprising, but for a minister to be speaking that way...it was jarring. And gut-wrenching.

He riffed on everything from California's forced school-children vaccines to the IRS shaking down nonprofits for their donor rolls. He promoted a new book that supposedly exposed "how the left has done a power grab to systematically dismantle religion and banish God from the lips, minds, and hearts of believers."

A middle-aged couple in front promptly whipped out their phones. Gina could see the Amazon app on each, then the book, then a one-click purchase.

She scoffed and shook her head. Boomers.

"You know," Baron went on, gripping the microphone with both hands and smiling, offering up a chuckle, "we had a visitor a few Sunday mornings ago to my Kentucky church—"

Gina threw a quick glance at Eli. His face was pinched and red, jaw muscles pulsing with anger. She understood the feeling.

"They says to me, 'Pastor Billy, it's really refreshing to hear a minister like you talk about issues like this.'"

More roaring, more cheers, more hoots and hollers. Billy Baron basked in it all with a wide, toothy grin.

"And you know what I told that couple?" he boomed. "I says, 'I'm okay talking about these things. I don't give a darn tootin' if the IRS cancels me for these diatribes. Because I speak the truth.' And as we all know—"

"The truth shall set you free!" the crowd roared, quoting the eighth chapter of John's Gospel—and horrendously out of context!

"We are born for such a time as this. God is raising you up to do something. We have a country God wants us to get back." He paused, shaking his head. "That ain't far enough, is it? Because we have a country—yes, I'll say it—to *take* back."

"By force!" a lone voice shouted from behind.

That was quickly followed by more voices, a growing cry that became a chant.

"By force! By force! By force!"

Billy Baron stretched out his hands and pressed them toward the ground to silence the growing anthem, a grin playing across his mouth.

"Now, let's not give the Santos administration a reason to

bring out the brownshirts!" He laughed, not at all phased by the dark turn of things.

"This vibe," Dana said, rubbing her shoulders. *"No me gusta…"*

"Dark," Gina agreed. "Real dark."

"Not just dark," Eli added, "Demonic."

A shiver ratcheted up her spine at the revelation. Dead on the money, Eli was.

"Think back with me," Billy Baron went on, shouting like the Baptist preacher he was, "to the Philistines of the Old Testament. They up and stole the Ark of the Covenant from the Israelites. The very footstool of God! Why? Why'd they go and do a thing like that?"

He waited a beat, then another, searching the crowd for an answer.

"Because they knew the only way they were going to defeat God's chosen people was if they separated them from God! If they erected a separation between God and Israel. The same thing has happened in America! Liberals have devised dastardly plots to erect a wall of separation between Christians and God, between the Church and State! And too many Christians have let it happen!"

"Oh my cheeps," Eli exclaimed, "Did that bozo just equate God with the US government?"

Gina nodded, saying nothing.

"You know what I say to that?" Billy Baron shouted. "Mr. Santos, tear down that wall!"

Her partner snorted a laugh. "Cue the Regan reference."

Gina said, "Suppose you can't have a Republican political rally without one."

"Interesting choice," Dana added, "equating the religious wall of separation with the Berlin Wall."

"Let me tell you something, tribe," Billy Baron shouted, pacing the stage, "Debby Gallego is the only one who has the backbone to tear down that wall! She's a godly woman and a patriot, standing against the tide of socialism and satanism to take America back again! But what does the media do? Demonize her patriotism by calling it nationalism and associating that with Hitler. Then it's white Christian nationalism, so they'll make it sound like y'all are the ayatollah. It is all designed to demonize you. And Debby Gallego won't stand for it!"

Another round of hoots and hollers, giving Billy Baron a window to wipe his sweaty face and get a drink of water.

"My 11th great-grandfather escaped religious persecution on the Mayflower, and look at what his godly passion built—America! You may never see the fruit of your labor, but I can tell you this: God will use your obedience to change this great nation."

He pointed at the crowd, jabbing his finger at his soldiers.

"We've got a window of opportunity, right now, this election, to convert millions of Americans to the principles of liberty and to biblical values because of the insane chaos of the last four years thanks to that man Santos. Standing before me is a tribe of warriors, under the direction and command of Jesus Christ! He is King of Kings and we are going to lawfully, peacefully, and democratically take back this country and our culture in his name."

He stepped to the edge of the stage, face sweaty and blotchy from his diatribe. Then he gripped the mic and bellowed: "And hear this, President Santos," he spit, "there ain't nothing you or any of the other powers and principalities can do to stop us!"

"*No me gusta...*" Dana said again, shaking her head.

Had to agree.

Billy Baron stepped back just as a man in an American flag cowboy hat and shirt stepped over to him, joined by Debby Gallego. Patriot Cowboy was holding something that Gina couldn't make out.

"Sweet mother of Melchizedek," Eli exclaimed. "Is that a sword?"

Gina squinted, the light catching the object just right as Gallego took it from the man.

Yup. Sword. A long thing of gleaming polished metal.

"Billy didn't know I was going to do this," Gallego said, gesturing to the sword, "but I've got a little present for you."

Baron clutched his heart with both hands with dramatic flare and shuddered backward a few steps, mouth wide and face flashing the crowd a look of surprise.

"I present to you this sword, partner, inscribed with the words *'For God and country.'* Because you've been cutting a lot of heads off lately!"

The crowd went wild, laughing and cheering and hooting their approval.

She continued, "Lord knows you are fighting for our religious rights in Christ Jesus, and so we wanted to bless you with that sword of David!"

Baron took the sword's hilt and raised it high, eying it and grinning widely.

"Debby, dear, aside from a heart-felt thank you, I just got one thing to say."

"What's that, partner?" she said.

"Where's Goliath?" he roared.

The crowd ate that line up, throwing up a thunderous reply as Baron waved the sword around in one hand, his Bible in another.

Then he turned toward the Capitol Building.

"There it is!" he shouted, receiving another thunderous applause and chorus of hoots and hollers. "There they are—all the Goliaths, the uncircumcised Philistines coming against God's people. Daring to stand against and defy God's army!"

"What's going on?" Dana asked. "*Qué es esta tontería?*"

Billy Baron threw up a guttural cry of defiance—of war. Like a Berserker ready to unleash the full fury of his bloodlust.

Or an army…

"I'll tell you what this nonsense is," Eli answered. Before he could finish his sentence, Baron did something entirely unexpected.

Taking a few steps back, he leaped from the stage into the crowd—a sea of hands catching him, the reverend body surfing his followers.

"The Great Awakening has begun!" he screamed. "Onward, Christian soldiers, marching as to war. With the sword of the Spirit going on before!"

"Oh my cheeps," Eli exclaimed. "That's not how it goes!"

"What goes?" asked Dana, a cry of bloodlust echoing all around.

He turned to her. "The Baptist hymn. The words are: *'Onward, Christian soldiers, marching as to war, with the cross of Jesus going on before!'* A song about enduring hardship for the sake of the gospel, not launching a crusade against the government!"

Gina seized his arm, then promptly let go, the turn of things making her forget herself, and their aversion to physical touch.

"I don't think they got the memo..." She pointed at what had startled her so.

That sea of followers Baron was still riding was indeed marching.

Past the stage and on toward the white marble reflecting pool, the crowd surging around them with the same war cry and threatening to sweep them off their feet.

"*Dios mío,*" Dana cursed. "What are they doing?"

Gina said, "Storming the Capitol Building, what else?"

"The worm has turned," Elijah said. "Bigly."

"What do we do about it?"

CHAPTER 30

'll tell you what we do about it," Elijah said, the surging sea of bodies carrying them farther on. "We join them."

"What?" Gina exclaimed.

"*Estas loco, muchacho!*" Dana agreed. "Who knows what's about to go down? They could be planning to storm Congress for all we know!"

"Exactly," Elijah said, the Capitol Building looming large now as they passed the reflecting pool, raindrops dancing upon the dark water as the engorged storm clouds rumbled overhead. "Something's driving these wackadoodles. A vibe, a force that's more wicked and supernatural than I've felt in a while. I want to be there when it's unleashed."

The crowd flowed past a forest of naked trees, a few of the oaks and maples still clinging to their leafy dignity but most barren and haunting, their scraggly arms reaching out as if to yell Halt! A large statue of some general riding a stallion high upon a boxy marble foundation tried in vain to offer the same warning, his pair of bronze lions acting as useless guards against the mob driven to the brink by Billy Baron's sermon mainlining fear and anger into their veins.

The Capitol grounds were straight ahead, the dome dark and

the shadowy facade hiding a looming presence that promised wicked things to come.

"*Dios mío...*" Dana cursed before throwing a pointer stage right. "Look!"

Took a beat to get her meaning, but then Elijah did. A whole army of men and women were dashing forward, from behind and toward a long walkway leading straight toward the People's House—guarded only by a short metal security barrier and a pair of Capitol Police officers looking like cows at a railroad crossing with a locomotive barreling their way.

A warning was raised to halt from the pair, but the mob overtook them in an instant, the bodies enveloping the cops.

Rage raced through Elijah at the violence. As a former FBI agent, he still bled blue for his fellow officers of justice.

"Come on!" he called out, racing to help—

When he was interrupted by an insistent vibration at his leg. His phone.

Skidding to a stop, he whipped it out.

Group X HQ. Probably Abraham Patel.

"Hello?" he answered.

"Why hello there, Mr. Fox! A right banger of a day, isn't it?"

"Who is it?" Gina asked.

"Abraham," Elijah replied, then returned to his granny phone: "You could say that, Abe, but we're sort of in the middle of it."

"Ahh, yes. Your *inexplicitus* case with the most intriguing of circumstances—and evidence."

That's right, the photos from Gina's mama's house!

He punched it to speaker, announcing Gina and their friend Dana as the mob continued to swirl past them, threatening to carry them away in the tide of violence.

Elijah said, "Whatcha got for us, Abe? Who are they?"

"The lovely lady in both pictures is a woman by the name of Gwen Anderson."

"We already knew that."

"Ahh, yes, well, at any rate, I was curious: Any relation to our intrepid agent Gina Anderson?"

Elijah threw her sympathetic eyes; hers cast down to the ground.

"You could say that," was all he replied. "What about the others, the men?"

"Well, the one is none other than Billy Baron."

Gina snapped her head up. "For reals?"

Elijah raced a hand through his hair. "Sweet mother of Melchizedek!"

"*Imposible,*" Dana said. "That *muchacho* with the mustache looks nothing like him! Especially with that port-wine stain birthmark on the right cheek."

"Ahh, the beauty of disguises," Abraham replied. "Sophisticated algorithmic software striped the bloke of his ruse to uncover the truth."

Gina sucked in a startled breath. "That's right…"

"What's right?" Elijah asked.

"When you grabbed for him, back in Kentucky, your hand swiped some makeup off from his face, revealing a birthmark underneath. Didn't put it together until now, especially with the crazy disguise."

"It's confirmed, then. Your mama was in cahoots with Billy Baron."

She nodded, saying nothing more.

Dana asked, "What about the other *hombre loco*?"

Elijah nodded. "Right, the black man."

Abraham replied, "That took a bit more digging, but I managed to find an identification photo for a one Deshaun Johnson."

"What photo?"

"Old driver's license from Harrisburg."

"Harrisburg?" Gina exclaimed, jaw dropping.

Elijah turned to her. "That ring a bell?"

"That's where Mama is from…"

"Another Keystone State resident, eh?" Abraham asked.

"Keystone?" Gina scoffed. "Try Buckeye."

"Sorry, mate. You're a right confused one. Pennsylvania is the Keystone State. There is also a Harrisburg, Ohio, but not where Johnson is from."

Elijah smirked. "That's 'Merica for you. No originality."

"Wait," Dana said to Gina, pulling out her phone, "*tu madre* is from Harrisburg? Ohio or Pennsylvania?"

She nodded, then shrugged. "Mama's parents had long passed, and I'd always assumed it was Ohio. Now…"

The reporter thumb-tapped her way across some app, Abraham clattering on the other line as well, then showed it to her companions.

It was the map app—showing Harrisburg a hop, skip, and a jump away from York.

Gina squinted, shaking her head. "I don't under—"

"I do," Elijah said. "James Maxwell introduced Billy Baron as a former student!"

"For the love…"

"And it appears," Abraham said, continuing his *clickety-clack* keyboarding, "Gwen Anderson is also a former resident of the Keystone State Harrisburg. Another DMV record, from high school."

"Welp," Elijah said, "I'd say that completes the triangle of connection."

Gina smacked her head. "The bleepin' picture…"

He nodded. "Word."

"Speaking of—" Abraham cleared his throat "—bleepin' pictures…all three matched the images of the people in the Polaroid as well."

"There it is. The whole taco. The love triangle."

Dana asked, "Who is he, this Deshaun Johnson character?"

Abraham answered, "The Legislative Director for a congressman."

Gina flashed him wide eyes. "Which one?"

"Congressman Calvin Dobson."

Elijah whipped his head up toward the Capitol Building, the mob having mounted a rising wall up to the second story, as well as scaffolding flanking the western facade. Like rats swarming a carcass.

Readying to devour it without mercy.

"What if that's the end game?" Gina said. "Taking down Caldo the Magnificent!"

"Who?" asked Dana.

"Cal. A pet name I had for—oh, it doesn't matter! No way it's a coincidence one of his congressional staffers is snapped canoodling with Mama—from now and then!"

"*Yo no sé*," Dana said. "Why would Dobson's staffer be plotting to bring his boss's ruin? And why would she be playing both sides—canoodling, as you put it, with Billy Baron?"

Gina sighed. "I don't know…Clearly they knew one another from decades ago, but—I don't have a bleepin' clue."

Neither did Elijah.

Abraham said, "I might have something on that front. Johnson's financials show he started only recently, a few months ago. And long story short, with lots of digging, I also traced him to a shell corporation that brought me to another entity he's the president of."

"What's that?" Elijah asked.

"Something called America First USA."

He gasped. Sweet mother of Melchizedek…

Spinning to Gina, the pair locked eyes and said in unison: "*A mole!*"

"*Dios mío*," Dana said. "The off-shore political action committee Chester found funneling money to *tu madre*."

"Giving us motive, means, and opportunity," Elijah said, shaking his head.

"The criminal case trifecta," Gina said. "Makes sense how that carcase could end up in Cal's congressional office."

"Which means the Democratic veep candidate could be in

danger, if this Johnson guy is so committed to this wackadoodle ideology that he would try and scare him off, or worse—with two sidekicks mainlining supernatural, demonic fear."

"Caldo…" Gina moaned, face falling.

"Except, aren't they all on the campaign trail?"

"*Hoy no,*" Dana said. "Not today. There's a special session of Congress this afternoon. An emergency vote on sanctions against China for the Taiwan invasion and a debate on a declaration of solidarity with the island nation."

"Oh my cheeps…" Elijah said. "So Dobson really could be in danger!"

Gina said, "All of them could be with the way this mob is running."

"Surely their security is prepared," Dana replied.

Elijah hooked a thumb at the two officers who'd been trampled. "Given what just went down, not likely."

"*Dios mío…*"

Thanking Abraham for his work, he said goodbye before ending the call and shoving his phone into his pocket.

"We better get the show on the rollercoaster. Pronto."

He led Gina and Dana dashing up the brick walkway toward the People's House. Which looked more like the monkey exhibition at the Smithsonian National Zoo!

Both sets of massive steps running up along both chambers to the first floor below the Rotunda were filled with people. Men were hanging from stone railings and that scaffolding rising up the building facade. Others were stacking up debris—wood planks, pieces of that metal security barrier, benches—and helping other men and even women climb onto the landing that was the west front before a fountain bubbling as if there wasn't a care in the world.

Crashing sounds were heard, the breaking of glass chief among them. And was that gunfire?

Elijah's back pulsed with his own piece, and he felt like he was violating a bazillion laws carrying it onto the Capitol Hill grounds. Didn't care. Crazy times called for concealing and carrying.

Just hoped he didn't end up in the clink for it.

A thunderous whooping and hollering was thrown up just as they reached the base of the stairs ascending the House side of the building.

Right before the boiling crowd of insurrectionists began funneling inside the Capitol Building's wounded side.

Gina gasped. "Did they breach the bleepin' thing?"

"Looks that way…" Elijah said.

Dana cursed in her foreign tongue. "Such sacrilege, busting into the People's House in this way."

Poor lady. Had to imagine she was gutted seeing her former place of employ stormed like Normandy.

He asked, "You know of any other way inside?"

She nodded. "*Sí.* But, given the breach, I have to imagine it's sealed tight and the entire place is on lockdown. Experienced those a time or twelve thanks to suspicious packages in the years after 9/11."

"So follow the mob, then?" Gina asked, edging up the stairs.

Dana took a breath and nodded, taking the lead with Elijah and Gina close behind.

Didn't take long before they reached the seat of the U.S. government, the trio racing up the wide white marble stairs on toward the crowd of bodies funneling inside an entrance that had been broken through.

Joining the mob, the river of bodies swept them inside a darkened vestibule and took them up a set of polished stone stairs edged with bronze railings into the Rotunda—a massive space soaring high above, with a cloudy fresco of hovering cherubic, angelic beings high above through the dome's oculus.

Following his gaze, Dana explained, "The Apotheosis of Washington."

"As in George Washington?" Gina asked.

"*Sí.* You can fit the Statue of Liberty in here, you know?"

"Thanks for the nickel tour," Elijah said, spinning around and eyeing several massive oil pantings of famous scenes from America's founding. "But we don't have much time until Calvin Dobson and his colleagues join our first president in his celestial abode."

Nodding, she darted back toward where they'd come from. "Follow me. I have an idea."

They pushed through the stragglers back down the stairs and circled around behind, shoving into a cramped, round space directly beneath the Rotunda, the ceiling low and held aloft by short, squat limestone columns as round as sequoias.

A smattering of people were milling about, unsure what to do. Some were toppling displays of the building's history. Even a model of the Capitol had been upended, its dome shattered. Others were marching around carrying flags—some American flags, but most representing various states of the Union. Caught some of those crazy Eye shirts—the triangle bisected by a line looking like an I at the center. But most were sporting pleated pants and high-waisted jeans and septuagenarian velcro shoes of various shades of oatmeal and licorice.

"What is this place?" Gina asked as Dana hooked a right toward the Capitol's south wing.

"The Crypt."

"The what?"

"Crypt."

Elijah asked, "As in for dead bodies?"

"They don't call it the Crypt for nothing," Dana replied. "Time was that Washington himself was interred in a chamber beneath the center down below."

"Eww!"

"Come on."

A short distance stage right and they came into a small, round clearing, with a view above to the second floor. Same plain, faded limestone columns and floor polished to a shiny sheen, walls painted pistachio and salmon. Very plain spoken.

Far less fancy than Elijah would have thought for the center of American power.

"This way!" someone shouted. A woman.

Glanced up to see a familiar face wearing a familiar Old Glory dress, joined by another familiar character.

Goat Man. The brute with the furs and painted skin and goat's skull mask.

"Gina…" Elijah said, pointing up.

She glanced at him, then craned toward the second floor.

And gasped.

"Mama?"

Gina skidded to a halt, her mother racing around the railing, ginger hair laced with silver whipping behind, while a group of hoodlums in white T-shirts followed close behind. Presumably Eyes.

She called out again, but it was no use. The woman disappeared from view.

"Where does that lead?" Gina asked Dana, eyes wide with desperation.

"Down past the Speaker's office and on toward—"

The reporter faltered, her throat stumbling over itself before swallowing and heaving a breath.

"On toward where?" Gina demanded.

"The House Chamber."

"Can they get inside?" Elijah asked.

"*Yo no se,*" Dana replied. "I wouldn't have thought they'd been able to breach the Capitol Building, but—" she swept her arm behind, the roving mob at the rear trashing the Crypt saying all she meant.

"How do we get there?" Gina asked.

Dana looked apprehensive, eyes shifting around and hands going to the top of her head.

But she nodded and started off. "Follow me."

She led them through a narrow, nondescript hallway of

brown limestone, edged by mahogany wood doors and keypads. Looked like offices. All closed, all sealed tight.

Dana raced past a set of ornate elevators of wood and gold, clumps of insurrectionists boarding them for higher ground with a few police officers cajoling them to come out. No weapons drawn, not yet anyway. Looked flat stunned at the turn of things, uncertain what to do.

Hooking a left, unabated by any sort of law enforcement force, Dana took them down another long hallway lined by office doors and to a set of wide stairs.

They took them, shouts of hoots and hollers echoing down from above as they reached the second floor into a hallway of boring beige walls with a bust of some Congressman chilling inside the wall. At least the floors looked descent, tiled in bright rust diamonds and sky blue circles and with larger yellow vines forming large circle patterns down the center.

Old men in dark suits raced by in a panic, trailed by equally panicked younger ones, presumably their staff.

"That's Congressman D'amato, from New York!" Dana said. "And was that Congresswoman Hildebrand in the red dress?"

Elijah said, "Looked like they were getting out of Dodge real quick."

"Def running away," Gina said.

A muffled *pop-pop-pop* erupted. Down the hallway, around the corner.

He instantly whipped out his Glock, toting his trusty sidearm of choice from back in his FBI days.

"Was that gunfire?" Dana asked on a shaky breath.

Elijah didn't answer, instead running toward the sound, which led him into a large outer room painted light mint and paved in more of that attractive tile, leading to a set of open mahogany double doors—where more of those *pop-pop-pops* were coming from, joined by the hoots and hollers of a mob drunk on mayhem.

"*Dios mío…*" Dana moaned. "The House Chamber. It's been breached!"

Didn't even think about what came next. Just headed into the breach, coming into an ornately decorated chamber of dark wood walls about the size of a high school gymnasium. Was smaller than he imagined, with rows of leather-cushioned wood chairs all dutifully lined up across bright navy carpet with orange blooms. All arrayed facing a large dais of wood desks standing high like a tiered cake, crowned by the Speaker of the House's oversized leather chair. Behind, the Stars and Stripes hung proud on a beige marble wall, flanked by two bronze classical Roman fasces, a bound bundle of rods with an axe gleaming in the light. Above ran the words "In God We Trust" and a gallery that normally sat members of the press and touring public, along with large digital displays tallying the legislative vote count.

Not this day.

Legislators weren't the only ones occupying their chamber, some cowering in corners wearing gas masks looking to escape the marauders, others shouting red-faced at the barbarian intruding horde.

The scene was surreal.

Men and women in fatigues, some sporting those Eye of God shirts, were rummaging through the leather satchels left behind on the chairs and stacks of papers on massive wood tables at the front. Others were tossing the contents of those cases to the floor, laptops and books clattering across the carpet. Still others were throwing those stacks of papers high into the air, the pages fluttering about like frantic birds as others overturned tables and flipped over the leather-padded wood chairs, some tearing down priceless oil paintings—destroying the Hall of the House of Representatives.

"What a desecration…" Gina moaned, a hand covering her mouth, tears slipping down her cheeks at her former world turning to ruin.

"Yuppers. But where's your—"

A howl from the front cut him off.

Sent his bowels to the floor and his arm reaching toward the sound with his Glock. Sounded like the menacing call from the Unseen Realm, the one that had haunted them the past few missions.

In many ways, this was far worse.

Goat Man had mounted one of the dais desks, a barrel-chested shirtless black man clutching Old Glory and a revolver with the other. No doubt Dobson's staffer.

The man let another set of pounding *pop-pop-pop* shots ring out—aimed high into the ceiling without ill intent, just for show —before howling again through that Baphomet skull mask of his.

That wasn't all.

Next to him was a wrinkly version of Gina colada, sitting in the Speaker's chair and looking like she was having the time of her life!

"Mama…" Gina whispered before yelling: "*MAMA!*"

A joyous noise erupted from the woman. A cross between elation and euphoria.

"You've come, Bug! You've come!"

Bug?

Elijah turned to her but realized it was neither the time nor the place to venture into that nickname. His partner's face was stricken. Pained and pinched. Doused by an equal measure of tears and fury, her cheeks blazing red beneath blood-shot eyes and above quivering lips.

Just like last time.

Her hands flew to her head like before as well, those ginger locks of hers squeezed through her fingers like Play-Doh. But before Elijah could intervene, she tore down the aisle.

"Gina—"

Beelining it for her mother, who was giggling like a drunken fool. Arms raised and twirling in that overstuffed leather chair on her knees.

He took off after his partner, reaching her just as Gina reached her spinning mama—

And screamed bloody murder!

Right before she shouted, in a whimpering cry: "*CALDO!*"

Didn't register at first.

Until it did.

"Oh my cheeps…"

There he was.

Calvin Dobson.

Hogtied with duct (not duck) tape covering his mouth.

And a big, fat I drawn in black marker across its shiny silver sheen.

"*Dios mío!*" Dana cursed. "What is this?"

Good question.

Was about to ask it, too, but Gina beat him to the punch.

"*What the hell have you done!*" she screamed, hands clenched into a fist and arms ramrod straight against her slim body.

That sucked the wind from her mama's sails!

She stopped spinning. Face fell. Shoulders shrugged.

"Why, taking American back again," Gwen replied, "what else?"

A wicked grin spread across her face, and she returned to spinning, a cackle rising high.

Before Gina could respond, a terrifying roary, snorty, skittering screech resounded through the House Chamber. Small at first before quickly crescendoing, as if emerging from a tear in the fabric of reality itself.

Elijah's breath caught in his chest at the sound, a cold dread spreading through him, sending every hair on his body standing at attention.

It was back. The thing of nightmares.

A bassy blast suddenly roiled the room, as if a concussion

device had detonated in the center, sending an aftershock racing through the chamber and carrying with it another deep moan.

Before all at once ceasing into an eerie void.

"What the heck is that thing?" Dana said, bracing herself against one of the rows and staring wide-eyed, pointing to the gallery above.

"Nothing from this world," Elijah replied, following her gaze, "I can tell you that."

"What do you mean?"

Before he could answer, the chair where Gina's mama was sitting started shuddering with intensity, her body vibrating like a marionette.

Gina gave a frightened yelp. Same for the others in the chamber.

Elijah took a step toward the supernatural display, keeping his eyes fixed on the Being from the Unseen Realm that had breached their own seen one.

"The Devil is with this one…"

Before Dana could further interrogate him, the door to the House Chamber slammed shut with such force that a crystal sconce anchored to the wall fell to the floor with a crash. The instruments of congressional sausage-making—laptops, glasses of water, pens and paper, books—startled rattling around the chamber. A pitcher of water jumped from the ornate desk where Mrs. Anderson was seated and crashed to the floor.

Then all hell broke loose.

Literally.

CHAPTER 31

t was back. The thing of nightmares.

The Being that had haunted *Gina's* nightmares the past few years.

A Watcher-spirit, as Eli had called it.

A Fallen One…

Out of nowhere, something emerged from the shadows of the House Gallery—from another dimension, even. A hulking figure, with a bulbous head resting atop wide shoulders corded with muscle, sauntered toward the railing above. Skin rippled in scaly waves with an iridescent glow as it reached the edge behind Goat Man and Gina's mama.

Something straight out of a Stephen King fever dream!

And yet…

Gina couldn't take her eyes off the Being—which was all at once beautiful and hideous. There was something attractive about it. Enticing, even. As if it was what she had been waiting for her whole life—to give meaning and definition and purpose to her identity as a woman, as a human.

An Angel of Light. Come to save humanity.

Come to save America.

Or bring it to its knees.

"Who—" Gina faltered on a shaking breath, then: "—or what is that?"

"The puppet master," Elijah answered. "One of the Watcher-spirits. Or perhaps America's cosmic Prince himself."

"*Dios mío…*" Dana squeaked, covering her face.

"No. Not your God. A son of God. Semjaza is my guess."

Gina went to reply when—

With sudden, supernatural levitation, Mama's body began moving with a wicked arch. Her arms stiffened with outstretched reach and belly rose dramatically toward the ceiling, body bent like a wishbone.

A crying shudder ricocheted around the chamber at the sight.

"*Mama!*" Gina screamed with terror.

She started for her, but was held back by Elijah.

"Let me—"

He was cut off by Mama falling and flopping down to the floor in a dramatic twisting of limbs.

Before anyone could react, her mother started screaming a frantic, hysterical howl—eyes bulging from their sockets and mouth wide with horrifying abandon.

"Mama…?" Gina said, wide-eyed with panic yet frozen with indecision.

Not Eli. He activated without a thought. Knew exactly what was needed.

She liked that about him. Because she was at a loss. She was done.

Flat undone!

Her partner stepped forward on cool, cautious steps. "Stand back. All of you."

Shoving his Glock at his back waist, he spread a commanding arm, pushing Dana out of the way while inching closer to Gina's mama. With his other one, he brought out a gold crucifix from the inside of his shirt.

Mama was jolted backward at the sight, skittering into the

chair and sending it rolling off the end of the dais. She bowed her head toward the Christian icon and fixed it with a penetrating gaze Gina had never before seen from her, eyes narrowed and dark with glaring ill intent.

Then a sound emanated from her being. Which sounded eerily familiar.

A terrifying roary, snorty, skittering screech. A cross between a strangled sheep and irate mama grizzly bear.

The same one Gina had heard throughout her FBI career, and then again in their two previous Group X cases—and moments ago.

But now it was coming from Mama!

She growled and glared at Elijah, then gnashed her teeth at him.

In a burst of jumbled words, she started muttering on about good and evil, God and the Devil, repeating those crazy I-Og phrases they'd seen scrawled across her living room.

Elijah stood resolute, unmoving. "The Lord rebuke you, O Satan!" he said with a commanding voice, taking another step and holding the crucifix with an outstretched arm.

Mama shuddered backward and lashed out with a wicked gnashing of her teeth again.

"What is going on, Eli?" Gina said with strain, her lips quivering with a mixture of shock and horror and fear at the woman who'd given her birth, raised her and bathed her—her flesh and blood babbling and gnashing and flailing in the face of her partner inching closer with his outstretched crucifix.

He replied with a choking whisper, "The Devil has shown himself. And in your dearest mama—"

All at once, she fell silent. No more muttering, no more screaming. No more writhing and flailing about.

The House Chamber went silent, all movement and motion seeming to hang in one dramatic suspension of time.

But then Mama began talking again. When she did, a new persona emerged. Something rose up within her, guttural and gravelly, like that of a deep-throated man whose voice was being masked from identity on those undercover news shows.

And the most unexpected thing happened.

The Being, the Watcher-spirit—it floated down below, taking its place behind Mama!

"She is mine, this one," the Voice hissed from her mama's mouth, the Being's own mouth unmoving. *"Mine!"*

Gina brought a hand up to her mouth, head swimming with confusion at the truth of what it all meant.

Was her mama possessed?

By the Devil himself?

She snarled and bared her teeth at Eli, who thrust the crucifix in her direction again, repeating his command: "The Lord rebuke you, O Satan!"

Then he added a prayer, pleading with the Holy Father, Son, and Spirit for assistance: "Oh God, come to my assistance! Oh Lord, make haste to help me! Oh Everlasting God, who have ordained and created the ministries of angels and men in wonderful order: Mercifully grant that, as your holy angels serve you in heaven, they may help and defend us on earth at your command. Through our Lord Jesus Christ, your son, who lives and reigns with you in the unity of the Holy Spirit, one God, forever and ever. Amen."

Another guttural moan followed by a high-pitched screech echoed throughout the chamber. The familiar grizzly bear strangling the sheep.

Lord Jesus Christ, Son of God…do something!

All at once, the Being raised a scaly arm, and Mama's head started flailing from side to side, cocking back at odd, inhuman angles—in sync with the Watcher's motions!

Gina rushed forward to hold her steady, but was held back by her partner still planted firmly to the floor.

"Stand back, Gina colada!" Elijah commanded.

"But we must do something!"

"We are."

"But—"

She was cut off by another screech slicing through the confusion, followed by a weak cry.

"*Help me!*" came a familiar voice, meek and mousy and full of trapped dismay, trailed by wracking sobs that heaved the woman's body up and down with a mournful shudder.

It was Mama, the real one, in all of her glory. Trying to break free.

Then the Voice returned, the one of demonic intent: "*You humans have your own sense of time,*" it hissed with the same guttural growl. "*I have plenty of time. I have all the time in the world. I've been biding it, saving it, stashing it away with this one…With this nation!*"

Gina's head swam with wide-eyed horror. Mama had done it. Opened herself up to the Devil, allowing him to gain a foothold in her very soul!

The voice shifted into a staccato whisper now: "*It's your mother I want,*" the Voice said through Mama, staring straight into Gina now with those haunting, slitted eyes brimming with a menacing wickedness she recalled from past investigations.

The Voice continued, "*Not only her, but America's soul!*"

As the Voice spoke, Mama jerked her head from side to side, as if carried along on strings by a halting puppeteer until Gina thought her head would pop off.

"That explains it then," Elijah said matter-of-factly, hand still gripping the crucifix.

Gina couldn't even speak what was wedged in her throat questioning what the hey-ho day Eli was talking about.

Dana voiced it for her: "Explains what, *muchacho?*"

"The Watchers were using her to sow chaos and fear in 'Merica—your mama literally possessed by Fear."

Mama's motions suddenly slowed. Her head began swaying from front to back like a viper hypnotized by the fabled snake charmer.

"The Nameless One can't save her," the Voice within Mama screeched. *"Do you understand that? She's mine, Gina Anderson!"*

The mention of her name by that hideous voice sent a frigid shudder through her bowels. Thought she'd lose them then and there!

Then Mama went silent. Just the HVAC hum and the distant mayhem outside the House Chamber echoing their way.

"Who are you?" Eli asked, not backing down.

A bassy cackle erupted—not from Mama but from the Being still standing behind her.

Holding the crucifix outstretched, he pressed, "In the name of Jesus Christ, what is your name?"

The Being staggered back, as if sucker-punched or hit by a sledgehammer, doubling over and bracing a hand against the desk.

Then again: "I command you in Jesus' name—reveal yourself!"

It finally relented.

"FEAR!" the Voice erupted from Mama in a roary, snorty, skittering screech before the Being threw its bulbous, scaly head back in a high-pitched yet growly and rumbly wail—the chamber shaking and quaking again under the unholy, wicked weight of the Unseen Realm, in the flesh.

Gina recoiled at the name, but it made perfect sense.

Fear.

It also seemed right on the moolah. The last two cases they'd learned something about these—Beings or demons, the Watcher-spirits or whatever. Their strength and power seemed to come from their name. So this one was Fear, wielding the same power.

Which had been unleashed against America, holding it in its grip.

And through Mama!

Eli pressed further: "What is your business with this woman?"

A laugh erupted from the Being, the sound cackling from it like a strangled goat. Bleating and braying, strutting even.

Then: *"To sow the seeds of discord in our land through the bonds of fear!"*

"Our land?" Elijah said with a start, glancing Gina's way. "Whose?"

Another laugh, guttural and horrifying before: *"Semjaza..."*

Recognition swept through Gina. Eli was right; there it was. A revelation of the cosmic geography he'd surmised.

"And we found an all-too-willing vessel for our designs. Several, in fact, the tinder of our spark to inflame our nation with fearful discord and tear it apart—limb from limb!"

Bile rose hot and heavy at the back of Gina's throat. Sour and tangy and threatening to escape without notice.

It was all too much. Mama was that vessel. So was Baron, and Eli's childhood church. Along with all the Eyes strewn across the land who had followed their breadcrumbs straight into the fearful Abyss.

If recognition had hit her partner, about how the cosmic powers of supernatural darkness had leveraged his daddy's church, he didn't show it. Just stoic and steady, like always.

No one moved, no one made a sound, no one thought to breathe lest they crack the truce that seemed to spread between the parties. Even Eli had ceased his prayers and supernatural fighting words.

Until Fear raised an arm and curled its long fingers that were more like tentacles—all six of them!—into a fist.

Another bassy rumble overtook the chamber. More glass and laptops and books clattered to the floor, followed by bulbs in those crystal sconces splintering all along the wall.

In the middle of the melee, Mama suddenly arched her back. Her face transformed into a series of menacing poses—her cheekbones and lips and eyebrows contorting in ways not thought possible.

The lights above dimmed and flickered before brightening

back again, sending jolting bolts of fear skating up Gina's spine and terrified panic blooming in her skull.

"*Dios mío!*" Dana cursed, throwing her hands over her head.

The writhing continued. It was almost as if Mama was fighting within herself. As if something inside of her was fighting for her very soul.

"Eli…" Gina yelled, not able to take it any more. "End this!"

Elijah took a careful step forward and began praying aloud, beseeching Jesus Christ and his blood to combat the very forces of hell.

"Almighty and eternal God," he shouted with all of the authority given him by Jesus Christ himself, "who appointed your only-begotten Son the Redeemer of the world, and willed to be appeased by his blood: Grant, we beseech you, that we may so honor this, the price of our redemption, and by its virtue be so defended from the evils of our present life, so as to enjoy its fruit in heaven forevermore, through the name of Christ Our Lord. Amen."

Another guttural moan followed by a high-pitched screech echoed throughout the House Chamber. The grizzly bear strangling the sheep—the roary, snorty, skittering screech that had come from the psycho at Cracker Barrel their first mission.

Then it changed, on a dime.

A cackle broke out from Mama in response. Which turned into hysterical giggling, almost like a spoiled child. Soon, her body started heaving with guffawing belly laughs from deep inside her being.

Gina's partner switched to praying a familiar, trusty portion of Scripture for such supernatural confrontation—a version of Psalm 40: "*'Do not, O Lord, withhold your mercy from your servant; let your steadfast love and your faithfulness keep them safe forever. For evils have encompassed your child without number.'*"

The cackling continued, but moaned and groaned something fierce, as if the Voice within Mama was recoiling from the Word of God being proclaimed against it.

Eli took sturdy steps forward until he came face-to-face with Gina's mother and the Watcher puppet master. Then continued directing his prayers at the Being: "*'Be pleased, O Lord, to deliver your servant; O Lord, make haste to help her. Let the forces of darkness be put to shame and confusion who seek to snatch away her life; let those powers be turned back and brought to dishonor who desire her hurt.'*"

The cackling continued, but seemed to be more pained the more Eli spoke.

Then Eli's finale: "I rebuke you, Fear, and command you in the name and authority of Jesus Christ to come out from this woman, to leave this chamber, and to retire from these lands."

That turned things real quick!

"I. WILL. BE. BACK!" the Voice suddenly screamed. "*Mark my words, we will meet again—both of us!*"

The Being disappeared into the shadows with a thunderous shudder. Mama slumped down on the dais.

She suddenly twisted toward the floor and vomited, letting loose a stream of green and brown liquid that seemed far more than her body could have held. It arced in a climactic splash on the navy carpet, then dribbled down her chest.

All at once, she wilted to the floor, disappearing behind the wood desk.

"*Mama!*" Gina screamed, racing past Eli.

Her mother was moaning, and her eyes were fluttering open. Gina reached for her, finding her cold to the touch yet clammy and damp with sweat, her hair matted to her head.

"Wha...where am I?" she moaned. "What have I done?"

She looked as though she had just wrestled an alligator or grizzly bear to the ground. Which, in many ways, she had!

"I am so sorry," she panted, "So sorry..."

"Shh, it's alright," Gina whispered, cradling her and kissing her head. "It wasn't your fault."

"I don't know what came over me."

Fearful dread swept through Gina. She looked at Eli with worry, wondering what had come over her mother.

Except they all knew what had come over her.

Even Dana seemed positively shaken by the encounter, her face fixed with horror and staring at Mama as if she were an alien.

Cradling her, Gina pleaded with Eli, "Help her…"

He went to respond when the lights dimmed to sudden darkness.

A beat later, yellow emergency lights from across the chamber flickered on, casting eerie shadows across the room.

"For the love…More demons?" Gina complained.

"That was no work of the Devil," Eli said, stiffening before stepping back with worry.

A sudden muffled cracking of *pop-pop-pop* shots echoed outside through the closed chamber doors. Then another, a more violent and violating series of shots.

Different tone, different timbre.

"We've got company," Eli said. "And it's not the demonic kind."

Before they knew what was what, men in black tactical gear came rushing into the chamber.

They'd stood against the darkness.

And lived to tell about it.

Today at least.

But Mama…

Gina looked down at her slight frame, then up at the agents swarming the chamber.

This could get ugly.

CHAPTER 32
ELECTION DAY.

Welp, the dreaded day had finally come.

Election Day.

Gina didn't know much—especially who would win. She did know one thing for sure: A major throwdown was in order! And she knew how to bring it.

Thankfully, only for two—five if you counted her cats. After all the mob cray-cray, a quiet night watching the returns come in was in order. Just her and Elijah, who took some cajoling (aka teeth-pulling), but gave in when she promised libation would flow like the salmon of Capistrano. Beer, wine, whiskey, a mean gin and tonic with some Southern charm, made with wild-grown Kentucky elderflower, smelling like honey and lemon.

She was an election hostess with the mostest—which wasn't even touching on the donkey burgers (aka bison burgers) and elephant dogs (aka Oscar Mayer wieners), joined by a mustard potato salad that was her mama's recipe (thought it fitting, given the past week) and a fresh-baked apple pie for dessert (which she knew was Eli's dad's fave; again, fitting).

Gina had just finished stringing the last of the red streamers to join the blue and white ones racing across her living room ceiling when the door *ding-donged*.

She checked her watch. 6:30. Which was odd. Eli was nothing if not punctual, and he wasn't supposed to arrive until seven.

Throwing open the door, she was stunned to silence at who was standing on her stoop.

The man smiled. "You came through. Like I knew you would."

Gina clutched her chest. "Caldo the Magnificent!"

Then promptly threw her arms around the man's neck, forgetting herself—not only that he was a happily married man, but also the Democratic veep candidate with a gaggle of Secret Service agents throwing her the stink eye from behind.

She giggled, pushing her ginger locks back into place. "You're right, I came through. And not a moment too soon. You were about to become demon bait!"

His face darkened, and he leaned in closer. "What was that thing?"

"You don't want to know."

He went to respond, but nodded instead. "Suppose all that matters is that democracy lived to fight another day."

"And you too."

They shared a laugh.

"What are you doing here?" Gina asked. "Shouldn't you be at some election party?"

"I was, but needed a break. Nerves and all."

"I bet."

"Wanted to personally thank you for saving my life."

She scoffed. "Wasn't me. Not in the slightest. Thank my partner Eli. Should be arriving any moment now."

Caldo checked his watch and frowned. "I should go. But tell you what, when we win tonight, I'll give you both a tour of the West Wing."

"Can I sit at the *Resolute* desk?" Gina asked.

"Even I can't sit at the *Resolute* desk! For the Commander in Chief only."

"Fine. But I want to stand at the podium in the press room."

"I think I can arrange that."

Gina and Congressman Dobson shared a brief embrace before he was led back into his government-issued Suburban and whisked away.

She watched the reds and blues fade into the DC evening, wondering what could have been.

Then shook herself from such flights of fancy and darted back inside. Went to finish decorating when the day's *New York Times* caught her attention—and the headline.

INSURRECTION NEARLY TOPPLES AMERICA.

Gina scoffed. Way too inflammatory for her tastes, but their new friend Dana Diaz had snagged the above-the-fold exclusive, so she was happy for her.

For Mama, which the article didn't spare from its punches, that was a different story. And a sorry one at that. Filled with everything from the WeChan posts to their discoveries at Presidential Estates to her arrest in the House Chamber when it was discovered she was on a domestic terrorist watch-list when the FBI sorted through everyone inside the chamber.

Who knew? Gina sure hadn't.

Thankfully, their former special agent in charge, Agent Pendergast, had been assigned to process the detainees, and she and Elijah were released and led out of the Capitol Building.

What she saw made her wish she'd stayed behind.

They'd been on the east front, the skies having opened up to a hopeful blue, with those storm clouds shoving off to bother another town, rays of sunlight dancing across the wet pavement. The storm had been upon them, and they lived to see another day. Democracy had as well, those storm clouds parting with optimism. Perhaps there was something to her woo-woo weather vibes.

Escaping no uncertain supernatural doom, she and Eli had stood against a towering Corinthian column to catch their breath, the white marble steps awash in blue and red from a gaggle of law enforcement vehicles swarmed down below.

Everything from the FBI to the National Guard, with SWAT team vehicles and ambulances, command centers and fire engines—even a few mass casualty triage trucks were anchored to the parking lot, which was most unnerving. And snaking through a gauntlet of royally pissed agents were several figures being led into the back of a paddy wagon.

Including two very familiar faces.

Eli had found at least some redemption for his daddy's legacy, that Billy Baron character one of those persons of interest carted away in cuffs. The dude's political career was over before it began. Who knew what would happen, but at least it looked like one charlatan minister mainlining fear into his parishioners' veins and peddling a political antidote to the addiction was out of the picture. At least Eli had that going for him, and he seemed grateful he'd brought resolution to Seventh Baptist Church of Paducah—some resolution for his mama.

Gina on the other hand…

"Look at what I've done," she moaned, her throat catching with emotion at the sight of that slight woman wearing Old Glory slinking into the van.

"Nope. What your mama did," Elijah reassured her.

"But I put her in the clink!"

"She put herself in the clink, along with all the others she led staging an insurrection against 'Merica, putting their hope—*her* hope—in the wrong powers to set the country right."

She just sighed, watching the car pull away with her mama. "What am I going to do, Eli?"

"Look on the bright side. With the way she was possessed like that, a marionette dancing to the strings of that Watcher-spirit, I'm sure she's got a good insanity defense."

"Not sure that makes me feel any better."

"Suppose not."

"Especially since this is the way she'll be remembered. This is her legacy, forever the poster child for Christian-political syncretism."

"Nothing Christian about it. More like supernatural syncretism, the way the cosmic powers of this present supernatural darkness had harnessed the fears and hopes and political dreams of the masses, but I get the point."

She turned to him, eyes wet and red. "I suppose you do, don't you? With the way Seventh Baptist Church of Paducah was made the poster child of the same. That Billy Baron character dragging your daddy's legacy through the mud like that."

Elijah said nothing.

"Can tell you one thing, though," she went on, "this country's never gonna be the same after today. The divisions are too stark, too dark."

He turned to her. "You know what my daddy used to say? *'God doesn't bite his fingernails over any of this. Neither should you.'*"

"Wise words. Sort of like what Jesus said about not worrying about your life, about what will go down tomorrow."

"*'For tomorrow will bring worries of its own,'*" Elijah quoted from Matthew's Gospel. "*'Today's trouble is enough for today.'* That was Daddy's point, especially when it comes to our culture, with all of its injustice and wickedness."

"Suppose that's the truth of it."

Then the soft slam of a pair of heavy steel doors put an exclamation point on their *inexplicitus* case. The back of the paddy wagon carting away Gina's mama. A case that had been way too personal for the both of them, challenging their parents' legacy like that, what they lived and stood for.

Challenging the Church's witness during these fraught, divisive times.

The Enemy almost scored a victory on that front of things, too.

Almost.

Standing against the darkness—against these fear-mongering powers, of all stripes—was exhausting.

Gina shook herself from the memory and got back to decorating.

When a *ding-dong* sounded.

Now it was seven o'clock. Right on the nose.

Throwing open the door for a second time, there was Eli. Cradling a Crock Pot of something with one arm and holding a bottle of some red wine with his other hand. Then he threw up a frightful screech.

"Oh me cheeps!" he said, wrinkling up his face and pointing. "What the heck are you wearing?"

Gina feigned a frown, but a giggle was hot on the heels. She knew exactly what he meant. Her T-shirt.

"You like it?"

"I don't know what *it* is! Notorious RBG? What's that, some dead rapper?"

Now she laughed. "That's B.I.G.."

"Well, who is that wrinkly geezer woman wearing a crown— and what's she doing on your chest?"

She scoffed. "Ruth Bader Ginsburg!"

"The dead Supreme Court lady?"

"Justice. And yes. Shows how much you know. Come in."

She led him to an antique wood mini bar cart with a white marble top veined with black. One of her prized possessions, given to her from Daddy's mother when she passed.

"A drink?" she asked.

"Yes, please! Elections give me the heebie-jeebies. But I came carrying."

He held up his bottle of red.

"Meritage," he said proudly. "Was sort of snooty about it at first, given it was an American invention to skirt import laws concerning French Bordeaux-style wines."

She smirked. "That's U.S. capitalism for ya."

"Can always count on 'Merica to rape and pillage the culture and customs of less-fortunate nations."

"At least it's the French."

"Word."

He uncorked the bottle and poured himself a glass of the dark crimson.

"So, what's with the T-shirt?" he asked, sipping his wine. "Knew you were political, but not *that* political."

Taking a breath, Gina grabbed her drink (a nice Viognier white wine) and downed a mouthful—the fragrant, powerful notes of tangerine and lemongrass and fresh flowers dancing across her tongue settling her mood.

Swallowing, she answered, "She was Mama's hero. Figured I owed it to her, given…"

She trailed off, the pain of putting her mother in the clink still stinging. Even though she had led an insurrection that sought to overthrow the U.S. government!

Elijah nodded, putting up a hand of solidarity.

She joined him, a few millimeters of space between them. Didn't say a word; didn't need to. His eyes said all he needed to say.

Burgers and dogs were waiting, along with her potato salad. Eli had lugged some Kentucky family recipe of baked beans along. Didn't ask questions, just went along with it. They were tasty though, made with black strap molasses and bacon. She squirreled those tasty details away for a rainy day when baked beans was called for.

They watched the results roll across CNN in silence, eating and mulling what it all meant.

After scarfing through dinner, Gina carried over the pie she'd baked, the bottom still warm, and two plates and forks.

"That smells amazeballs!" Eli said.

"Figured an American election night wasn't complete without apple pie."

"Good call."

Gina dished out two massive pieces and handed off Elijah's, then plopped down for the home stretch.

She shoved a bite in her mouth, the cinnamon and tart apple tang sending a shiver through her jaw. Chewing, she wondered about something that had been nagging her from the start of this mess.

"Gina…" Eli said, "you're chewing."

"Uh…yeah." She held up her fork and shoved another bite into her mouth.

"No, not that. I mean, over an idea."

She smiled. He knew her too well.

"You caught me."

"So, what were you chewing on?"

She turned toward him, setting down her plate. "I was just thinking, what do you think Jesus would be like if he ran for president?"

Eli shook his head. "Nope. Ridiculous question."

"Hey, it is not!"

"Yuppers. It is."

"Why?"

"Because he didn't run for president. Or emperor, for that matter. His kingdom was not of this world, as he himself said."

"The Gospel of John," Gina replied, "chapter 18. I'm aware."

"Look at you, all Bible-answer gal!"

"I still think the question is a good one. If not simply as a mental exercise. An object lesson even, for his followers."

He considered this, tilting his head and furrowing his brow.

"Alright, I'll give you that."

"Ha! Did I just get the venerable Doc Fox to admit he was wrong about something?"

"No, you got the venerable Doc Fox to admit you were right about something."

Gina frowned. "Isn't that the same thing?"

"Nope."

"For the love…" She grabbed her plate back and stuffed a bite of pie down the hatch. "Anyway, let's hear it. If the historical Jesus were running for president, what kind of candidate would he be? Republican or Democrat? For or against the death penalty, war, immigration?"

"None of the above."

Chewing again (on the tart apples, not the idea), she asked, "Then what, pray tell, would he do?"

Eli shrugged. "Easy. Jesus would challenge power, not run for it."

She hummed and settled back into the couch. "Do tell…"

He shrugged. "Jesus was a different kind of ruler, of a different kind of kingdom. Didn't originate in this world, but it was meant for it. To transform it, to heal it. The Messiah would have challenged it all. What government spends money on, the cult of personality, how it tramples the needs of the poor. I think the real question would have been what sort of a cross would our government have used to kill Jesus."

"Whoa, truth bomb," Gina said, catching her breath.

"Truth bomb diggity," Eli corrected. "No matter which necktie wins the White House tonight, we'll be alright."

"Maybe shirt or skirt is a better analogy," Gina said, "but I get your point."

Kai Renolds, that dreamy CNN anchor, just announced the final numbers had been tallied and the results were ready to announce.

She slid to the edge of her seat—literally, her backside barely on the couch.

"Here we go…"

Eli just leaned back and sipped his wine, saying nothing but saying all he needed.

Didn't matter a lick.

Fine. Whatev. Jesus was King and all that jazz. Didn't mean us jokers down on Earth didn't have to live with the consequences of which bone-headed leader we put in the Lincoln Bedroom!

"And the winner is…" Kai crooned as a splashy red-white-and-blue graphic of the stars-and-stripes flashed across the screen.

Gina held her breath and closed her eyes, but then she let one eyeball peek for a look-see.

Right before a big, fat purple screen was thrown up with both Santos's and Gallego's mugs on either ends.

And the number 269 chilling underneath each of their photos.

Half of the 538 possible Electoral College votes available.

And one vote shy of the White House.

"Oh my cheeps," Elijah exclaimed, sliding to the edge of the couch now. "Is it a tie?"

"Egads, the election was just 2020ed!" Gina said, mouth open and eyes wide.

"Sounds about right," Eli muttered. "Why not add an Electoral College split to the mix of a viral pandemic and self-inflicted recession?"

"And a Senate split," Gina said.

"What?"

He nearly choked on his wine spinning back to the big screen. Sure enough, the Upper Chamber was divided right down the middle between the Blues and Reds.

"Even after all the cray-cray we exposed," Gina said, shaking her head. "Us and Dana, with her exposé on the matter. People still voted for—" She gestured at the TV "—*this?*"

Elijah shrugged. "Like I said before. The people desire nothing more than bread and circuses."

"Not sure about the bread part, but they sure got the latter!"

"Now what happens?" he asked with amusement.

"Well, the Vice President is technically the president of the Senate, and that chamber casts the deciding vote. So in the event of a fifty-fifty split, the majority goes to that party."

"But if there's no VP while the Electoral College is split, given the last joker was given the boot, then what?"

"Good question."

Gina's head was spinning with it all. She was a political

junkie through and through. Blamed Mama for that one. But even this one stumped her.

"Meh," Elijah threw back his wine and sauntered to the kitchen for more. "I'm not worried."

She stood, joining him. "Not worried? Why the hey-ho day not? We could be headed to a governmental stalemate."

"Meh," was all he said again, nearly draining the bottle of Meritage he'd brought—

Before Gina snatched it from him.

"Hey, that's my Meritage!"

"*Our* Meritage," she corrected him, finishing what was left in her own glass. "Don't forget I fed you."

"Touché."

Throwing back a swig, she asked, "So give it to me. Why aren't you worried?"

Eli shrugged. "Presidents come and go. Party power ebbs and flows. I mean, look at tonight! We've got a split right down the middle with no end in sight, both in the White House and in the Senate. And after what I saw and experienced, in my view it just doesn't matter at the end of the day."

"Then what does?"

He motioned with his arms between the pair, then outside. "This. Us. Community. Together, having drinks and talking about life. Doing life. And if I could put a Christian spin on it—because I am the son of a preacherman, after all."

She grinned, liking the sound of that. "Alright, preacherman, carry on."

He did, saying, "What matters is loving God and loving people. Everything else is just window dressing."

"To love God and love people," Gina said, "that's your solution to the country's cray-cray?"

He smiled and shook his head. "Not mine. Jesus'. The real King this day. All of our centers of power will be brought low when Jesus Christ returns in all his glory to topple the kings and queens of this world and take his rightful place to rule and reign for all eternity."

Boy, did Gina like the sound of that.

She said, "Suppose we might as well make that a reality now. Not through powerful institutions but through powerful lives, living out the two commands Jesus said summed up the entirety of God's desires for humanity: Love God and love others."

Elijah nodded. "And that starts with me. With each of us. Today. Besides, remember what the Book of Daniel says. *'He changes times and seasons; he deposes kings and raises up others. He gives wisdom to the wise and knowledge to the discerning.'*"

Gina nodded. "Reminds me of our new friend's dream, about all of our American government institutions burning to the ground someday."

"No reason why they can't be burned to the ground this day."

She shushed him. "Uncle Sam might be listening!"

They shared a laugh.

"But I understand what you're saying," Gina said. "No reason the good Lord couldn't lay to waste our presidents—here and now."

"And set up a whole other set of rulers. A whole new country, even."

She didn't want to even think about that—any of it. Was quite content with the American system as it was, and as screwed up as it was. At least it was predictable. You could count on the crazy, because it was *our* crazy.

Maybe that was the problem. Perhaps it was not only time to comfort the afflicted from the fallout of the knuckleheads in Washington whose policies ravaged everyday Americans, but also afflict the comfortable. Felt like someone said that about God's job description once—comforting the afflicted, afflicting the comfortable. Or was that journalism? Couldn't remember.

They returned to the television, Kai now yammering with that blonde bimbo Mara Mitchell about the implications of the stalemate—what it meant for the presidency, what it meant for the country.

Gina wondered herself. She flat didn't have a lickin' clue. About any of it, especially what it all meant for the Church.

Christians had been played, and played good. Everyone had, all across the political spectrum, the executors of the Enemy's plans for sowing fear and discord into America nearly sending it over the edge and into the Abyss. Perhaps they'd succeeded, dishing out a perfectly divided government with no winners and only losers on all sides.

What a mess.

How it would all pan out, how it would all be resolved…she flat didn't have a clue. Flat doubted whether anyone else had a clue!

All Gina knew was that the good Lord above was sovereign. He was in control. The Lord Almighty raises up kings and disposes others.

And that was good enough for her.

For another election.

EPIOLOGUE

merica the wretched, you did not fail to disappoint! We were so close to making magic together, had it not been for those imbecile investigators of the Nameless One.

And his people were the ones driving the cart off the cliff!

No worries, however, because Semjaza ain't through with you. Not by a long shot! Neither am I. Given his designs for the land—*his* land, *his* nation—I imagine you'll see me again soon.

Until then, I have some parting words.

So, pull up a chair and grab your drink of choice, for the tale I'm about to recall is rich!

As the story goes, recounted in that Gospel of that louse Luke, one day the Nameless One *'full of the Holy Spirit, returned from the Jordan and was led by the Spirit in the wilderness, where for forty days he was tested by the devil.'*

Yes, you heard right. The Big Kahuna himself, the Shining One tested He-Who-Shall-Remain-Nameless. Well, not tested. It was much more an invitation, as you shall see further on.

During this…invitation, the Nameless One *'ate nothing at all during those days, and when they were over he was famished. The devil* said to him, 'If you are the Son of God, command this stone to become a loaf of bread."

How did the Nameless One respond? He answered: 'It is written, 'One does not live by bread alone."

Bah! Here is the Shining One, full of power and might, authority and glory, offering living bread—and the Nameless One bites the hand that feeds him? What a moron!

Anyhoo, the story continues: *'Then the devil led him up and showed him in an instant all the kingdoms of the world. And the devil said to him, 'To you I will give all this authority and their glory, for it has been given over to me, and I give it to anyone I please. If you, then, will worship me, it will all be yours."*

That's right. The Shining One then offered to hand over his rightful claim to the nations. For a mere whispering nod of reverential supplication he could have ruled the world! Didn't even have to mean it, either. Our kind certainly could appreciate fingers-crossing lip service.

Now, any rational being in the universe would have leaped at the opportunity. Positively danced a jig at being gifted the keys to all Earth's kingdoms.

No no no! Not the Nameless One! Instead, get this, he responded: *'It is written, 'Worship the Lord your God, and serve only him."*

I guffaw in the face of such a pathetic, worthless, short-sighted retort! Guffaw, I tell you. *Guffaw!*

After such a rejection, it's any wonder the Shining One didn't dispense with the Nameless One altogether. But he is merciful to the weak willed; he is patient with the retarded. So, one more opportunity the Shining One gave him.

Again, as the story goes: *'The devil led him to Jerusalem and placed him on the pinnacle of the temple and said to him, If you are the Son of God, throw yourself down from here, for it is written, 'he will command his angels concerning you, to protect you,' and 'On their hands they will bear you up, so that you will not dash your foot against a stone."*

An apt offer, if I may say so myself. Apparently, the Nameless One disagreed. *'It is said, 'Do not put the Lord your God to the test,''* was his retort.

Can you imagine? Rejecting not only the raw power of the Shining One, on top of his helping hand, but also his permanent protection!

You think sheltering under the wings of Elohim the Most High is where it's at? *Bah!* He's got nothing on the Shining One, nothing on even the Watchers and their spirits who still command the nations.

Nothing on *me*!

Our power is matchless, a 100-proof living water. And it was almost yours, America. *Yours!*

You can blame those mousy followers of his all you want—those cowering, cowardly agents of his Church—but you wasted your chance getting drunk to your heart's content.

Just remember, America: Behold, I stand at your door and knock. He (or she, as the case may be) who hears my voice and opens the door—I will be more than thrilled to let you suckle from my teats and take you under my wings.

Even after those retards thwarted my plans.

Think of all that we could have accomplished together!

If our people who are called by our name shall only submit themselves to us—bowing down, seeking us out, turning to our life-giving ways, then we will hear them from the Unseen Realm and will forgive their shortsightedness—ravaging their land.

Alas, it was not to be. Not this go around, at least.

But do not despair, for Semjaza has asked me to stick around for another show of things. Who knows what the future holds?

Mark my words, America: I will have my way with you. We will accomplish great things together! One way or another.

One election at a time.

ACKNOWLEDGMENTS

I want to give a sincere, heart-felt "Thank you!" to someone who helped make this story happen thanks to their generous support through the Kickstarter campaign that helped launch this book: Dana Day, after which our intrepid reporter character Dana Diaz was named and dedicated.

Backing this project not only helped me finalize the story in order to put it out into the world, it also gave me a shot in the arm with a goodly dose of encouragement. So, thanks for both! This kind of fandom and support is why I'm able to do what I do.

ENJOY AGAINST THESE POWERS?

A big thanks for joining Elijah Fox and Gina Anderson on their investigation saving the world! **Here's what's next:**

Want to join Elijah Fox and Gina Anderson solving more supernatural mysteries? Dive into solving more Group X cases: www.groupxcases.com.

A prequel case from their FBI days, *Luck Be the Ladies*, is ready to solve at:
solve at:
http://bouma.us/luck

If you loved the book and have a moment to spare, **a short review is much appreciated.** Nothing fancy, just your honest take. Spreading the word is probably the #1 way you can help independent authors like me and help others enjoy the story.

AUTHOR'S NOTE

They say that you should avoid two topics at all cost in the interest of polite dinner conversation: politics and religion.

This novel is about both.

As you might imagine, I'm not all that popular for dinner!

This story is near and dear to me because I served for half a decade on Capitol Hill in Washington, DC. It was quite the experience, one I look upon fondly—mostly. Because during my tenure serving America's government, I had quite the vantage point perched at the intersection of Church and State. And much of what I witnessed still makes my stomach turn just thinking about it.

Hence this story.

It seems that we are at a pivotal moment in this historically tenuous Church-State relationship, on multiple levels. In many ways, it's always been this way. However, in the late '70s and early '80s through to this decade, there has been a concerted effort to marry politics and religion in a way that would make the early Church fathers turn over in their graves.

That's what this story is about. It's a political mystery that considers not only the relationship between the Church and

State, but also what's authentically Christian and what's worth fighting for. A controversial proposition, I know.

When I wrote this story, I recognized people would probably either love it or hate it, given the two dicey topics it addresses: politics and religion. But I was fine with that, because both are near and dear to me, given my own personal experiences with them, and I hoped to start a conversation about Church-State dynamics and authentic Christianity.

This is a political mystery with a religious, supernatural edge. While it centers on the right wing of the political spectrum, and the Religious Right's involvement, the same commentary on the Church's involvement in the political arena could easily be said of the Religious Left. It was just easier to use them as the springboard into the conversation given its more overt history with playing politics—as well as my own history with the movement as a conservative Evangelical. Let me explain.

As I mentioned, I spent half a decade working in politics. First as a congressional aide to a U.S. Senator, then later as a sort of pastor to politicians severing the spiritual needs of Members of Congress and their staff. No, we weren't lobbyists for Jesus. We were a nonpartisan, non-political organization that sought to serve the spiritual needs of those serving in America's capital. (Although, our group was part of a larger entity founded by someone who was intimately involved with the Religious Right in the 1980s.) I led prayer groups and Bible studies for those serving in our government for Christians and others interested in spirituality. It may surprise you, but there are over 20,000 congressional staffers working to support the 535 congressmen and senators and their committees. And get this: the average age (at least when I worked there over a decade ago) is 27. It's a tough environment with long hours and short tempers, and so we sought to be a safe place for them to receive counsel, prayer, and support in their important roles. It was a great vocational gig that afforded me super-cool opportunities to attend a State of the Union Address and presidential election party.

With that said, I also saw the seedy underbelly of the relationship between Church and State, and how Christians from both sides of the political spectrum vie for power—spending money and doing what is necessary to secure a seat at the table. One poll conducted shortly after the 2004 election put this relationship in perspective: a number of Members of Congress were asked which political group they would ignore if they didn't have to worry about the political ramifications. At the top of the list for Republican members was the Religious Right.

Which told me that the Church of Jesus Christ has been reduced to a lobbying group on par with the NRA and AFL-CIO. I saw, up close, how the Church whores herself to either political party for the lowest bid—and how both Democrats and Republicans use the Bride of Christ to further their own political agenda. What I saw then, over a decade ago, has continued to play itself out on the American political scene (Yes, shades of my story and perspective showed up in Dana Diaz's own story.)

I wrote *Against These Powers* in the summer of 2020, during a tumultuous election year and after another tumultuous year of political revelations. If you've followed such things, there were contours of the story that were probably recognizable.

First, if you read *American God* from my Order of Thaddeus thriller series, you'll recognize some of the elements I established from that world—like President Robert Santos and Freedom University, led by James Maxwell, along with the Faithful Majority and their complicity in the Christian-political syncretism from the last go-around four years ago in my fictional world. Also, that "Breakthrough" song was featured in a story about a pair of charlatans peddling deadly hope, in another OT book with the same title.

Then there're the candidates: Debby Gallego and Billy Baron are a wink and a nod to President Orange Hair (as Gina called him); both Gallego and Baron were *nom de plumes* of the former 45th president. And that's because I wanted to focus on the second aspect of the story: I-Og, which is modeled after the remarkable phenomenon of QAnon that has enraptured conservatives, non-religious and Christians alike.

If you are unfamiliar with the conspiracy theory that's more of a movement, now you are. Because everything about I-Og is true of QAnon—from the Eddy Lee stand-in searching for a pedophile ring in a Virginia diner run by President Santos (mirroring a sad soul searching for the same in a DC pizza joint, with Hillary Clinton as its supposed ringleader) to insights Dana Diaz had dug up on WeChat (a stand-in for 4Chan and 8Chan online networks) and shared with our intrepid heroes in chapters 26 and 28, and culminating in the breach of the Capitol Building (an obvious nod to the same sad episode from our nation's history in January 6, 2021).

The research for these chapters, along with much of the background comes from a few sources: A revealing book on the QAnon phenomenon by Mike Rothschild, *The Storm is Upon Us* (Melville House, June 2021), along with a deep-dive article from *The Atlantic* by Adrienne LaFrance, "The Prophecies of Q" (June 2020 issue), informing chapters 7, 26, and 28. Tim Alberta, in an exhortive article to the Church from *The Atlantic*, offered much of the inspiration for what went on in both Elijah's childhood church and the political-religious rallies. It also inspired the Billy Baron character based on a profile of a similar minister featured in the article, and all the ways his (Eli's dad's) church became entangled in politics. "How Politics Poisoned the Evangelical Church" (June 2022 issue) is a sobering clarion call for Christians of all stripes to be vigilant and on guard when it comes to giving our awe and worship away to anything other than King Jesus (the bit about fear, being anything we give our awe and worship to, parroted by both the demon Fear and offered by Dana Diaz, was taken from an insightful quote in this article, among other things inspiring the prose). His commentary informed chapters 14, 15, 22, and 29.

Also, in case you think I'm overplaying the Christian-political syncretism angle of the story, the song featured in 14 and 22, with the chorus "Take America back again" is based on an actual hymn written and sung at First Baptist Church of Dallas. Titled "Make America Great Again," it was sung in service of a Republican presidential campaign—one of the starkest illustrations of such syncretism. I riffed off this song but re-wrote its lyrics to serve the story but also create a connection to the real world; sometimes life really is stranger than fiction.

Finally, as with my previous two books exploring the Unseen Realm and its supernatural connection to our seen world, I leveraged the insights of Michael Heiser and his excellent work in this area from his book *The Unseen Realm*. The content on the sons of God and their rule, especially the concept of cosmic geography, from chapters 25 and 27 tapped into Heiser's book, particularly chapter 15.

This book isn't about Trump and Trumpism, or even QAnon. Rather, it's a warning to Christians in particular and citizens more broadly for how fear grips the heart and drags it into terrifying realms. I know I myself have been griped by such a Force the past few years, for a variety of reasons with which perhaps you yourself can empathize (hello: murder hornets, to say nothing of political maneuvers on both sides of the spectrum).

Here's that quote on fear again, this time direct from Alberta's *Atlantic* article:

"Biblically, fear is primarily reverence and awe. We revere God; we hold him in awe," [Pastor Ken] Brown told me. "You can also have reverence and awe for other things— really, anything you put great value on. I think, in conservative-Christian circles, we place a lot of value on the life we've known. The earthly life we have known. The American life we've known … If we see threats to something we value, we fear—that is, we revere, we hold in inappropriate awe—those who can take it away."

May those who have ears to hear listen and take to heart— myself included.

One final thing to mention: It is always a risk for any writer to represent characters from certain walks of life. Naomi Torres (from my *Order of Thaddeus* series) is one such character, a Latino woman; same for Dana Diaz in this story. Elijah and Gina were two more, autistic people whose characters came to me in the writing process of a different story, *Fallen Ones*. I spent time reading autistic people's stories and getting to know their experiences in the world to get them right. I particularly wanted to listen to their pain points when it comes to representation in the media, not wanting to fall into the same traps.

Hopefully, I represented them justly, writing unique, individual characters that shed some light on how they image their Creator in the world and their unique challenges expressing their personhood. However, if I fell down on the mark, and you yourself are autistic who can offer me insight into better representation, do contact me and help me understand how I can better write the stories of autistic Image Bearers.

I will also say that writing these two characters and exploring their stories in these first two books gave me a chance to explore my own story. During the course of research, I myself tested for autistic tendencies. I also placed along the autism spectrum in a way that gave me further clarity about myself and also gave me interest in delving deeper into this aspect of my own story. While I would not claim to be an autistic person, nor have I been clinically diagnosed, this process writing these stories was an interesting journey for me personally.

As with all of my stories, I like to take elements of the real world and spin it in a way to tell a compelling, propulsive page-turner. I hope you enjoyed this foray into supernatural suspense with a dose of political thrill.

Thanks for joining Elijah and Gina on their adventure investigating the crazy from the Unseen Realm breaching our seen one.

I have a hunch there will be plenty more cases to investigate in the coming years!

GET YOUR FREE THRILLER

Building a relationship with my readers is a joy of writing!
Join my insider group for updates, giveaways, and your free novel—a full-length, action-adventure conspiracy mystery in my *Order of Thaddeus* thriller series.

Just tell me where to send it. Follow this link to subscribe: www.jabouma.com/free

CONTINUE YOUR NEXT CASE!

Read *Deliver Us From Evil* **today: bouma.us/gx4**

ALSO BY J. A. BOUMA

Nobody should have to read bad religious fiction—whether it's cheesy plots with pat answers or misrepresentations of the Christian faith and the Bible. So J. A. Bouma tells compelling, propulsive stories that thrill as much as inspire, offering a dose of insight along the way.

Order of Thaddeus Action-Adventure Thriller Series

Holy Shroud • Book 1

The Thirteenth Apostle • Book 2

Hidden Covenant • Book 3

American God • Book 4

Grail of Power • Book 5

Templars Rising • Book 6

Rite of Darkness • Book 7

Gospel Zero • Book 8

The Emperor's Code • Book 9

Deadly Hope • Book 10

Fallen Ones • Book 11

The Eden Legacy • Book 12

Silas Grey Collection 1 (Books 1-3)

Silas Grey Collection 2 (Books 4-6)

Silas Grey Collection 3 (Books 7-9)

Backstories: Short Story Collection 1

Martyrs Bones: Short Story Collection 2

Group X Cases Supernatural Suspense Series

Not of This World • Book 1

The Darkest Valley • Book 2

Against These Powers • Book 3

Luck Be the Ladies • Novelette

***End Times Chronicles* Sci-Fi Apocalyptic Series**

Apostasy Rising / Season 1, Episode 1

Apostasy Rising / Season 1, Episode 2

Apostasy Rising / Season 1, Episode 3

Apostasy Rising / Season 1, Episode 4

Apocalypse Rising / Season 2, Episode 1

Apocalypse Rising / Season 2, Episode 2

Apocalypse Rising / Season 2, Episode 3

Apocalypse Rising / Season 2, Episode 4

Antichrist Rising / Season 3, Episode 1 (May 2023)

Antichrist Rising / Season 3, Episode 2 (June 2023)

Antichrist Rising / Season 3, Episode 3 (July 2023)

Antichrist Rising / Season 3, Episode 4 (August 2023)

***Faith Reimagined* Spiritual Coming-of-Age Series**

A Reimagined Faith • Book 1

A Rediscovered Faith • Book 2

***Mill Creek Junction* Short Story Series**

The New Normal • Collection 1

My Name's Johnny Pope • Collection 2

Joy to the Junction! • Collection 3

The Ties that Bind Us • Collection 4

A Matter of Justice • Collection 5

He Will Direct Your Paths • Collection 6

Find all of my latest book releases at: www.jabouma.com

ABOUT THE AUTHOR

J. A. Bouma believes nobody should have to read bad religious fiction—whether it's cheesy plots with pat answers or misrepresentations of the Christian faith and the Bible. So he tells compelling, propulsive stories that thrill as much as inspire, while offering a dose of insight along the way.

As a former congressional staffer and pastor, and award-nominated bestselling author of over forty religious fiction and nonfiction books, he blends a love for ideas and adventure, exploration and discovery, thrill and thought. With graduate degrees in Christian thought and the Bible, and armed with a voracious appetite for most mainstream genres, he tells stories you'll read with abandon and recommend with pride—exploring the tension of faith and doubt, spirituality and culture, belief and practice, and the gritty drama that is our collective pilgrim story.

When not putting fingers to keyboard, he loves vintage jazz vinyl, a glass of Malbec, and an epic read—preferably together. He lives in Grand Rapids with his wife, two kiddos, and rambunctious boxer-pug-terrier.

www.jabouma.com • jeremy@jabouma.com

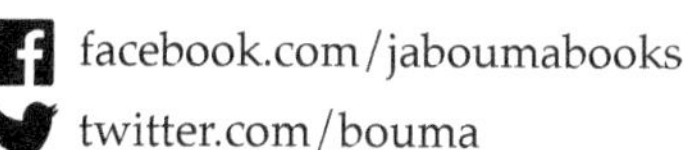

facebook.com/jaboumabooks
twitter.com/bouma
amazon.com/author/jabouma